Presented to

Nash Community College

in memory of

J.          Margaret Harper

~y

William L. Everett

January 13, 1999

# COOLMORE

*A Historical Novel of*
*Destruction, Reconstruction*
*and Reconciliation*

*By William L. Everett*

**E&E**
PUBLISHERS

Printed in the United States of America

Library of Congress Catalog Card No. 95-90243
ISBN 0-9646745-0-5

E&E
PUBLISHERS

From The Press of Walker-Ross Printing Co. - Rocky Mount, N.C.

TO . . .

*My wife, Len, for over 40 years of encouragement.*
*William L. Everett, Jr., for confidence in this*
*venture.*
*Cynthia Sykes Everett, for the attributes of a good*
*mother to  my three grandsons.*
*Gresham Jerome Everett, Seth Sykes Everett and*
*Andrew McGuire Everett for great expectations*
*of tomorrow.*

*A man' s family is his most cherished asset and a*
*country's best hope for a future civilized society.*

## ACKNOWLEDGEMENT

Braswell Memorial Library

Confederate Military History
Clark's N.C. Regiments
Official Records - Operations in the East

Without the patience and editing of Faith J. Lehman,
this book would not exist.

# PROLOGUE

In July of 1863, North Carolina experienced the tightening of "Scott's Anaconda." General Winfield Scott, a Mexican War veteran, recommended the tactic of blockading and occupying the Confederate States' ports and harbors at the outbreak of hostilities in 1861. This strategy was to deny the Confederacy the use of its port and harbors, thereby squeezing the life from the newly formed nation.

Plymouth, Hatteras, Washington, New Berne and Beaufort were occupied. Wilmington was blockaded. North Carolina was strangled. Scott's tactical serpent was producing the desired effects.

The Roanoke, Tar, Neuse and Cape Fear rivers provided access from the coast to inland rail lines. The *Ram Albemarle* was being built on the Roanoke, the *Ram Neuse* was being built on the Neuse and an iron-clad was under construction on the Tar. If completed, these new iron-clads could help open and secure the occupied ports.

From their positions, the Union armies raided strategic locations in eastern North Carolina. New Berne, at the convergence of the Neuse River and the Pamlico Sound, was the largest Union-held area. The staff of the commanding general of the Department of North Carolina and Virginia was quartered in many of New Berne's private dwellings.

The story of *Coolmore* is drawn from the "Official Records, War of the Rebellion," and "Clark's N. C. Regiments," reports and accounts of a raid into eastern North Carolina to destroy the manufacturing and transportation facilities providing supplies to the Army of Northern Virginia.

The destruction, reconstruction and a reconciliation through a love story are woven into an ironic narrative of the times.

Any correlation, with the exception of those names listed in the "Official Records," to any individual, living or dead, is coincidental.

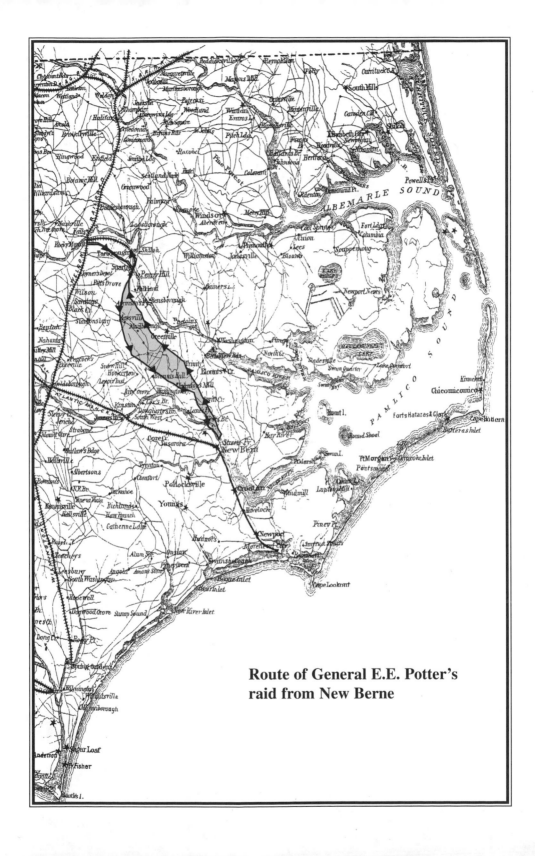

**Route of General E.E. Potter's raid from New Berne**

# CHAPTER ONE

The Josiah Alcock house cast a long shadow toward the south bank of the Neuse River. Captain Chamberlain stepped onto the porch and looked toward the river, sweeping broadly and turning on its journey toward the Pamlico Sound. Below the house on the river's bank, a quay had been constructed to load and unload the packets and steamers which now frequented the waterway. It gave the New Berne waterfront a bustle unlike anything the old port city had ever experienced.

The captain mopped his brow as he stepped off the porch and walked toward the quay. The heat was oppressive. He wondered how anyone could bear this summer heat year after year. Winters in New York were cold, but handling the cold was a lot easier than dealing with this intense heat. He could put on more clothes to stay warm, but he could not take off enough to stay cool.

The perspiration on his face attracted the mosquitoes, and he swatted constantly to keep them out of his eyes. Still Captain Chamberlain remembered and looked forward to the brisk winter days when the "skeeters," as most of the inhabitants called them, were nowhere to be found. New Berne was his home now and had been since his arrival shortly after General Burnside was relieved by Major General J. G. Foster.

As he moved farther from the rear of his quarters toward the quay, Captain Chamberlain remembered having overheard some of the Negroes working at the quay refer to it as the South Quay; it was located on the south side of the river.

The pathway from the rear of the Alcock house was well worn. Narrow, it was shaded by pine trees. Autumn was not far away bringing gentle breezes stirring the evergreen pines and gently mixing the yellow of the sweet gums with the orange of

1

the maples. The Carolina winters were much less harsh than the New York variety.

The water reeds began to thicken as he neared the water's edge, and he could feel the slight abrasiveness as his boots moved through the low growth. As he approached the quay, the captain could hear the mumbles of the Negroes as they labored under the burden of removing supplies from the Lake Ontario. The side-wheeler was belching out her contents on the backs of the Negroes, while soldiers, bare from the waist up, sweating and swearing barked instructions.

"For God's sake put that barrel of beef over here on this wagon, not back in the water," Private White yelled out in frustration. George White, a slender lad and a lover of horses, was just twenty-three years old. He had not wanted to leave Binghamton, but he realized the only way to guarantee a cavalry position was to volunteer early in a cavalry unit while it was being formed. Private White had heard that Colonel James Jourdan was forming a cavalry unit in Albany, so he made the train trip to volunteer. Right now, Private White doubted the wisdom of that decision.

Captain Chamberlain observed that the Negroes, all freemen from some of the small farms in eastern North Carolina, were not accustomed to making even the slightest decision. Not the smallest detail could be left to them. He shook his head in disbelief.

"Is this detail getting the best of you, Private?" Captain Chamberlain inquired.

"Yes, sir, and I don't know if this waterlogged paddle thing will ever get her guts out and gone. It took a mighty good river pilot to put her this close." The private stopped, looked at the bobbing side-wheeler and sighed, "Ain't you glad you don't have to ride this thing?"

"I'd be mighty glad to take her to Baltimore just to be closer home. The thought of being so far away from home sometimes makes it difficult to take," responded the captain.

Private White continued to make motions with his hands to direct the Negroes in unloading the heavy boxes. Beads of sweat glistened on the black torsos as they moved from the ship to the waiting wagons. Even the mules hitched to the wagons were listless, only the switching of their matted tails at the ever present flies stirred the air, then only enough to stir the odor of the straw-filled droppings that lay everywhere.

Captain Chamberlain, detecting the aroma of newly cut cypress, was refreshed as he looked at the recently built quay. It wasn't an engineering marvel, he thought, but under the circumstances, it served the purpose. The cypress logs had been put down into the river bottom at low tide. In an upright position they supported the boards and logs. Extending over the bank, a landing was formed. At least it supported the supplies being off-loaded. The captain moved from the quay, deftly dodged the mule droppings, turned and yelled to Private White, "I'll remember you when a good detail comes along, believe me!"

"Thanks, Captain, I need all the help I can get." White looked back to the moving black mass and yelled, "Look where you are goin' for God's sake."

Private White heard a rough voice from the docked boat. The boat master called out, "Private, will you get them darkies moving so's I can ketch the tide tomorrow and get the devil outa here!"

White moved closer to the boat, and wiped sweat with a red bandanna. "If you can get it done any better, get on over here. I'm in the army and you ain't."

The captain heard someone call him from the house. "Hey, Seth!" That could have been only one person, Major Ferris Jacobs. The major had volunteered in Albany the same day he had, and they both had been together from the time Colonel James Jourdan formed the Third New York Cavalry unit. Major

Jacobs was older than most of the volunteers of the Third Cavalry Brigade and was appointed second lieutenant upon volunteering and had moved quickly to major.

"Come on down, Ferris, I want to show you something." Despite the differences in their ages, the two men had developed a trusting relationship. Captain Chamberlain would soon be twenty-four, but Major Jacobs would never tell his age because he had frequently been told that he looked younger than he actually was. The officers stopped at a well-shaded opening of the path, shook hands and exchanged the customary civil greetings. "Come on with me a little closer to the river; I want to know if you can smell something before you see it."

Jacobs had no idea what Seth was talking about. Maybe Seth wanted to check out his instincts. As they neared the quay, Jacobs thought he might have the answer as the unmistakable odor of freshly cut cypress filled his nostrils. "Is it the Carolina cypress?"

"No," answered the captain.

"Is it the tar resin?"queried Jacobs.

"No," responded Chamberlain.

"Is it the fishy smell from the nets in the river?" asked Major Jacobs.

"No," Seth answered.

Suddenly the major saw the quay bustling with sweaty Negroes and soldiers and exclaimed, "Good heavens, man! It's last month's sweaty clothes and just plain stinking, moving bodies!"

Their conversation then took a strange turn. "Captain," asked the major, "of what religious persuasion are you?"

"I couldn't say with any certainty about any of them, sir." The captain hesitated, "Why do you ask?

The major, not wanting to emphasize his Jewish heritage,

said, "You're about to witness a Baptist conversion. Do you want to fetch a Baptist preacher, or do you want to make like one?"

Seth was puzzled. After all, it was he who asked the major to accompany him to the river. Now it was the captain following the major onto the quay.

"Private White!" called Jacobs loudly. "Private, stop all these men at once!"

White recently had been given some military responsibilities. He had shown some affinity for military life, especially when he could show some of what he thought was his dashing side. The private yelled out, "Ease off, you Mr. Lincoln Misfits! The major here has something in mind for you miserable devils to do, so keep still and listen."

Jacobs smiled as he directed the soldiers and workers to line the edge of the quay on two sides. "Get closer to the edge of the planks," he called. Observing their reluctance to get to the edge, he called again, "I said get closer! Get closer and look down!"

The cypress landing was about three feet above the water, but it looked farther as the men stood on the edge and looked down into the water. Jacobs walked up slowly behind the first man, "Have you ever been baptized?"

"Yassur, when I was a young'un."

"Well, you got it again." The major pushed the man off the side of the quay. "Wash behind your ears while you're in there!" Jacobs moved along the U-shaped line and pushed the back of each one just enough to take him off balance to ensure he fell into the water. "The Catholics might call it a Mass. The Baptists might call it a baptizing. Let's call it a mass baptizing!" Laughing, Major Jacobs quipped, "If John could do it in the Jordan, Jacobs can do it in the Neuse! Private White, be sure none of our converts drown."

White thought he'd seen about everything, but this, well

this was something he'd tell his grandchildren about.

Major Jacobs leaned over the side and looked down in the water at the men and called to them, "Sorry! The army ain't got no soap!" Then turning to Seth and with a grin, he said, "Let's go, Captain, I've got something to talk with you about."

Turning, Major Jacobs and the Captain made their way back to the Alcock house. They pushed back the limbs hanging over the path. Major Jacobs, ahead of the Captain, said, "Seth, I know when you volunteered you didn't expect to be assigned to this occupation duty, and neither did I and it doesn't seem there's anything we can do about it. But it looks like some things are about to take place that you might want to be a part of, or I think you will want to be a part of."

"You're right, Ferris, I'm darned bored with this occupation of New Berne. I joined to be a part of this army that would be fighting, and I really thought by now it would be over and done with. Now I've come face to face with the plain truth, these Rebels believe just as strongly as I do about their country. I really didn't realize how devoted they are to their state."

The major paused, and looked directly at the Captain, "I'm sure you've heard the news from Pennsylvania. From what I understand, Lee and his boys took a real licking at Gettysburg and have gone back closer to Richmond. This is making Washington a little bolder and we may be called on to push out farther into Carolina."

"This is good news, Major. Do you think this is a reliable account, or is this just another camp rumor?"

"No, I have reason to believe that this might be for sure, and if it is, do you want to take part?" Major Jacobs inquired.

"Yes, indeed I do, so be sure I'm included." Just the thought of mounting his horse and moving from the confinement of New Berne was exciting enough. "Thank you, Ferris, you can be sure I will keep this quiet, if that is expected."

"It is expected."

Seth looked through the trees toward the house now occupied by himself and some of the officers of his cavalry brigade, smiled and started toward the back porch, now completely shaded and more inviting than in the hot afternoon sun. He was glad now that General Foster, the commander of the departments of Virginia and North Carolina, had confiscated the Alcock house for the duration of the war.

Seth turned to the Major, "I thought when General Foster confiscated our quarters, it was an unnecessary thing to do, but now I don't much care."

"Yeah, you're right," responded Jacobs. "The people are hostile, the weather is hostile, the bugs are hostile, the whole wretched place is hostile, and the sooner we get this over, the better."

"Maybe tomorrow I'll have some information to share with you, we'll see," said Jacobs as he moved away from Seth.

Each went in a different direction. Seth headed for the back porch. The major walked around to the front of the house and into the dirt street.

Seth stepped onto the porch, turned and looked at the river and thought how it would have been so much better if the packet *Muskegon* was there unloading mail. It seemed so long since he had held a letter from his sweet Melissa. He longed to look into her eyes, to touch her skin, kiss her lips, caress her auburn hair. This rebellion be hanged for separating him so long from Melissa. If only a letter would come! If only a letter would come!

A pall of smoke from the fires of soldiers' cooking hung low, and with no wind stirring, Captain Chamberlain started for the 'Grub section'. He gasped for breath. As he neared the heavy concentration of smoke and complaining, sweaty soldiers, he heard, "Looking forward to dining tonight, Captain?"

Seth stopped and turned in Colonel Jourdan's direction, "No, sir, but it's either this or perish to death here in hell. When I joined up with you in Albany, I didn't think we would be involved this long."

Sarcastically, Colonel Jourdan bowed and jestingly quipped, "May I join you for dinner, this lovely evening?"

The captain, not wanting to be outdone, responded with a curt bow, "By all means, Colonel, join us for dinner."

"Would Miss Melissa mind this intrusion?" asked Colonel Jourdan as he pretended the captain's beloved Melissa was in his presence.

"Not at all, Colonel, not at all."

Captain Chamberlain, remembering to bring his tin plate and fork and knife, hesitated as Major Jacobs moved ahead in the line beside the mess wagon. Salted beef was better than the army biscuits, at least when a mess of beans had been thrown in.

The mess steward dipped the ladle into the black cast iron pot and brought out what he labeled, "Triple B, Captain, and hits 'aworth ever bite, the best beef south of Boston." The captain held his plate beneath the dripping ladle and cringed, knowing Boston Baked Beef and Beans was despised by every man in the regiment.

"Yeah, Private, I know all about your refined culinary expertise."

The captain noticed some of his fellow officers stooped around a gum tree, with balanced plates in their hands, trying to get the rations to their mouths. Captain Chamberlain and the major moved to join them. "Join us, major, the atmosphere is delightful, and the rations fantastic," one of the group wisecracked.

Major Jacobs and Captain Chamberlain settled into a stooped position and began to lift their forks in concert with the crouched officers. Silence prevailed and only the sound of metal forks against tin plates was audible.

The steadiness of the forks scraping the bottoms of the plates suddenly stopped as the sound of moving men made room for the orderly of General Potter to pass. Major Jacobs looked up from his plate and saw the orderly approaching his group of officers. Great Scott, what now? he thought. Major Jacobs looked at the stooped officers. "I hope it's one of you boys Old Potter wants and not me."

One of the officers began to laugh. "Yeah, you would want it to be one of us and not you, but you outrank us, so you go and face that weird-talking buffalo." "Buffalo" was a derogatory term used by the rebels to identify a person who sided with the Union cause and joined in with the Federal forces. General Potter, a native of Pamlico County, had at the beginning of the war raised a company of volunteers for the Union army. He had been given a brigadier star as a reward and assigned to the staff of Major General J. G. Foster, the commander of the department of Virginia and North Carolina, headquartered in New Berne.

Potter's orderly stopped to salute, and addressed Major Jacobs, "Major Jacobs, General Potter desires your presence at his quarters after mess tomorrow morning."

Major Jacobs, plate in hand, responded, "Thank you. Inform General Potter I will report as ordered."

Captain Chamberlain looked at the Major and sighed, "If the heat won't keep you awake all night, this order surely will, just dreading for the morning to come to find out what that old buffalo wants."

Captain Chamberlain scraped his plate into the wooden trough and turned with a weary gesture, "Gentlemen, I am calling it a day and I'm glad to see it go. Maybe tomorrow will bring some change." The captain turned and slowly walked toward the river and his quarters.

He approached the house from the front, stopped, looked up, and knew the open windows on the front and rear of the house would afford little comfort. Even now the breeze from the river was still. He paused, opened the door and slowly ascended the stairs to the bedroom at the top of the stairway. The darkened room was still and foreboding. He dreaded another night with a steady concert of river frogs and an occasional owl plus the foul smell of rotting fish at the water's edge.

In the darkened room, the captain fumbled for the oil lamp on the table beside the bed. He reached with one hand to steady the lamp and with his right hand, lifted the chimney from the base and gently placed it beside the lamp. Chamberlain reached into the table drawer and found only one match. This one must light the lamp, he thought. In the dark he raised his foot and turned the boot sole over his knee, and quickly rubbed the match across his boot. It sputtered, then flamed, and the captain thanked the Almighty for little things. His steady hand moved to the wick and a flickering flame illuminated the darkness. Black smoke billowed from it. He turned the wick down and the flame became smaller and the smoke disappeared, but the smell of coal tar prevailed.

The captain pulled the straight back chair up to the desk, opened the drawer and took out a sheet of paper. He was going to write a letter to his dear Melissa. He had not received a letter from her in two months. Thoughts of her accompanying someone else in Albany were unbearable and he was determined to keep his mind occupied, even here in New Berne. The captain wanted to tell her of his love. They had been engaged for only a few months before he had volunteered for the army.

The flickering light from the lamp cast an eerie shadow on the walls, almost a distinguishable pattern of waves rolling onto a beach and disappearing into the sand, one after another, hypnotically in repetition. All was quiet. Seth opened the ink well and dipped his pen.

My dear Melissa,

The mail packet has not docked here in over a month. Every day I have walked down by the river and looked toward the Sound in hope of seeing the *Muskegon* appear on the horizon. Every day I have been disappointed and the wait is almost unbearable. I think of you constantly and my mind wanders back to Albany and the precious moments we spent together.

Sometimes, I must confess, I have thoughts of you being with someone else. How tortuous are those thoughts! The very thought of us not being together and that someone else might be looking into your lovely eyes, touching your delicate hands, caressing your beautiful skin and sitting beside you is more than I can endure while the distance separates us.

I am comforted by the remembrance of the words you last spoke to me—your assurance that you would be waiting for the time we would be united in matrimony so that we might spend our lives together. Oh, my Love, what a sustaining thought! You may be assured that I constantly have you in my thoughts, and my affection for you has not diminished. I long for the day when we shall be together as one. That thought is the one thing that makes the days and nights more bearable.

Rumors are circulating that we might be venturing out into this part of North Carolina since the Rebel troops are in short supply. It appears most of the available men have been transferred to Lee's army in Virginia. We have received reports of a great victory at Gettysburg, and it has encouraged us that this war will soon be over. It can't end soon enough for me.

Major Jacobs received orders today to report to General Potter in the morning. We are hoping we will be relieved of this occupation duty and put into another operation. General Potter is not well-respected among the officers. Even though he wears the Union uniform, we know he deserted his own, and we have heard he can be quite ruthless when he thinks it will be to his advantage.

I will be looking for the packet tomorrow in the wonderful expectation of having a letter from you as I need reassurance from you to make this separation more bearable. Separation is too painful to endure at such a distance.

Please be reassured of my enduring affection for you and the longing in my heart to be by your side once again, to breathe the fresh fragrance of your hair and touch the delicate softness of your hands.

My fondest regards to your family, I am yours in  eternal love,

Seth

Seth folded the paper to fit the only envelope he could find. He addressed it and pulled the drawer open to see if there were wax enough to seal the envelope. As he fumbled in the drawer he felt the stick of wax, half used, but enough to seal the letter. Softening the wax over the lamp chimney, he daubed the envelope in three places and sealed it.

Seth pushed back from the desk and leaned over to turn down the lamp wick even farther, and the room dimmed to almost total darkness. Weary and depressed, the captain allowed his galluses to slide from his shoulders and leaned back in the straight chair and slipped off his boots.  For a moment he thought, what's the need to get to bed? The heat and the constant noise of the river frogs will go on all night. As he rose from the chair, he leaned over and cupped his right hand around the top of the lamp chimney and with a quick puff blew the flame out.

In the darkness, he removed his trousers and placed them over the chair, and as he lay down, pulled the pillow under his head. Sleep might come, but old thoughts would come,  too. His mind wandered back to Albany and Melissa. He said to himself, in a low, barely audible voice, "Good night, my love."

# CHAPTER TWO

The aroma of freshly boiled coffee filled the still morning air. Coffee was in short supply, even for the Union army. It was considered a nonessential for an army in the field. Even more out of the ordinary was the fire begun so early in the morning. The aroma was reminiscent of better days in Albany.

Captain Chamberlain arose from his bed and realized he had slept through the night in spite of the noises and the heat. The sun, partially risen above the tree tops, cast a shaft of light through the window that only a few hours before was dark and still.

Seth moved slowly to the open window, leaned out and viewed the top of the veranda leading from the house to the kitchen. The kitchen was not connected directly to the main house. Seth saw a wisp of smoke from the chimney at the rear of the kitchen and called out, "I'll be right there, hold some for me!"

Captain Chamberlain knew the kitchens of the homes in the south were separated from the main houses because of the incidence of fires from the wood-burning stoves. Before the war he had begun an apprenticeship with an architectural firm in Albany, and many of his friends thought him well suited for the profession. The call to arms by Mr. Lincoln had interrupted all those plans.

Seth leaned again through the opening of the window and yelled out, "Don't use it all up, you greedy alley cats!"

Seth slipped into his trousers hurriedly and sat in the chair still near the desk. He reached for his boots, pulled on the first boot and sat back almost as if resting, then pulled on the other. He pulled his galluses to his shoulders with his thumbs and gently tucked them into place. His mouth was dry from the long night. He thought how great a fresh splash of water would feel to his face, and a dipper full for his mouth to start the day.

Seth dashed down the stairs, turned quickly from the stairway bottom and headed for the rear door leading onto the porch. He stopped on the porch where a bucket with a protruding dipper rested on a wide plank nailed between two porch columns. Seth looked into the bucket expecting fresh water and found it empty.

"Who's the lazy rascal who used this last?" he called out. "Don't you remember the agreement about who uses the last of the water, fills it up?"

Not hearing any response from the kitchen, he hurled the empty bucket toward the kitchen door, "One of you lazy rascals fill this thing up."

As the bucket rolled to a stop a short distance from the door, Major Floyd Clarkson appeared in the doorway and braced himself between the facings, "What's all the ruckus out here? Contain yourself, Captain."

The major's presence had a calming effect on Seth. "Yes sir, but the last one to use this bucket when it was emptied was supposed to fill it."

"Really now," replied the major, "which do you think is the most reasonable—the last one to use the bucket, or the last one to get out of bed?"

Seth, realizing he was the last one out of bed, quietly reached down, picked up the bucket and started walking toward the well at the rear of the house. The wooden structure surrounding the well supported the overhead beam holding the pulley, through which a worn chain was threaded and attached to the bucket. Seth knew the well had been dug by men with shovels, and consequently a barrier had to be made to keep thoughtless children from falling into the well.

It was dark in the well as Seth watched the bucket descend,

finally hearing it drop into the water. He waited a few moments for it to completely fill before he pulled the chain through the pulley to hoist the water-filled bucket. As the captain reached over the well, he grasped the bucket. The water made it heavy. Seth used both hands to pour the water into the pail he had brought from the house. As he lifted the pail by the handle he began walking back toward the house, balancing himself by raising his other arm.

The captain paused, then stepped onto the veranda and moved onto the porch. A wash basin was still on the plank that held the bucket of water. He poured first into the basin and then placed the bucket on the suspended plank. With cupped hands he splashed water onto his face, first once and then twice. A linen towel was hung on the porch column within reach of the basin and Seth drew it to his face.

"Come on in and have some coffee, Captain, now that you've gotten your frustrations out," said Major Clarkson, as he stood in the doorway to the kitchen. "You can believe it's hotter in here than outside. The Alcocks left this old iron wood stove here when they packed up and left. I heard he lost his wife, Lily, and he didn't want to stay here anyway." The coffee excited the senses of the captain. The heat in the kitchen didn't really matter.

"Pull up a chair. I brought this table down from my room this morning, just for this elegant breakfast," quipped Major George Cole, also a New Yorker, who volunteered at the outbreak of the war.

"I have been hiding this slab of salt bacon and now seems as good a time as any to put it to good use." Looking around Cole inquired, "Who'll fry it on the stove, if I slice it?

Lieutenant Caleb Henderson, realizing he was the last officer to join the unit, hesitated, then volunteered. "I will, if somebody can produce a frying pan."

Major Cole headed toward the pantry. "I think I saw one here a few days ago, maybe it's still here. Let's hope so, I'm hungry!"

The major looked inside the empty pantry and saw a pan hanging low under a shelf, "We're in luck, boys, here it is."

Cole lifted the pan from the peg, handed it to the lieutenant, who quickly dusted it and placed it on the hot stove.

"The bacon is ready when the cook is ready, ain't that so, son?" Cole said to Henderson.

"Yes sir," responded Henderson, as he took a few slices from the major and placed them in the hot pan. The bacon instantly started to splatter hot grease in all directions and Henderson backed away quickly, "Hey man, that's hot!"

It began to sear. Smoke from the bacon filled the kitchen. An enticing odor of frying bacon penetrated the nostrils of the officers. Major Cole yelled in glee, "The aroma of the gods, ah yes, breakfast like she ought to be!"

Cole pushed the lieutenant from the stove and moved the pan from the hottest part of the stove. "Give it a little break, son, not too fast."

Captain Chamberlain, quickly opening and closing the kitchen door trying to ventilate the kitchen, called out, "This may be a little messy, but the smell is fantastic! Keep 'er going, lieutenant!"

"Grab a chair, boys, and we'll all sit at the breakfast table," invited Major Cole. With his cup lifted he added, "And we'll raise a cheer for the brigade chef, our very own Henderson."

The smoke gradually cleared from the kitchen, and Henderson with his knife lifted each individual piece of bacon out of the pan and onto the plates of each officer, "Here you are, and the gentleman who complains, be hanged."

Major Cole held his plate in Henderson's direction and motioned to the lieutenant, "Pour a little of that hot grease on this hardtack biscuit, Lieutenant; that ought to soften it some, if anything can."

"Who else wants to try this Carolina hog topping?" asked the lieutenant sarcastically. "The southern boys seem to thrive well on it."

Major Clarkson looked at Captain Chamberlain, "Have you heard we might finally be venturing out from this dull duty anytime now and taking on something that might be important in this God-forsaken place?"

"Yes, sir, I have. I was with Major Jacobs last night when General Potter's orderly came with orders for him to report to the General this morning."

"Have any idea what about, Captain?"

"No, not the least, Major."

Cole leaned back in his chair, and steadying his cup observed, "We can't walk on water, so we can't go east. Washington just north of here is occupied, and Wilmington to the south is blockaded—where else is there to go?"

Captain Chamberlain thought a moment and asked, "Why not west?" All the officers looked at Chamberlain as he added, "After all, that's a part of Carolina that has not seen much of this accursed war."

As he leaned forward in his chair, Seth continued, "And I've heard that many supplies have made their way north to Lee from that section."

"You may just be right," Clarkson said, "And right now that part of the state is pretty well left to itself, with all the troops with Lee in Virginia."

Major Cole informed the officers, "I hear the Seventeenth North Carolina is bogged down with sickness at Fort Branch on the Roanoke River."

"That don't leave a whole lot left to make eastern Carolina feel good about it," added Henderson.

"That ought to make old Potter a little more venturesome,

knowing he will not have much to face," stated Chamberlain. "Yeah, he might like that" added Clarkson, getting up from his chair.

The leisure breakfast was interrupted by the sound of running feet on the veranda. "Major! Major!" Private White called out while bursting into the doorway of the kitchen, "General Potter wants all of you at his headquarters, quick step!"

"All right, all right, private! We got the message. You can calm down."

"Yes, sir," replied the private, "I got to git back, the man's a-ravin' like a wrung-neck chicken."

Captain Chamberlain, opening the door to allow the other officers to exit the kitchen, exclaimed, "This is what we've been talking about! Hallelujah! Let's get with it!" Leaving the smoldering wood in the stove, all of the half-dressed men made a dash for their quarters.

Seth, knowing to appear before Potter in less than proper attire would be disastrous and slowing a bit to take care of the details in putting on his uniform, called out, "You fellows better be sure you're fully uniformed. You know how fussy old Potter can be!"

The early sun began to heat the dirt streets and the dust was stirred by every moving thing. The wagons, the horses, the mules—everything was stirring dust. Major Clarkson broke the silence as he asked, "Who all do you think might be there when we get there? To be sure, old Potter called in somebody else, too."

"Yeah, we ain't the only losers who have to put up with that old sorehead!" Captain Chamberlain muttered, as he remembered the summons the evening before for Major Jacobs.

As he moved briskly to the side of the dusty street, Lieutenant Henderson, following behind the other officers, gestured with his hand, "Who in torment ever called this a street? It's a path to the valley of dry bones, and it's my bones."

Between the officers and the headquarters of General Potter appeared a wagon in a cloud of dust, moving slowly toward them. When they came more clearly into view, Major Cole saw that the regimental chaplain and driver occupied the wagon seat and they were heading to the cemetery. Abreast of the wagon, Major Cole looked at the chaplain, "Was it the grub or the boredom that got the best of the boy?" The plain wooden coffin was in full view in the wagon bed.

"Be a little more respectful, lads. This could be one of you," responded the chaplain.

The driver spit tobacco juice to the side, flipped the reins onto the back of the mules and mumbled, "They'uns don't give a dang, no siree, they'uns sure don't."

General Potter's headquarters were just ahead and Captain Chamberlain began to fall behind allowing the others to be first to approach the house.

"We see what you're up to, Captain," Clarkson noted. "It won't do you any good; old Potter can smell a snake at thirty yards." The door was open and Colonel Jourdan and Major Jacobs could be seen in full view standing beside the table occupied by Potter. Silent and still, Potter stared at the open doorway until the officers stopped.

"Now that ya'll are finally here, how about coming on in?" barked Potter. "It took you long enough all right!"

Captain Chamberlain turned his head slightly upward and rolled his eyes backward and whispered, "I knew it, I knew it."

The captain, as the last one to enter the doorway, stopped and closed the screen door. He briefly noticed the scroll woodwork securing the screening in the corners of the door. There was something special and elegant about this house. The columns were decorated at the top with scroll woodwork that seemed to support the porch roofline. Every decorative touch echoed gently from the past.

A feeling of remorse settled on Seth, almost as if he were intruding into the privacy of someone's life. The room, which now served the army, still maintained its own distinct personality. A damask covered settee, marble-top tables, gilded plaster of Paris frame holding a portrait of a matron from the past and the worn and faded Persian rug—they added to the condemnation of this unwarranted intrusion.

The parlor emitted an aura of past gentility, now crying to be remembered, not rejected. A sense of orderliness overcame the captain. There was something out of place. Something here was not right.

"Chamberlain, you might as well move on up here with Major Jacobs, you're gonna be spending a lot of time with him from here on," Potter barked, "and you had better understand how this operation is going to work."

There was a shuffling of boots as the officers made room for the captain to move to the front. Major Jacobs stepped from beside Colonel Jourdan and joined the captain. Potter was sitting on one side of the oak kitchen table in a matching table chair. The other chairs were lined against the walls, unoccupied. As he stood on the opposite side of the table from the general, Colonel Jourdan said, "I believe this is all the staff officers, sir."

General Potter rose slowly from his chair, rolled open a map and turned it to a correct position for the officers to find out exactly what it was. A paper weight was placed on one side and an inkwell on the other to hold the map open. Potter pointed with his finger. "And what do you see, gentlemen?"

The staff gathered more closely and glared at the spread map. The silence seemed forever. All the officers leaned to be sure what they were viewing. They knew it was a map of North Carolina, but they did not know what answer the general wanted.

"Didn't you hear me? I said, 'What do you see?'"

"Yes, sir," responded Colonel Jourdan, "I see a map of North Carolina."

"Colonel Jourdan," the general asked, "if you were General Lee, what on this map would be the most important thing to you? Look at it very close again and tell me what you see."

The colonel leaned over the table, placed his finger on the Wilmington and Weldon line. He moved his finger along the route of the Wilmington and Weldon rail line to the Virginia border. "The Wilmington and Weldon railroad!" replied the colonel.

"That's right, Colonel, that's the lifeline of the Army of Northern Virginia. Break that and we take away the breadbasket of the Rebels."

"But we've tried that before," said Jourdan, "and as fast as we tear it down, they build it back."

"Not this time, Colonel, not this time. This will be one thing that will be well remembered; either your name or mine will be cussed for generations to come." Potter looked at Jourdan, his finger pointing inward.

Potter walked away for a short distance. "What else do you see, Colonel? Do you see anything else of real consequence?"

Colonel Jourdan, puzzled as to the questioning, leaned over the map again, "I see the roads leading into New Berne and I know they are blocked with artillery and abatis."

"You boys just don't know the value of waterways," Potter stated. The general went on, "Now I was raised to appreciate what the water can do for you, if you use it right." The general continued his self-appointed lesson, "Do you think these Southern boys don't know how to use the rivers to their advantage? I know they do."

The general pointed again to the map, "There's the Neuse. It starts up near Raleigh and it ends right here. You've heard about the ironclad they're building near Kinston? And how do you suppose they plan to get it out into the Sound?" asked the general.

"They will use the river, of course," Potter informed the officers.

Potter paused, gazed out the window, his finger on the map, "And here's the Tar, it empties into the Sound at Washington." Slowly he moved his finger and pointed to Plymouth, "And here the Roanoke ends in the Albemarle Sound."

"Now do you see the possibilities?" asked Potter. "Do you think the boys are sitting idly by and not using the water? No, sir, you better believe they ain't."

"Major Jacobs, have you heard what's going on up the Roanoke, just south of Weldon?" inquired Potter.

"Yes sir, I heard a new Ram is being built," responded Jacobs.

"Well," asked the general, "do you have any thoughts as to what might be going on at Tarborough on the Tar River?"

"No, sir, I don't have any idea."

"Well, Major Jacobs, maybe it's about time we found out."

General Potter walked back to the opposite side of the table. "General Foster will be giving a general order for a detachment of cavalry, along with all the necessary equipment, to move out. Rocky Mount, a station on the Wilmington and Weldon line will be the objective. The aim is to destroy the trestle over the Tar River and anything else that I think necessary."

Captain Chamberlain discerned the emphasis Potter put on the I, and he thought, he's trying to put himself at the head of this operation. Well, why not, he's the brigadier!

Potter looked directly at Colonel Jourdan, "Colonel, remain here." He turned to the remaining staff and nodded, "Gentlemen, you are dismissed. Thank you."

Captain Chamberlain walked to the open door, turned as if bidding the room a final goodbye and realized what was missing. He said to himself, How uncultured to mingle the simplicity of the plain kitchen table with the elegant furnishings of civility and social graces!

With his hand the captain closed the screen door behind him. He again admired the scroll work securing the screening of the door.

As he stepped onto the porch, he looked up and down the street to detect which direction the officers had taken. With a grasp on the column he swung onto the steps and then onto the street. The captain increased his gait to join the staff before they reached their quarters.

"Colonel Jourdan, now that it's just you and me, may we speak frankly?" asked General Potter almost apologetically.

"Yes sir, if that is your wish," responded Jourdan with a look of amazement. It was unusual to hear the general being so humble, thought the colonel.

"Would it offend you if your brigade were used in a feinting movement to draw attention away from the real objective?" inquired Potter again, apologetically.

Jourdan hesitated, and realizing he didn't have much of a choice, responded, "Well, no, sir, but my brigade is getting pretty restless, and it would be a rather disappointing assignment, but we would obey our orders."

"Thank you, Colonel, I appreciate your frankness."

The general continued, "This is the plan I will put into action on the 17th. I know July is a hot month, but it is also a good time to destroy the maturing crops before any possibility of harvesting. You will be directed to cross the Neuse at Street's Ferry with your brigade and proceed to Swift Creek. You will wait there for my arrival. On the morning of the 18th you are to take your brigade toward Kinston," the general continued, "but you will return to New Berne with your brigade the following day."

Colonel Jourdan was well aware of this military tactic, but it was still distasteful; nevertheless, he responded, "Yes, sir, I understand." Further the colonel asked, "Will we be in a bivouac at Swift Creek overnight?"

"Yes, we will because there is fresh water readily available from the creek, and it is far enough from the cannons at Barnwell." Potter continued, "I will be using the Third New York Cavalry, two companies from Mix's Regiment, three companies from the Twelfth New York Cavalry, and one company of my North Carolina cavalry." After rising from his chair the general turned the map in his direction, adding, "And two sections of Mountain Howitzers."

"Colonel, don't you think the artillery could use some activity also? They're restless, too."

"Indeed, General, they need to be a part of this assignment."

"Then it's settled, Colonel."

Potter walked around the table, again viewed the map, "I will notify you and the staff when to assemble for final instructions," and added, "you will already know your objective."

"Yes, sir," responded Jourdan. "Will that be all, sir?"

"For today, that will be it. Have a nice day, Colonel," the general nodded.

Colonel Jourdan came to attention and saluted, "Thank you, sir, I will be awaiting your word."

Turning from the general, the colonel walked briskly to the door, paused a moment, opened the door and stepped onto the porch. He mopped his brow, put on his hat and positioning it, made his way down the dusty street in search of the staff.

# CHAPTER THREE

Julia loved to climb the steps leading from the hallway on the second story to the cupola. Situated on the middle of the A-roof, it towered above the ornately designed house.

The windows of the four sides of the cupola were arched at the top corresponding to the windows of the lower portion of the mansion. The cupola windows were covered by extended A-shaped gables, supported by hand-carved modillions. The cupola provided a panoramic view of Coolmore in every direction.

The oak tree tops below the cupola provided a carpet-like appearance surrounding the entire house. It appeared entirely safe to walk from the roofline onto the lush green of the leaves.

Where the carpet of leaves seemingly ended, the tassels of ripening corn waved in the morning breeze as rippling waters in a gust of wind. Nature's bounty bowed to the wind. Beyond the waves of tassels, now golden in the morning sun, the pale blossoms of the cotton plants were gradually changing the field of green into a true harbinger of a bountiful crop. From every bud now dotting the field would come a boll of cotton. The rains had come and at the right time. This had been a good growing season.

The windows of the four sides of the cupola gave a grand view of the harvest to come. Field hands had begun their labor much earlier. They moved down the rows of cotton pulling the weeds that had grown quickly between the cotton plants, alternately leaning and rising as they shook the soil from the roots of the weeds.

Julia had heard from her father, Frank, of the use of this cupola as a tower to keep watch on the field hands. It was not uncommon for slaves to make an effort to escape, and from this vantage point they could be watched.

Farther from the house at the outer edges of the corn and cotton, a small tobacco patch could be seen. Tobacco was interesting and if it could be sold, it fetched a goodly price.

This crop year was promising, even in the midst of the ever worsening war situation. The demands of the new confederation were burdensome, but to maintain the necessary methods of the southern agricultural life, it must be upheld, at all costs.

Julia could hear the mournful whistle of the approaching train in the distance. The rail tracks from Rocky Mount to Tarborough passed through the dense woods immediately behind Coolmore. The curveless rails gave the appearance of a tree-lined tunnel as far as the eye could see, looking both east and west.

Miss Julia, as she was called by the Dupree slaves, stood many times on the tracks in the morning looking east at the sunrise and west in the evening at the sunset. The sun seemed to rise and set at both end of the tracks. Looking toward the front of the house beyond the tree tops, Julia could see the dusty road connecting Rocky Mount and Tarborough. Coolmore was situated almost halfway between the rail line and the road. There was dust from the front and smoke from the rear, but never at the same time. The schedule of the train appeared to be only twice a week.

"Julia, where are you, girl?" vibrated through the morning air.

She knew it was her mother calling and she knew well she had stayed too long alone in the cupola daydreaming. The chores of the day would not wait.

"Juuulia!" now there was the emphasis on her name she recognized as being immediate.

"Yes, Mama, I'm coming!"

The stairway from the cupola was a short distance to the second floor. Julia dashed down the stairs from the second floor and was breathless as she emerged at the bottom.

"Will you ever learn to accept your share of the responsibilities in this home? At nineteen, you really ought to be about more than daydreaming."

"Yes ma'am," replied Julia.

Julia knew it was difficult for her mother and father since her older brother Willis had enlisted in the Confederate army. 'Willie,' as he was called, had been away from home nearly a year with the Edgecombe Rifles. Their last letter was from Fort Fisher near Wilmington.

"Your daddy is taking some corn to Mewborn's Mill to get ground for cornmeal today, do you think you can find the time to give him a hand?" her mother asked sarcastically.

"Will he let me drive the team?" asked Julia as she hurried out the back door to join her father. The corncrib was getting empty, but from the appearance of the height of this year's corn, it would be filled, come winter.

"Daddy, can I drive the team to the mill? Mama said I could."

"Your mama said no such a thing, but yes, little lady, you can drive the team. But you've got to promise not to wander off while the corn is being milled."

"I promise, Daddy, I promise," Julia gleefully exclaimed.

Frank Dupree held out his hand for Julia to grasp. She reached for the wagon side to pull herself onto the seat. Swinging her long skirt over the top of the wagon seat, she settled onto the seat. "Let's go daddy, give me the reins." She twisted her cheek, uttered, "Gick! Gick!" and the team moved forward down the path to the Tarborough road. Frank, walking alongside the wagon as it passed the main house, called out, "Mama, we'll be home 'fore dark!" Frank pulled himself up into the wagon seat while the wagon moved slowly and settled in beside Julia.

"Alright, girl, you wanted to drive to town, so let's go, it's all yours now."

Julia felt secure now with her daddy alongside, and the road ahead left nothing to watch for except the deeper ruts to the side of the one-lane road. Keeping the team in the middle was easy enough.

Josh Mewborn, the son of the mill owner, Julia thought, will surely be there today. He always was, and Julia knew he could not keep his eyes off her. She had observed every time she and her daddy went there, he seemed to neglect his work and watch every move she made.

The road became monotonous with only the wagon wheels squeaking with regular rhythm. Frank was quiet. The team was steady.

Julia's thoughts were centered on what she might do in a flirting manner to attract Josh's attention. It would be fun to see just how she might entice him to see what a fool he might make of himself. Yes, she thought to herself, that might be fun.

Arrival at the west side of town had not taken very long. It was still well before noon and Frank began to greet people he knew as they passed through toward the river bridge. Mewborn's Mill was across the bridge from Tarborough, on the Tar River. The river provided plenty of water to flow down the flume to drive the waterwheel.

Frank took the reins from Julia and reined the team to the front of the millhouse near the door leading to the milling operation itself. Even from outside, the rumble of the millstones could be felt and heard.

"You did it alright, young lady, now we'll tie the team and I will unload the corn," her father added. "And don't git too far, cause we got to be home 'fore dark."

Julia with her right hand, lifted her skirt to raise her leg over the top of the wagon. She put her foot onto the wheel hub, and with both hands lifted herself from the bed of the wagon onto the ground. She thought Josh might be somewhere out of sight, but if he were here he would be surely looking. He always was and now would be no different.

Julia stood next to the wagon trying to look uninterested. She brushed off the front of her dress from top to bottom and turned away from the millhouse while bending slightly toward the wagon. She suspected Josh's eyes were peering at her every move. As she leaned even more to check her shoe laces, Julia deliberately remained interested in her laces long enough to be sure Josh had become attracted.

The wide door at the loading platform led into the milling room. Mewborn's milling room floor showed the effects of wear produced by dragging bags of corn to the area of the giant millstones. The exposed rafters and beams, coated with the yellow dust of years of grinding the yellow kernels were now supporting spider webs. The webs were fully yellowed and seemingly undisturbed by years of neglect.

Mr. Mewborn, his eyelashes and beard also yellowed by the dusty operation, called out, "Just put your corn on the platform; we'll get to it shortly, Mr. Dupree."

With his gnarled hands he brushed off the front of his yellowed clothing as he walked to the platform door to speak to Mr. Dupree.

The millhouse, vibrating from the turning of the massive millstones, and the sound of rock against rock was deafening. Mr. Dupree had to raise his voice above the level of the sounds, "How long do you think it will be afore we can go home?"

"Maybe two hours," Mewborn yelled back.

Julia strolled into the mill room, stopped and looked around. The vibration seemed to stimulate her feet. It feels good she thought. Glancing around the yellowed mill room she spotted Josh behind the giant moving stones, peering as if he didn't want to be noticed.

Now motionless, Julia waited for Josh to make his appearance. Josh, too, was covered with cornmeal dust. His hair was yellowed even though it was brown in color. He looked pale yellow from head to toe.

As Josh walked toward Julia, he began brushing off his clothes and mussing his hair to remove the cornmeal dust. He smiled and stated, "Hit's good to see you, Miss Julia. It's been quite a spell since you've been around. How you been?"

"Right tolerable, Josh, how 'bout yourself?"

"All's 'bout the same, nothing seems to change."

Julia noticed how Josh was looking at her and thought to herself, he's right, nothing has changed. He is still looking at all the same places.

"Will you be waiting here for your daddy's corn to be ground?" asked Josh.

"Yes, I reckon so. I might walk down by the river after a while if it gets tiring in here."

"Josh, get back to watching the bags! They're getting filled up," yelled Josh's father.

Barely able to hear the order, Josh walked back to his job and turned to get a glimpse of Julia.

Julia glanced around the millhouse, spotted a closed door, turned slowly and started toward the door. She stopped short of the door, put her hands in the front pockets of her dress and drew the back part of her dress tight. She turned slowly to be sure Josh was looking.

Josh was staring and Julia put more pressure on the front pockets of her dress with her hands, further tightening her dress across the back of her body. She knew the tightness of her dress was emphasizing the shape of her figure.

As she took her hands from the pockets, her dress relaxed, and Julia turned in Josh's direction and smiled.

Josh's face became flushed. He felt it, but the cornmeal hid the change of color. He felt his temples begin to throb with every beat of his heart. His heartbeats quickened and the throbbing in his temples became more intense. He could barely keep his mind on the job he was supposed to be attending.

Julia again looked toward Josh, smiled and moved toward the closed door.

The vibration of the millstone's constant turning drowned the sounds of the partially stuck door as Julia pushed against it with her shoulder. She stopped again and looked in Josh's direction. Julia smiled as the door closed behind her.

Josh could feel his face flush with every beat of his heart, and the very thought of being alone with Julia was stimulating to his seventeen-year-old body.

Young Mewborn looked around the milling room and saw Mr. Dupree and his father walking onto the platform to join other farmers. He was sure to talk about the conduct of the war. From experience, Josh knew it would be a while before they would return inside.

Josh checked the funneling troughs that guided the freshly ground corn into empty sugar sacks. Josh thought he would not be absent from his work position too long and his father would never notice anyway.

He turned and looked again to the platform as he moved to the room where Julia had disappeared into. He knew the room contained only sacks of shelled corn and some empty sugar sacks.

Gently he pushed against the badly warped door and looked inside the room. Standing in the narrow opening of the doorway, he looked to his left and saw Julia leaning against the inside wall. Looking outside again, Josh closed the door behind him.

"Julia, I don't know what to say," Josh stammered. "You are just about the purtiest thing I ever saw!"

"What do you mean 'just about,'?" Julia responded, prodding Josh for more compliments.

"I mean you are the purtiest girl I ever saw!" Josh moved closer to Julia, stopped and said, "Yes, ma'am, the purtiest girl I ever seen."

The cornmeal dust in his hair and on his clothes didn't matter now, the only thing that mattered now was to touch Julia. His heartbeats were pulsating in his head as he placed his arm around her waist. Then with his other arm braced against the wall, drew Julia toward him.

Julia slowly moved her waist to his and lifted her head upward to meet Josh's face.

Josh, lost in the moment, did not realize Julia had raised her hands to his lips and touched them and said softly, "No, not now and not here."

The vibration of the turning millstones made Josh even more aware of the weakness in his legs. He backed away, too embarrassed to say a word. The disappointment glared through the cornmeal dust.

Julia looked shyly at Josh and whispered, "Don't feel foolish, I still like you."

Suddenly the vibrations and rumbling sounds of the millstones stopped and a voice rang out, "Josh, where in the name of God are you?"

Josh's father clambering at the door, now stuck, yelled out, "Josh, get out here!"

As Josh pushed inside the door and his father pulled from the outside, the door burst open, exposing Julia and Josh, alone together.

Julia's father, enraged at the sight, screamed, "Julia! Get in the wagon and, by God, stay there!"

Josh's father looked at him saying, "Just look at this damnable mess!"

Josh's gaze was fixed where the bags had filled and the cornmeal had poured over onto the mill floor. All the sacks were filled and a pile of cornmeal lay beneath each filled sack.

"I'll deal with you later," his father yelled, "and get this cleaned up and I mean right now!"

"I'm sorry about this, Frank," Mewborn said.

"No need to be, I'm sure it ain't all Josh's doings."

Julia was waiting in the wagon as her father came from the millhouse and loaded the wagon for the return home. She knew he was mad and dreaded the long wagon ride back to Coolmore.

Frank emerged from the door onto the platform with a sack of cornmeal. He placed it onto the platform and returned inside to bring out another sack of cornmeal. Before he returned inside, he paused and looked at Julia, shaking his head in disgust.

The wait seemed an hour, though it took only a few minutes for Frank to settle with Mr. Mewborn. Julia was silent as her father stepped down from the loading platform.

Unhitching the lines from the platform rails, Frank walked, lines in hand, to the front of the wagon. Before lifting himself onto the seat he looked again at Julia and mumbled, "God help us."

Grasping the side board of the wagon, he pulled himself first onto the wheel hub, then onto the seat board and without saying a word, snapped the lines and the team moved into the road.

The rumble of the wagon wheels crossing the river bridge sounded even louder in the silence. Julia's father was alone with his thoughts as he urged the mules on with a constant snapping of the lines.

The ride through Tarborough earlier in the day had been a pleasant experience, speaking with everyone, but the return journey on the same road westward seemed endless. Julia, in dread, remained silent.

An hour passed and finally Julia's father, without looking at her, said, "I am plain ashamed that my daughter would make such a fool of herself." Frank continued, "And I ain't exactly blind neither, I saw how you baited that boy, and you ought to be ashamed of yourself, too."

Julia knew what he was talking about, and the more she thought about it, the more she regretted her actions, but thinking about what happened did give her a sense of power and that felt good.

The sun appeared to be disappearing at the end of the road casting a long shadow behind the wagon. The wooded land beside the road offered no shady spots. The sun was directly ahead in such a position it was blinding to view the road. Julia had to turn her head from one side to the other to keep her eyes in focus. She caught a glimpse of her home and the trees in the front in the distance. She thought how good it would be to get back home again and the safety of the cupola.

Frank pulled on the left line. The team turned into the path leading from the road around the house to the rear where the barns were located.

Passing by the rear of the house, Frank stopped the team and turned to Julia, "Your mama needs some help with supper. I'll put up the team and be in after a little bit."

Julia grasped the side board of the wagon, leaped over and onto the ground. She was glad to be home and greatly relieved when she heard her father say, "There ain't no need to mention what happened today to your mama."

"We're home, Mama," Miss Julia yelled out. Julia was happy her father wasn't going to tell her mother what happened. "I'm coming on in to help with supper."

As Julia ran into the kitchen that was attached by a short porch to the main house, she began singing "We're marching to Zion, beautiful, beautiful Zion, we're marching upward to Zion, that beautiful city of God."

Bursting into the kitchen, Julia raced and grabbed her mother and swung around her, joyously exclaiming, "Home, home, home sweet home!"

Dolly, the Negro slave, still in the kitchen with Julia's mother, looked at Julia in amazement. "What ails that young'un, Missus Ada? She axs plum dizzy!"

"I don't know, Dolly, she's been gone all day with her daddy and God only knows what she's been up to. You know how it is with young'uns at her age," answered Ada.

"Julia, set the table for supper. Dolly has to go fix her husband his supper, and she ain't got all night to do it," her mother instructed.

Frank, stopping on the porch to wash up for supper, called out, "Ada, is supper 'bout ready? I'm perished. This ain't been a easy day; no, it ain't been easy ah-tall."

"Come on in, Frank, everything's 'bout ready, the biscuits are ready to come out of the stove and everything's on the table."

Frank opened the screen door and realized how hot it was in the kitchen. The wood cookstove was putting off heat and the sun had been shining in the backyard all day. Ada was wearing a high necked dress and long sleeves. Frank sympathized as she moved through the kitchen.

The aroma of freshly fried chicken, squash, butterbeans and string beans along with the baking biscuits invigorated Frank as he sat at the table.

Relaxed in the chair at the table, Frank asked, "Well, Ada, how was your day? We got a fairly good yield from the corn and old Mewborn didn't take so much for grinding it this time. He must know how much Richmond and Raleigh is taking from us now. "Frank continued to bemoan the needs of the newly formed confederacy, adding "It seems every day there's somebody here from Richmond wanting more and more. The government is taking all we can make and expects the land to do more and more," adding, "and taking our boys, too, and they ain't getting back home."

Ada, finishing putting supper on the table, said to Julia, "Come on, girl, take your place at the table so your daddy can return thanks."

Frank pulled himself closer, bowed his head and intoned, "Lord, what's here and what all we got is your goodness to us. Make us thankful and mindful of it all. Amen."

"How long this chicken been off the ground?" Frank asked.

Ada responded, "Just this morning and there ain't many left. I don't know if they've been taken off or running off, but they're getting scace."

The heat from the iron stove was less intense as Frank, Ada and Julia finished supper. Frank took a spoonful of bean "likker" and spread it over a biscuit, sighing, "Ain't gonna let this biscuit be left for the chickens."

"Julia, go on the porch and fetch a potful of water and put it on the stove, so's it can get warm to wash the dishes," her mama directed. "I'll clear the table."

After clearing the table and putting the leftover beans, chicken and biscuits in bowls, Ada spread the white cotton tablecloth over the entire table, and  murmured, "If the flies won't so bad, this wouldn't have to be done."

The dishes finished, Julia asked, "Daddy, can I go watch the sunset from upstairs?"

"Yeah, I suppose so. Your mama and me will be in the yard for a spell."

Julia hurried through the kitchen, into the main house and up the stairway to the cupola. There she paused with her arms supporting the upper part of her body as she leaned from the west side window of the cupola. The sun was disappearing beneath the treetops leaving what looked to be half an orange ball glowing over the green woods. The dust in the air partially obscured the outer edges of the brilliant ball of orange, as Julia was absorbed with her private thoughts. This day had proved something to her even though it had been embarrassing and frightening. She had learned of the influence and power she could exercise. That felt good; it made her feel important, and to feel important was to be important. But there was also a feeling of bitterness as she thought of the comforts and pretty things girls of her age were supposed to enjoy. The war was depriving her of that part of her life.

Darkness slowly engulfed Coolmore and the night would bring sleep and forgetfulness.

# CHAPTER FOUR

T he shadows lengthened as Frank and Ada paused on the back porch and gazed down the pathway through the trees to the barns. The Duprees spoke of the slave quarters near the barns. The two small wooden dwellings were home to Nathan and Dolly and Nero and Esther. Frank placed his arm on Ada's shoulder and wearily observed, "I hope the corn makes better this year than it did last year." Corn in the crib was being depleted rapidly. Hay in the loft of the mule barn would soon be gone. Willie was not home to help with the harvest.

Nathan and Dolly considered Coolmore home, and from all appearances were content. Neither could remember living anywhere else. Nero and Esther had been at Coolmore since the spring of 1862. Esther looked to be in her late twenties, but Nero looked older. Frank, a short time after Esther and Nero arrived, saw to it that they were married. Elder R. D. Hart, from the western part of the county stopped in on his way to Tarborough, and as a favor to Frank, joined Nero and Esther in Christian marriage.

Frank and Ada walked toward the barns. "Ada, do you think it would do Julia good to go visit with your sister Mattie over in Nash County for a few days? She's getting to the age now where she might need to talk with somebody other than us."

Ada stopped and looked at Frank, "You know I've been thinking the same thing. The poor girl ain't got nobody near her age around here to talk to and Mattie's a mite younger than me and she's always took a liking to Julia."

As he thought how he could get word to Mattie the quickest, Frank said, "I could ask Elder Tucker at church Sunday to tell Mattie when to pick her up at the station at Nashville. Brother Tucker has to pass close to Mattie's place on his way home. To be sure Julia can change trains at Rocky Mount. It wouldn't be too far for Mattie to ask her neighbor to go to pick her up at Nashville. Castalia ain't that far from the train station." Frank looked toward the mule barn, stopped and said, "Wait here a minute for me to put some more corn in the mule trough, then we'll go back to the house."

Frank hastened to the barn, removed some corn from the barn storage and placed the dry ears in the trough. He briskly walked back and joined Ada in the shade of an old oak tree.

Ada, noticing the back porch was well-shaded, suggested, "Let's sit on the porch 'till bed time. It ain't all the way dark yet, and it's a mite cooler here than upstairs."

Frank responded, "You're right, there ain't much air stirring right now, but maybe directly it will be." The two leisurely walked back and stepped onto the veranda. Frank placed two chairs side by side, sat down and leaned back against the wall with his feet propped on the chair rung. Ada adjusted her chair beside Frank and quietly lowered herself into the chair.

"I saw a lot of things going on in town today that I didn't realize was going on," Frank whispered to Ada, almost secretly. Ada reflected, "It's been so long since I've been to town, I ain't got the foggiest notion what you seen. We stay so busy here, we don't have the time to take notice of what's going on."

"We go to church, but we never get far enough to see what's happening on the river," Frank added. "You wouldn't believe your eyes. They're building boats, and I mean big boats. Why there's one so big it looks like they got stilts holding it up on all sides. The thing is propped up all 'round like hit's balanced on 'bacco sticks. The cotton press is getting a good working over, I suppose for the coming crop. Lord knows we need a good crop this year," lamented Frank. He went on, "What the weevil don't get, the gov'ment will."

Julia opened the back door quietly. "I think I'm going to bed now; it's too dark to see anything."

"Go ahead, your mama and me will be upstairs directly."

Julia stopped at the bottom of the stairs to give her eyes time to adjust to the darkness inside the house. She grasped the wooden handrail leading up the stairs. Pulling with her right hand, she slowly placed her foot on the first step, then the next until she arrived at the top. She paused again, then turned down the hallway to her room. She walked slowly as she groped her way along the wall until she came to the door of her room. The door was open and the moonlight filtering through the window offered enough light that Julia could make her way to the bed.

As she sat on the edge of the feather mattress, Julia raised her foot and unloosened the laces of her shoes and dropped them to the floor. Falling back onto the bolster, she thought, Oh God, another long hot night. Julia realized she must undress. The night would be even more miserable sleeping with a dress on. She sat on the edge of the mattress again and unbuttoned the front of her dress. As she stood, she let her dress drop to the floor and stepped from it. Only her plain pantalettes remained. Even this is too hot for a night like this. Take it off, she thought. Why not?

Julia slipped the vest over her head and shook her hair back into place. She tossed the top onto the dress and stepped farther from the window, unbuttoned the pantalette and pulled her legs up one at a time and removed the bottom of the pantalettes. Julia could not restrain a giggle as she remembered seeing chickens in the yard standing on one leg.

The mellow light of the moon flooded through the open window. Julia stood motionless. Her body was silhouetted on the wall between two family portraits. She turned slowly from side to side and watched the shadow respond. She wondered from whom she took her body. Did any of her ancestors have such definite curves? Is this what caused Josh to forget his work today?

Moving back to the bed, she rolled back the spread, and fell onto the mattress. The sheets felt cool to her naked body. Pulling the bolster under her head, Julia stared at the light flooding in the open window, remembering the day and remembering the power she felt in the presence of Josh.

Frank did not try to be quiet as he closed the bedroom door. Julia knew they were going to bed. Only the staccato sound of the crickets and an occasional guinea roosting in the trees broke the still night air. Julia closed her eyes. Sleep came slowly and then oblivion.

A loud shriek broke the silence. A sound of pain and a cry for help startled Julia from her sleep. She sat up in bed and braced herself with both hands, and again the blood curdling scream, "No! No!" and again a scream, "Help me! Help me!" Julia detected the cries were coming from the rear of the house. A dull thud and again a shriek, "Help me, please!"

Julia quickly leaped from the bed, put on her crumpled dress, and ran to the top of the stairs. Frank and Ada were making their way down the stairs, and Julia followed. "Daddy, what was that? It scared me to death."

"It sounded like Esther to me," Frank said as he reached for the lantern hanging on the back porch door facing. "Julia, get the lantern on the kitchen table," Frank called out as he held up the lantern in one hand. With his other hand he pressed the lever exposing the wick. "Ada, get me some matches."

Julia returned to the porch with the lantern and pressed the lever to raise the chimney. "Light this one at the same time, Daddy, I'll go with you and Mama."

Ada returned with the matchbox in her hand. She struck the match on the sandpaper side of the box, raised the flame to the lantern in Frank's hand and then to the lantern in Julia's hand.

Julia lowered the lantern chimney and adjusted the wick as she held the lantern level with her eyes. Again a scream came from the back of the house. "No! Please don't!" Another dull thud and the screams became more desperate. "Please, please, no, no!"

Frank, barefooted, started down the path to the slave quarters. "That sure sounds like Esther!" Holding his lantern before him, Frank broke into a run. Julia, barefooted, raised her lantern high and followed her father into the darkness. Frank called out as he hurried toward the quarters, "Ada, you stay at the house. I'll send Julia if I need you."

As they neared the log house of Nero and Esther, Frank recognized the form of Nero in the darkness, moving outside the open doorway.

"Is that you, Nero?" Frank yelled. "Nero! Is that you?"

"Yassur, hit's me," Nero responded as he moved from the open door into the darkness. "Yassur, hit's me."

Frank lifted the lantern above his head and leaned inside the open door. The flickering light against the log wall exposed Esther, on her knees in the corner. Her face was bloodied, her lips swollen. Her cotton night clothes were spattered with blood. Esther screamed and shrank into the corner.

The sight of Esther cowering in fear and screaming from pain enraged Frank and turning to Nero, he screamed, "Good God, Nero, did you mean to kill her? If I'd brung my gun, I'd put a ball in your black head!" He turned to Julia, "Go tell your mama we're going to be here for a while, and stop and tell Nathan and Dolly to get here with some water and cloths."

Frank assured Esther she was safe, looked at Nero angrily and demanded, "You black heathen, what got into you to do such as this?"

Nero, almost childlike, responded, "She wouldn't do her wifely duties."

"That don't give you no cause to do this to her," Frank pointed to Esther, as she cried softly.

Frank detected the odor of whiskey on Nero's breath. "Where'd you get the spirits this time? Every time you get hold of some whiskey, the devil gets in you!"

Nero dropped his head in shame, "Some of Coker's boys left a mite with me when you borrowed them to help us crop 'bacco."

"Why ain't you tending the barn like I told you? Get yourself down to that barn right now, and, by God, you stay there!" barked Frank.

Esther on her knees in the corner sobbed, "Misster Frank, I can't do what he wants every time he wants."

"Hit's all right, he won't bother you no more tonight."

Julia approached Nathan and Dolly's quarters. "Dolly, Nathan, are you in there? Daddy needs you. Nero has beat Esther awful bad. Bring some water and some cloths!"

"Yessum, we's here, Miss Julia," answered Nathan, "I'll get my lantern and Dolly will take the water bucket and cloths." He excitedly added, "We'll be right wid you." Julia waited as Nathan and Dolly joined her at the doorway of the cabin. Julia lifted her lantern above her head and ran toward Esther's quarters followed by Nathan and Dolly.

Dolly entered the door of Esther's quarters. Nathan held the lantern above his head. The light flowed into the corner where Esther was cowering. Dolly knelt and wiped the blood from Esther's face with wet cloths. She comforted Esther, "We'll have to keep cool water on this for a spell to keep it 'suaged down. I'll bring over some poke salve in the morning."

Esther rose from the floor with a groan. "He's a mean one when he's had the likker. One of dese days he's gonna have me in my grave."

Dolly helped Esther to the bed reassuringly. "But not dis night he ain't."

Nate, as Nathan was called, asked Dolly, "Do you think you need stay with her fer the rest of de night?" She answered, "I don't b'leve so, if she'll do like I say."

Esther moved slowly onto the shuck mattress. "I surely will,

I surely will."

Dolly, offering a damp cloth, stared at Esther. "Now you stay put and keep this on your face for de rest of de night and I'll be back at first light."

Julia realized her feet were bare, looked down and said, "I'd better get back. Esther, you keep the lantern for the night. I don't need it to find my way back."

Frank looked at Nate and Dolly and acknowledged, "I just don't know how we'd make it without you. I'm much obliged to you both." Nathan nodded at Dolly and looked at Frank. "You welcome, Mr. Frank."

Julia and her father walked slowly back to the house. "Girl, I know this ain't much of a life for you and I'm sorry." Julia assured him, "That's all right, Daddy."

Ada waited in the darkness on the porch. "Did Nero beat on Esther again?" Frank answered, "Fraid so, Ada, fraid so; I just don't know what to do with that buck. He's worth more alive than dead, but that ain't saying much."

Frank touched Julia on her cheek. "Run along back to bed, little girl, maybe tomorrow will be better."

As her bare feet touched the stair step, Julia realized she was not wearing her underclothing. She stopped and thought, well, it's dark, what's the harm? In the darkness she fell onto the feather mattress again, only this time without removing her dress. The bolster tucked to her neck, she turned her head toward the window. The moon had changed position in the night sky and the reflected light was now dim. There were no shadows on the wall to admire. Julia closed her eyes and tried to forget Esther's bloody face.

The early morning sunrise cast its bright light through the open window causing Julia to slowly open her eyes. It seemed only a short time had passed from darkness to morning light. Julia raised herself and swung her legs off the side of the bed.

She realized she had fallen onto the bed in the darkness while still partially dressed. She saw her clothing strewn on the floor from the night before.

Julia walked toward the dry sink. She thought how helpful it was that she had taken the time the previous afternoon to fill the pitcher with fresh water. Standing in front of the sink, she slipped her dress off her shoulders and allowed it to drop to the floor. With her foot she slid it from beneath her feet. Opening the dry sink drawer, she chose a patterned cloth that had been cut from a sugar sack. Laying it beside the porcelain bowl, she lifted the pitcher from the bowl and emptied half the water from the pitcher into the bowl. Julia soaked the cloth in the water and began to freshen her face.

The door was still ajar from the night before and Julia heard her mother call from the bottom of the stairs, "Julia, breakfast is almost ready, if you want anything to eat, you better not be late in coming."

The wet cloth felt so refreshing that Julia thought, why not bathe now? Events of the night before had left her uncomfortable enough, and she was still undressed as well.

With the wet cloth in hand, she reached for the soap in the colorful dish beside the bowl and lathered the cloth. She began to rub the cloth over her body, alternately rinsing the cloth to remove the soap residue from each part of her body.

The early morning breeze through the second story window dried Julia's body as quickly as she finished each arm and leg. Still undressed, she walked across the room to the mahogany veneered bureau topped with a mirror and began to brush her hair. She saw her reflection in the mirror as she brushed her hair. She thought to herself how she might look with some fancy clothes and wondered if she might turn a few heads.

"Juulia!" her mother called out again, "Do you want any thing to eat or not?"

"Yes, Mama, I'm coming."

The bureau drawer fully open, Julia lifted out some older pantalettes and quickly put them on. From another drawer she chose a black skirt and gray blouse. A blouse with an open collar would be more comfortable today than a high necked one.

Julia moved to a chair, sat and began pulling on her cotton knee-high stockings. Then she leaned forward and pulled her pantalette legs over the stockings. Near the door she stooped to pick up the clothing on the floor and remembered her shoes were on the porch. Glancing at the bowl of water she thought, I'll clean it all up later.

Julia dashed down the steps, one hand on the railing and the other clutching the soiled clothing. She ran through the doorway to the porch, pausing only to toss the clothing aside. Rushing into the kitchen she called out, "Am I too late?"

"No, not quite," her mother responded. "Take a chair and go ahead and eat with your daddy."

Julia adjusted her chair at the table as Frank began to pick up the bowl of grits and spoon them into his plate. He passed the bowl to Julia. "Julia, your mama and me think it might be good for you to visit your Aunt Mattie for a few days. She's been after you to come and stay with her a spell."

The fried side meat was within Julia's reach. "But I don't want to go to Aunt Mattie's. There isn't anyone to see and nothing to do over there. All she can talk about is scripture and what the preacher preached about at the last meeting."

"I know all that," Frank said, "But hit'll do you good to get away from here for a while. She's your mama's sister and besides that, she's a widow woman. You know her husband was killed at Cold Harbor up in Virginia and she ain't got no thought as to where he's buried." Frank stopped eating momentarily, "You know very well it ain't easy for your Aunt Mattie. Losing her spouse and with the Yankees about to take everything we worked for, it ain't getting any easier. You might be able to ease her burden a bit."

Julia interrupted, "But, but." Before she could utter another word, her father stopped her with, "No 'buts,' you're going and that's the end of it."

Ada came over to the table. "Your daddy will see Elder Tucker from Castalia Sunday at church, and ask him to tell your Aunt Mattie to have somebody pick you up at the station in Nashville."

Frank added, "The preacher has to pass close by her place on his way home."

"How will I change trains in Rocky Mount? I've never done it before," Julia asked, hoping to discourage Frank and Ada from giving it any more thought.

Frank looked at Julia, "You are old enough to take care of yourself for a little bit. You've been there before with us. To be sure you can do it by yourself. You ask enough questions around here, you can ask questions at the station."

"But somebody will have to take me to the station at Tarborough," Julia complained.

"No we won't. I'll flag down the train when it passes behind the place. I know the conductor and he'll see to it that you get on the right train," Frank responded. "You can tell your Aunt Mattie when we want you back home. She will see to it that you get on the right train," Frank added.

"But who will help with the work as Esther is about dead?" Julia asked. "Mama and Dolly can't do it all."

"Just never you mind, girl, we'll manage alright."

Frank pushed from the table with a sigh. "I better be 'bout seeing what kind of shape Nero's in. God knows I can't do without him now, what with the harvest coming. Julia, see 'bout Esther and tell your mama how she is."

Julia sat on the edge of the porch and dangled her legs for a moment before she raised her foot to pull on her shoes. With her knees close to her face, she laced her shoes then went to check on Esther. The path looked different in the light. The weeds, not visible in the darkness, now lined the path to the barns and slave quarters. Esther's crying wasn't vibrating the morning air, all seemed calm now.

She approached the cabin, which the night before, had held such awful and horrible sights and sounds. Julia pushed open the door and called, "You here, Esther?" Hearing no response, she pushed the door slightly harder and with a louder voice called, "Esther, you here?"

"Miss Julia, is that you?" a faint voice responded. "Yes, Esther, it's me. Can I come in?" answered Julia. In a strained voice Esther replied, "Yessum, you sure can."

Julia opened the door wider, stepped in and looked toward the bed where Esther was lying. "Good God, Esther, I ain't never seen anything like this before, you must be in pure misery."

"I kept wet rags to my face all night and Dolly rubbed some poke salve on me this mawning, and hit feels a mite easy. Things look a bit fuzzy," Esther said in a weak voice. "But I ain't seen Nero here since last night."

"He ought to be 'shamed to show himself," Julia declared. "Esther, what can I do to ease you some?" asked Julia.

"If'n you would, Miss Julia, would you tell Dolly I could use a mouthful of sump'n t'eat?"

"Surely I will. I passed Dolly going to the house as I was coming here. There's plenty left on the table."

As Julia left Esther's cabin, Frank was on his way to the curing barn. "Daddy, tell Nero Esther wants to see him. She's doin' some better."

Nearing the barn, Frank saw Nero and Nathan trying to appear busy tying tobacco leaves on sticks, getting them ready to go in the barn. "No need for you two bucks to act like you can do without Esther and Dolly, cause you can't." Frank stared directly at Nero. "And you, you worthless jackass, if there was a sheriff around I'd have you hung!" The glare from Frank continued. "Lincoln thinks you're worth freeing, but you ain't worth hanging. You better stay at what you're doing, cause Dolly and Esther can't help you none," muttered Frank as he turned and headed for the mule barn.

Every time Frank thought about the government in Washington sending the army into Virginia, and invading all North Carolina from Wilmington to Cape Hatteras, it infuriated him. North Carolina was a separate state and Washington ought to leave it alone.

Stopping at the well, he looked down into the darkness and thought, maybe there would be enough water to last until the rainy season in the fall.

The morning sun was higher in the sky and the heat of July began to intensify. Frank walked to the back porch to get his straw hat from a nail in the porch post. Julia was coming from the kitchen, "Do I really have to go visit Aunt Mattie?"

"Yes, you do, and I don't want to hear about it any more," Frank grumbled. "Come Sunday I'm going to make the arrangements with Brother Tucker to let your Aunt Mattie know when to be expecting you."

Ada listened as Julia pleaded with her father. Julia returned to the kitchen and asked, "Mama, do I have to visit Aunt Mattie?" Before she could finish, her mother said, "Stop right there, girl, you heard your daddy and that's the end of the matter." In a pouting mood, Julia muttered, "Alright! Alright! Alright!"

Sunday morning came too quickly to suit Julia. She did not care to go to church. Breakfast was very quiet, as Frank asked, "Mama, have you made up your mind about church today? If you're going, we've got to be leaving before seven."

Ada, realizing it required at least one hour for the wagon ride into Tarborough, responded, "No, I don't believe I'll try to make it today. This week has been real difficult. Maybe Julia will go with you."

"No, I don't want to go either," Julia added, knowing her father intended to ask Elder Tucker to pass a message to her Aunt Mattie about her visit next week.

"Well, since it's only me going today, I might as well use the cart and one mule instead of a team and give one mule a day off," observed Frank, as he got up from the table and started to the stairway.

He knew it would not require much time to dress and hitch the mule to the cart. Frank moved a little more relaxed, knowing he did not have to wait for Ada and Julia.

The morning sun was bright as the cart disappeared at the end of the path. Ada called out, "Julia! Just because you got out of going to church today, don't mean you can lay around all day." Her mother quickly added, "Get yourself back in here and help me clean up the table."

Julia returned to the kitchen. "Do you think daddy will take dinner with somebody at church today, and not be back home 'till about dark?"

"To be sure he will. I don't expect him to turn down going home with somebody for dinner and getting a chance to talk," Ada said with confidence.

Sunday passed quickly for Julia and late in the afternoon she climbed to the cupola to watch for her father to appear from the east. Looking to the west she could almost measure by the tree tops the rate of descent of the sun. Her sight began to blur from viewing the brilliance of the departing rays. Julia stepped to the east window and peered toward the road. She could barely view the dust in the distance but she knew from experience it would be her father prodding the mule to get home before dark. Julia dreaded to leave the solitude of the cupola. The thought of visiting her Aunt Mattie was depressing.

She could hear the cart rumbling down the path to the barn as her mother called, "Julia, your daddy's home, you better get in here and help me with supper. It won't take your daddy long to feed-up." In no time at all Frank was wiping his shoes at the back door.

Frank entered the kitchen wearily. "Well Julia, you'll be taking the train Wednesday morning for your Aunt Mattie's place, and she'll be expecting you. Brother Tucker will pick you up in Nashville and take you to your Aunt Mattie's." Frank dusted off his clothing with his hands and pulled a chair up to the table. Julia dreaded hearing this announcement, but it was what she expected, and she knew there was no need to complain about it.

"Something smells good," Frank said and pulled his chair closer to the table. Supper was quieter than usual as Julia resigned herself to the visit she did not care for.

Julia finally broke the silence of supper. "Daddy, I have heard you and your friends talking about a Section Nine of some kind of constitution. I don't understand what you are talking about."

"Oh yes, little lady, we have talked aplenty about that part of the constitution and it's likely to take up more talk," Frank responded to Julia. Frank looked calmly and sympathetically at his daughter. "I know you have been deprived of a lot of the nice things a little girl ought to have because of this war. You have lost a lot of your kin and I know you don't understand why. I also realize you need to know why we have been asked to go through so much hardship and I intend to explain it all to you, but right now I feel like I have pulled a plow all day and this can wait for a more convenient time," Frank sighed.

"That's all right, Daddy. I know mama and you are worn down," acknowledged Julia.

Julia usually enjoyed the longer hours of daylight during the summer months, but on this day the sun appeared to stop in its course. The pain of the thoughts of the trip was prolonged as the day lingered. Sunday evenings were usually pleasant with talk of the coming week. Tonight Julia did not want to hear anything that concerned her having to take the train Wednesday morning.

Monday melted into Tuesday, and Wednesday dawned with the early morning sun obscured by the lingering dust of the work of the previous day. It was another dry and sweltering July day. She loathed the journey that was ahead of her.

"Julia," her mother called out loudly from the bottom of the stairway, "You better be up and about now."

"Yes, Mama, I'll be right down," answered Julia wearily.

Julia, remaining motionless on the mattress for a few moments, realized she might as well get started. She remembered her mother often telling her, that the hardest part of any job was getting started.

Atop the trunk at the end of the bed she saw the valise she had packed the evening before. Julia made her way to the dry sink and poured water from the pitcher into the bowl. Perhaps some fresh water would invigorate her to take that first step. Finished at the dry sink, Julia brushed her hair for a few minutes. She flipped the freshly brushed strands off her shoulder and placed her hands behind her head. She began twisting one half of the locks toward the back of her head. Her arms dropped to her side in frustration. Julia looked into the mirror above the dry sink and thought, oh God, what's the use?

"Juuulia!" her mother called loudly, "What's keeping you? If you want any breakfast before you leave, I would suggest you hurry."

"Yes ma'am, I'm on my way," replied Julia.

Julia began to twist the remaining strands of hair into a second bun behind her head. With a long sigh she pinned it into place beside the first bun. With a final look into the mirror, Julia thought, well this old gray skirt and blouse will just have to do. I don't intend to wear a hat either. Julia walked to the end of the bed, took a last look at the unmade bed and thought to herself, let Dolly take care of it. She will be in the house for the rest of the day.

Closing her valise, Julia jerked it up and swung it toward the door. She stumbled on the loose shoe laces she had not taken the time to tie. Julia stopped on the top step and sat lacing her shoes completely.

"Julia, for heaven's sake, girl, are you deliberately trying to be late so's your daddy won't put you on the train?" her mother asked from the bottom of the stairs.

Julia answered sarcastically, "No, no, no, no, I'm just putting it off as long as I can."

"Don't get smart with me, girl, get on downstairs and eat a little something," Ada snapped, and added, "I'll wrap you a ham biscuit to take with you for dinner."

Julia stopped, put down the valise and entered the kitchen. She walked by the table, reached and clutched a biscuit in her hand and began to eat as she walked to the porch.

"Julia, ain't you going to take the time to sit at the table and eat some breakfast? It'll be a mighty long time 'fore dinnertime!" insisted her mother.

"No, daddy wants me on that train and I don't want to disappoint him," Julia said in a sulking manner.

"There's that smart mouth again, girl, you better mind what you say!" her mother reminded Julia.

Julia heard her father talking to Nate as they came onto the back porch. "Nate, I want you to take Miss Julia's valise down to the railroad at the end of the path from the barns, and wait for us there. We'll be there directly."

"Yassur, Mr. Frank," answered Nate.

Nate picked up the valise from the porch, walked a short distance toward the railroad, turned and asked, "Mr. Frank, does you want Dolly to come and help Missus Ada while Miss Julia is gone?"

"To be sure I do, Nate. Tell Dolly that Miss Julia is leaving for a spell and we want her at the house," Frank answered.

Frank looked directly at Julia. "You ready, girl? It won't be too much longer and we ought to hear the train whistle between here and Tarborough."

Frank turned and faced Ada. "I won't be gone long. I've got a lot of work to do today that won't wait."

Leaving the kitchen, Julia hesitated on the porch for her father. Together they stepped into the path leading to the railroad tracks. The early morning sun on its journey through the southern sky gave no hint of rain. It would be another hot and sultry July day. Frank slowed his steps and turned to Julia. "Do you remember asking me about a Section Nine of the Confederate Constitution?" Julia looked at her father. "Yes, sir, I remember,"

"I suppose now is as good a time as any to explain it to you; that is, if you still want to know," Frank asked.

"I do still want to know, Daddy. I've heard a lot of talk about it and I don't understand what they're talking about," replied Julia.

Frank stopped and looked directly at Julia. "We'll have to go back in history a little bit so's you can get a better grip on it, or you might not really understand what's going on in this war today."

"That's all right, Daddy, we've got the time. The train is never on time anyway. I watch it from the house and it never passes at the same time every day," observed Julia.

"Well, child," Frank continued, "we in the southern states, and we in North Carolina, don't see why if we came into the central government of the United States of our own doing, why we can't get out the same way. If our state wants out of the federal government, we don't see why we can't get out. The state was here first and we don't see why we have to listen to somebody else in Washington tell us what we got to do. Now I know," Frank added, "that holding a man in bondage ain't right and it ain't according to the scriptures. This way of life won't started by me and I can't stop it all at once. This land was handed down to me from my father and this way of life was handed down, too. I don't know anything else to do."

Julia looked at her father and asked, "But what do other people want you to do? Everybody seems to have a notion as to what to do, but nobody can tell us how to do it."

"That's right, child, and those folks up north don't understand what a mess it would put us in if we had to get shed of all our field hands at one time and start trying to hire hands. We feel like we have the right as a state to get out of the union and form our own country, just as much as we had the right to get in the union." Frank continued, "Julia, I want you to remember this real good. We in North Carolina got out of the Federal Union and formed our own country with a lot of other states and we are the Confederate States of America. We got our own Congress and we got our own Constitution, just like the federal government." He continued emphatically, "And in that constitution it says in Article Nine that the importation of Negroes of the African race from any foreign country other than the slave holding states or territories of the United States of America is forbidden. Our Confederate Congress is required to pass such laws to prevent such things and to stop the trading of slaves from any state not a member of this confederacy."

"Now, child, this ain't fast enough to suit some people up north who think we ought to change right now, no matter what happens to our crops and our property. We'll do away with the wrong fast enough, if they'd give us time. But they ain't willing to wait and we ain't willing to sacrifice everything at one time. Mr. Lincoln sent his army into Virginia first and we considered that an invasion of our country. We didn't have any choice but to defend our country, since we are a state first. Our state don't have to listen to any federal government that is trying to force us to do what we ain't able to do." Frank began to display his irritability. "The northern people, they don't understand our farming ways. They have all those factories and some of them politicians think they can force their ways on us, and we ain't going to have it. We know holding a person in bondage ain't right, but they ain't willing to give us time to set it right." Frank added, "I'm scared we ain't seen the worst of it yet."

Near the tracks where Nate was waiting, Julia heard the mournful train whistle in the distance. In almost perfect sequence the whistle sounded, each time becoming louder as the engine drew closer.

Frank stepped into the middle of the tracks and faced east. Approaching from the east, he saw a small black object with a funnel-looking stack, belching black smoke with every stroke of the engine piston. The sounds became louder and the locomotive with its "cow catcher" front became more distinct. The pride of the Atlantic and East Carolina Railroad came into view. Frank pulled a white cloth from his pocket and began waving it from side to side above his head. As he moved from the center of the tracks he heard the locomotive releasing steam as it prepared to stop.

As the locomotive slowly came to a stop, Frank walked with Julia and Nate to the rear of the train. Conductor Hugh Speight approached from the last rail car.

"What's the problem, Frank?" asked Speight with a look of bewilderment. "You don't usually flag us down. You normally wave as we go past. What's wrong?"

Frank answered, "Not a thing, Hugh. I just need a favor, and you need a passenger." The conductor replied, "You are right about that. Who's the passenger?"

Frank took Julia by the arm. "My little girl here is going to Rocky Mount and then to Nashville to visit her aunt. Do you think you can see to it to get her to the station?"

"Sure can, Frank, but I'll have to charge you thirty cents for the ticket," reminded Speight.

Frank nodded, "I expected that and I'm sorry to stop you out here, but it saved me a wagon trip to Tarborough. I'm much obliged to you for stopping."

"Well, with all the supplies we are carrying, I don't want the superintendent to find out about this unscheduled stop," said the conductor.

Frank grasped Julia by the arm, giving her a lift onto the steps at the rear of the passenger car. "Grab the top railing and pull yourself on up, girl."

Julia pulled herself onto the rear platform and turned toward her father. "Don't forget my valise, Daddy."

"Nate, put Julia's bag up on the platform for her. She can handle it from there." Frank turned to the conductor, "Much obliged, Hugh."

Conductor Speight reached for the iron railing, pulled himself onto the bottom step, leaned outward as he held to the railing and waved his arm.

The engine began to puff steam from its sides and with a sudden jolt the train of cars vibrated one against the other. The last car snapped like a whip. Its giant wheels slipped on the rails momentarily then settled onto the iron ribbons. The wheels gripped with each revolution simultaneously with the venting pistons. Slowly the cars began to move in front of Frank and Nate.

Frank waved to Julia as the passenger car passed, "We'll be waiting for you next Tuesday. Have a good visit!"

Frank moved to the center of the tracks. He watched as the train became smaller and smaller, disappearing in a plume of smoke into the trees. Frank turned to Nate, "Let's get back. There's a lot to be done this day."

# CHAPTER FIVE

The Third New York Artillery with its cannons lined wheelhub to wheelhub, the limbers unattached in a straight row behind the cannons and the caissons in line, gave the appearance of perfect positioning according to the official artillery manual. The artillerymen's tents reflected the same order of straight lines. Stacked cannon ammunition continued the same correctness. The entire artillery camp mirrored the official manual.

Rays of early morning sunlight reflecting from the polished bronze barrels lightened the chalk-colored tent encampment, giving the appearance of arrival of all newly-manufactured equipment.

Sergeant Thomas Utz, section chief of the Mountain Howitzers, on morning rounds noticed General Potter's aide enter the tent of Captain Snyder. The sergeant had heard camp rumors that some artillery might be moved out along with some cavalry units to destroy some vital Confederate supply lines in eastern North Carolina.

As Utz continued, he observed Sergeant John Rudisill, another section chief, making his rounds. "John Rudisill," Utz called loudly, "can I have a word with you?"

"Sure thing," replied Rudisill, "meet me at the front of the formation."

The two sergeants stopped their inspection, started toward the front of the cannon formation and simultaneously met in front of the artillery display.

Utz looked directly at Rudisill. "Did you see General Potter's aide going into Captain Snyder's tent?"

"Sure did," snapped Rudisill.

"What do you think it means?" questioned Utz. "Don't know," responded Rudisill.

"Well, don't let yourself talk too much, John," Utz said sarcastically to Rudisill. With an exasperated expression, Rudisill replied, "How in blazes do you expect me to know, Utz?"

Sergeant Utz looked at Rudisill directly. "Well, haven't you heard the rumors about our batteries being used by Potter?"

"Sure have, but I've about given up on it since we seem to have been forgotten."

Utz spotted Captain Snyder and the aide as they emerged from the captain's tent. "Look yonder, there they come. They're heading this way."

As the officers approached, the two sergeants came to attention, saluted, and stood rigid for a few moments. They relaxed as the captain suggested for them to be at ease.

Captain Snyder, looking at the kepis the sergeants were wearing, asked with a smile, "This is Battery K of the Third New York Artillery, is it not? If it is not, then I have the wrong section chiefs in front of me." The captain recognized the insignia on their kepis and knew what battery they were in charge of.

Captain Snyder looked at the formation of ready artillery. "Have two sections of Mountain Howitzers ready to move in a column of cavalry on the morning of the 17th at first light."

Snyder looked at Rudisill, then looked at Utz and shook his head, "I don't know why old Potter requested for you two to be a part of this raid," and continued, "but he did, so that is that! And that's the end of that!"

"Yes, sir!" the two sergeants responded simultaneously.

Captain Snyder, walking from the rows of cannons with General Potter's aide, turned and ordered, "Carry on, sergeant."

Utz smiled as he stared at Rudisill, "You hear that, John? Both of us will be taking part!" and with a reluctant sigh added,

"Good Lord, I hope the brigade don't hear old Potter asked for us!"

"Suppose we will, suppose we will," mumbled the reticent Rudisill and he continued, "if they know, they know!" Sergeant Utz focused his eyes on Sergeant Rudisill, "Maybe Old Potter doesn't think these old Mountain Howitzers are worth a captain's presence."

"Come on, John, let's take a look at the back side of the depot. I want to see where the best sections are," Utz said as the sergeants turned downhill toward the rear of the area.

"This must be a fearsome sight from the other side of the Trent River," Rudisill remarked. He continued, "This is a lot of iron and brass on this side of the river."

New Berne, situated where the Neuse and Trent rivers converge, gave the town strategic importance to the Federal forces now in command of most of the Carolina coastline.

Sergeant Utz began to move uphill from the river. "John, do you think we need to check with the livery quartermaster to requisition the horses? This operation will require twenty-two horses by my figuring."

"With two spares, that would be twenty-four," added Rudisill.

"I don't know if Potter is aware it takes three horses for a section of a Mountain Howitzer. With two sections and the crews for two sections, that's sixteen men with their sixteen horses," Utz reminded Rudisill.

"Yeah, I reckon we better see about it," Rudisill concurred.

The two artillerymen left the armory area and walked slowly to the livery stables. July's heat began to intensify as Utz and Rudisill neared the stable area. No one had to remind them they had reached their destination. They braced themselves on the corral timbers. The sergeants were admiring the animals when two cavalry officers approached from the opposite direction.

"Sergeants," Chamberlain interrupted, "I am Captain Seth Chamberlain and this is Lieutenant Caleb Henderson of the Third New York Cavalry."

"Very good to make your acquaintance, sir," responded Sergeant Utz. "This is Sergeant Rudisill and I'm Sergeant Utz of the Third New York Artillery."

Captain Chamberlain did not want to suggest his knowledge of any impending operation. "Have you gunners by any chance been advised of any operations you might be a part of?"

"Yes sir, in fact, we have just been ordered by Captain Snyder to have in readiness for the 17th two sections of Mountain Howitzers," answered Sergeant Utz.

Chamberlain smiled approvingly at the answer. "That's good, it looks like we'll be in the same operation. Six companies of the Third New York and three companies of the Twelfth New York along with one company of Potter's North Carolina volunteers have been alerted to be ready for the same operation."

"Thank you, gentlemen," added Henderson.

Seth looked approvingly at Henderson and smiled. "Let's get back to quarters; this really is shaping up for sure."

Near their quarters the officers saw Major Jacobs and Major Cole standing on the Alcock front porch. Jacobs remarked in a loud voice, "Gentlemen, you're right on time to learn of our orders. Cole and I have just learned from Colonel Jourdan about the raid we're going to take part in on the 17th."

Major Cole added, "Yes indeed, come on to the back where there is some shade and we'll pass the information on."

The officers walked to the rear of the house and found a well-shaded spot. Major Jacobs quickly spoke first. "The good news is we're moving out to destroy some vital Confederate supply lines," Jacobs hesitated, "and the bad news is Potter is going along, too."

A look of disappointment surfaced on their faces as Captain Chamberlain said, "I had hoped for Colonel Jourdan to command. I'm not so sure Potter knows what he's doing."

Major Cole injected, "And Potter can be downright mean, especially when he wants to prove his point."

The trees provided shade and a gentle breeze from the river rustled the green leaves for a moment, then silence fell over the group.

The stillness was broken by the loud voice of Private White as he rounded the corner of the house and ran in the direction of the two officers, "Captain Chamberlain! Major Jacobs! General Potter wants you at his headquarters." Private White added excitedly, "And you, too, Lieutenant Henderson. I believe the general's entire staff has been called in."

"Thank you, Private, we'll come on immediately," Captain Chamberlain acknowledged. "Lieutenant Henderson," the captain asked, "do you think this may be the beginning of the operation we have been hearing about?"

"I certainly hope so," answered the lieutenant and added, "we have been waiting long enough."

The two officers, though reluctant to leave the shade, rounded the house, increased their strides and started for the headquarters of General Potter. The dusty narrow street was no different from a few days before when they had been summoned by General Potter. This time Captain Chamberlain did not feel the dread.

As he stepped onto the porch of General Potter's headquarters, Captain Chamberlain again admired the scroll woodwork and the columns supporting the front porch. At every projection and overhang appeared detailed scrolled woodwork to support the appearance of weight. The captain was reminded of his days in Albany as an apprentice architect. He knew the importance of appearance in a well-designed building. He had also used the gingerbread decorations in his early designs. Chamberlain hesitated, turned and motioned for the lieutenant to come onto the porch. He could see the entire staff was already in the front living room with General Potter.

With a rap on the door, Seth again was overwhelmed with a sense of intrusion into the privacy of some unknown presence from the past.

The gruff voice of General Potter vibrated through the doorway. "Come in, Captain, and you too, Lieutenant." Just as quickly as the sense of a past presence came over the captain, it was dispelled by the incivility of the general's tone of voice.

The room, unchanged from the gathering earlier, still spoke to the present of its past elegance. Captain Chamberlain, as he looked at General Potter, thought, what an incongruity!

General Potter got up from the chair behind the table and shoved the chair back with his foot and removed the cigar from his mouth. "Gentlemen, I believe we're all here. Let's get on with the details of this operation." Looking at all the officers, Potter continued, "And I think you brigade commanders have maps for your own use. I won't go over this but one time with you, and you should be briefed enough to know what our objectives are." General Potter pointed to the map on the table. "We are going to destroy the trestle bridge of the Wilmington and Weldon Railroad over the Tar River at Rocky Mount, and whatever we find of stores and transportation, we will also destroy. I am determined that nothing of any value will be left to Lee's army." With great delight in his new-found authority, Potter added, "And then we're going to burn the bridge over the Tar River at Tarborough and destroy any thing of any use by anyone who supports this rebellion." The general reiterated, "And I mean to level everything that might be of any value, and that includes private property." Potter paused, as if to gain more courage for his next statement, "This section of North Carolina has been spared for the most part, but that is about to change, and change drastically. When we return, I expect to see the smoke of destruction in our rear and fear in the eyes of the enemy." The general with bravado continued, "And anything that can't be brought back or used by our forces I expect to be destroyed. Before we go any further, is that understood?" asked Potter, bracing himself on the desk. "And I will not tolerate any timid souls in this operation. Is that understood?"

"Yes, sirs," sounded like falling dominoes around the table.

"Colonel Jourdan," Potter called out, "you are to take your brigade on the afternoon of the 16th and cross the Neuse at Street's Ferry and proceed to Swift Creek, and wait there for my arrival. I will follow on the morning of the 17th with a column of cavalrymen and two sections of artillery and artillerymen." The general looked at his staff and assured Jourdan, "And we will join your brigade at Swift Creek on the 17th. Swift Creek should provide fresh water and protection for an overnight bivouac," the general continued.

Potter walked slowly to the side of the table and placed his finger back onto the map indicating Swift Creek, "And there on the night of the 17th you will all be given final orders and destinations. Colonel Jourdan," General Potter reminded, "don't neglect to take a voucher with you for Mr. Street at the ferry." The general glanced at the men, "I don't recollect that he ever carried anything over the river that he didn't charge a fancy price for." Potter looked at Major Jacobs, "You do know the units I want for this expedition, do you not, Major?"

"Yes, sir, I made note of your instructions when you first informed us of the possibility of this operation," responded the major.

"Major Cole, I presume you have the same information?" asked the general.

"Yes, sir, we will have all units in readiness at your directive," Cole answered.

Potter paused and looked slowly around the room. "Very

well, gentlemen, then the operation will proceed."

From the back side of the table General Potter looked directly at the officers at the front of the table, "Tomorrow, the 17th of July, you will assemble the specified units of cavalry at seven o'clock on the road to Street's Ferry. We will use the Carrowan Farm wheat field as a staging area. I have ordered Captain Snyder of the Ninth New York Artillery to make ready two sections of Mountain Howitzers and their crews. Again, let me emphasize we will take a line of march to Street's Ferry. From there we will proceed to Swift Creek, and there we will join with Colonel Jourdan for an overnight bivouac." Potter continued to emphasize the movements in slow and deliberate words, "And Colonel Jourdan's brigade will be detached for a feinting movement toward Kinston on the morning of the 18th. The column under my command will proceed on the morning of the 18th on the road to Greenville and from there to the community of Sparta. We will at all times remain on the south side of the Tar River. At no point will we be required to cross the Tar River. We will destroy all bridges crossing the Tar, as we will not have to use them on our return to New Berne."

General Potter again guided his finger along the route of the Tar on the map. "I know it sounds odd, but we do not have to cross the Tar to destroy our objectives at either place. We can hold the enemy from crossing the Tar to attack our front very easily at Tarborough." Potter continued, "When we reach Sparta, we will bivouac again, and on the morning of the 20th I will direct our column divided into two columns. One column will proceed to Rocky Mount and one column will proceed to Tarborough." The general paused for a moment. "On the night of the 19th I will issue detailed orders to Major Jacobs, who volunteered for the raid at Rocky Mount, and also to Major Cole, who volunteered for the raid on Tarborough. If there are no questions, you are dismissed, gentlemen."

Only the sound of shuffling boots was heard. The staff officers turned in the direction of the door. In single file they began their exit from the presence of General Potter. The general began to handle his cigar again and reached for a match in his vest pocket. "See you in the morning, gentlemen."

Captain Chamberlain sought out Lieutenant Henderson. "Lieutenant Henderson, hold a minute. Do you mind my walking back to quarters with you?"

The lieutenant hesitated as the other staff officers moved ahead and waited for the captain to join him. "Well, Captain, we've got our work to do today, getting all the units together and ready for tomorrow."

"Yes, we do and we'd better get to it," responded Chamberlain.

The front porch of the Alcock house was in the sunlight. Chamberlain and Henderson hesitated in the morning sunlight as Henderson said, "Let's go to the back, this front is just too hot."

Morning quickly passed to afternoon. Afternoon quickly passed to evening. The late afternoon sun again caused the Alcock house to cast a shadow toward the south bank of the Neuse and the day quickly merged with all other days. Darkness slowly engulfed New Berne.

Nature's river symphony began to intensify as the inactivity of night silenced the noises of the day. The rain frogs of summer and the immature crickets began their nightly overture to darkness.

Captain Chamberlain considered another letter to Melissa but dismissed the thought as there were too many other activities to keep his mind occupied. Tomorrow would be the beginning of a long and difficult operation and the captain realized he should try to get as much rest as was possible this night. Without attempting to use the oil lamp, Seth removed his uniform and boots. He placed his boots beside the bed and laid his uniform on the chair near the bed. The captain knew tomorrow would begin early. The room was dark as the clouds of the July night obscured the light of the moon. Sleep was the only opiate for the pain of separation. Melissa was so far away, yet so near in the captain's thoughts. Oblivion finally engulfed the captain as time and space became irrelevant in sleep.

The early morning activity awoke Seth. For a moment his confused thoughts suggested he had not awakened on time for the operations of the day. The frightening thought caused his heart to race as he jumped from the bed and ran to the window. Leaning on the window sill and peering through the open window, he realized light was just beginning to dispel the pall of the night before. Thank God, he thought, as he withdrew from the window.

He listened as the horses stirred and stretched the limits of the tethers that secured them to the trees behind the house. Seth was glad they had made some preparation the night before for the horses to be near at first light.

Seth dressed hurriedly in full uniform and side arms even though he knew the weight of his side arm and saber would add to the discomfort of riding in the midday heat.

After a dash down the stairway, he felt compelled to stop on the back porch. He must at least splash some water on his face to clear the sleep from his eyes. His beard, which had not been trimmed in days, began to irritate his skin. Maybe this operation would be over and he would be back at quarters by Saturday night. The Saturday bath was always refreshing.

Fully dressed, he stepped from the back porch and headed for the wooded area where the horses were tethered. He and Lieutenant Henderson had readied their saddles the evening before and left them on the ground near the well. Seth thought his horse could use some fresh water. Before he reached for his saddle, he lowered the bucket into the dark well until he heard it splash. He waited a few minutes as it filled before he pulled on the chain to hoist the bucket to the top of the well. Captain Chamberlain saw Lieutenant Henderson as he approached. "Henderson, bring me that bucket from the watering trough. I need to see to it that the horses are watered."

"Good thinking, Captain. This may be a long day and the horses will appreciate it," said Henderson.

Chamberlain emptied the bucket into the trough and watched the horses as they began to drink. "Henderson, when was the last time this trough was filled? It looks like it's been neglected."

Henderson, leaning to lift the saddle upon his horse, responded, "I don't know. The privates assigned to it don't care, and it looks like the longer we stay here the less anyone cares."

The captain raised the saddle onto his horse. He noticed the troopers were beginning to saddle up. Again he observed the cavalrymen were in full uniform. All were carrying sabers and the newly issued Colt revolvers. Chamberlain called out to Henderson, "Lieutenant, I haven't seen this many weapons in a long time. I knew we had them available. Looks good!"

The captain and lieutenant mounted simultaneously and adjusted themselves in the saddle and Henderson asked, "Ready, Captain?"

With his cavalry-issue hat adjusted, Chamberlain called out, "Sergeant, let's move out!"

Dust began to rise as the horses and riders moved onto the narrow street and began the short ride to the staging area. Seth felt the excitement as he reached into his saddlebag for a piece of hardtack. Some morning start, he thought, and no coffee either, only the tepid canteen water.

The staging area glittered as sunlight danced from bright saber hilts and sheaths as rippling waters reflecting the brightness of the sun on a windy afternoon. Seth marveled at the affect of orderliness. The column began to take shape. General Potter's staff issued commands as to where the companies were to position themselves.

Captain Chamberlain heard Major Jacobs call, "Chamberlain, over here! We're forming to follow General Potter."

Captain Chamberlain guided his mount in the direction of

Major Jacobs, barely able to hear amid all the rattling of cavalry equipment. With every movement of the horses, the sounds of metal meeting metal intensified to one rhythmic, deafening roar.

The column began to take shape and was taking on the appearance of a massive military movement. Potter and his staff were entering the road to Street's Ferry with the general at the head of the column. Like a giant snake, the column began to wind from the staging field onto the road behind Potter and his staff as they proceeded up the road.

In a column of two abreast, the companies of troopers began to lengthen the column. They joined in one company behind another. The column of mounted troopers with glistening equipment reflected light with every movement. A glare of blinding light reflected from the sun. Company after company of mounted blue clad troopers wound their way off the staging field. The gold insignias mingled with the blue trappings.

Captain Chamberlain looked over his shoulder. "By God, it looks like the column is two miles long."

Henderson alongside, turning in the saddle, responded, "Good heavens, this is the longest column I've ever seen. Maybe Old Potter does know what he's doing."

As the column passed a curve in the rutted road, the rear of the column was hidden. The two sections of Mountain Howitzers mounted on six horses entered the road behind the cavalrymen.

The artillerymen, forming an orderly column of their own, brought up the rear guard. Two mounted artillerymen led a howitzer section, followed by six mounted artillerymen. Dust began to cloud the horizon in all directions as the column snaked its way to Street's Ferry on the Neuse River.

General Potter began to realize the massive crossing was going to take more time than he had accounted for. He thought for the first time where Colonel Jourdan might be and the difficulties he might have encountered on the day before.

Potter remained upright and silent until the ferry came into view as the column rounded the final turn. The general excitedly broke the silence. "There's old Street's operation! It looks like he's been waiting for us. Come on ahead with me, Major Cole, and I'll tell him how things are to be handled."

Potter and Cole spurred their mounts and raced ahead of the column to alert Street to be ready when the column arrived.

General Potter quickly dismounted. "Mr. Street, did Colonel Jourdan cross here yesterday afternoon?"

"Yes, he did and it was gittin' kinda late," answered Street.

"Did he cross without incident?" queried Potter.

"He crossed without anything happening, but he didn't cross without complaining," answered Street.

"I'm not concerned with his attitude, only his success," growled Potter.

Street responded, "Sure, sure, he's on the other side."

Potter turned in the direction of the approaching column and pointed with his hand. "I've got over three hundred mounted troopers heading here at this very time and I want them all across before dark."

"I ain't taking no riders on horses across on my ferry," Street retorted.

Potter angrily interjected, "I didn't say they would stay mounted during the crossing. I know very well each trooper will have to steady his horse. Do you think I'm stupid?"

"Your sense ain't in question here, General, just yer loyalty," Street added sarcastically.

Major Cole saw the flush in the general's face and deliberately moved between Street and Potter. "The main thing here is to get to the other side."

General Potter realized the situation immediately. "You're right, Major, you're right."

Major Cole had not observed a ferry before. It appeared to be nothing more than a raft of logs spiked together and topped with rough hewn planks, just enough to float. Posts had been added at the four corners to support a rail around the outer edges.

Major Cole doubted the reliability of the crude contraption to transport the column across the river, though it was positioned at the river's most narrow point. The major observed there was only a large rope secured to the ferry on one end and pulled through a pulley attached to a large oak tree on the opposite bank. A mule on the north side of the river pulled it across. A mule on the south bank of the river pulled it back by a rope and pulley. Very simple.

"You want to go first, Mr. Potter?" grumbled Street, "From the dust being kicked up in the distance, your boys are 'bout here."

Potter viewed the gradual incline from the water's edge. He knew it would be easy enough for the troopers to dismount and lead their horses onto the ferry.

General Potter stared directly into Street's eyes, "Get as many as you can on each trip. I can't be here all night waiting on you."

The column slowly approached the ferry landing as Potter called out to Major Jacobs, "Major, follow me onto the ferry and the rest will follow as Street directs."

The general and his staff dismounted, gripped the reins of their mounts and slowly led the animals onto the ferry. Jacobs observed how Potter wanted it accomplished.

The major looked at Captain Chamberlain and nodded. "We'll do it the same way, Captain."

Captain Chamberlain and Lieutenant Henderson neared the platform of the ferry as Henderson said, "This is my first time at such as this."

"Mine too," Seth acknowledged.

As he led his mount onto the ferry, Seth felt a bit uneasy. Street's ferry rocked with every movement of the animals. The waves created by the bobbing craft returned from the opposite side of the river and rocked the ferry even more.

The ferry quickly filled to its capacity. All of the troopers held the reins tightly to calm their horses.

Street called to General Potter, "Are you ready, General?"

"Ready!" answered Potter.

Mr. Street walked to the front of the ferry and waved his arms to attract the attention of his helper on the opposite bank.

"Start the mule!" Street yelled across the river.

Seth felt a jolt, then a rocking motion. He looked around, all the troopers were trying to balance themselves as they held the reins of their horses tight in their hands. Slowly the ferry began to bring the opposite bank closer as it neared the incline of the water's edge.

Lieutenant Henderson looked at Seth and smiled, "That wasn't all that bad."

"No, it wasn't. It was over before I ever realized it had started," answered Seth.

General Potter waited for the mule to be tied to a tree. He yelled to Street's helper, "Get this board off the front; we need to be on our way."

Potter and Cole gripped the reins of their horses, stepped off the ferry and led their mounts onto the river's edge and up the incline to dry and level ground.

General Potter turned and looked toward the ferry, "Come on! Get unloaded and follow me."

"Major," the general said, "I think we would be well advised to move toward Swift Creek slowly. It will take some time to move the column across the river and we don't want to have any gaps in the column."

"Very true, General," the major responded.

# CHAPTER SIX

General Potter raised himself from the saddle as he put pressure on his feet in the stirrups. He stiffened his legs, turned and looked back at Major Cole, "Major, on our return to New Berne we will not cross on Mr. Street's ferry. Before I have to go through this again, I will exhaust every manner possible to recross the Neuse."

Cole looked back at the ferry being reloaded, saw the awkward movements the troopers were having to make to move their horses onto the ferry. "To be sure, General Potter, there has to be a better way. We will be darned lucky if we don't lose some men and equipment in this crossing."

The general spurred his mount, gently tightened the reins, and turned again to Major Cole, "Major, move Lieutenant Henderson and his company to the front of the column with instructions to move forward to Fort Anderson by two's."

"Yes, sir," responded the major as he reined his horse and turned around to wait for Henderson to move from the ferry landing.

Henderson, upright on his saddle, approached Major Cole as his company followed close behind. The ferry had begun its return trip to the opposite bank to load again as Lieutenant Henderson and Company C moved from the river's edge.

"Lieutenant!" yelled Cole.

"Yes, sir," responded Henderson, as he reined in his horse to hear the major better.

"General Potter said for you and your company to move to the front of the column and move along the road to Fort Anderson by two's," instructed the major.

"Yes, sir," Henderson answered loudly.

Slightly turned in his saddle, the lieutenant raised his arm and motioned the company to move forward. "Company C, forward ho!"

Cole waited for the company to pass to the front of the column before he rejoined the general. The column began to take shape as Henderson and Company C moved to the lead position. The forward movement to Fort Anderson had begun.

General Potter waited for Major Cole to join him before he urged his horse to follow the lead company in the column. Major Cole tightened one rein to ride alongside the general. "General, I hope to God we don't lose the artillery pieces at the end of the column. If we meet any resistance, we'll need to clear the way ahead of us or we'll be caught between thick woods on both sides of the road."

"Yeah, yeah, I can see that, Major. I suppose Jourdan got to Fort Anderson all right. I don't see any evidence of much disturbance on this road. At least not yet."

"Have you ever been to Anderson before, Major?" asked Potter.

"No, sir, I have not. I've heard it's nothing more than an old abandoned fort just a little south of Vanceboro on Swift Creek. I believe it was used at one time for overnight protection."

"Well, Major, let's hope it gives us a little protection this night," said the general.

Potter, as his horse moved haltingly, raised himself from the saddle, stood upright in the stirrups, turned and looked behind. "Major, I can't see beyond the bend in the road behind us. I trust the crossing was completed without incident."

"I think it was, Sir, or we would have received word by now. We've been on the road well over an hour, and so far all has gone very well," Cole encouraged the general.

"Yes, perhaps you're right, Major. I know we've been just over an hour on this road, but it seems like we've been on this rutted road all day. The woods on both sides just won't let a breeze blow through. It's stifling and dust is covering everything. My God, this heat is miserable!" lamented Potter.

The lead company under Lieutenant Henderson kept a steady pace. A pillar of dust rose from its rear. General Potter and Major Cole tried to remain behind to escape the dust before it rose into the air behind the advancing column.

As the road turned in a westward direction, the late afternoon sun cast its brightness directly into the faces of the advancing troopers. The cavalrymen all turned their heads to keep from looking directly into the sunlight as they prodded their horses into the brilliant sunset.

Potter's lead troopers, almost blinded by the light, did not realize they had advanced into the rear guard of Colonel Jourdan's brigade. The road became crowded quickly; the column began to slow and finally stopped.

General Potter rose up in his stirrups and called out, "Lieutenant Henderson, what the devil is going on?"

The general looked directly at Major Cole, "Cole, for heaven's sake find out what's going on!"

With a heel prod to his mount, Cole dashed to the head of the company. He quickly saw their lead column had caught up with the rear guard of Colonel Jourdan. The major reined in his horse, galloped back and stopped abruptly abreast General Potter, "We've caught up with Colonel Jourdan. He's not all the way to Fort Anderson yet. His columns are still moving ahead."

"Pass the order to halt to the column," yelled Potter.

Captain Chamberlain heard the order, rose in his stirrups, turned around and yelled, "Halt the column! Halt the column!"

Like an echo around the bend, toward the rear of the column the command resounded from one company to another. The dust began to settle and stillness filled the late afternoon air. The troopers remained still in the road. Towering pine trees that lined the road gave some semblance of shade. The troopers edged their mounts closer to the side of the gutted road to take advantage of the shade.

"Major Cole, get word to Colonel Jourdan to get his brigade off the road and into the fort. We're vulnerable here in the middle of this road. I hope to God the Rebs don't know we're caught in this bottleneck!"

Cole galloped quickly past the rear guard, into the fort and yelled, "Colonel Jourdan! Colonel Jourdan! Where the devil is Jourdan?"

"Over here, Cole," came the reply from behind the rotted railings of the abandoned outpost.

"Raise the ensign, Private," called out Jourdan. "I don't think the major can see with all my brigade's dust in his eyes."

"General Potter said get your men off the road, immediately, Colonel, we're caught in a bad spot," called Cole.

"All right, all right, we're moving just as fast as we can. Give us time to get inside the perimeters," responded the colonel.

Cole returned to the general, reined his horse abruptly to a stop. "Colonel Jourdan is inside the fort perimeters now. We can move forward again, General."

"Very well, Major, pass the word to advance."

Cole looked to the company behind him. He saw Major Jacobs and Captain Chamberlain waiting. "The general said to move forward."

Major Jacobs observed the lead column advancing, raised his arm and commanded, "Forward, ho!" and continued moving his arm in the direction of General Potter.

Captain Chamberlain gently nudged his horse with the side of his stirrups and with a slight forward motion on his saddle coaxed his mount forward.

The abandoned outpost, once known as Fort Anderson, showed all the evidence of neglect. It had not been used for anything except as a location on the map to indicate a position. The log building had long ago fallen and only rotted logs remained. New growth could not be distinguished from old growth. The only usable asset was the winding creek that twisted its way to the Neuse River.

Potter's horse turned from the road into the area designated for the bivouac. General Potter looked at Major Cole arrogantly. "Well, Major, I made the decision to use this spot and by all that's holy we're going to use it. Order all company commanders to find any place they can to set up for the night."

"Orderly," yelled the general, "locate my position inside the perimeter of the old stockade and come and get me. I'll be right here when you get back."

His slouch hat removed, the general wiped perspiration from his forehead with his sleeve. He looked as the cavalrymen entered the perimeter two by two. With a loud grunt he lifted himself from the saddle, held to the saddle pommel as he pulled one leg over the rump of the horse and lowered it to the ground. Motionless in that position momentarily, he removed his other foot from the stirrup and stood with both feet on the ground.

Potter was unsteady. He held onto the front and rear of his saddle and lowered his head. "Thank God to get out of that saddle for a while."

Major Cole, arriving in time to hear the exclamation, added, "Yes, sir, my rear feels like I've been astraddle a pine burr all day."

"Major Cole," the general said, "direct all units to dismount and set up camp for the night. We'll be leaving at first light tomorrow."

The low scrub brush showed the previous enclosure perimeters. The low growth began to disappear as the troopers scuffled to the pines and gum trees that surrounded the abandoned outpost.

Saplings were cut and scrub brush was cleared. The cavalrymen quickly turned the density of the forest into cleared areas, scattered around the old fort.

Private White wrapped the reins of his horse loosely around a gum tree and walked to the edge of Swift Creek. As he looked toward the west, the rays of the setting sun glimmered on the slow-moving water. He wondered why it was called Swift Creek. The deeper water was black, yet along the shallow edge it appeared as clear as any he had seen before. White walked back toward his mount. He saw the artillery units as they entered the clearing, and yelled out, "Utz, any place you can find is yours."

Sergeant Utz tightened the reins in his hands, brought his horse to a stop and looked at White. "Where in blazes do you expect us to unload? You boys have already filled the whole place."

"I don't know, Sergeant. My mama used to tell me to do the best you can with what you got. And this looks like what you got," Private White said with a chuckle.

"Well, now, Private, we'll just stop right here and take all the space we need and let you boys scatter to the woods," retorted Utz.

The sergeant dismounted and stood motionless for a moment and then barked to the gunners," Get those howitzers off the horses' backs and give those animals a rest before we break away. See that the tubes are secured to the carriages."

Utz realized that Private White watched intently as the unloading went on. "What are you waiting for, Private? You waiting for the spirit to move you?"

"Oh, no, Sergeant," responded White, "I was in amazement how you fellows fixed it so one horse carried the barrel and another horse carried the carriage and still another horse carried all the shot and shell."

The sergeant, feeling his sharpness was uncalled for, meekly said, "Yeah, some talented leathersmith fixed a special saddle to carry the tube on the horse's back. But the other horse, he ain't so lucky. That animal has to carry the carriage on his back and that takes a mighty special contraption to even the load."

Private White continued to observe the unloading. "Yep, and it looks like the third horse gets off easy just carrying shot and shell."

"Don't let that fool you, Private. The ammunition can be just as heavy as the carriage," answered Utz.

The artilleryman again assured the private, "Tomorrow we'll limber the howitzers so the horses can pull them and that ought to make you feel better about the welfare of the animals."

Utz observed the gunners attaching the barrels to the carriages and said to Private White, "These things ain't been used much since the war with Mexico. I suppose they're all Foster would let Potter bring along. Yeah, old Potter had to take what he could get."

The twilight began to dispel the light. The dust settled as movements in the area began to slow. Evening settled over the bivouac and smoke from the small fires began to rise above the trees. The aroma of boiled coffee permeated the camp. Only the early evening activities of an army in their bivouac stirred around the edge of the woods.

Weary troopers leisurely led their horses to the bank of the creek for water and to fill their canteens. The sloping bank of the creek provided easy access as the cavalrymen held the reins loosely for the animals to freely drink the clear water.

Suddenly from the opposite side of the creek the brilliant orange glows from a hundred places at once illuminated and reflected off the black water. The rattle of muskets rumbled across the creek.

A blue clad trooper at the water's edge crumpled to his knees.

The reins fell from his hand. The cavalryman collapsed into the water, face first. His frightened horse broke and ran from the water's edge. The trooper's hat began to float with the current as a small ribbon of red blood followed from his bare head.

The noise of the horses as they broke from their riders and ran from the creek muffled the sounds of the wounded cavalrymen.

Painful groans quickly intensified as the wounded men realized what had happened. The numbness of their wounds turned into reality. Cries of agony echoed through the air.

Major Jacobs heard the musket fire, rushed to the creek and stood in a wooded area near the water's edge. He reached for his field glasses, quickly placed them to his eyes and scanned the opposite bank in both directions. Nothing! The major looked in both directions on his side of the creek. He saw fallen troopers and listened to the calls of the wounded who had managed to make their way to the safety of the trees along Swift Creek. Jacobs again put the glasses to his eyes and swept the opposite bank more slowly than before. He saw no movement.

"Captain Chamberlain," called the major, "get your company down here quick."

Chamberlain yelled as he rushed to the creek bank. "Henderson! Get the men down to the creek with the Major and me."

Chamberlain joined Major Jacobs. "Do you see anything on the other side? Can you tell how many there may be?"

"No, I don't see a single one. It looks like they all fired at once and then pulled back into the woods. Blast it all! They can hold us down all night and be gone at light."

"Captain, report what happened to General Potter," ordered Major Jacobs.

"Yes, sir," replied the captain, and added, "shall I send for the hospital steward?"

Major Jacobs surveyed the water's edge and viewed the wounded troopers. "Yes, get some help to remove the wounded troopers from the exposed position."

General Potter was near enough to Swift Creek to hear the sudden crack of the muskets. He was already standing outside his partially erected headquarters' tent. Chamberlain rushed up and reported, "General, sir, we have been attacked from the opposite side of the creek and have taken some casualties. Major Jacobs is there now with Company C, but he can't see anything on the other side."

"Good God! Captain, I thought Lee had all the boys in Pennsylvania. By Jove! I'll not take any more casualties. Captain, tell Major Jacobs to pull back from the creek. My objective is not here and I'll not fight here."

Potter turned to Major Cole. "Order all the fires extinguished. There will be no light for the Rebs to see by this night. It's only about thirty yards across the creek."

"Yes sir," replied the major.

Cole disappeared into the bivouac and the general heard him barking, "Douse those fires and stay where you are!"

Captain Chamberlain, out of breath, reappeared at the general's tent, "Sir, we need to remove some of the wounded from the creek bank. Major Jacobs and C company are still watching the other side of the creek."

"Very well, Captain, secure some stewards and do what you can to clear the wounded, and tell Major Jacobs not to press the attack. Remember, do not press the thing, Captain."

"Yes, sir," responded Chamberlain as he headed toward the now silent creek.

Captain Chamberlain rejoined Major Jacobs, "The stewards should be here shortly to start removing the miserable fellows back to the camp and to the ambulance area. I only trust old Potter brought along some regimental surgeons with the one ambulance I saw."

The stewards deliberately moved in a low posture. As they checked the groaning troopers, the stewards motioned for others to come and remove them into the woods lining the creek.

Major Jacobs stood along with C company and watched as one by one the wounded were moved to safety.

Captain Chamberlain removed his hat to his side. "Major, it looks like some won't be going all the way with us. That one volley across the creek had its affect. There will be some burial details this night."

Jacobs raised his field glasses to his eyes and again scanned the opposite bank, "They've disappeared back into the swamp. Maybe that's all for tonight."

The smoke from the smouldering fires hung like a pall over the bivouac and the odor of wet burned wood filled the night air. There would only be cold hardtack biscuits and water tonight.

Quietness came as suddenly as the musketry. Only the restless horses on their tethers broke the stillness of the evening.

Captain Chamberlain, slowly settling for a night under the Carolina pines, heard a faint call, "Captain! Captain Chamberlain! Are you there, Captain?" Recognizing Lieutenant Henderson's voice the captain answered, "Over here, Lieutenant."

"I just rolled out my blanket. What in heaven's name do you want?" asked Chamberlain.

"General Potter wants you and Major Jacobs at his tent. He sent for Cole and Jourdan, too."

The captain had removed his cavalry saber and revolver. There was little preparation for lying on the open ground. A few hours of rest under the canopy of the tall pine trees was to be delayed.

"Lieutenant, I'll be right with you. Can you find the way to the general's tent without stepping on some poor unsuspecting trooper who may be lying on the ground?"

"Yes, sir, I think I can. I didn't walk on a single one coming this far," the lieutenant emphasized.

The captain walked slowly from the edge of the pine trees into the clearing that earlier had been trodden down by the incoming horses. It was now occupied by the gunnery units. The two moved closer to the remnants of the abandoned stockade.

The stockade logs which earlier displayed the evidence of neglect and deterioration now in the dark appeared protective and forbidding.

Chamberlain stopped to step over a fallen log. "Lieutenant, you go ahead and I'll follow in your steps. You have been here before and I have not."

The captain peered into the darkness and viewed the outline of a tent. A candle inside General Potter's tent flickered from side to side. It illuminated one side and in a moment the flame danced to the opposite side, illuminating another side of the tent.

A silhouette of a short, stocky frame moved in and out of the tent opening. Passing between the flickering flame and the inside  wall of the tent, the general gave the appearance of an animated shadow, imprisoned inside a box, searching for a way of escape.

Nearer the headquarters' tent the captain viewed the form of Colonel Jourdan and Major Jacobs. As Chamberlain moved closer, he clearly identified Major Cole and Major Clarkson.

General Potter abruptly stopped his conversation with the officers as the captain emerged from the darkness and turned in Chamberlain's direction. "Captain, I trust this will be the last disturbance for this night, but I wanted you and Lieutenant Henderson in on this briefing."

Potter lifted the front tent flaps and tossed the corners onto the topside of the tent, lowered his frame and walked inside.

"Gentlemen, come on inside where there is a little light. We are too far from the creek to be a good target in the darkness."

General Potter stood at the small table in the middle of his tent. The officers lowered their heads and removed their hats as they entered the tent.

The single candle flame flickered high and then low, first to one side and then to the other. A dim light was cast onto the table. Exposed was a small map, opened to the area they were advancing toward.

"Move up close to the table, gentlemen," invited Potter, "I want every one of you briefed on the entire operation. After tomorrow Colonel Jourdan will no longer be with us. He will have another assignment."

Potter removed an unlit stub of a cigar from his mouth. "Colonel Jourdan, I take it you understand you are to take your brigade at first light and move in the direction of Kinston. You are to cross the bridge over the Neuse above Fort Barnwell and return to New Berne on the main road."

"This movement should give the indication you are moving on Kinston and draw attention from our advance toward Greenville," added Potter. "Do you understand, Colonel?"

Colonel Jourdan did not like the order, but he had earlier agreed to it. "Yes, sir, I understand."

"Major Clarkson," the general continued, "you will accompany Major Cole and me behind the squadron of cavalry under Lieutenant Henderson, who will take the lead."

Potter put the cigar stub, unlit, back into his mouth, "Major Jacobs, you and Captain Chamberlain will fall in behind us in the column. And two by two again, we will take the road to Greenville."

"If we do not meet any resistance and proceed unmolested to Greenville, I will detach a squadron of cavalry to reconnoiter the Greenville defenses," the general continued.

As he moved slowly to the wall of the inside of his tent, the general again removed the cigar stub from his mouth, "If there is no opposition, we will burn the bridge over the Tar River at that place."

"Our principal objective is still the railroad trestle over the Tar at Rocky Mount and the work going on in Tarborough on the river," emphasized Potter.

Again at the table, General Potter placed his finger on the map at Sparta on the Tar River, "By late tomorrow afternoon we should reach Sparta. There will be plenty of fresh water and from what I hear there are no defenses in that part of the state. We will bivouac there."

Potter rolled up the map and placed it to the side of the table. "Gentlemen, Colonel Jourdan will be detached in the morning but the rest of you will receive your final orders for the raid on Rocky Mount and Tarborough at Sparta tomorrow evening."

General Potter stopped and remained motionless for a moment as if trying to remember something. He raised the unlit cigar stub to his lips, but suddenly lowered his hand back to his side. "Oh, yes, Colonel Jourdan, I was about to forget something. I will have my aide prepare a request that I would like for you to deliver to General Foster on your return to New Berne."

"Yes, sir, I will be giving my report when I return."

The general looked at the officers and smiled. "Do you want to go through another crossing at Street's Ferry?"

"Major Jacobs, what do you say?" asked Potter.

"No, sir, not if it can be avoided. That experience this morning took entirely too long."

"Major Cole, did you enjoy the crossing at Street's place?"

"Not in the least, sir," responded Major Cole.

Potter walked to the back side of the tent and turned in the direction of the staff officers, "And neither did I. And furthermore I don't intend to do it again."

"Colonel Jourdan will carry my request for steamers to deliver a pontoon bridge from New Berne to a point downstream from Street's Ferry. I fully expect to have more to make the crossing on my return than we had today."

Major Jacobs hesitated before he asked the question he was thinking about, "More? More of what?"

Potter stopped and stared directly into the eyes of Major Jacobs, "More prisoners, more slaves, more wagons, more chickens, more potatoes."

"Yes, Major Jacobs, more for us and less for them. We free the slaves and we free the chickens. How does that sound to you?"

The major regretted having asked the question. "Yes, sir."

General Potter placed the cigar stub back into his mouth, walked to the tent opening, turned and looked at the officers. "Goodnight, gentlemen. Perhaps we can secure some rest before daybreak?"

Major Jacobs placed his hat on his head and looked at Captain Chamberlain, "After you, Captain. Let's find a little quiet."

Captain Chamberlain walked slowly and deliberately in the direction he thought he had left his horse and bedding to give his eyes time to adjust to the darkness.

The moon above the top of the pine trees provided the captain with some guidance. He reached the spot where he had tethered his mount and prepared his blanket for a night of sleep on the ground.

Chamberlain knelt on one knee and removed his sidearm belt. Laying it by his blanket, he removed the revolver and carefully placed it near the edge of the blanket.

The leaves the captain had earlier gathered and placed under one end of his blanket were better than nothing, but it did not feel like a feather pillow. His thoughts began to turn again to New York and Melissa.

The moonlight was interrupted as the clouds moved unseen from horizon to horizon. The monotonous symphony of tree frogs reached its nightly crescendo as Captain Chamberlain closed his eyes to the night.

# CHAPTER SEVEN

T he early morning fog filtered the emerging light. It gave the appearance of night refusing to give way to the day as the notes from the bugler startled Captain Chamberlain. Instinctively the captain jumped to his feet and looked around defensively. Slowly his consciousness awoke to the reality of the dampness of the early morning. Another day had evolved from the stillness of the night.

Chamberlain looked to reassure himself of the presence of his horse. Excellent, the captain thought. Blue Boy was still tethered to the rope suspended between two large pine trees along with the mounts of other officers.

Major Jacobs entered the edge of the woods from the cleared area of the old compound with the reins of his horse in his hand, "Seth, old boy, you must have been worn to a frazzle. Some of the men have been stirring for almost an hour."

"You're right, Major."

Seth stooped to pick up his saddle and with a subdued mutter lifted the saddle and moved toward Blue Boy, "I know you're glad you didn't have to wear this leather all night long." With the saddle raised higher, Seth placed it securely on Blue Boy's back. "Old boy, you've got to wear this another day."

Jacobs stood silently by as he looked at Chamberlain and inquired, "Talking to your horse now, Seth?"

The captain tightened the saddle straps and moved to the horse's head to arrange the bridle and bit. Ignoring Jacobs' question, he commented, "Maybe today won't be as tough as yesterday."

Major Jacobs waited as Seth completed the saddling procedure, "Think you ought to take your sidearm and saber, Seth?"

With a look of exasperation Seth leaned over and picked up his saber and revolver belt, "Yeah, I reckon I'd better take it along."

Captain Chamberlain wiped his eyes, placed his saber sheath against a tree and swung his revolver belt and holster around his waist. With a quick pull he buckled the belt and reached for his saber sheath.

With a wide swing of the sheath, Seth wrapped the belt around his waist, "By God, that added a weight my friend Blue Boy has to share." Seth gripped the saddle pommel with one hand and placed one foot into the stirrup and with the reins in the other hand pulled himself up into the saddle. "Well, Major Jacobs, are you ready to start the day?"

Jacobs led his horse into the cleared area and in the manner prescribed by military regulation, mounted his horse. "Yes, Captain, I am ready."

The officers moved their horses slowly toward General Potter's tent but stopped side by side as Colonel Jourdan's brigade passed before them on their way out of the area. Seth looked at Jacobs and smiled, "Tonight ought not to be so crowded with Jourdan gone."

The last of Jourdan's brigade passed and the officers nudged their mounts toward the general's tent. As they approached, the two men saw they were the last to arrive.

"I have already directed Lieutenant Henderson to begin moving his company onto the road north to Greenville," advised the general as he walked to his mount.

The orderly held out the reins for Potter as he stopped to brush the forehead of his horse, "General, everything is ready."

"Thank you, private."

"Gentlemen, are you prepared for the ride to Sparta?" asked General Potter.

Henderson had proceeded north earlier on the Greenville

road. The blue cavalry column began to form by twos as it had the day before. General Potter and Major Cole followed Henderson and Jacobs and Chamberlain reined behind the general.

Captain Chamberlain glanced to the side as he passed out of the perimeter of the fort. "Look, Major Jacobs, I pray they will be the only graves we leave behind."

The day began with only a dry hardtack biscuit and water. That didn't set well with Captain Chamberlain. It would be a long day before he reached Sparta. The opportunity of heating a can of beans in the metal pan he stashed in his saddle bag would have to wait.

The sun was well advanced in its arched journey to the western horizon and the clouds of the night before had dissolved into the blue immensity of space. Pine and Gum trees that lined the rutted road of yesterday vanished as cultivated farms began to appear along the roadside. The small modest houses that dotted the small farms caught the attention of Captain Chamberlain.

Seth noticed the dwellings were plainly constructed as more farm houses came into view. "Major Jacobs, have you noticed the absence of large plantations? It looks like there are more small farms than large plantations in this part of North Carolina."

"Yes, Captain, and I have observed that there are no blacks in any great numbers working the fields either. Do you think that strange, Seth? We were sent here to free the slaves, yet there are not that many in this particular section."

Chamberlain, removing his cavalry hat and wiping his brow with his sleeve, responded, "It appears to be more families working the fields than slave hands."

Major Jacobs raised himself from his saddle by straightening his legs and putting pressure on both stirrups. He turned and looked to the rear of the dusty column. "Captain,

I'm glad to see the two sections of Mountain Howitzers being pulled instead of carried by those animals. I can understand why the cannons have to be carried in rough terrain. I'm sure it has to be done in mountains." After lowering himself back into his saddle, the major looked ahead at the straight road before the column, "But these roads are not in the mountains."

The sun indicated midday as the hours had melted into oblivion. Only the rattle of the harnesses broke the sound of the dull hoofbeats of the horses. The dust had long been accepted as an unchangeable lot.

Major Jacobs spurred his mount, pulled out from the column, put his horse in a gallop and moved forward alongside Major Cole. "Major, do you see a grove of trees ahead to right of the road?"

Cole raised himself high in the saddle. "Why, I believe I do. It looks like a good place to stop and refresh ourselves."

"What do you think, General Potter?" asked Cole.

Potter, who had been silent for some time and alone with his thoughts, quickly asked, "Think about what, Major?"

Major Cole stared at the general, "There looks to be a grove of trees ahead on the right. What about resting the troopers there?"

The general looked down the straight road with fields of corn on both sides, "Very well. Direct Henderson to lead us into the shaded area ahead."

Major Cole turned to Major Jacobs, "Since you're already out of the column, advance and instruct Henderson to turn into the grove of trees on the right of the road."

"Thanks, Cole," responded Jacobs as he spurred his horse to the head of the column.

"Henderson, turn in at the grove of trees on the right side of the road just ahead. The men and mounts need a rest," instructed Jacobs.

"Yes, sir," answered Henderson and added, "and from here I believe I can see a well in what looks like a churchyard."

"All the better," responded Jacobs as he pulled the reins to ride back to his position with Captain Chamberlain.

The lead company began to turn into the grove of trees and Lieutenant Henderson immediately noticed the shutters of the church windows were closed. The building did not resemble a church nor did it resemble a dwelling. Its architecture was simple and the boards were painted white. The northern exposure of the roof exhibited an extensive growth of slow growing moss giving it a green cast in the sunlight. Lieutenant Henderson continued toward the rear of the building in an attempt to give more space for the incoming column. He rounded the rear of the structure and saw a graveyard with narrow marble markers identifying the graves. Henderson was convinced this must be a church building. He reined his mount to a halt and pulled the lines to turn completely around. "General, this is a church. Surely we can rest here a spell without fear of molestation."

"Very well, Lieutenant."

Potter drew on the reins to halt his horse. "Major Cole, have the column dismount and rest. There's enough shade for the entire column. These oak trees will give us rest and sanctuary from the midday heat."

"Major Jacobs," the general called out as he tied his horse to a small water oak, "I don't want to remain here very long. We will need to get to Sparta before nightfall."

Captain Chamberlain walked to the building and looked up at the corners of the roof line. He thought this was about as plain a building he had ever seen. Well built, but still plain.

General Potter walked to the rear of the building, leaned with his hand on the corner and looked at the small cemetery. "This is a Primitive Baptist Church. I've seen them before and those plain folks don't hold to anything fancy in their places of worship. We had best be on our way quick. They don't like intruders either." He walked quickly back to his horse, "Major Cole, hurry the boys up a bit we need to be on the road."

The general pulled himself into the saddle and called directly to Major Clarkson. "Major, take company B and ride ahead on the road to Greenville. Report back as quickly as possible what you find the situation to be. We will be on our way in your direction and have to pass through Greenville."

Major Clarkson mounted his horse and called out, "Company C fall in behind me!" The troopers of C company quickly mounted their horses and the single column entered the Greenville road on the gallop.

Potter pulled himself into the saddle, reached for the reins and called to Major Cole, "Let's get on the road. I don't know what we will find in Greenville. If there is no resistance we will at least destroy the bridge over the river before we leave."

With a quick squeeze of his feet to the side of his horse the general moved to the front of the church building. He turned his mount toward Lieutenant Henderson and Company C, "Let's move out, Lieutenant. Take the lead."

"Yes, sir," responded Henderson as he nudged his horse onto the Greenville road. The early afternoon dust began to rise as C company entered the road ahead of the general.

Major Cole reined his horse beside General Potter and for a few minutes rode in silence.

General Potter broke the silence, "Major, Greenville should be just around the next bend in the road. At least according to the map I looked at when we stopped at the churchyard. We can't waste much time there. I want to be at Sparta before the edge of night."

The column entered the bend of the road and headed almost due north. General Potter's attention was drawn to a rising cloud of dust. "That must be Major Clarkson headed this way.

With good news, I trust."

The rising cloud of dust neared the approaching column. The general and Major Cole felt the ground rumble beneath them as the squadron closed the gap between them and the lead column.

Major Clarkson passed the lead company on the gallop and reined his horse to a halt beside General Potter. "It looks like the earthworks have been abandoned all around Greenville."

Potter called loudly to Henderson, "Stop the column, Lieutenant!"

Henderson stretched his arm upward and shouted, "Column, halt!"

The column reacted like a train of railroad cars. Two by two the troopers halted. The first company halted, then the next company halted and on down the column to the last company. The artillerymen with the Mountain Howitzers slowly halted. The line settled and the halt became complete.

Major Clarkson explained excitedly, "General, beyond the abandoned earthworks there is only a field hospital and just a few wounded in the area. It looks like the town has been abandoned."

"Excellent, excellent!" Potter exclaimed.

General Potter turned to Major Cole and smiled, "We'll pass through on the gallop to the road toward Sparta. Direct Company K to stop at the bridge over the river and build a brush fire under the opposite side of the bridge. When they have returned to this side, then build another brush fire under the bridge on this side." The general continued to issue orders, "And order the company to remain at the bridge until the fire is burning out of control. They can rejoin the column before we reach our destination," added Potter.

With an air of excitement, General Potter looked to the column in his immediate front, "Proceed on the gallop,

Lieutenant Henderson."

Dust began to rise from the narrow street as the column of thundering horses passed through the deserted town. The wounded Confederate soldiers could not hinder the advance.

It was only a matter of minutes and Greenville was to the south of the advanced column. Major Cole stiffened his legs and raised himself in the saddle and turned toward the rear. "General! Black smoke is beginning to rise above the trees in the vicinity of the Tar River bridge."

"Excellent! By Jove, excellent!" General Potter exclaimed happily.

The rays of the late afternoon sun glared into the eyes of the cavalrymen as they continued the advance west by northwest. The horseback riders constantly moved their heads from the direct sunlight and pressed on.

General Potter squinted his eyes as he looked ahead through the rising dust, "We'll make our objective this day, Major. We should be far enough from any enemy camps to rest in peace tonight."

Major Cole raised himself in the saddle and turned toward the rear of the column, "It appears that Major Clarkson is about to rejoin us, sir."

"Splendid! Thank you, Major," Potter acknowledged.

The steady hoofbeats droned on. The sun began to ebb into the western horizon of tree tops. General Potter was silent. Major Cole was in deep thought. The silence was broken as Lieutenant Henderson raised himself in the saddle and raised his arm above his head, "Column, halt!" Lieutenant Henderson turned in the direction of Potter. "There's a crossroads ahead, sir."

"Very good, Lieutenant, that must be Sparta," the general responded. "Go on past the crossroads to the river."

General Potter turned to Major Cole, "When we pass the

crossroads, Major, move to the head of the column and choose a good area for the bivouac tonight."

Major Cole pulled his horse's head to the side and moved out of the column and in a trot outdistanced the column as it passed the crossroads.

The major reined his mount to a stop and looked to both sides of the rutted road. There were pine trees on both sides as tall as he had seen. Yes, he thought this would provide a pine straw mattress for the night, and it would be better than the night before. Tugging the bridle reins, the major spurred his horse into the wooded riverside area. It looked good, he thought. Much better than what Potter had chosen. Yes, this would be superb, he thought.

The major raised himself from the saddle and with one foot in a stirrup he lowered himself to the straw-covered ground. Pine needles felt good to his feet. Towering pines looked good to his eyes. Gripping the halter of his horse, the major led the steed back onto the road leading to the river's edge. The worn slope toward the water suggested the use of a ferry in the past. The major looked across the river and viewed another worn sloped bank area, confirming his suspicions of the use of a ferry. At the very least, he thought it would be an open and safe position to water the horses and replenish fresh water supplies.

Cole turned and looked in the direction he had come and saw the column as it closed the distance quickly. "This side of the road," the major motioned and began to lead his own horse into the wooded area.

The blue and gold column with its ensigns and glittering weaponry were quickly engulfed by the tall pines, sweet gums and hickory trees. A serene and quiet paradise, if only for one night.

A brilliant southwestern horizon opened her golden gates to receive the bright yellow god of the heavens. The gates would close and the light guarded until the glowing red eastern gates of the morning opened for it to begin again its westward journey.

The forest swallowed the blue column as if it had never existed. Darkness engulfed the forest. The safety of nature covered her with an unseen mantle of security. A sallow moon light filtered by the needles of the pines reassured the weary bodies of nature's safekeeping.

Captain Chamberlain secured his horse to a pine tree, loosened the girth strap of the saddle and removed the leather burden from his mount. With the saddle tight to his waistline he moved away from the horse and lowered the saddle to the ground. The captain felt the sponge-like leaves and pine needles beneath his feet. He moved farther from his horse and thought how good the soft needles would feel for the night ahead. Seth spread his blanket on the welcoming forest floor. He walked back to the open area where he had noticed small fires as the cavalrymen began their evening preparations.

As the captain moved near the open road, he saw Lieutenant Henderson. The bouncing flames from the small fire illuminated the lieutenant as he leaned over to stir the burning wood. "Lieutenant, mind if I heat a pan of beans over your fire?"

"Sure, be my guest," responded Henderson, "but you better hurry, General Potter wants us at his quarters at nine o'clock."

"I hadn't heard that, Lieutenant, but I reckon I'd better make as if I had. Thanks for letting me know."

Seth cut into the can, pried open the top to reveal the contents and emptied the beans into the pan. "Now I know why the cavalry issued these knives. They won't inflict much damage, but they will open one of these cans."

Seth stooped and placed the pan over the flame. The pan began to heat and became warm in the captain's hand. The beans began to bubble as the heat intensified emitting an aroma reminiscent of stale and damp swamp air. "Not too great to smell but better than nothing at all," the Captain quipped.

Chamberlain stood upright and moved away from the fire with the warm pan in his hand. His metal fork scraped the pan. Its grating noise continued as he moved back to the area he had chosen for the night.

The captain finished the beans, put the cooled pan on the soft pine needles and started for the quarters of General Potter. He stopped and thought, I'll clean the pan by the moonlight when I return from the general's quarters.

As the captain approached General Potter's quarters, he saw the staff in front of the general's tent. A lantern hung from the lower limb of a sweet gum tree. The dim light outlined the staff officers as they stood quietly around as Potter unrolled a map.

Chamberlain neared the staff officers and maneuvered beside Major Jacobs. "Good evening, General. Good evening, gentlemen," the captain nodded to the general and again to the staff.

"Yes, Captain, this may be a good evening. This may be the evening you will be given something to do to break the monotony you have been complaining about. Yes, yes, we all know you want to get on with this war. Well, now you may get a taste of what you can do to your enemy and where you can hurt him the most," Potter emphasized.

Captain Chamberlain, embarrassed that the general knew of his discontent, remained silent.

"Yes, Chamberlain, I know of your dissatisfaction with your duty. Tomorrow I want to see if you're up to what will be expected of you. Tomorrow will determine if you have the mettle to destroy," continued Potter.

The general moved near the hanging lantern. The dim light of the flame flickered. "Gentlemen, these are verbal orders. Nothing will be committed to writing. You can elaborate in your reports when we return to New Berne." Potter turned in the direction of the staff officers and looked at each directly, "Tomorrow morning all companies will assemble at the crossroads. I know I have been referring to it as Sparta, but it looks like the people want to call it Old Sparta. So be it. It doesn't really matter to me." General Potter continued to issue verbal orders, "Major Jacobs, Captain Chamberlain, you will take companies A, D, E, G, I and L and move on the road to Rocky Mount by way of the Kingsboro Road. Your objective is to destroy the rail yards and trestle bridge over the Tar River as well as the cotton mill. You are to spare no aid to the enemy." The general continued, "And when completed with that objective, you will rejoin me at Tarborough by way of the Rocky Mount to Tarborough road. A Mountain Howitzer section will be assigned to you," the general added.

Potter walked away from the lantern, turned and moved directly in front of Major Cole. "Major Cole, Major Clarkson and Lieutenant Henderson will be with me." The general deliberately added, "And companies B, C, K, M, F and H."

"We will move on the Tarborough Road to Tarborough and there do as much injury as possible until the squadron from Rocky Mount rejoins us," the general directed. He glanced at the staff officers, "And when we have regrouped, we will return to Sparta the same way we came. Is that understood? Are there any questions, gentlemen?"

The staff responded, "No, sir."

"Then, gentlemen, get some rest. Tomorrow may be a little arduous."

Chamberlain returned to the site he had previously prepared, walked to his horse and with a gentle pat said quietly, "Rest well, old friend."

Seth placed his side arms beside the spread blanket, sat on the blanket and removed his boots. Slowly he lay down on the bed of layered pine needles and leaves.

The stars sparkled as a million flickering candles. Nature was pressing humanity to its breast. Nature's bed was secure.

Captain Chamberlain slowly opened his eyes to the early morning darkness. The years of accumulated pine straw provided a better than expected night of forgetfulness. The eastern horizon had not opened its gates to free the brilliant golden globe to commence its daily arc through the southern heavens.

Captain Chamberlain sat up and braced himself with his arms behind him. Sleep was slow to allow his eyes to focus as he stared into the darkness. The figure of Blue Boy began to clear as Seth's vision adjusted to the morning blackness. Night still held the troopers captive. The symphony of the water creatures of the evening before was silent.

Seth turned and with one knee on his blanket raised himself to his feet. He stretched his arms upward, groaned briefly and dropped his arms. He walked to the side of Blue Boy, stroked his steed gently and uttered, "Well, old boy, it's going to be a long day. A long day for both of us."

Chamberlain walked back to his blanket-covered pine needle bed and began to roll the blanket. Suddenly he realized he was bootless. He leaned over, picked up his boots and walked to a large pine. As he held his boots, he paused and listened as the sounds of morning began to penetrate the stillness. Braced with his back against the tree, Seth lifted his foot and pulled on his first boot. With his foot lowered, he paused, sighed and thought of the long hours that daybreak would introduce. He lifted his other foot and slowly pulled on the boot.

The eastern heavens began to reflect the approaching light as the tops of the trees became more visible. A mist hung low over the surface of the river as the inhabitants of the water vibrated the silence returning to the murky depths of the river's secrets.

Seth wearily leaned over and lifted the saddle to his waist. He hesitated momentarily, and with a muffled groan raised the leather seat onto Blue Boy's back. The captain stooped to grasp the leather girth and with a sudden pull he tightened the saddle on the mount's back.

Seth stepped back to be certain the blue saddle blanket was according to regulation. The gold stripe outlined the blanket to meet cavalry manual standards. The captain knew Potter was a stickler for regulations. Captain Chamberlain reached for his canteen hanging from a tree limb and lifted it to his mouth. With a big swallow he swished the water in his mouth and spewed the tepid liquid onto the forest floor.

Lieutenant Henderson, bridle reins in hand, led his mount in the direction of Captain Chamberlain, "Maybe you'd better fill your canteen with some fresh water before we leave. That didn't seem to appeal to your taste." The lieutenant continued, "General Potter has directed all companies to assemble at the crossroads at Old Sparta. Potter's aide is passing the word to all company commanders."

Seth acknowledged the lieutenant. "I know now what old Potter has in mind for us. I don't think we are far from our objectives. I'll be glad to get this mission over and done. I never thought I'd be glad to get back to New Berne, but after being on the move for two days with more to go, I'll be glad to get back to civilization."

Chamberlain grasped the saddle pommel and with a heavy tug pulled himself into the saddle with one hand. He secured his boots in the stirrups and reached for the bridle reins, "Lieutenant, let's get to the river for some fresh water and then back to the crossroads."

Henderson raised his foot quickly into the stirrup and pulled himself with both hands into the saddle. "After you, Captain. This may be your lucky day."

Chamberlain and Henderson spurred their horses and joined the assembled companies at the crossroads.

Captain Chamberlain pulled Blue Boy alongside Major Jacobs as Lieutenant Henderson directed his horse beside Major Clarkson and Major Cole.

General Potter turned in his saddle, and with an overhead motion of his arm commanded, "Major Clarkson! Take the lead."

Clarkson tightened his feet against his steed and galloped around the general. He reined in beside Lieutenant Henderson, "Lieutenant, move onto the road to Tarborough."

Henderson lifted his arm and gave a forward gesture, "Column, hooaaa!"

Major Jacobs and Captain Chamberlain watched as the column disappeared in the dust of the Tarborough Road. The edge of the tree tops became distinct as the eastern gates of the heavens announced with brilliant red the opening of another day.

Major Jacobs looked directly at Captain Chamberlain and smiled approvingly, "Let's move out, Captain."

Chamberlain secured his feet in the stirrups, raised himself in the saddle and with a long overhead sweep of his arm, yelled "Column, Ho!"

The column moved orderly onto the Kingsboro Road. Sparta's crossroads became silent. Early morning dust began to rise behind the columns as they moved toward their objectives.

# CHAPTER EIGHT

Julia stepped cautiously up the wooden steps onto the front platform of the depot. She stopped and watched the railroad men as they walked the distance of the connected rail cars. At the end of each car they leaned and checked the couplings. The stack of the engine was dominant as smoke ascended from its wide top. The passenger car and two freight cars were still. Rocky Mount's station was quiet. The door to the office was open. Julia heard the clicking of the telegraph as she moved inside the station. The odor of freshly-cut pine drew her attention to the wide rough-cut boards that lined the wall and ceiling.

Julia gripped her valise as she approached the counter between her and the station agent. The narrow iron bars on the high counter required Julia to stand on her toes. She placed her valise beside her on the floor, raised her hands onto the counter and watched the agent.

The clock on the wall above the agent struck eight times. The telegrapher looked up from his desk as the telegraph stopped clicking. As the agent placed his pencil on his ear, he turned, looked at Julia and got up from his chair. He walked to the inside of the counter and leaned toward the iron bars. "Young lady, can I be of any help to you?"

Julia glanced at the clock and looked at the station agent, "Am I too late for the train to Tarborough?"

"No, ma'am, you are not. It will not leave until about eight-thirty. That is, if the fireman can get the steam up by that time." The agent observed the bag beside Julia. "Do you want to take the train to Tarborough?"

"Yes, sir, I do. I want to get home before dinnertime," replied Julia.

"Where do you live, young lady? I know most of the folks in these parts," inquired the agent.

"I live between here and Tarborough. I live at the Coolmore place," stated Julia proudly.

The station agent took a closer look at Julia. "You must be Frank Dupree's girl. Lord, it's been a long time since I've seen you. You've really done a piece of growing. "You got thirty cents?" the agent asked.

"Yes, sir, I think so. Let me get my purse."

Julia stooped, opened her valise, removed her small purse and stood with it in her hand. "Yes, sir, here is the money for the ticket."

She placed the confederate coins on the counter and pushed them toward the agent. "Will it be alright if I wait on the platform till the train is ready to leave?"

"Sure it will. It's the only train headed east toward the sun. You can't miss it. Just be sure to get on board before eight-thirty."

Julia picked up her valise and walked toward the open door, "Thank you, sir."

The outside platform surrounded the station. An extended roof protected the platform on all sides. Rough cut posts supported the overhung roof. The enclosed storage area of the station emitted the odor of guano. As she looked at the wide perpendicular boards that covered the outside of the station, Julia noticed the batten strips that covered the uneven joints. The strips, at the very least, made it look finished, she thought.

From the station platform Julia watched a wagon approaching with two men on the seat. A team of mules passed close to the steps leading to the office and slowed. "Whoa," the driver called out as he pulled the lines tight.

Julia watched as the younger man raised his foot with difficulty and positioned it outside the wagon seat. She continued to watch as he lifted his other leg and with both hands lowered himself to the ground. Clad in a worn butternut-colored uniform, the young boy stood motionless on the ground, "Thank you, Uncle Simon. I'm much obliged to you for letting me stay a few days with you. Maybe after I'm healed up I can come and visit longer. Your place is a whole lot better than that hospital in Wilson."

Julia saw the insignia on the boy's uniform and recognized him as a captain. She was not able to identify anything else about the soldier. He climbed slowly up the steps to the platform. With a noticeable limp he passed in front of Julia, "Excuse me, ma'am. I've got to get me a ticket to Tarborough."

Julia walked behind the captain to the door of the office. She looked at the clock, saw it was fifteen after eight, returned to the platform edge and picked up her valise. Gripping it tightly, Julia descended the steps to the dusty ground. She paused and looked across the short distance, covered with brown grass and weeds to the still rail cars.

With one hand she lifted her skirt from the top of her shoes and began to walk to the passenger car of the train. As she neared the train, Julia stumbled, regained her stance and continued to the steps of the rail car.

As she stood beside the passenger car, she felt a tap on her shoulder. Startled, Julia quickly turned.

The young uniformed boy stood directly behind her. "Pardon me, ma'am, can I help you with your valise?"

"Captain," Julia answered, "I'm the one that needs to help you."

"Oh, no, ma'am, I'm just a little sore. That ain't no reason not to help a lady," the captain stated.

Julia looked sympathetically at the soldier, "I can climb the steps. If you would hand me my valise, I will help you pull yourself on the steps."

"That would be mighty kind of you, ma'am," added the captain.

Julia, on the platform above the steps, reached for her valise and placed it inside the door to the car. She walked back onto the platform, leaned toward the captain and extended her hand. The captain grasped her hand and cautiously pulled himself onto the steps. He stepped deliberately one step at a time until he was on the platform with Julia.

"Might I ask your name, young lady?"

Julia felt sympathetic toward the captain. "Yes, captain, my name is Julia Dupree. Might I ask yours?"

"John Dancy, ma'am," the captain answered.

Dancy looked at the open doorway of the passenger car and extended his arm toward the entrance. "After you, ma'am."

Julia entered the narrow doorway into the car, stopped, picked up her valise and proceeded down the center of the car. The slatted wooden seats on both sides of the car were vacant.

Dancy followed Julia as she walked through the middle of the car, "Looks like we can sit most anywhere we want to."

Turning her head, Julia responded, "Yes, it does."

Julia stopped midway the car and looked to an open window, "I think I will take this seat beside the window."

She placed her valise on the seat and moved past it into the space beside the window. The captain observed she had taken both seats with her valise and herself. "I think I would like the window on this side. It will be nice to see some of my home county again for a spell," announced the young captain.

Captain Dancy looked out the window toward the station. He saw two lieutenants and more privates as they approached the rail car. The captain thought to himself that he should know them, but with the Seventeenth Regiment taking new enlistees he realized he could not know them all.

The captain and Julia sat silently as they watched the passengers enter the small door into the car. The privates dressed in the same butternut colored uniforms walked to the rear of the car.

As the two lieutenants passed Captain Dancy, they spoke, but continued to the rear of the car.

Julia heard the soldiers talking as she stared out the open window. Black smoke rose from the stack of the engine and wafted downward into the window. The acrid smell of the smoke caused Julia to cough. She opened her valise, removed a white handkerchief and wiped her eyes.

Dancy glanced at Julia as she wiped her eyes. "That smoke can be downright bothersome."

"And dirty, too," Julia responded.

Dancy turned in his seat and looked toward the rear door of the car, "It must be about time for the train to pull out. Here comes the conductor."

Hugh Speight entered the rear door and began moving down the middle of the car. "Have your tickets ready please; we're about ready to leave."

Speight stopped beside the seated privates. "You boys going back to your units or going on furlough?"

The young soldiers handed their tickets to the conductor. "Furlough," two of the privates responded.

"Back to Fort Branch," answered two of the last soldiers to enter the car.

"Well, are you two lieutenants going home?" asked the conductor as he moved through the center of the car.

"Yeah, but it ain't the home we want to go to. It's back to camp," responded one of the lieutenants.

The conductor continued through the middle of the car, stopped beside Julia, looked at her and smiled. "How did you get from Nashville so quick this morning? Weren't you 'sposed to spend some time with your aunt in Castalia? You must have got on the road early this morning."

"I did spend some time with my aunt. One of her neighbors had to come to Rocky Mount yesterday so I came and spent the night with a cousin here. I'm sure glad I didn't have to make that trip back to Nashville and then here."

"I 'spose you'll be glad to get home?" Speight asked.

Julia looked up at Speight and smiled. "Yes, sir, I sure will be happy to get back home. Back to a little peace and quiet. My aunt nearly talked me to death."

Speight reached for Julia's ticket. "It won't be long now."

Captain Dancy slid to the inner edge of his seat, handed the ticket to Speight and said, "I suppose you'll be wanting this one, too."

"Yep, you're right. I want yours, too."

Speight heard hurried steps at the rear of the car, turned and saw two more privates enter the rear door and take seats at the back of the car.

The conductor looked at the two late arrivals. "You boys got your tickets? It's time we were leaving."

"Yes, sir, sure do," one of the privates replied.

Speight walked quickly to the side of the two late soldiers. "Let's have the tickets and we'll be on our way."

The two privates handed their tickets to the conductor simultaneously, one smiled and said, "Yeah, let's go home."

As he walked back through the middle of the car Conductor Speight called out, "It's eight-thirty, let's be on our way!"

Speight quickly moved to the front of the car, walked onto the platform and stepped on the lower step. With one hand gripping the iron railing of the rail car, he leaned outward, "All aboard!" The conductor looked toward the engine and with a wide overhead sweep of his arm, motioned to the engineer to move ahead.

The passenger car jerked, the couplings became taut as the

train began its forward motion. Black smoke began to billow from the high stack, steam began to vent from the pistons and red burning ash spewed behind the locomotive.

Julia pushed herself away from the window to escape the ash being pulled through the open window. "Good Lord, this will set us all afire!"

"No, ma'am," assured the captain, "the ashes will burn out before they do any damage. Just try to keep it out of your eyes. Pretty soon the wind will blow the smoke over the top of the cars."

Julia felt reassured and settled into her seat.

The car moved slowly. The iron wheels of the passenger car began to roll quicker over the rail joints. The sounds of the wheels as they rolled over the joints began to quicken into a constant click, clack, click, clack.

Rushing early morning air felt good to Julia as she thought of going home. The train slowed as it approached the Kingsboro Siding. The engineer, relaxed in the coolness of the early morning, was unaware of Major Jacobs and Captain Chamberlain as they loosely reined their horses along the Kingsboro Road. Towering thick pine trees on both sides shaded the troopers from the early morning sun.

The crossroads of Old Sparta was only a distant memory in the mind of Captain Chamberlain as he peered into the distance. "Major, I think I see a clearing ahead. It appears at least to be an end to the trees."

"Very well," responded Jacobs and he added, "Captain, halt the column. We best be sure exactly what is there before we expose the column in the open. This is somewhere we have not been before."

"Yes sir, you are probably correct to take all precautions," answered the captain.

Chamberlain raised himself from the saddle, stood erect in

the stirrups and raised his arm. "Column, halt!" The sounds of the moving column became still as the mounted cavalrymen brought their horses to a halt. The horses began to snort, shake their heads and prance in a backward motion. Their halt became complete.

"Captain, direct a trooper to go on ahead and report the situation," ordered the major.

Captain Chamberlain turned in the direction of Company A, "Private White!" the captain shouted.

"Yes, sir," George White responded as he spurred his horse in the direction of the captain.

Private White reined his horse beside Captain Chamberlain, "You called me, sir?"

Chamberlain turned and looked directly at the private, "Ride ahead into the clearing, check in all directions and report back."

"Yes, sir," White responded as he urged his mount from the halted column.

White snapped the reins in his hands and in a fast gallop advanced to the clearing. The private stopped at the edge of the woods and proceeded slowly from the protection of the trees.

As he prodded his mount from the woods he quickly observed the railroad tracks. The private cautiously urged his horse closer to the road bed of the tracks.

He reined his horse to a complete halt and looked in both directions along the rail line. The private looked east and saw nothing along the road bed. He looked west, away from the sun into the early morning mist. What is that, he thought? Again he peered through the mist. Yes, it is! Yes, it is a train, White thought to himself. Private White pulled tight on the reins, turned his horse back in the direction of the halted column and gouged his steed with both feet. In a fast gallop the private returned to the column.

"Major!" the private excitedly reported, "There's a train

approaching from the west. There is no sign of anything in the other direction. There's no sign of activity at the siding up ahead."

"Very well, private. Thank you. Return to your company," ordered the major.

Jacobs nodded at Chamberlain. "Move to the head of the column and go on to the clearing."

The captain snapped the bridle reins of his horse and reined the mount into the road at the head of the column.

Chamberlain lifted himself above the saddle, turned and raised his arm in a forward motion. "Column, ho!"

As the captain cautiously moved from the protection of the wooded terrain, the rails suddenly appeared. He prodded his mount into the center of the tracks, stopped and looked westward. The captain stood in the stirrups, placed both hands on the saddle pommel and leaned forward.

Yes, it was a train. He could see the black round front of the engine as it emerged from the convergence of the trees. The black smoke billowed from the funnel-shaped stack as the locomotive waddled closer.

Seth lowered himself from the saddle, reins in hand, he quickly walked his horse to the edge of the trees. "Major! There is a train approaching. What do you want to do?"

Major Jacobs raised himself high in the stirrups and turned to Company A, "Company A, block the rail tracks! Captain Chamberlain, flag down the engine!"

The major continued his sharp orders, "Companies E and G dismount and line the side of the road bed!"

Jacobs reined his horse around in the direction of the column, "All other companies remain in position."

The major snapped the reins and galloped to the side of the rail tracks. Jacobs observed the mounted cavalrymen lined across the tracks.

"Captain Chamberlain, move to the center of the tracks and flag the train to a stop," Major Jacobs called out.

The captain gripped the reins of his horse's bridle, turned and faced west. Seth looked toward the west as the engine slowly closed the distance between the  plume of black smoke and the troopers. Company A troopers blocked the tracks as they lined abreast from one side of the road bed to the other.

Chamberlain removed his hat and began waving it over his head, from shoulder to shoulder.

The engine continued to advance, the smoke became thicker, the engineer was in full view as he leaned to the outside of the engine cabin. The sounds of the steam venting became louder and louder, the vibration of the rail bed became distinct.

Seth, quickly detecting the engineer had no intention of stopping, reined his horse from the tracks. "Good God! Get off the tracks, boys! That engine is not slowing down! Move quick!"

The cavalrymen quickly pulled the reins of their mounts and split the line to both sides of the tracks. They remained mounted as the captain called out, "Stay clear of the tracks! That engineer is crazy!"

The engine passed the troopers as it belched embers and smoke in its wake. The rail cars rolled quickly in front of the blue clad troopers as the smoke settled behind the final passing car.

Major Jacobs looked confused as the rear of the train passed his position, "Private White!" the major yelled, "Stop that engine."

George White gripped the reins, sharply spurred his horse and began to race his mount alongside the moving train. With another squeeze to the side of his horse he moved faster, closing the distance between him and the engine. The road bed of the tracks was smooth. Private White moved closer to the engine.

Julia looked out the window as the trooper raced past the passenger car. "Oh my God, it's Yankees! Oh my God, it's Yankees!" Her heart began to race, fear filled her mind and she began to scream. Her screams became more intense as she rose from the seat and grasped the back of the seat ahead of her. Julia screamed again. "Oh Lord, it's Yankees!"

Private White reached the engine and galloped along beside the cab. He loosened the reins from his hands, stood upright in the stirrups and leaned toward the opening of the engine cab. His mount raced on alongside the hissing engine. The private grasped the two iron railings of the engine cab and pulled himself from the saddle and onto the steps leading into the cab. His horse continued running alongside the engine.

Private White pulled himself inside the engine cab and drew his revolver from its holster and placed the barrel directly at the head of the engineer, "Shut this thing down or your brains will be lining the side of the train!"

The private placed the barrel closer to the engineer's temple, "I ain't foolin', fellow, stop this thing!"

The engineer reached for the throttle and released the steam vent as he called to the fireman, "Stand by to brake the train!"

Private White watched as the two trainmen began to pull on the levers that put pressure on the iron wheels. The engine began to slow as the steam began to vent.

The private pointed his revolver directly at the engineer again, "You boys stay where you are."

"Captain Chamberlain, board the passenger car!" yelled Major Jacobs.

Seth dismounted and pulled his revolver from its leather holster, approached the steps of the passenger car and with one hand pulled himself up the steps onto the platform. With his revolver in one hand he entered the front door of the car and glanced from the front to the back.

"Well, what have we here?" the captain asked loudly.

Julia, her heart pounding inside her breast, remained silent.

Seth looked to the rear of the car, then to the middle of the car. "Well, boys, the war's over for you. Looks like we got us some officers and some privates. Just stay where you are and don't give me any trouble!" demanded Chamberlain.

Chamberlain walked to the window directly in front of Julia. He leaned out the window and shouted, "Major, send in some troopers to hold these soldiers!"

Julia's face became ghostly white, her heartbeats pulsed in her temples. She grasped her valise with both hands. Her eyes remained on the captain as he moved back to the center of the car. He looked directly at Julia, placed his revolver at his side and smiled broadly, "I don't suppose you can be considered a prisoner. From the look on your face you probably are no danger to anybody."

The troopers began to crowd into the passenger car. Major Jacobs appeared in the doorway, looked down the length of the car, placed his revolver back into the holster and announced, "This train is going back to Rocky Mount!"

The major leaned out an open window and commanded, "Sergeant, tell Private White to order the engineer to reverse this thing back to Rocky Mount!"

Julia watched as the soldiers stood with pointed revolvers. She observed the helpless Confederates. Slowly her fear turned into anger as she thought of what her father had told her before she began this trip. This was her country, she thought. These Yankees were the intruders. Her anger began to intensify as she remained silent.

Julia felt the jolt under her feet as the engine began to make its movement. "I'm not going back to Rocky Mount! I bought a ticket to Tarborough and I'm entitled to get to Tarborough!" The anger began to redden Julia's face as she stood and looked at Chamberlain directly, "You don't have any right to make me go back to Rocky Mount. You don't have any right to make me do anything! I don't have a way to get home from Rocky Mount, and you can't make me do anything I don't see best."

Seth placed his hand on her shoulder and gently pushed her toward her seat. "Will you sit down and be quiet? I really don't care how you get home! That's your problem, not mine."

Captain Dancy rose from his seat and angrily gripped Chamberlain by the arm. "Can't you blue bellies be civil?"

The captain raised his revolver above his shoulder and with a twist of his body came down with his revolver in his hand, striking Dancy in the face. Captain Dancy reeled backward onto the floor. Blood began trickling down his lips as he pulled himself into the seat. Chamberlain looked down at Captain Dancy with contempt. "You ought to know better than to interfere, you contemptible Rebel!"

The rage in Julia exploded as she screamed at Captain Chamberlain, "You Yankee devil! You son of hell! You come to our home and try to make us do your bidding! I hope you rot in hell with Lincoln and all of his mean Republicans!"

Captain Chamberlain turned toward the cavalrymen and laughed, "Would you look at this little Dixie wench? What do we think she can do? Yeah, what can she do but squeal?"

Julia looked down on the floor between the seats, spotted a sawdust-filled brass spittoon, stooped and picked it up. Rapidly she raised it above her head and darted toward the captain. The brown colored sawdust spilled onto the floor and seats.

A yell sounded from the troopers, "Captain! Watch your back!"

As the captain suddenly turned around, Julia brought the brass spittoon solidly against the side of his head. Seth recoiled from the impact. Stunned, he staggered backwards into the mass of troopers. Seth, numbed, grasped the back of a seat and steadied himself.

The captain placed his revolver back into the holster, steadied himself again and yelled, "You little wench! I don't know where you live, but this train will never take you home! It's a good thing you are not one of these soldiers or I'd crack your head open."

Captain Chamberlain looked at the valise on the seat where Julia sat, reached and grabbed the bag, "Watch as I throw this bag just as far as I can send it!" He walked quickly to the platform of the rail car; with a long underhand swing he threw the valise over the road bed into the scrub weeds.

Still shocked from the sudden blow to his head, the captain returned to the angered Julia, "Now, by God, I'm going to fling you in the same place, and you can get home the best way you can!"

Chamberlain gripped Julia's arm at her elbow and pulled her toward the platform. "You're lucky I don't slap the daylights out of you!" he proclaimed.

Julia held back, pulled against the grasped hand of the captain, "You're hurting me, you Yankee scoundrel!"

"I don't care; you're getting off this train right now!" shouted the captain.

Chamberlain pulled Julia by the arm onto the platform, released his hand and pointed toward the open valise. "Get out there with your grip and go!"

Julia started down the steps, stopped and looked back at the captain, "You miserable son of hell! I hope you rot in torment!"

Captain Chamberlain watched as Julia walked toward the edge of the trees and began picking up the contents of her valise.

The captain walked to the opposite side of the platform,

leaned out and looked for Major Jacobs. "Major, everything in here is secure. I'll leave our prisoners under the sergeant of Company I," he shouted.

Chamberlain grasped the railing next to the steps and leaped onto the ground. He called for the corporal to bring his horse. Blue Boy looked good to him as the corporal handed the reins to the captain.

"Corporal, ride to the engine and tell Private White to start putting this train in reverse," commanded the captain.

Chamberlain turned his horse in the direction of Major Jacobs, slowly joined the major as he rubbed the side of his head. Seth thought, good Lord, that lick hurt!

The rail cars began to move slowly in the reverse direction. The sound of the pistons grew louder as the iron wheels of the locomotive rolled past the officers as they remained mounted beside the track.

"Where are we taking this train, Major?" asked the captain.

"Back to the railyard and station in Rocky Mount," answered Jacobs.

Captain Chamberlain snapped the reins and urged his horse into the narrow path alongside the tracks. "Then what will it be, Major?" Jacobs responded, "Then it will be the destruction of our objectives!"

Major Jacobs and Captain Chamberlain rode ahead of the column as they made their way along the tracks behind the reversing engine. The black smoke rose into the air, then sank to cover the troopers as their horses reacted to the stifling cloud of black ashes and smoke.

Captain Chamberlain turned in his saddle and saw Julia as she made her way eastward along the rail tracks.

# CHAPTER NINE

Major Jacobs loosened the bridle reins, twisted the straps around the saddle pommel, removed his hat and with his sleeve wiped his brow. "My God, it's already hotter than the hinges of Hades."

Captain Chamberlain turned in the saddle, removed his hat and began to use it to fan below his face. "This smoke would stifle the devil himself. How far do you think the railyards are?"

"Judging from our map, it should be about a mile farther," answered the major.

The major placed his hat back on his head and looked at the captain. "Captain, dispatch a company to the lead part of the train. The rear of the train will arrive first. We will need a guard to proceed ahead into the railyard."

Seth drew his mount to a stop, pulled the reins hard and turned the horse around. "Sergeant Wentz, take Company L to the other end of the train and lead it into the railyard."

"Yes, sir," responded Wentz as he motioned for his company to move past the side of the moving train of cars. "Company L, to the front of the train!" the sergeant called out.

Wentz moved to the last car of the train as it moved slowly toward the railyard. Company L followed the sergeant as he constantly prodded his horse to remain in the lead.

"I believe I can see the water tower of the yard!" called out Major Jacobs. "Captain Chamberlain, ride to the front and order Sergeant Wentz to take the station and evacuate any nonmilitary persons from the building."

Chamberlain snapped the reins, guided his mount along the sides of the moving cars, and maintained the pace alongside Sergeant Wentz. "Sergeant, evacuate the depot, cut the telegraph lines and put the torch to the station. There should be plenty of dry kindling in the station to get a good fire started. Be sure that what you start, nobody can stop. Take the company and go on. I will take over from here."

The sergeant rode ahead, turned and motioned, "Company L, on to the station, on to the station!"

Captain Chamberlain observed the rail yard workers as they came out of the buildings, stopped, stared at the reversed train as it entered the yard and began to scatter. He heard their shouts as he neared the shops. He saw the frightened men turn and run into the nearby swamp.

Very good, the captain thought, we can go on without interruption. Seth saw Company L as they entered the telegraph office. The railcars began to slow, the sounds of the engine indicated the reverse movement was coming to a stop.

The captain turned in the direction of Major Jacobs and quickly galloped to the side of the major. "What now, Major? L Company is putting the torch to the station. The telegraph lines have been cut and it looks like we have no resistance!"

Major Jacobs halted his horse and glanced at the entire area. "Captain, take the other companies and set fire to the shops and all the buildings in the yard. Pull down the water tower with ropes and horses. Rip up as much track as you can. I will take care of this train of cars."

Jacobs spurred his horse, galloped to the side of the stopped engine. He looked up at Private White, still pointing his revolver at the engineer and raised his revolver over his head. "Well done, Private, well done!"

The major placed his revolver back into its holster and called out to Private White, "Private, close the steam pressure valve and order the fireman to fill the firebox with wood. Then get just as far from this thing as you can!"

White with his revolver at his side looked at the engineer

and smiled. "You heard the Major! Close the valve and tell your fireman to bank the firebox with plenty of dry wood. And I mean now and I ain't foolin'!"

The engineer glared at the private and in an exasperated tone said, "But that will build up pressure and blow us to kingdom come."

The private grinned and laughed, "Then I would suggest you put as much distance between you and this monster as you think necessary for your own good."

The engineer yelled to the fireman, "You heard the man! Fill up the firebox and get the devil away from here!"

Private White demanded, "And where is the pressure valve?"

The engineer pointed to the valve handle and looked at the private.

Private White pointed his revolver at the engineer. "Well, close the thing and get out of here. Or stay if you want; I don't mind."

The engineer raised himself from the seat beside the cabin opening, walked to the middle of the engine, reached above the firebox and turned the valve to a tight closure. "I hope you know what you're doin', soldier. When this blows, it's mighty likely to scald somebody."

Private White looked directly at the sweaty engineer, "Then we best be out of the way, huh?"

The private placed his revolver in his holster. He moved quickly to the door opening, grasped the outside rail of the cabin door and swung onto the bottom step. He began running as his feet touched the ground.

Private White's horse had followed the engine instinctively. As the private approached his mount, he grabbed the reins with one hand and with his other hand grasped the pommel of the saddle. He raised one foot and quickly inserted it into the stirrup.

With his hand tightly gripping the saddle pommel he pulled himself into the saddle. With a quick adjustment of the reins, the private urged his mount in the direction of the railyard.

Major Jacobs observed Private White as the private approached the railyard, raised himself in the saddle and called loudly, "Private White, over here! Over here, Private!"

Private White saw the major as he motioned to him, rode quickly toward Major Jacobs and reined his horse to a stop. "Yes, sir, Major. You called?"

"Private, ride and tell Captain Chamberlain to search for some rope or chain in the shops and pull down that water tower," the major directed.

"Yes, sir," answered the private as he galloped toward the railyard shops.

Private White saw Captain Chamberlain as he guided his horse in and out of the large open roundhouse doors. The image of a steam engine being turned in another direction on the rails quickly passed through his mind. This roundhouse will be useless, he thought, as he raced to the scene of destruction.

"Captain Chamberlain!" the private called out as he tightened the reins and halted, "The major said to look for some rope or chains and pull down that water tower!"

"Alright, Private, you go find enough rope and we'll do just that. Be sure to get enough rope to get far enough away from the tank," the captain called out.

White quickly galloped to the open door of what appeared to be a tool shop, dismounted and dashed inside the building. The private glancing from side to side, spied some large stained rope coiled in a corner. White stooped, lifted one side of the coiled rope, and placed his arm under the entire coiled line. The private looked toward the open door, rose, pulled the coil over his arm and dashed out the door.

"Captain! Captain! Here's the rope, Captain," the private

yelled as he ran toward Chamberlain.

Chamberlain reined his horse and held his mount in check. "Very good, Private! Do you see that ladder nailed to the front leg of that tower?"

"Yeah, I see it, Captain," responded the private, and added loudly, "and it looks like a barrel on legs."

"Get up that ladder with one end of the rope and tie it to the leg at the top of the ladder and make it secure," ordered the captain.

The private reached down, grasped one end of the coiled rope and started up the ladder. "Yes, sir!" the private called out as he made his way up the narrow ladder rungs.

White glanced toward the flume that protruded from the bung opening, observed the open top and quickly wondered how the barrel-like tank was filled. He knew the steam engines required a lot of water. At every station along the rail line there had to be a supply of water beside the tracks.

The private reached the top of the ladder, held himself erect with one hand, leaned around the tank leg and guided the rope around the backside of the wooden support. As he held tight with one hand on the ladder, he pulled the rope toward him. With the line in both hands, his feet secure on the ladder rung, the private held himself upright as he tied the rope loosely around the wooden support. With a hefty tug on the tied knot, the private placed both hands back onto the ladder and began his descent.

Captain Chamberlain called out loudly, "Private, I've got the other end of the rope! Get away from that tank and get over here with me! It's going to take both of us to pull that tower down!"

Private White ran to his horse, with precise accuracy pulled himself into the saddle and called out, "Captain, how are both of us going to pull that thing down?"

"Stay where you are, Private!" the captain called out.

Chamberlain prodded his mount behind the private, began to coil the rope in his hand and twisted the uncoiled line around the saddle pommel. "Private, steady yourself to catch this line!" Private White turned in his saddle and saw the captain take a long swing as he hurled the coiled line. The private caught the loose line and began to search for the end.

"Private," the captain yelled, "twist that end through your saddle pommel and pull! I'll be behind pulling at the same time! Between the two of us we ought to be able to bring that thing down!"

White squeezed his boot heels into the side of his mount, snapped the reins and urged the animal forward. The rope between the private and the captain became taut. Captain Chamberlain spurred his horse forward, the line attached to the top of the ladder rose from the dusty ground and began to bounce in the air.

"Let's pull, Private!" yelled the captain.

The private spurred his horse in rapid foot movements; the animal leaned forward and the line tightened.

The captain snapped the reins, tightened his feet into the side of his horse and the rope strained.

"Keep pulling, Private!" the captain called out.

White urged his mount even more as he snapped the reins on the animal's mane.

Chamberlain spurred harder into the side of his horse and with a verbal outburst, "Pull, Blue Boy, pull!"

The timber support began to creak as the horses' hoofs slipped in the dust with every strain on the taut line. Suddenly the line became limp, the horses leaped forward and a cry went up from the troopers. "Auhhhhhh!"

The water tower leaned, shuddered, and with a thunderous

123

crash, shattered on impact. Water splashed in every direction into the dry, parched ground.

"Private, let the line loose!" yelled the captain as he unwound the line from his saddle pommel. Private White loosened the line from the saddle pommel, reined his horse in the direction of Captain Chamberlain and pulled the prancing steed to a stop. "Where do we go from here, Captain?"

Chamberlain raised himself high above the saddle and pointed to the open doors of the engine roundhouse. "Get inside those doors and find the lanterns and lamps! By God! Use their matches to light them! Then, Private White, throw the lanterns far enough inside to start a good blaze," yelled the captain.

The private dismounted quickly, handed his mount's reins to the captain with some hesitation, "Mind holding my horse while I get inside the roundhouse, Captain?"

Chamberlain reached forward and grasped the leather reins with a loud response, "Make it quick, Private; we got a lot more to do this day!"

White dashed toward the open doors of the roundhouse and thought as he entered the structure, where will I likely find any matches, or any fire for that matter. The wooden structure was empty, tools and chains lined the outer walls and the exposed rafters were covered with soot from the engine stacks.

The private stopped, looked around the interior, spotted a desk and noticed the lamp. What good luck, the private thought, just what I wanted! White ran to the desk and in a rush pulled the drawer from its guides. There they were, the wooden matches inside the small tinder box. The matches scattered from the box as the drawer crashed to the floor.

The trooper bent his knees, reached for the matches and scooped them  from the stained wooden floor. The tinder box with the striking exterior lay open, but empty, beside the splintered drawer.

The private, the tinder box in one hand, sulphur-tipped matches in the other, quickly spread the matches onto the desk and reached for the lamp. As he removed the chimney, the private thought it would be best if the chimney were put back on after the wick had become ignited. He did not want the flame to be extinguished as he threw it to the middle of the structure.

White placed the lamp chimney beside the lamp, turned the wick up from its lowered position and reached for the box of sulfur-dipped wooden matches. As he scraped the sulphur tip against the rough side of the small tinder box the sparks ignited the wooden end. The private hesitated as the flame began to consume the match stick. The black smoke reeked of sulfur.

The trooper leaned over the lamp and touched the slender stick to the blackened wick. The flame from the match moved onto the wick. A narrow pillar of black smoke danced upward. Private White recognized the odor. Coal oil. Very good he thought, this will burn excellently.

The cavalryman reached for the chimney, looked around, leaned over the lamp and placed the chimney securely in place. Its wick burned higher within the chimney as the private extended the lamp from his side and with a deliberate side arm swing tossed the lamp onto the floor. The glass chimney shattered as the coal oil spread from the force of the toss. The flame from the wick touched the coal oil and began to spread along the pattern of the spilled oil.

Private White watched as the flames began to engulf the middle of the wooden floor. Black smoke reached the ceiling and curled as it returned to the floor. He ran back to the desk, reached for the splintered drawer and with a long underhanded swing tossed the drawer into the leaping flames. Brilliant orange flames began to spread into the ceiling and lunged outward from the center to engulf the roundhouse. The pungent smoke filled the structure as Private White ran from the building, closed the massive doors behind him and ran to mount his horse alongside Captain Chamberlain.

Chamberlain leaned over and handed the reins of the private's horse to him. "Excellent, Private White, excellent!"

The captain pointed to the train of cars. "From here it looks like the major has put the fire to the railcars. The engine could blow at any time. Let's get out of here!"

Private White looked toward the station. The heavy black smoke billowed high into the sky; the odor of burning pine tar filled the air as the flames began to break through the round house roof. "A good day's work, wouldn't you say, Captain? A very good day's work!"

Captain Chamberlain lifted himself above the saddle, stood erect in the stirrups and turned in the direction of the fallen water tower and burning roundhouse. "Yeah, Private, a very good job! Everything seems to be burning pretty steady now. We'd better join the major. Do you see him and the rest of the troops?"

"Yes, sir, I saw the major leading our column northward from the station. I think we'll find them along the tracks just beyond this smoke. Maybe we'd better get out of here before the engine blows."

Captain Chamberlain tightened the bridle reins, turned his horse in the direction of the railyard and observed the destruction of the shops and railyard. The flames danced from structure to structure, reached upward and gave off a black cloud of smoke and sparks, returned again to the tops of the roofs. With greater brilliance the flames leaped higher into the blackened sky.

The captain felt the heat from the blazing inferno as he observed the station and the rail shops as they began to crumble from the onslaught of the fire.

He pulled the bridle reins tight; his mount began to move back from the heat as he viewed the train of cars, now engulfed in smoke and flames. The engine, now barely visible through the smoky haze, emitted a towering plume of black smoke and ashes. The scene was somber and desolate.

The captain gasped as he motioned to Private White. "Move out, Private, north along the tracks!"

Chamberlain spurred his horse and guided his mount alongside the tracks and away from the burning railyard. "Move to the other side of the tracks, Private. I see the major and the other companies just ahead. They must be waiting for us. We seem to be the last to leave."

The captain and Private White galloped in the direction of Major Jacobs and the column as they waited on the tracks.

Major Jacobs watched as Captain Chamberlain and Private White approached. "Very good, Captain, very good. I brought out the companies when I saw you had everything well under control. I can see from here everything is burning out of control."

Captain Chamberlain reined his horse to a stop, pulled tighter on the reins and turned his mount in the direction of the towering flames and smoke. "Major, that is what I would call total destruction!"

Jacobs pulled the reins of his horse as the mount pranced in place without moving forward or backward. "Yes, Captain, that is total destruction. And there is more to come, yes, much more to come!"

The vibration of the ground caused the column to look in the direction of the smoke. A roaring blast echoed from the direction of the steam engine. A tower of white smoke ascended and spread into a mushroom-like cloud, covering the haze of black smoke. The heated water from the ruptured boiler spewed upward into the vaporized smoke, the clouds from the engine fire became gray as the steam mixed with black smoke.

A plume of black smoke glided upward from the prostrate giant of the Atlantic and East Carolina Railroad. Another explosion ripped through the black iron boiler, and like a dying animal, it settled into stillness. The earth beneath the horses became still. A calm satisfaction engulfed the troops as they viewed the devastation.

Major Jacobs relaxed the reins in his hands and settled in his saddle. "Captain Chamberlain, take Companies A, E, and G and the howitzer section west on the Hilliardston Road. There is a cotton mill and a  county bridge over the Tar River at that position. Destroy as much as you can!" Major Jacobs added, "There's a flouring mill, somewhere in this area, too!

"Yes, sir," answered Chamberlain, "and where will I meet you when we're finished?"

"I will take the remainder of the column to the trestle bridge over the river," responded the major.

Jacobs turned his horse northward and looked ahead along the rail tracks. "We will burn the rail trestle at both sides like we did in Greenville and rip up the rails in the middle. When we are finished, we will wait for you where the Hilliardston Road crosses the tracks. Be about your assignment, Captain!"

Chamberlain turned in his saddle and motioned forward with an overhead sweep of his arm, "Rudisill, fall in behind with your howitzer! Limber the piece if you want to, the road looks right good."

"Right with you, Captain," the sergeant replied.

Sergeant Rudisill dismounted, looked at the three animals loaded with the carriage, barrel and ammunition and instructed, "Battery K, limber the section and follow the troopers."

The captain rose in the stirrups, turned and with a raised voice called out, "Company A, Company E, Company G, move in behind me!"

Chamberlain snapped the leather reins on the neck of Blue Boy and began to move west on the Hilliardston Road.

Major Jacobs watched as the column began to form behind the captain. The dust from the horses began to rise upward into the noontime sun as the troopers moved toward the river. The Mountain Howitzer lumbered from side to side, rut to rut, as it disappeared into the dusty road.

Major Jacobs knew the river trestle was north of their position as Chamberlain moved into the distance. He held his horse in check as he viewed the terrain. Jacobs looked to the south, the smoke billowed high above the tree tops.

Major Jacobs scanned the cleared area of the tracks where the Hilliardston Road intersected. He observed a large, plain, wooden building, four floors in height, and thought this would be looked into on Captain Chamberlain's return. The present objective was the important thing now, he reflected.

The major pressed his feet tight in his stirrups and raised himself above his saddle and motioned with his arm above his shoulders, "Move north along the tracks! Column hoaaa!" he commanded.

# CHAPTER TEN

The early morning sunlight began to penetrate the sparse growth of pine trees that lined the tracks. Julia had retreated into the wooded terrain after she was certain her clothes were in her valise. She stood motionless in the security of the trees. Her anger and humiliation were hidden from the cavalrymen by the distance and the forest. The rage within caused her entire body to tremble as she suppressed the urge to scream unholy oaths at Captain Chamberlain.

Julia watched in silence as the cavalrymen began to fade into the distance. The black plume of smoke from the reversed engine obscured the troopers. The sounds of the reversed locomotive diminished. Julia was alone. The quietness was broken by the sounds of circling crows, searching for their morning meal.

She stooped, picked up her valise from the brushy growth and stepped through the growth toward the rail tracks. A briar vine tugged at her skirt as she lifted her foot over the low growth of weeds and scrub grass. As she gripped her valise in one hand, Julia pulled at her skirt with her other hand. The briar vine held firm. She tugged again and she heard the tear. My God, she thought, is there no end to this misery? She knew she was not far from Coolmore. Julia had walked these tracks often in the past. Now they appeared desolate and foreboding.

With her hand tightly squeezing the handle of her grip, Julia stared along the tracks leading to Tarborough and behind Coolmore. The rails appeared to disappear into the distance. Julia's eyes remained fixed on the disappearing tracks. The morning heat was visible as it radiated from the rail bed. Coolmore seemed so far away!

Julia began to walk toward the Kingsboro Siding. She moved to the side of the tracks to avoid the rail ties and with a slow, discouraged gait began her journey home.

The weight of her tapestry bag began to strain her arm; she switched the bag to her other hand and continued toward the siding. July's merciless heat bore onto Julia's face. Now she wished she had worn a hat when she left Coolmore for her visit with her aunt. She focused her eyes westward along the tracks toward Rocky Mount; only the radiated waves of heat ascended from the tracks.

There was no activity at the Kingsboro siding. The covered platform beside the tracks was empty. Guano stains from the leaky burlap bags spattered the platform. The heavy spring rains had dispersed the residue over the edges of the platform flooring. A faint odor of the Peruvian import lingered in intermittent sensations.

Julia turned, faced east, and in the glare of the open space, decided there was only one way to return to Coolmore. The rutted wagon path crossed the rails in a north to south direction. North was the only choice Julia concluded was available. She looked again around the cleared area of the Kingsboro Siding, noted the wooded terrain and with resignation began to walk north.

The thick pine trees provided very little relief from the penetrating rays of the morning sun. Its long southern sweep, to its disappearance in the west, lengthened the day. The withering heat of the sun concentrated on the tree-lined road.

Julia moved slowly away from the tracks, the glare of the sun to her back and the rutted narrow road in her front. The creatures of the forest stilled their voices as Julia moved closer to their space and raised their voices again as Julia passed in silence.

Beads of perspiration formed on Julia's cheeks and forehead. The valise weighed heavily in her hand, the ruts of the road twisted her feet; her long skirt became entangled in her steps as Julia pushed farther along the forsaken road. She burst into tears, and ran into the thicket beside the road. She released the valise, allowed it to drop to the forest floor, kneeled on the ground covered with pine straw and began to cry uncontrollably.

Julia, lost in her tears, was unaware of time and space in the stillness of nature. The solitude of the forest provided security and forgetfulness; she placed her hand on the soft bed of leaves and raised herself upright. Her desolate weeping had brought composure.

The sounds of rattling animal harnesses penetrated the stillness. The dull thuds of turning wagon wheels accelerated. Julia heard the excited urgings of the driver as the wagon neared. She observed the two wheel ruts, separated by high weeds in the center of the narrow road. She gripped her valise, stood at the edge of the wooded area and looked in the direction of the wagon sounds. She felt more secure as she stepped from the cover of the trees into the road.

Julia saw the driver as he pulled tight on the leather reins and called out loudly, "Whooa! Whoa!"

The horses drew to a halt. The driver looked at Julia as she stood, valise in hand, partially hidden by the trees. "Good God, girl, don't you know there's Yankees 'round here? They stopped the train and took it back to the station, and they took some prisoners on the train, too! What in heaven's name are you doin' out here by yourself?"

The driver looked directly at Julia and pulled the reins tighter, then inquired, "Ain't you Frank Dupree's girl? Does your papa know you're out here by yourself?"

Julia moved closer to the wagon, passed the team and looked up at the driver. "Yes, sir, I'm Frank Dupree's daughter. I was on that train and I got put off back there at the siding. I saw everything that went on. A Yankee soldier made me get off the train and walk home."

"Put your bag in the wagon and get on the back of the wagon," directed the driver. "You ought to know me anyhow.

I'm Joe Edmondson and I'm headed close by your papa's place. You best hold on tight! This ain't the best road I've ever been down."

Julia lifted her valise above the side boards of the wagon, dropped it onto the wagon bed and quickly moved to the rear. She turned her back toward the driver, placed her hands behind her onto the wagon bed, and with a quick lift upward with her feet, slid onto the wagon floor. Then she spoke, "I know my daddy is worried. I was supposed to be home early this morning. I sure am glad to see you come along, Mr. Edmondson. Yes, sir, I am glad to see you."

Edmondson snapped the reins onto the backs of the horses once, then again, and instructed Julia, "Hold on tight back there! We got to get away from here and get you home. I don't know where them Yankees might be!"

Julia gripped the wagon bed with her hands, stiffened her arms and braced herself as the wagon began to move in the ruts. Mr. Edmondson snapped the reins quicker and verbally urged the team, "Glick, glick, move, move, you old rascals!"

The two horses broke into a trot; the wagon began to bounce from side to side as dust from the wheels rose and disappeared into the trees.

Thick pine trees began to disappear as Edmondson saw the Heartsease crossroads ahead and informed Julia, "Miss Dupree, I ain't gonna stop anywhere. I'm goin' on down the Tarborough Road close to your daddy's place."

Edmondson pulled on the reins, turned around and looked at Julia. "Did you hear me, girl? I said I ain't stoppin'; I'll have you home in a little bit!"

"Yessir, I heard. Never mind me! Keep going!"

The wagon turned east on the Tarborough Road. The driver snapped the reins in rapid succession; Julia held tight as the wheels turned faster. The wagon bed rattled and metal rimmed wooden wheels strained as they bounced in the ruts. Julia stiffened her arms and tightened her grip. The vibration of the wagon radiated through Julia's body and she held tighter.

Edmondson drew the reins tight, leaned back to tighten the reins more and yelled, "Whoa, whoa!" The wagon came to a halt. Julia remained gripped to the wagon bed as she heard Mr. Edmondson speak to the team, "You fellows need to take a breather. I don't need two dead horses on my hands."

Edmondson turned and saw Julia, her legs dangling from the rear of the wagon, rigid and silent. "You can ease some, Miss Dupree, I've got to rest the team a spell before we can move on down the road."

Julia relaxed her grip on the wagon bed, turned toward the driver and smiled, "Mr. Edmondson, I'll be glad to walk the rest of the way home from here. It's not much farther and I know you got chores to take care of."

"I can take you a little more on the road, but I do have to turn off this road up ahead and go to the Cox place," added Edmondson.

After a brief rest, the driver snapped the reins onto the backs of the team and goaded the horses with gentle tappings of the leather straps. The wheels began to roll in and out of the ruts. Julia bounced from side to side as she balanced herself with her hands. Edmondson turned around and called to Julia, "I'll be turning off the road up ahead. You get on home and tell your papa what happened to you. Give your mama my best."

Mr. Edmondson pulled the slack from the lines; the wagon rolled to a stop. One horse of the team shook his head, snorted and jerked the wagon forward. Edmondson pulled the lines taut and assured Julia, "It's all right; you can get off. Don't forget your grip! And for God's sake, get on home!"

With her hands firmly on the wagon bed, Julia lifted herself slightly and with a thrust, leaped onto the ground. She reached for her valise, pulled it toward her and backed away from the wagon. She walked to the front of the wagon, stopped and looked up at Mr. Edmondson, "I'm much obliged to you, Mr. Edmondson. If you hadn't happened along, I'd have been on that road all day. Yessir, I'm much obliged to you!"

Edmondson looked down from the seat of the wagon and compassionately addressed Julia, "You ought to see yourself, Miss Dupree! You remind me of a stray cat what's been out all night and waiting at the kitchen door for a mouthful of sump'n 'teat. Be on home now, girl, and don't stop!"

Mr. Edmondson flipped the reins in rapid succession; the wagon jerked forward and moved away from Julia. The ever-present dust rose from the rumbling wagon as the sound of turning wheels dissolved into the distance.

Julia quickened her pace toward Coolmore. The Tarborough Road was not as rutted as the road from the Kingsboro Siding; walking was much easier. She constantly switched her bag from one hand to the other. The midday sun concentrated on the barren road. A bright glare from the light-colored ground blurred her vision and Julia turned her eyes toward the trees along the road. She walked closer to the side of the road and stopped in the shadow of the tall pines. Her vision began to clear and she thought it couldn't be much farther. She moved from the shade of the wooded terrain onto the road and with renewed enthusiasm anticipated home and safety.

The tall oaks of Coolmore came into view. Julia felt her pulse speed up; she instinctively increased her pace and rounded the final turn in the road that led home. Her beloved cupola appeared above the majestic treetops. Julia felt secure again!

The wagon path from the road to the house looked like home to Julia. She stopped, gripped her valise and began to run toward Coolmore, shouting, "Daddy, Mama! Mama, Daddy! Esther! Nero!"

Frank Dupree ran from the back to the side of the house and

stopped in the wagon path. "Oh, thank the Lord, Julia's back! Yes, thank the Lord, my little girl's back!"

Julia dropped her valise and jumped into the waiting arms of her father. "Oh Lord, Daddy! You just don't know what has happened to me!"

Frank Dupree lifted Julia from the ground and embraced her, inquiring, "Have you been harmed? Have you been hurt? Are you all right? We've been worried sick, not knowing your whereabouts!"

Ada Dupree, hearing the commotion, ran from the kitchen, saw Julia embraced by her father and screamed, "Thank you, Lord! Thank you, Lord! Oh, praise God!" She lifted her skirt with both hands and ran to Frank and Julia exclaiming, "Oh, thank the Lord, my girl's home!"

Julia ran toward her mother, embraced her and wrapped her arms around Ada's neck. "Mama, I've been scared half to death! I'm so glad to be home again! It will take me forever to tell you and Daddy what happened! I don't ever intend to leave Coolmore again!"

Frank leaned over, picked up Julia's bag, and joined Ada and Julia. He placed his arm around Julia's shoulder and said happily, "Let's go to the back porch. I know my girl is half starved, and from the looks of her, she's been through something!"

Ada took Julia by the hand, patted her cheek and said lovingly, "I've been worried to death about you. The train didn't come this morning and we've heard nothing but bad things since the sun came up. Lord, am I glad to see you safe!"

Frank added excitedly, "Yeah, we've heard there's Yankees in the area. We can hear thunder noises coming from Tarborough way. Now and again we can see clouds of smoke rising! Something bad's going on over there!"

Nathan and Dolly heard the screams from the main house as

they cropped the yellow leaves from the bottom of the tobacco stalks. "You hear dat, Nate?" Dolly asked.

"Yeah I did. What do you reckon it might be?"

Dolly looked puzzled as she stared at Nate with his leaf-filled burlap sack. "We better be findin' out what de 'sturbance is 'bout!"

Nathan walked to the edge of the tobacco patch, put the sack down and called out to Dolly, "I'm goin' right now to the house. You come on directly! Wees better see what's goin' on!"

Dolly followed Nathan as he ran to the rear of the main house. Nathan saw Frank, Ada and Julia, stopped and blocked Dolly as she approached. Nathan grabbed Dolly's shoulders and said excitedly, "Hit's Miss Julia! She's come back home! Miss Julia's home!"

Dolly raised both of her arms above her head and shouted, "Praise de Lawd, praise de Lawd! He done brought de young'un home! Oh, glory! de Lawd done worked a miracle!"

Nate and Dolly ran to greet Miss Julia as she walked to the back porch with Frank and Ada. Dolly excitedly grabbed Miss Julia, pulled her close and wildly exclaimed, "Lawd, child! We wuz worried sick! Oh, glory, the Lawd done brung you home!"

Dolly lifted a corner of her apron to Julia's eyes and wiped the dust away. "Miss Julia, you look jus' like you been in the flour sack. I knows you must be hongry; you look famished. Git to the kitchen so's I can fix you sump'n t'eat!"

Dolly started for the porch, turned and looked at Nate. "Nate, you best be 'bout finishin' dat job in de field." With a scowl on his face, Nate stared directly at Dolly and meekly answered, "Alright, woman! I knows what needs bein' done!"

Julia, Frank and Ada followed Dolly to the porch. Dolly lifted her skirt and stepped onto the porch. "Lawd, am I glad to see dat child back home! Y'all come on in de kitchen and sit down at de table. I'll have sump'n t'eat directly," Dolly declared.

Frank took his usual place at the table. Julia pulled back a chair from the table, sat down and with a sigh said to her mother, "Mama, you won't believe the things that have happened to me this morning! I made the trip to Aunt Mattie's all right, but coming back home this morning has been pure frightening! If it weren't for old man Joe Edmondson, I'd be on the road right now."

Frank placed his calloused hand on Julia's shoulder. "Child, you just take your time and tell us all what has happened to you. You go right ahead and eat a little something and don't worry about a thing now. You're back home now and everything's going to be all right. Just put your feet under the table and eat," Frank directed.

Julia reached for the damp cloth lying at the corner of the table and wiped her hands and face and asserted, "Oh, it's so good to be back home! I've seen some mean things this day. I've seen how mean them Yankees can be. Oh, I hope I never see another Yankee! Never!"

Dolly opened the oven of the wood stove, removed the warmed over biscuits and placed them on a plate in front of Julia. "Dis ought to give you a little help. De fried ham and cold gravy will be jus right with de biscuit."

"Thank you, Dolly, I'm starved to death."

Julia nudged her chair nearer the table, reached for a warm biscuit, crumbled it with her fingers and asked, "Mama, will you pass the gravy bowl and the ham meat, too?"

Julia arranged the fried ham beside the crumbled biscuit and spooned the gravy over the plate. The conversation at the table absorbed the time. Frank and Ada listened as Julia recalled the events of the morning.

"Good Lord," Frank exclaimed as he looked at the shadows on the kitchen porch. "It's well past noontime and time to be back in the field. Julia, you best take some rest for the balance of the day. I know you're worn out from the ordeal. You go on upstairs and rest."

Ada looked at Julia, saw her tattered dress and scratched shoes and lamented, "Good Lord, girl, you must have walked through a field of briars. Take those clothes off! Dolly will put them in the pot for wash day. There is some fresh water in the bucket beside the back door of the house. Refresh yourself for a spell. Don't fret about your grip, we'll take care of that. Be off with you, now!"

Julia pushed her chair away from the table, placed her hands on the table and braced herself as she rose from the chair. She started for the door, paused and sighed, "Lord, I'm glad to be home!"

The sun was high in the southern sky. The porch columns cast a short shadow on the porch. Julia stood for a moment in the shade of the porch and looked for the bucket of water. It was usually on a table beside the door that led into the rear of the main house. Thank God, she thought, as she saw the dipper handle protruding from the bucket. Julia looked again and saw the empty enameled basin beside the bucket.

Julia looked down at her tattered skirt and instinctively brushed the front with her hands. She thought, oh, what's the need, this old skirt is ruined anyway. As she walked to the table, the bucket looked full, and that looked good to Julia; fresh water for her face would feel delightful. She gripped the dipper, plunged it to the bottom of the bucket, held it momentarily on the bottom, then lifted it over the basin. The clear, cool water looked refreshing as she turned the dipper to slowly empty the contents into the basin.

Julia cupped her hands in the basin of water and splashed the water on her face. She felt the invigorating effects immediately, shook her hands over the basin and looked for a drying cloth. As she rubbed the dry cloth over her face she remembered her dusty shoes. They would not be worn in the main house, especially not in her bedroom.

Julia moved to the side of the porch, stepped from the porch onto the ground and sat on the edge of the porch. She lifted one foot over her knee and unlaced her shoe from top to bottom and removed her shoe. With one bare foot on the ground, she raised her other foot over her knee and loosed the laces and pulled off her shoe. She sat for a moment with her bare feet on the ground. The cool ground of Coolmore felt good!

Julia looked up into the direct sunlight, gripped the porch column with one hand and pulled herself back onto her feet on the porch. As she held to the column, she shaded her eyes with the other hand and looked toward the west. Were her eyes deceiving her, or was she seeing a towering column of black smoke on the western horizon?

Julia ran to the kitchen door, looked in and saw Frank, Ada and Dolly talking. "Daddy, I'm going up to the cupola! There's something going on over Rocky Mount way and I aim to see what it might be!" She bolted from the porch, raced through the rear door and dashed up the spiral staircase from the first floor to the cupola.

# CHAPTER ELEVEN

C aptain Chamberlain was feeling the exhilaration of the military operation. He felt in command of something and this gave him a sense of control, the real purpose of his presence in the Union army. Now, he thought, these rebellious secessionists would feel the consequences of war. This was his opportunity to strike at the enemy in their own territory. The captain was the commanding officer of this raiding party and he was the authority.

The captain snapped the reins of Blue Boy's bridle and prodded his mount ahead of the column. He pressed his feet in the stirrups, stood erect, turned and looked to the rear of the column and commanded loudly, "Close up! Close up!"

The stone structure came into view as Chamberlain rounded a bend in the Hilliardston Road. He observed the massive stone building. The captain counted the levels as he viewed the windows at each level. Six stories! My God, he thought, this is a tremendous operation! It appeared everything was normal; there was no indication of any protective military units. The cotton mill was an easy assignment. Captain Chamberlain raised his arm and motioned the column forward. Blue Boy felt the gentle squeeze of the captain's spurs and began a gallop.

Captain Chamberlain pulled the rein in his right hand, turned his horse from the road and into the wide path leading from the main road onto the mill property. Maple and pine trees lined the path to the smaller buildings of the mill property. Chamberlain reined his mount to a stop near the front steps of one of the buildings in the yard of the cotton mill. He dismounted and called out to the troopers, "Dismount! Dismount!" The captain, lifting his hat above his head, yelled, "All sergeants! All sergeants, right here!"

Three noncommissioned officers reported to Captain Chamberlain as he stood before the building entrance. The captain, holding the reins of Blue Boy, ordered, "Order your companies to secure their horses and report to me! Immediately!"

The sergeants hastily returned to their companies. All the companies dispersed into the trees on the mill property, tied their mounts and returned to Captain Chamberlain.

Chamberlain, holding the reins, looked around at the assembled troops. His heart began to race, excitement filled his mind as he confidently ordered, "Evacuate the mill! Leave nobody inside the mill! Order everybody out! Break up all the wood you can with your hands and pile it in the middle of the floor." Chamberlain continued to issue orders to the troopers, "Do not! I say do not! start any fire until I order you to do so! Sergeants, be about your assignments and report to me when you have evacuated the mill!"

The troopers quickly began to run toward the mill. The large double doors were open, exposing the massive interior of the cotton spinning operation. A deafening roar overwhelmed the cavalrymen as they entered the main mill building. The giant overhead wheels were turning as the wide leather belting bounced up and down from the rotations. The massive floor vibrated from the water wheel that provided the power for the spinning operation.

Sergeant Meyers of Company E glanced around at the busy scene, and called Sergeant Kutz, "Kutz! There ain't nothing but girls working in here! Get these girls out of here! Quick!"

Sergeant Kutz dashed up the stairway to the second level. "Get out of here! All of you workers, get out of here, now!" He bolted to the next level and shouted, "Clear the area! Clear the floor!" The waterwheel slowed, then came to a stop. The sergeant watched the girls move backward toward the security of the walls. Slowly the giant building began to settle into stillness. Kutz looked around at the still machinery and the frightened girls. "Get out of here! Everybody! Out of here!"

The stairway rumbled as the workers ran from the upper levels to the bottom level. Large belted wheels that turned the spinning operation at each level were motionless. Only trampling feet of the workers descending the steps was heard.

The open doors leading into the yard of the mill were filled with sunlight. Total terror gripped the young girls as they ran screaming for the open door. The pounding of their feet as they crossed the lower floor caused the building to vibrate.

The terrorized young girls disappeared into the trees and into the houses along Hilliardston Road. Battle's mill was vacated. All the machinery was stilled. The troopers were busy crashing wood and throwing the splintered pieces into the center of the floor.

Captain Chamberlain was startled as the front door of the building burst open and a well-dressed man dashed down the short steps onto the ground. "What in God's name is going on here? Don't you know this is private property? This is not government property! You have no cause to be on this property!" demanded the furious man.

Captain Chamberlain frowned at the excited man. "You're no fool! You know very well I'm going to level this mill! You know very well this mill supplies your Carolina boys in Lee's army. And who are you anyway? Are you the owner here? Is this your mill?" demanded the captain.

"Yes, I'm the owner! I'm telling you to leave, at once!" countered the indignant man.

Chamberlain glared at the middle-aged man with a neatly trimmed full beard and pulled on Blue Boy's reins. He drew his horse closer and continued to stare at the seething owner. The captain immediately felt he was intimidating the frightened proprietor. "Well, what is your name, Mr. Owner?"

"Battle, Jacob Battle," answered the frightened man.

"Well, Mr. Battle, I'll tell you what I'm going to let you do. I'm going to let you watch as my men put the torch to your mill. Then I'm going to let you watch it burn to the ground!" Chamberlain slowly dismounted and stood in front of the mill owner.

Jacob Battle, his face flushed with anger, stared directly into the eyes of Captain Chamberlain. His penetrating focus demanded the captain's attention. The captain turned quickly and looked directly at Battle, as Battle pointed at Chamberlain and angrily asked, "Captain? Are you off, or from?"

Chamberlain was shocked by the unexpected question. He knew the significance of it, however. The captain was well aware that Mr. Battle was using this unusual question to ask if he were a member of the Masonic fraternal order. He remembered the oath he had taken when he came into the fraternity; now his sacred oath was being put to the ultimate test. He recognized he was being asked for brotherhood consideration.

The captain's attitude abruptly changed, he looked Battle directly in his eyes and answered, "From!" Battle immediately recognized the answer; he knew the captain was a member of the brotherhood. Battle hesitated, looked intensely at Chamberlain and asked, "Well, brother, you know what I'm alluding to; what is your reply?"

Captain Chamberlain walked to the side of his horse, stroked Blue Boy's mane, hesitated and returned to Battle. "Mister Battle, I'm sorry. I have to obey the orders of my commanding officer. I wish it could be otherwise. But, I assure you, I will not be as enthusiastic as I might have been."

The captain did not want to dwell on the matter. He turned from Mr. Battle, pulled his horse by the reins and walked toward the mill. As he neared the opened double doors of the mill he observed the troopers carrying out his orders. A feeling of betrayal subdued his enthusiasm. He reached the open doors and shouted, "That's enough! Take the lanterns from the walls and throw them on the floor! Make certain the lanterns break and the coal oil is leaking!"

"Sergeant! Hurry to the office building! Find an oil lamp and some matches and get back, quick!" directed Chamberlain. He continued to direct the troopers to be certain no one was left in the mill.

The sergeant ran from the building to the wooden two-story house, bolted up the steps and into the building. Mr. Battle appeared at the door as the sergeant surged past. The sergeant reappeared at the door, oil lamp in hand, pushed Battle from the doorway and ran to the mill. Battle followed the trooper from the house to the mill.

The sergeant handed Captain Chamberlain the ornate box containing the matches, removed the lamp chimney and held the lamp toward the captain. Chamberlain opened the box, removed a match, struck it on the rough part of the box and placed the flame onto the lamp wick. Black smoke began to rise from the lamp wick and the captain passed the lamp to the sergeant, "Throw the lamp onto the floor! Be sure it ignites the coal tar!"

"Everybody out! Sergeant, get everybody out!" ordered the captain as he ran back to his horse. Mr. Battle was standing outside the large doors as Chamberlain ran past. "I'm sorry, Mr. Battle. I truly am sorry!" The captain grasped the reins of his horse, mounted Blue Boy and called loudly, "Men! On to the bridge!"

Captain Chamberlain tightened the reins, turned his mount out of the mill yard and onto the Hilliardston Road. The mounted cavalrymen drew their horses behind the captain and the column galloped along the Hilliardston Road toward the river bridge. Chamberlain pulled Blue Boy to a halt at the edge of the wooden bridge, observed the plank structure and looked to the opposite side of the river. The opposite side appeared desolate.

Captain Chamberlain stood erect in the stirrups, turned and looked at the companies behind him. "Company E, proceed across the bridge! Sergeant, pile brush under the bridge as heavy as you can get it and start it burning." The captain stopped the sergeant as the trooper passed in the lead of the company. "Take this fancy box of matches to start the fire!" The sergeant leaned toward the captain, reached out and grasped the tinder box and with one hand snapped the mount's reins and galloped across the bridge.

The sounds of the horses crossing the wooden bridge gave the audible impression of an entire brigade. It sounded good to the captain as he remained in the saddle and observed the cavalrymen at work above and below the bridge on the opposite side of the river.

Chamberlain pulled on the reins and turned Blue Boy in the direction of the other companies. "Company A, dismount and pile shrub and tree limbs under this side of the bridge. Sergeant, we will put the fire to it when the men come from the other side of the river!"

Blue Boy began to prance from side to side, not moving forward or back; Seth pulled on the bridle straps to soothe his impatient mount. He recognized the cause of Blue Boy's unsteadiness. Smoke was beginning to rise from the center of the mill and flames were breaking through the roof. The towering column of black smoke was drifting over the river, obscuring the dam that controlled the water for the waterwheel.

A wisp of smoke appeared through the gaps in the wooden planks; pale gray smoke began to rise along the edges of the bridge. The captain watched as the troopers remounted and followed the sergeant back across the bridge. The fire was burning well, the entire side of the bridge appeared engulfed as smoke rolled upward.

Captain Chamberlain called out as the sergeant passed. "Sergeant! Put the fire to this side, too!"

"Yes, sir!" the sergeant responded as he galloped past. The trooper pulled his mount to a stop, tightened on the reins and turned his horse in the direction of Captain Chamberlain. "You want me to use this fancy match box again, sir?"

"Just like you did on the other side, Sergeant! It looks like it's burning very well!"

The sergeant dismounted, scrambled down the embankment, lowered his head below the planking and struck a match against the box. He placed the flame onto the dry leaves of a tree limb crumpled under the bridge. The leaves began to smoke, a flame began to rise upward and the trooper withdrew from under the bridge.

The cavalryman scampered up the embankment, placed the ornate tinder box in the captain's hand and mounted his horse. The cavalry company was mounted and in place as black, pine-scented smoke rolled skyward. Chamberlain drew his reins tight and turned Blue Boy in the direction of the burning mill. He spurred him to the head of the column and away from the burning bridge.

Captain Chamberlain pulled Blue Boy to a halt, stood upright in his stirrups, looked again at the bridge and estimated the length to be about four hundred feet. The thick black smoke rolled skyward as the fire intensified.

Chamberlain tipped his hat to the sergeant and the troopers. "Well done, boys! Well done! Let's get back to the rail crossing! The major might need a little help."

Captain Chamberlain quickly spurred his mount. Blue Boy began to gallop past the burning mill. The captain saw the flames leaping from the open windows of the lower levels. He knew the fire was out of control. The captain observed the gray smoke as it turned black, rising above the treetops.

He maintained a steady stance in the stirrups and looked toward the wooden structure in the yard of the burning mill. He observed Mr. Battle and several well-dressed men as they directed the efforts to extinguish the inferno within the stone walls. Captain Chamberlain urged his horse faster, the column of troopers filed behind. The lumbering Mountain Howitzer section lagged in the rear. Sergeant Rudisill urged his battery on, but wondered why his unit was along. There had been no need for artillery.

Dust began to cover the Hilliardston Road behind the moving column as the troopers and artillerymen headed east toward the rail line. Captain Chamberlain prodded Blue Boy with a constant snapping of the bridle reins.

Chamberlain reached the rail track, halted his mount and looked northward along the track. He saw Major Jacobs atop his horse, directing the ripping of the track from the trestle. The captain thought he looked like he could use some help; I've got some experience now!

Applying pressure to the stirrups, he rose above his saddle and confidently called out, "Sergeant Rudisill, position your piece toward that flouring mill we just passed! Company sergeants! Follow me to the trestle! The captain settled into the saddle, whipped the leather reins gently on Blue Boy's neck and galloped toward the rail trestle. The companies of troopers followed single file alongside the track behind Chamberlain.

The captain tightened the reins of the bridle as he approached Major Jacobs. "Major! Looks like your boys are taking great delight in undoing what the Rebs have done! Those rails splashing in the river look good to me!" Chamberlain urged his mount closer to the major, "My boys are still in the mood to put our name on something else; what can we do?"

Major Jacobs turned his horse in the direction of Captain Chamberlain. "We raided a rail shack down the track for iron bars to rip up the track! Can you suggest how we can burn this trestle?"

"Indeed I can, Major! Look to the west and see the results of how I can put the torch to the enemy!" He pointed to the western treetops and added, "How does that look to you, Major? Yes sir, how does that look to you?"

Heavy black columns of smoke billowed upward in two distinct pillars. High above the tree tops the two shafts of roiling smoke joined and formed a flowing pall. The prevailing southern wind pushed the cloud northward. The turpentine odor of burning pines began to faintly infiltrate the atmosphere.

"Well, Captain, I suggest you get to the task! Use your own discretion," ordered Jacobs, "and you best hurry! We can't be here all day!" The captain answered, "Yes, sir!" and turned his horse in the direction of his detachment of companies.

"Sergeant Wentz, dismount your company and go across the trestle to the other side of the river! That was such a good job at the other bridge, do the same thing to this trestle!" Chamberlain put out his hand to stop Sergeant Wentz as he ran past and added, "Reach in my saddle bag and get the same tinder box. You know what to do with it!"

The sergeant ran to the trestle, motioned for his company to follow him and cautiously walked across the trestle using the trestle cross ties to steady his feet. Slowly and deliberately the troopers followed the sergeant to the opposite side of the trestle. Major Jacobs and Captain Chamberlain remained in their saddles and observed the busy cavalrymen on the opposite bank.

Major Jacobs lifted himself from the saddle, held the reins of his horse in his hands and walked nearer the trestle. "Captain! What in heaven's name are those men doing on the other side? It looks like they're putting abatis in place!"

"Hold on a bit, Major, and you might see a sight you'll mightily approve of. Those boys have done this before! They know how to take down the other side!" The captain continued, "Just watch for the flames to start after they finish!"

Captain Chamberlain grasped the reins of Blue Boy in one hand, dismounted and joined Major Jacobs at the trestle. "It won't be but a few minutes and you'll see my men coming back to this side of the river!"

The two officers observed intently as the troopers ripped the tracks from the trestle ties, pushed them off the trestle into the river and moved forward to rip up more tracking. Sergeant Wentz directed his company with equal fervor as the assignment continued. Major Jacobs walked closer to the edge of the trestle and shouted, "Enough! That's enough, men! Back to this side!"

Sergeant Wentz heard the command and opened the ornate box. He struck a match stick against the rough side of the box and held the flame to a dry pine needle bough. "Back to the other side, boys! and watch your step on those ties! I don't want to lose a single one!" The sergeant retreating from under the trestle, added, "The water is over your head, too!"

Wentz looked to be certain the troopers below the trestle were safe. He ran to the edge of the trestle, stopped and looked along the track to the north. "Don't rush this crossing! Be careful you don't fall through the weakened rail ties! Let's go, boys!

The sergeant stepped onto the trestle, took several steps, checked his position and began to watch every step he took. His head down, Wentz guided his every step deliberately as he moved cautiously across the trestle. In a single file the troopers began the crossing behind the sergeant. Wentz's company began to merge with the troopers that had been ripping the rails from the ties. The merged troopers carefully stepped back to the south side of the river.

Jacobs, holding the reins of his horse, looked at Chamberlain and grinned. "The men look like busy ants going back to an ant hill, don't they? I don't think a train will be able to cross here for quite some time! Do you, Captain?"

"No, sir, I don't think so!" the captain answered as he looked across the river. He pointed his finger, and continued, "Look over there, Major, the fire is already beginning to break through from under the trestle! That ought to take care of that side!"

"Oh, I almost forgot," shouted Chamberlain as he stepped into the stirrup and mounted his steed, "I ordered Sergeant Rudisill to train his cannon on that four-story mill we passed earlier! Excuse me, Major, I'd better see to that order right away!"

Major Jacobs had seen the tall wooden structure also. It was a few hundred yards from the railroad; he did not know exactly what it was used for. "Very well, Captain, see to it! I will assemble my men and join you at the Hilliardston Junction."

Captain Chamberlain prodded his horse into a gallop along the track toward the junction. As he approached the junction, he reined his mount to a slower pace. The captain observed Rudisill positioning the gun crew and stopped to remain at a safe distance from the artillery piece. He could hear the sergeant directing the crew into readiness. "You boys get into position! You've been practicing for this; I don't want any mistakes!" shouted the sergeant.

The five artillerymen of the crew assembled around the howitzer. Sergeant Rudisill looked toward the wooden flouring mill as he stood behind the barrel. "I hope to God, there ain't nobody in that building!"

Captain Chamberlain overheard the comment of Sergeant Rudisill. "Sergeant, hold your fire until I can find out for sure that the mill is empty!" The captain spurred Blue Boy, galloped quickly to the mill and pulled the mount close to an open window. He looked through the window and saw what he estimated was hundreds of barrels of flour and hardtack. The captain yelled through the open window, "Anybody in here? Get out! Get out, now!"

The captain turned his horse from the building, moved to the rear of the structure. He observed two small buildings at the edge of the wooded area surrounding the flouring mill. He urged his mount in the direction of the structures and guided his mount to each cautiously. By God, he said to himself as he looked through the window, this is a munitions storage!

Chamberlain pulled quickly on the bridle reins, turned Blue Boy in the direction of the artillery piece and galloped back to the howitzer crew. "Sergeant Rudisill! Throw some canisters into all those buildings! Nobody is over there! You don't have to be too careful; those buildings are not occupied. I reckon everybody has run off!"

"Sergeant!" one of the gun crew yelled out, "See if you can put a shell through the top window! You claim to be the best gunner around!" Another of the crew added loudly, "Yeah, ain't nobody shooting back at you now!"

Rudisill backed off from the howitzer and looked at each of the five crew members, "Get in your positions! Loader, get the canister shot from off the back of the pack animal!" The sergeant stood behind the cannon and looked toward the building. He stooped, looked along the barrel of the howitzer trained on the building and said confidently, "I think about thirty degrees ought to do it." He reached to turn the elevation screw, "Yeah, thirty degrees will be about right."

"Five-seconds fuse!" the sergeant called out. "Ram the load!" the gunner ordered. He hesitated, then ordered, "Insert the primer!" Sergeant Rudisill paused again and looked toward the towering unpainted wood building. "Fire!" Another artilleryman pulled the lanyard; a spark from the primer ignited the black powder bag attached to the canister. The carriage recoiled as the ground shook beneath their feet; the deafening blast stunned the gun crew.

Sergeant Rudisill moved quickly to the side of the howitzer and watched the projectile penetrate the wall of the wooden building. Simultaneously the fuse ignited the black powder and the canister exploded. A brilliant orange glow from inside the structure illuminated the windows as the report echoed back to the gun crew.

The gun crew rapidly repositioned the howitzer, reassembled in the proper military positions and readied the cannon. Sergeant Rudisill approached the rear of the howitzer, directed the trail to be moved to the left and reached to turn the elevation screw. "Not enough elevation! Ten degrees more for the next one!" instructed the sergeant.

"Can't you put one through the window, Sergeant?" a voice rang out, "What ails you, Sergeant?" Rudisill glanced quickly at the gun crew and rebutted, "Yeah, yeah! Wait for the next one!"

"Positions!" yelled Rudisill, "Man your positions! Loader! Insert five-seconds fuse! Ram 'er to the breech!" He continued, "Insert the primer! Stand clear! Fire!" Sparks from the primer ignited the black powder of the load and again the ground vibrated as the thunderous blast caused the cannoneers to flinch.

Captain Chamberlain watched as the gun crew quickly withdrew from the howitzer to watch the shell as it burst through the third story window of the towering structure. Again a brilliant orange glow filled the interior of the building, illuminating the windows and spattering the upper story with fiery sparks. The report echoed back and the gun crew broke into a cheer. "Three cheers for old Rudisill!" one of the crew yelled out, "Yeah, three cheers for the old Sergeant!"

Chamberlain tightened the reins to calm Blue Boy as his horse shied from the activity of the gun crew. "Easy! Easy, old boy, easy." The captain called out to Sergeant Rudisill, "Very good, Sergeant! I can see some flames beginning to start on that floor! I think that should take care of that old wooden building!"

"Sergeant, train your cannon on that building to the right of the tall one! I saw munitions in that one! We need to take care of that one, too!" the captain ordered. "Yes, sir," responded Rudisill as he turned to the gun crew, "You heard the captain! Get back to your positions!"

Sergeant Rudisill looked toward the small building to the right of the smoking structure. Moving to the rear of the howitzer, he leaned forward over the right wheel of the carriage. "That looks pretty level to me. Ninety degrees ought to do it!"

"Positions! Man your positions!" Rudisill ordered. The sergeant looked around at the gun crew and continued, "Loader, use a five-seconds fuse, quick now!" With quick movements he turned to the artilleryman behind him, "Move the trail twelve inches to the left!"

Sergeant Rudisill leaned over the breech of the cannon, peered along the top of the brass barrel and viewed the small building next to the smoking wooden structure, "Eighty degrees might be more like it!" The gunner reached and turned the elevation screw, "Yeah, eighty degrees will do just fine!"

Rudisill visually checked the positions of the crew, stood back from the howitzer and shouted, "Ram the canister to the breech! Insert the primer! Stand clear!" The sergeant looked over the howitzer barrel again, stood back and commanded, "Fire!"

A bright orange flash exited the muzzle of the tube, a deafening blast jolted the carriage wheels upward as the artillery piece recoiled toward the sergeant. A puff of black smoke exited from the vent of the breech. The cannon crew watched as the projectile exploded through the walls of the munitions storage. A loud report indicated a thorough explosion; the small wooden structure shuddered as an orange and red flash scattered flaming sparks. A moment of stillness prevailed as the artillerymen watched. Suddenly the structure exploded, hurling timbers and splintered wooden boards in all directions; an orb of roiling fire rose above the disintegrated structure, followed by a column of black powder smoke. The cavalrymen watched the thick cloud form over the wreckage and waited for a follow-up explosion. The column of black smoke rolled skyward; no explosions followed.

Sergeant Rudisill smiled and looked at Captain Chamberlain. "Looks like we got all the black powder in that shack! Maybe there ain't no more!"

Chamberlain, astride Blue Boy, lifted his hat to the gun crew, "Well done! Well done!" He put his hat back on and continued, "Sergeant, keep the howitzer limbered and be ready to move out when Major Jacobs joins us!"

The captain turned his horse in the direction of the burning trestle and moved to meet the major. Major Jacobs was in the lead of the file as the gap closed between the major and the captain.

Major Jacobs approached Captain Chamberlain, saluted and called out, "Very good! Very good, Captain!" The major pulled his horse to a halt, turned in his saddle and continued, "and I see the cotton mill is burning! That flouring mill is burning! and by God, that munitions shack is gone! Well done! Captain!"

Captain Chamberlain felt the flush of success, the pride of accomplishment with the compliment from Major Jacobs. He pulled the bridle straps of his horse and drew to the side of the major. As the two officers passed the artillerymen, the captain called, "Sergeant, file in behind the column!" and turning in the saddle continued, "We're finished here! Very well done, Sergeant!"

Major Jacobs and Captain Chamberlain held the reins loosely as their mounts moved south along the tracks toward the Tarborough Road. The heat from the midday sun radiated from the railroad bed. Chamberlain removed his hat, wiped his brow with his sleeve and with a sigh, remarked, "This heat is sure no better here than on the Neuse River! This Carolina weather is awful, here or in New Berne!"

Jacobs and Chamberlain gently urged their mounts along the tracks toward the Tarborough Road; the cavalrymen and artillerymen followed in a single file. Major Jacobs scanned the rail tracks in their front and stated, "Captain, it appears the smoke from the railyards is slacking off somewhat. It may be it has burned itself out. I hope so! We will turn to the east at the next road crossing and move to join General Potter in Tarborough."

Captain Chamberlain stood erect in the stirrups, lifted himself high above his saddle, turned toward the north and proudly commented, "Major! It looks like we're leaving a smoking and useless position here for the Southern boys." Major Jacobs stiffened his legs in his stirrups, raised himself from his saddle and concurred, "By God, Old Potter ought to be satisfied with this! Yep, he ought to be happy!"

Jacobs settled in his saddle, looked to Captain Chamberlain and smiled broadly, "We will turn and ride east just ahead." The two officers snapped the reins of their horses, sat erect in their saddles and in military formation turned onto the Tarborough Road.

# CHAPTER TWELVE

The fog of the early morning began to lift as the sun ascended above the pine treetops. The road to Tarborough was dry; the dust from the moving column began to cover the troopers before settling on the low-growing brush beside the road. The sounds of the crows circling above broke the morning silence. A wisp of high clouds failed to dim the brightness of the morning sun.

General Potter removed his hat and wiped his brow with his sleeve. "Good Lord, another hot and miserable day! It does look like by now, I would be used to these southern summers. I was born in Carolina! I ought to like it well enough."

Major Floyd Clarkson was in the lead with Company B of the Third New York Cavalry and Company L of the First North Carolina Union Volunteers. The artillerymen with the Mountain Howitzer section filled the gap between the lead companies and General Potter and Major George Cole.

Potter stiffened his legs, steadied his feet in the stirrups, raised himself from the saddle and looked behind at the trailing column. "Major Cole! Keep the column moving in double file," and the general added as he settled back into the saddle, "Keep the column closed up! I'll rejoin you after I have given Major Clarkson his orders."

"Yes, sir!" Cole responded. He adjusted himself in his saddle, snapped the horse's reins and moved to the middle of the road as the general spurred his horse out to the side of the road. Potter pulled his horse to a stop, watched from the side of the road as the column passed. The general quickly squeezed his legs into his mount's sides, leaned forward and galloped to the lead company, and reined his horse in beside Major Clarkson.

Potter slowed the gait of his mount, maintained his position beside Major Clarkson, and lifted his hat. "Major, Tarborough is a pretty little town. But we have our objectives here and we must not let our hearts overrule our judgment. I feel certain our presence is known by this time to all military commanders in the area."

Clarkson looked at the general and agreed, "Yes sir, I expect when we left Greenville yesterday, the word went out that we were in the area. By now I suspect Colonel Martin at Fort Branch knows exactly where we are."

General Potter and Major Clarkson rode steadily together as the general broke the silence with a question, "And if you were Colonel Martin, what would you do?" The general continued, "You do know that Martin is probably at Fort Branch at Hamilton on the Roanoke River with some companies of the Seventeenth North Carolina Regiment."

"Yes, sir, it's a well known fact there is a Colonel Martin at Fort Branch, and a General Martin at Kinston," stated Clarkson. He continued, "And if I were in Colonel Martin's place, I'd put some men on the road to Tarborough and I'd have them on the road now!"

"That's precisely what I would do, too! And I'm going to plan on Martin doing just that," said Potter as he settled into the saddle.

"Major," the general directed, "take these two companies and the howitzer section and post pickets on the road east of the bridge over the river. Should the enemy come, it would have to be from that direction," and the general added, "and I'm counting on that to happen!"

The general pulled his horse to the side of the road and called out, "See to the pickets, Major!" Potter waited as the column moved past, called loudly, "On the gallop, Major! On the gallop!"

Clarkson, raised himself above the saddle, turned to the

companies behind and with a forward motion of his hand called, "On to Tarborough! On to Tarborough, men!" The major pressed his horse into a fast gallop and took the lead as the companies of cavalrymen filed in behind, followed by the limbered howitzer and artillerymen.

General Potter, halting at the side of the road, waited as Major Cole approached in the lead of the remaining cavalrymen. The general urged his horse beside the major as the officer neared him. General Potter steadied his horse and rode silently beside Major Cole. The general turned and said confidently to the major, "Major! I really do think we might have some time to destroy our objective before we meet with any resistance. Things appear mighty quiet and peaceful so far." The general continued, "What do you really expect, Major?"

"General, since you have asked, I will say what I really expect," answered Major Cole, "and I will be perfectly honest about it. Things have gone far too easy for us! I'm afraid we might have a fight on our hands before this day's over." Cole snapped the reins of his horse and looked at the wooded terrain from side to side. "To be sure, General, they're not going to let us get away without a fight!"

"You may well be right, Major," Potter nodded in agreement and added, "This has been too easy. We had best keep our men close by and not take any chances of being surprised from another direction other than from the east. I have always found it better to remain close rather than scattered."

The major responded, "Yes, sir, we best stay together and get this work done quick and get away from here. I have a mighty uneasy feeling about this operation."

"Major," the general ordered, "pick up the pace! Let's move on into Tarborough! Clarkson ought to be in position by now! Move out, Major! Move out!" Potter whipped the reins on the neck of his horse, leaned forward, steadied himself in the stirrups and moved to the head of the column. His horse's galloping movements lifted him up and down in the saddle in rapid succession as General Potter advanced to the lead.

Major Cole turned quickly, looked at the trailing column, stood erect in the stirrups and looked at Potter riding off. "Column, hoah! On the gallop! On the gallop!" The major raised his arm, motioned and shouted, "Let's move out!" Cole snapped the reins quickly, settled in the saddle and galloped to the side of General Potter. The two officers, their horses in galloping sequence, moved ahead of the column into Tarborough. The column of six companies moved behind the officers into the town. War had come to this pretty little town on the Tar.

The dusty road from Old Sparta connected with a narrow street lined with small neat houses partially obscured by oak trees. The galloping column moved in a trail of dust behind Potter and Cole. Tarborough was quiet; only occasional venturesome residents opened their doors and stood watching on the shaded porches. The cavalrymen continued behind General Potter and Major Cole.

General Potter tightened the reins of his horse, slowed to a normal gait and pointed to the rail track ahead. "We'll cross the track and turn east and head for the river bridge at the next road. That ought to be the main road east and west through town." Cole noticed the men and women running inside the buildings as he approached the main road through Tarborough.

General Potter urged his horse ahead of Cole, approached the east/west road, halted in the middle of the road and looked east. "Well, Cole, there it is! Just look at that suspension structure. That's the bridge we came to rip up!" Potter motioned to Cole to follow him and continued, "And anything else of any value to the southern armies!" Major Cole prodded his horse behind the general. The two cavalry officers neared the west side of the bridge and Cole looked downstream. "Good God, General! There are two steamers docked at a wharf!" The major, with a look of amazement continued, "I didn't know this river was navigable this far inland!" Cole continued to scan the banks of the river above and below the bridge. "My God, General! they're outfitting an iron-clad! The darn thing is still on the stocks!" Cole continued.

General Potter tightened the reins with his two hands, leaned over the saddle pommel and looked over the river bluffs. "By God! I told you these southern boys knew how to use the waterways. We've got work to do!" The general ordered excitedly, "Major, dispatch two companies to burn the steamers!"

Potter stiffened his feet in the stirrups, raised himself and stared directly at Cole. "Major! Instruct your men when the boats are on fire to loose them from the wharf! The current will take the steamers downstream—burning!"

General Potter pulled on the reins, backed his horse from the bridge and turned in the direction of the town. The cavalry troops were entering the main road and headed for the river bridge. The general called to Cole, "Major! See to the destruction of the steamers and the ironclad! I'll dispatch Lieutenant Henderson to the rail depot with two companies!" Potter looked westward along the road through Tarborough and added, "I'll be here on the bluff with my aide! I can see Clarkson from my position." Potter motioned to his aide, "Lieutenant Smithson! Come with me!" The general and his aide urged their horses into the trees above the river. General Potter dismounted, reached into his saddle bag, fumbled and found a cigar. "Lieutenant! I can enjoy a good smoke while the boys do a little mischief." The general pulled a match from his vest pocket, leaned against a pine tree and standing on one foot raised his boot to his knee. "Lieutenant," the general said as he struck the match against the brass boot spur, "Issue Lieutenant Henderson orders to take two companies and follow the rail track west and burn the depot!" Potter raised the flaming match to his cigar; with several quick puffs the cigar smoke billowed above his head.

Potter walked to the edge of the tree-lined bluffs of the

river, looked down and acknowledged, "It's most unusual for banks to be this high above eastern Carolina rivers." The general continued to scan the bluff, "It makes it easier for boats to pass under the bridges when the banks are high." General Potter quickly turned to his aide and said in an irritated manner, "Didn't I just tell you what to do! Be about the job, Lieutenant!" The aide responded, "Yes, sir!" and reached for the reins of his horse. The lieutenant grabbed the saddle pommel and quickly pulled himself into the saddle, whipped the reins smartly and galloped off to locate Lieutenant Henderson.

General Potter was alone as he observed the activity of the cavalrymen. He had a good view of the river below and of Major Clarkson's pickets across the bridge on the Hamilton Road. The general could manage the entire operation from his position on the river's bluff.

Major Cole nudged his horse to a wooded area above the wharf, reined his horse around, stood erect in the stirrups and shouted, "Over here with me! All troopers over here!" Cole looked down at the two steamers docked at the wharf and continued, "Secure your horses and dismount!" Major Cole shook his foot from the stirrup and grasping the saddle pommel swung his leg over the back of his horse and onto the ground. He called out as he removed his foot from the stirrup and secured his horse to a small gum tree, "Companies F and H, follow me!" The major ran to the top of the bluffs, looked down at the wharf and shouted, "Let's go, men! Down the bank to the steamers!" Cole started down the embankment, felt himself off balance and leaned backwards as his feet dug into the dry soil. He quickly put his arms behind him to brace himself as he began to slide down the river bank. Cole looked to his right and left and saw the troopers, all in the same sliding positions, attempting to slow their descent to the water's edge.

Lieutenant Henderson watched as Major Cole and the two companies of cavalrymen made their way down the embankment and onto the wharf. The lieutenant turned to a company sergeant, grinned and said, "Looks like a landslide! This dust may never settle."

Major Cole took off his hat and began to use it to beat the dirt from his uniform and shouted, "With me, men! Over here with me!" The major walked to the edge of the wharf, viewed the two steamers and walked back to the assembled cavalrymen. "Steamers have boilers! Boilers have fire. The stacks are still smoking! Ah, yes, we're in good shape!" Major Cole continued, "Sergeant! Company F! Find the boiler in the larger vessel and empty the fire box on the lower deck!" and in rapid order, continued, "Sergeant, Company H, go below on the small steamer, find the boiler and shovel the ashes on the deck below!"

The two sergeants, followed by their companies, ran toward their objective.. Both steamers began to rock against the wharf as the troops jumped from the dock onto the top decks. They quickly disappeared from the top decks; the two vessels continued to bump against the wharf. Major Cole backed away from the rocking steamers and looked up the cliff to the bluff and waved to Lieutenant Henderson.

Suddenly a hatch burst open and two men rushed onto the top deck from below. One of the men yelled, "These are private steamers! You ain't got no right here! This is personal property!"

The two men rushed to Major Cole and continued, "We ain't soldiers!"

The major looked directly at the two oily-clothed men and laughed. "Then you'd better make your way up the bank and get back to town!" The men looked simultaneously at the cavalrymen atop the bank and without another comment scrambled up the embankment.

Major Cole watched the open hatch as one by one the troopers began to emerge from below. Gray smoke began to rise from the open hatch door. The major called, "Sergeant! Was there enough ashes to do any good?" The company sergeant excitedly responded, "Yes, sir! I mean it was enough! Just watch her for a spell!" Cole ran to the smaller vessel, jumped from the wharf onto the deck, ran to the open hatch, leaned inside and shouted, "Hurry it up! Get up here on deck!" He ran to the edge of the deck and jumped back onto the wharf. "Sergeant! When all men are accounted for, let me know!"

Cole observed the open hatch as the men stepped onto the deck. A wisp of gray smoke floated above the hatch opening as the last trooper exited the hatch. "Sergeant! Is that the last of the men?" The sergeant looked at the two assembled companies and answered, "Yes, sir! All accounted for!"

"Sergeants! Both of you sergeants! Listen up!" shouted Major Cole. The major continued with a loud voice, "Get back aboard the steamers and cut the mooring lines! Use your sabers!" Cole ran to the edge of the wharf, pushed the troopers aside and extended his orders, "Throw the lines back onto the dock! We can make good use of the strong lines!"

Major Cole watched impatiently as the sergeants drew their sabers on the vessels' decks and proceeded to sever the lines. "That's it! That's right!" the major shouted and without hesitating he shouted again, "Get back on the dock! Quick! Back on the dock!" The two sergeants, sabers in hand, ran to the side of the steamers and jumped back onto the dock. The current slowly moved the vessels from the wharf. The cut lines still attached to the dock cleats fell from the steamers and floated as the smoking vessels moved farther from the river bank into the middle of the river.

"Very good, sergeants! Sheath your sabers," ordered the major as he moved to the edge of the dock to observe with the troopers the drifting vessels. Cole removed his hat, shaded his eyes with his hand and surveyed the scene. "Very good! It looks like the steamers will be burning well very shortly, and with nobody on board to put out the blaze. Yes, very good!

"Sergeant! Both of you company sergeants! See that the lines are pulled from the water," ordered the major, and continued the directive, "and loose the lines from the dock cleats! I've got a good use for those strong lines!" The major motioned toward two corporals, "You two corporals each take a line and pull it along the water's edge to that boat on the stocks." Major Cole continued, "That's one iron clad that won't make it downstream to Washington!" Cole motioned to the two sergeants and indicated to them to follow him and called out, "Bring all men of your companies with me!"

Major Cole began to walk quickly toward the unfinished ironclad vessel. He observed the huge gap in the side of the high bank, well clear of the water's edge. The wooden stocks supporting the hull were secure on level ground in the excavated area. The major turned to the troopers and shouted, "Move on up closer! Move up closer to the stocks!" The major looked at the sweaty cavalrymen and quickly asked, "Who will volunteer to shinny halfway up one of those timbers and tie one of the lines to it? Do I have any offers?" The major hesitated and again asked, "Well, any volunteers?"

"I'll take one up the timber," answered one of the troopers as he stepped from the assembled cavalrymen. The major looked at the small bearded trooper and smiled, "Get the end of one line and secure it halfway the front supporting timber stock!" Another bearded trooper stepped from the grouped cavalrymen and took the other line and declared, "I'll handle the other one and you fellows better not pull while I'm off the ground!" The two soldiers began to shinny up the support timbers with the lines. With simultaneous precision the two troopers placed the lines around the timber stock twice and secured the line with a knot. Major Cole looked up, saw the two troopers descending and gave a congratulatory shout, "Bravo! Bravo!"

"Company F! All of Company F! Take hold of this line," the major ordered as the two troopers returned from tying the lines.

He continued, "Company H! Take the other line and stretch it as far as it will extend!" Major Cole moved quickly from the crowded troopers and directed the two companies with his arms, "Sergeant! Separate the companies! I don't want all the men together in one place!" The Major, energized by the activity, continued frantically, "Order the men to tighten up on the line! Not too fast!"

Major Cole watched as one company of troopers tightened the line and quickly turned to watch as the other company pulled their line taut. The Major saw the troopers were well separated and he shouted, "Now, pull! Pull!" Cole saw the men lean as the line strained and tightened, and called again, "Just one more pull! Just one more pull!" The line tightened again, a loud crack radiated from the timbers and the two timber stocks fell from their positions. The unfinished ironclad crashed into the shallow water as the remaining timber stocks crumbled toward the river. The impact of the vessel as it fell on its side sent monstrous waves radiating to the opposite side of the Tar River. "Ahhhh!" the troopers sighed as they let the lines fall from their hands.

Major Cole looked up the river bank, saw Henderson observing the operation, removed his hat and shouted, "We did it! We got it!" Henderson removed his hat and acknowledged the success with a low dip of his hat.

Cole looked again at the crumbled ironclad, put on his hat and shouted, "Back up the bank! Well done! Back up the bank!" The Major ran to the incline and started up the embankment. His feet slipped in the dry soil as he leaned forward to steady himself with his hands. He looked up and continued climbing.

Lieutenant Henderson, standing on the bluffs, looked down on the scrambling troopers as General Potter's aide approached. Lieutenant Smithson drew his horse to a stop, dismounted and called out, "Henderson! General Potter has directed you to take two companies west on the tracks and destroy the depot and any railcars you might find on the tracks! Take any two companies you want!" Henderson responded, "Very well! Thank you, Lieutenant."

Henderson looked to the clearing at the south side of the wooded area and noticed the terminal point of the rail line. He previously observed the pine timbers in the ground at the end of the tracks to prevent the cars from going off the end of the tracks. The lieutenant called, "Company K!" and motioned to the sergeant, "Sergeant, remove as many of these timbers as you can! I am taking Companies B and C with me to the rail depot!" Henderson pointed to the timbers at the track's end and continued, "You might not be able to get them all, but do the best you can!"

The lieutenant mounted his horse, secured himself in the saddle and called, "Company B! Company C! Mount up!" Henderson reined his horse to the rail tracks, looked west along the straight tracks, raised himself to his full height and with a long overhead motion with his arm, ordered, "Follow me! After me! West on the tracks!" Henderson spurred his horse to a fast gallop, snapped the reins on the horse's neck, leaned forward and bounced in the saddle as he rode toward the depot. The two companies followed in a single file. The cavalrymen's sabers rattled with the jolting movements of the horses.

Henderson looked up as he pulled the reins tight, saw three rail cars together at the depot and spotted yard workers as they ran from the depot. The lieutenant reined his horse to a halt, waited for the troopers to arrive, stood erect in the stirrups and pointed to the depot and ordered, "Company B! Check the depot contents—then burn it!"

"Company C!" the lieutenant shouted as he dismounted, "check those three freight cars! Be sure the couplings are secure! Sergeant!" the lieutenant called out, "locate some rope! I need two long ropes! Report back to me if you find it." The sergeant dismounted and ran to the depot, "Yes, sir!"

The cavalrymen ran up the depot steps, approached the

telegrapher's desk and rifled the drawers to locate the matches. As the drawers were emptied and thrown to the floor one of the troopers called out, "Here's the matches! One of you find a lamp with oil!" The company sergeant called out, "I've got one! I've got it!" The sergeant quickly removed the glass chimney, turned the blackened wick high and held it up to the trooper with the match box. The sweaty trooper struck the match against the rough part of the box and placed the flame onto the exposed wick. The company sergeant, his hand shaking, waited for the flame to envelop the wick, then shouted, "Stand back! Stand clear!" and with a slow movement he tossed the burning lamp onto the depot floor.

Flames began to soar from the spreading coal oil on the depot floor. The sergeant ran for the door and yelled, "Let's get out of here!" One of the cavalrymen stopped, picked up the desk chair and tossed it through the glass window. "Let's give 'er a little air!"

Lieutenant Henderson mounted his horse, sat erect in the saddle and calmed his horse. He looked at the cavalrymen descending the depot steps, leaned forward and called loudly, "Sergeant! Sergeant Mummer! Did you find any line?" Mummer approached the lieutenant and responded, "No, sir, there weren't none in the depot," and continuing to move toward the rail cars, he said, "Let me check these freight cars; sometimes there's some tie-downs left around."

The sergeant ran to the open door of one of the rail cars, stretched himself enough to view the interior of the freight car. He saw a pile of twisted hemp rope at the end of the car and turned to the lieutenant and shouted, "Yeah! Here is some line, Lieutenant." He reached and gripped the side of the door and lifted himself into the car. The sergeant stood in the open door and shouted, "Looks like right much, too!" He ran to the rear of the car and pulled the twisted pile of hemp rope to the open door.

Sergeant Mummer looked in the direction of Henderson and

motioned for his attention. "Lieutenant! Here it is. You will have to straighten it!" The sergeant scrambled around to locate one end of the line, found it, pulled it free of the pile and handed the end to the lieutenant. Henderson goaded his horse to the open freight car door. He grabbed the line, spurred his horse and rode away from the car pulling the line and the twisted pile from the open door. The sergeant jumped from the open door, hastily began an attempt to untangle the line as the lieutenant rode slowly away, dragging the loose line.

"Lieutenant!" shouted the sergeant, "don't move too quick! I can't untangle this mess that fast!" Henderson drew his horse to a halt, turned and looked as Mummer untangled the line. "Let me know, Sergeant, when you're ready!" Sergeant Mummer looked up and replied, "Yes, sir! I think if you move slow now, it will come clear!" Henderson pulled his horse in the direction of the first rail car and called out to Mummer, "Sergeant! Secure your end to the coupling of that first freight car!" Henderson prodded his mount eastward along the side of the tracks and continued to bark orders, "And Sergeant, put your men behind the cars and push them when I start to pull!" Sergeant Mummer responded to the lieutenant in exasperation, "No disrespect, sir! But are you crazy?"

Lieutenant Henderson rode back to the rear of the train of cars and assured the sergeant, "It's downhill from here to the river. If we get it moving, it won't take much pulling to get a good run going! Get your men behind these cars now and let's get this stock rolling downhill!" Sergeant Mummer looked up at the lieutenant and shook his head saying, "When the cars are moving good, we'll get back on our horses and let you have this thing!"

Henderson, with one hand holding the line and the other hand holding the reins, nodded to Mummer, "That's right, Sergeant! That's exactly right!" The lieutenant urged his horse to the front of the train of cars, turned and looked at the sergeant, "Get your men in position!" Sergeant Mummer raised his hand and called loudly, "Get over here, boys! The lieutenant needs your shoulders to the wheels!"

Lieutenant Henderson wrapped the hemp rope around the saddle pommel, spurred his horse deeply and moved toward the river. The hemp rope tightened, his horse hesitated and the lieutenant turned and shouted, "Put your shoulders to it, now!" The company of troopers with their arms, shoulders and hands pressed against the last car. They all simultaneously groaned as they pushed on the train of cars. Henderson snapped the reins with one hand, held the twisted rope on the saddle pommel and squeezed tightly with his feet into the horse's side. The cars began to vibrate, then a forward movement was felt as the troopers eased off from the rear of the cars. Henderson felt the line tighten and then loosen as the cars began to move. The lieutenant spurred his horse again; the line became taut and the movement became faster. The lieutenant prodded his horse again and increased the animal's gait as the load began to ease on the downhill grade.

Henderson urged his horse faster along the side of the tracks. The line became taut and Henderson prodded his mount even more. The hemp line suddenly relaxed, the lieutenant turned and saw the cars moving freely downhill. Henderson quickly unwrapped the line from the saddle pommel and with a quick movement tossed the line free of the saddle pommel and the horse. Lieutenant Henderson reined his horse to a slower pace, pulled away from the tracks and watched the train of cars as they passed.

Henderson looked toward the river, saw the troops as they scurried away from the tracks and raised his hat in triumph. He turned toward the approaching cavalrymen from the depot and with his hat still raised, shouted, "Just right! Just right!"

General Potter watched as the troopers scattered from the wooded area back toward the river bridge. He looked in amazement at his aide and asked, "What in heaven's name is going on? Surely we're not being attacked from that direction!"

Lieutenant Smithson quickly looked toward the scattering troopers and caught a glimpse of the moving train of cars. "Good Lord, General! It's some freight cars running wild!"

The general, moved closer to the bridge for a better view. He focused on the freight cars as the first car burst through the retaining timbers and tumbled down the embankment into the river. Potter continued to watch in awe as the second car left the tracks and impacted into the top of the bluff. The general's gaze remained fixed as the third car rammed into the second one and twisted off the tracks. General Potter ran to the edge of the woods, looked across the main road and  exclaimed gleefully, "By Jove, the lieutenant has done the job! By Jove! he did it right!"

Lieutenant Henderson reined his horse around and faced west. He saw a black column of towering smoke billowing skyward. Very good, he thought, that must be the depot. Henderson tightened the reins and turned his horse in the direction of the river. As he began riding to the river bridge, he could hear the cheering. That sounded good to him. Now he was more than the brigade chef.

General Potter called, "Lieutenant Smithson!" He turned in the direction of the lieutenant, "Bring my horse!" Smithson mounted his horse, prodded the animal to the tree where the general's horse was tied. He leaned to retrieve the leather reins of Potter's horse. With one hand gripping the reins of the general's mount and one hand on his reins, the lieutenant urged his horse onto the road where Potter was waiting. Potter turned as Smithson approached, reached for his horse's reins and quickly slipped his boot into the stirrup. With one foot on the ground and one foot in the stirrup the general grasped the saddle pommel and with a grunt pulled himself into the saddle.

The general adjusted himself in the saddle, reached into the saddlebag for his field glasses and put the glasses to his eyes. "Yes, sir! That is a pretty sight! Yes, sir! that is a sight to behold." Potter scanned the river again and continued, "The steamboats are burning smartly and the ironclad is lying useless at the water's edge. Excellent!"

Lieutenant Smithson observed the steamers, black smoke rising from the wheelhouses as they moved slowly with the current and out of control. The aide looked at the general, reined his horse closer to General Potter and complimented General Potter. "A well-executed plan, General! Well executed!" Potter looked at his aide, smiled broadly and responded, "Thank you, Lieutenant."

General Potter gently touched his horse's sides with his heels and rode back to the bluffs overlooking the river. Lieutenant Smithson reined his horse behind the general and joined Potter as the general raised his field glasses to his eyes. Potter began to scan the horizon to the east, noticed Clarkson's position and fixed his sight on the tree tops in the distance. "I was afraid of this! There is a cloud of dust a few miles to the east!" the general declared and without lowering his glasses he continued, "Lieutenant! Alert Clarkson of the situation!" Smithson reined his horse from the wooded terrain and galloped across the bridge.

# CHAPTER THIRTEEN

Jonathan Lamb had been referred to as Colonel Lamb since his promotion to lieutenant colonel earlier in the spring. He had served in the Seventeenth North Carolina Regiment from the date of his enlistment in Wilson County. Colonel Lamb was ordered by Colonel Martin to command a detachment to intercept the Federal force known to be headed for Tarborough. Major J. T. Kennedy with two companies of the Seventh Cavalry from Greenville, arrived earlier and alerted the ailing Colonel Martin of the Federal presence. Colonel Lamb, Major Kennedy and Captain J. T. Edgerton assembled the cavalry companies and wagoners for the infantrymen. They quickly began the advance toward Tarborough.

Colonel Lamb realized he had pushed his horse fast and hard for most of the early morning. He reined his mount to a slow gait, and motioned for Major Kennedy and Captain Edgerton to join him. Lamb, steadying his horse in the middle of the road, called out, "Join me off to the side of the road!" The three officers slowly urged their horses to the side of the road. The tall pine trees cast a section of shade in the morning sun. Colonel Lamb reined into the shady space and looked at Kennedy and Edgerton."I don't know what to expect. Before we rush into a situation we don't know about, I want Captain Edgerton to move ahead of us with a company of mounted scouts." The colonel restrained his horse and continued, "I will determine the time and place when we will make our presence known," Lamb removed his hat, leaned on the saddle pommel and added, "but wait for me to give the final order!"

Lamb turned his horse around and looked at the approaching wagons with the infantrymen. "I suppose the wagon ride may be better than walking; it doesn't look to be such a good thing from here." The colonel turned his horse around in the direction of Tarborough. Placing his hat onto his head, he reminded the officers, "We'll wait here for the detachment to catch up with us. Our animals need a spell of rest."

The cavalry companies came into view as they rounded a bend in the road; wagons with the infantrymen lumbered behind the mounted troops.

Colonel Lamb raised his arm and motioned the column forward. "Let's move on, men! It's not much farther to our destination. Forward, hoaa!" The rattle of the harnesses and the moans of the infantrymen with each bump in the road gave notice to the creatures of nature of the approach of danger. All the wildlife sought security in the density of the forest. The Confederate column moved closer to Tarborough.

Colonel Lamb leaned forward, spurred his horse, moved ahead of Kennedy and Edgerton and reined his horse to a stop in front of an unpainted wooden schoolhouse. The colonel scanned the terrain and observed a pine thicket behind the building. Lamb turned his mount in the direction of the approaching column and motioned to the officers to join him. The colonel rose above his saddle and shouted, "Bring the column behind the school house! Lead them on into the piney woods!" Lamb lowered himself into the saddle, pulled the reins and prodded his horse into the pine trees behind the schoolhouse.

Colonel Lamb dismounted, stood and watched the column of cavalry and two wagons of infantrymen file into the security of the pine trees. The colonel held the reins of his horse, walked to Kennedy and Edgerton and directed, "Captain Edgerton, take five men and approach the Tar River bridge; find out the force in our front and report back to me, here." Edgerton responded, "Yes, sir," and urged his horse in the direction of the mounted cavalrymen. The captain looked at the squadron of cavalrymen and stated, "I need five men! The first five to present themselves in front of me will do just fine!"

The horses began to stir and spread into the pine thicket as five mounted troopers reined their horses in front of Captain Edgerton. The captain looked at each cavalryman and declared, "We must drive the invading marauders from our state! We must do our duty!" The captain continued, "And we can start here and now! Let's see what we have in our front!"

The captain prodded his horse onto the road, turned and motioned with his hand for the cavalrymen to follow him. All five mounted troopers snapped the lines of their mounts and filed behind Captain Edgerton. The captain turned in his saddle and motioned for the cavalrymen to move ahead. Edgerton reminded each trooper as he passed, "Don't use your weapons! This is only reconnaissance!"

Captain Edgerton flipped the leather reins on his horse's neck, moved ahead of the cavalrymen again, held his arm upright, turned in the saddle and watched the troopers halt. The captain pointed toward the river bridge, warning the troopers with hand gestures of the pickets ahead. Edgerton's mounted troopers pulled on the reins to still their horses. Captain Edgerton saw everything he needed to see and pulled tightly on one rein to turn his mount around. Before his turn was completed a musket shot broke the silence. The Federal pickets converged in the middle of the road, began to yell and formed into a firing line. Edgerton yelled at the trooper, "Blast you! You were to hold your fire!" Edgerton completed his turn to the rear and called loudly, "Get back to the schoolhouse!"

The captain spurred his horse and raced back to report to Colonel Lamb; his five mounted scouts followed in the dust. Captain Edgerton turned his horse in front of the schoolhouse and proceeded to the rear. He saw the troops dismounted, their horses tied to the trees and the wagons well out of sight. Edgerton pulled the reins tight, halted his horse and with a sudden lurch leaped from the saddle. "Colonel Lamb!" the captain shouted, "we've been spotted! There's a picket line and a cannon blocking the bridge!"

Colonel Lamb responded, "Very well, Captain! We can take care of that. Calm yourself." Lamb looked at Edgerton, pointed and ordered, "Get back on the road—move toward the pickets and make a show of force. Open fire on the pickets!" The colonel continued, "Then, by God, fall back! I want to draw them in this direction!" Colonel Lamb emphasized, "Do you understand that, Captain? Fall back!"

Captain Edgerton responded, "Yes, sir! Yes, sir! You can rely on it! We will have them behind us very shortly!" Captain Edgerton motioned to the mounted cavalrymen and yelled out, "Let's get back to the road and engage the Yankees!" Edgerton spurred his horse, entered the road and galloped toward the river bridge. The five mounted troopers followed in a cloud of dust.

Colonel Lamb called Major Kennedy and ordered all the cavalrymen dismounted. Lamb quickly issued orders for Major Kennedy to position the cavalrymen and infantrymen along the side of the road. "Major!" the colonel shouted, "place your men three paces apart on each side of the road!" Colonel Lamb continued, "About fifteen paces from the road and hidden in the woods!"

Major Kennedy answered, "Yes, sir! That will be done!" The major ran to the cavalrymen, "Get your weapons ready! Company L! Take to the opposite side of the road and get back in the trees! Keep about three paces apart and wait for the command to fire!" The major continued, "Company K! Keep on this side of the road! Keep about three paces apart and stay in the trees!" The troopers began to take up their positions. All of the horses were hidden from view. Two infantrymen remained with the livestock and wagons. The piney green grounds became quiet as the wait began.

Colonel Lamb snapped the reins, rode to the center of the road, looked to both sides and ordered loudly, "Do not fire until ordered! Do not fire until ordered!" the colonel emphasized. He continued his orders with persistence, "Do not aim above the stirrups! Do not aim above the stirrups! Wait for the order to fire!" Colonel Lamb scanned both sides of the road, pulled hard on the reins and turned his horse into the trees.

Colonel Lamb steadied his horse, looked at Major Kennedy and said confidently, "Now, we wait! We wait for the sound of musketry." Kennedy looked at Lamb and excitedly asked, "Then what?"

Lamb stroked the mane of his horse, patted the animal gently and responded, "We wait for Edgerton to clear the road and then we bring down the Federals—horses and all, with one well-placed volley!"

Captain Edgerton approached the Federal line at the river bridge. He reined his horse to a halt and scanned the road toward the Union picket line. The captain ordered the troopers to aim their rifles and fire into the advancing cavalrymen. The five men raised their muskets and fired into the line. Edgerton yelled, "Now fall back!" The gray-clad troopers turned their horses, pressed the side of their animals with their heels and galloped toward the schoolhouse where Colonel Lamb waited in ambush.

Captain Edgerton turned quickly as his horse bounced under him. He saw the bright orange flash of exploding black powder from the muzzle of the Federal howitzer. He heard the shell as it passed overhead. Captain Edgerton flinched at the explosion to his front. The thunderous orange and red burst of sparks spattered the road ahead.

The captain spurred his horse and led his five men past the Confederate infantrymen waiting on both sides of the road.

Colonel Lamb shouted, "That's it! That's it, Major!" and added excitedly, "watch for the mounted troopers to be in our sights pretty shortly!" Major Kennedy steadied his horse, looked at Colonel Lamb and quickly asked, "You going to give the order to fire, Colonel?" Colonel Lamb, erect in his saddle responded, "Indeed I am! It will be my pleasure!"

The sound of galloping horses became louder; the thundering horses neared the Confederate trap about to be sprung. Colonel Lamb waited; looked at Major Kennedy; waited again, and then suddenly, as the Federals moved into the sights of the waiting men, Colonel Lamb raised high above his saddle and shouted, "Fire!" The orange and red bursts from the muzzles of the muskets stopped the Federal charge. The horses fell forward; the cavalrymen fell to the sides. Stunned, the Union cavalrymen jumped to their feet, drew their revolvers and looked to both sides of the road. The Confederates, muskets in hand poured into the road, ran among the fallen troopers and began to smash them back onto the ground with the butts of their muskets.

Major Clarkson drew his saber, grasped his revolver and ran to the center of the road. "Hold your ground! Hold your ground!" The major turned in time to aim his revolver in the face of an oncoming Confederate private. The private recoiled from the blast of the revolver in his face; fell to the ground lifeless. The major continued to move quickly among his men. An infantryman with lowered bayonet, charged the major. Clarkson dodged the rushing man and brought his saber sharply down on the trooper's back. Major Clarkson quickly surveyed the carnage and shouted, "Pull back! Fall back! Fall back to the bridge!"

Colonel Lamb observed the hand-to-hand brutal attacks and shouted to Major Kennedy. "Major Kennedy! Cease the attack!" Kennedy hearing the colonel echoed, "Cease the attack! Cease fire!" The mass of fighting and bleeding men became still. Suddenly from the wooded roadside, the remaining infantrymen in reserve rushed onto the road and demanded the surrender of the men unable to retire to the bridge. The Confederates moved the wounded and the prisoners into the schoolhouse. The Union cavalrymen retired to the bridge; the Confederate cavalrymen retired to the piney woods behind the schoolhouse. As quickly as the chaos began, it ended. Blue-clad bodies filled the center of the roadway in grotesque positions of life's final convulsions.

Colonel Lamb prompted his horse onto the road and scanned the road to the west. The colonel saw the Federal forces being reinforced from the opposite side of the river. He rose high in his stirrups and called out, "Captain Edgerton! Major Kennedy! Retire all your men to the piney woods!" Colonel Lamb yelled to the Sergeant Major, "Sergeant! Clear our wounded from the road! Retire to the school house!" The colonel gazed at the bloody scene and directed, "Sergeant! Take care of their boys, too! Bring them with you!"

Major Cole heard the musketry, galloped across the bridge, lifted his arm and motioned for the troopers to follow him. The major dashed down the Hamilton Road and viewed the results of the clash. He halted in the center of the road and turned his horse. Upright in the saddle, he raised his hand overhead to stop the advancing cavalrymen. Major Clarkson galloped to Major Cole's position, pulled his mount to a halt and demanded, "Are we stopping here? Do we press the thing?" Cole steadied his horse, focused his eyes on Major Clarkson and declared, "Potter sent word to break off!"

Clarkson responded angrily, "Potter sent word to do what? I can't believe what I heard!" Clarkson stared directly at Cole and added angrily, "I believe he's scared of getting caught and getting hung! The Rebs might do us a favor to hang him!"

Major Cole moved quickly away from the angry Clarkson. He urged his horse into a gallop in the direction of the river bridge. Cole turned and shouted to Major Clarkson. "Retire to the bridge!" Major Cole still shouting as he galloped past the troopers ordered, "Form a skirmish line at the bridge!"

The Federal cavalry force began to pull their horses around, formed into single file and galloped back to the river bridge. Cole held up his hand to prevent the troopers from crossing the bridge and directed the mounted troopers to block the bridge. Major Cole stood erect in the stirrups above his saddle and shouted, "Sergeant Utz! Sergeant Utz!" The gunnery sergeant approached excitedly, "Yes, sir!" The major motioned to Utz and ordered, "Position your piece in  front of the line!" The bridge was  blocked. There would be no crossing by the Confederates.

Major Cole turned in the saddle as he heard the hoofs of a single horse crossing the river bridge from the west. He observed Lieutenant Smithson approaching on the gallop and looked toward Clarkson and asked disgustedly, "I wonder what Old Potter wants us to abandon this time!" The general's aide pulled his horse to a stop and called to Cole, "Major Cole! General Potter says to retire across the river—immediately!" The major acknowledged the aide with a salute, called to Sergeant Utz and ordered, "Sergeant! Throw another shot down the road to let those boys know we're still here!"

Sergeant Utz lined the gun trail straight with the road, ordered the gun crew with military precision to take positions and began the firing sequence. The crew in position, the sergeant reached and adjusted the elevation screw to sixty degrees, backed off from the howitzer and shouted, "Fire!" The Mountain Howitzer recoiled as the bright orange and red glow extended from the muzzle. A deafening roar of the blast echoed down the Hamilton Road as the missile whistled through the air. The explosion of the shell in a brilliant red burst scattered the spherical shot.  A black powder cloud floated above the road and then stillness. Acrid black smoke dissipated over the road. Major Cole scanned the road with his field glasses and exclaimed, "They won't be coming this way, now! No, they won't come this way!"

The major shouted, "Over the bridge! Over the bridge!" He motioned to the cavalrymen to follow as he pressed his horse across the river bridge. He turned in the saddle as he reached the opposite side of the river bridge and shouted, "Back to our positions!"

General Potter remained in the wooded area atop the river bluffs. He lifted his field glasses to his eyes and observed the Federal troopers as they crossed back to the west side of the Tar

River bridge. The general remarked to Lieutenant Smithson, "Our objectives have been met! No need to fight on their ground." Potter turned to his aide and directed, "Inform Major Cole to begin withdrawal back onto the Sparta Road!"

General Potter watched as Smithson galloped to transmit the general's orders to Major Cole. Potter reached for his horse's reins, loosened it from the tree, pulled his mount closer, placed his foot in the stirrup and pulled himself into the saddle. The general scanned the river, snapped the lines and galloped to the center of the road that led back into Tarborough.

"Major Cole! Major Clarkson!" the general shouted, "Join me on the road back!" The general stiffened his legs, lifted himself high above the saddle, removed his hat and motioned forward. Cole and Clarkson watched Potter and pressed their horses behind the general.

The Federal cavalry column, the Mountain Howitzer section and the walking troopers fell in behind General Potter and the cavalry officers.

# CHAPTER FOURTEEN

Julia ran to the staircase leading to the cupola, grasped the rail of the staircase and looked up into the center of the cupola ceiling. With each grasp of the rail she pulled herself to the entrance of the dome that gave Coolmore its individual character. She darted from the staircase to the east window of the cupola, looked toward Tarborough and viewed the columns of smoke rising above the town. Julia quickly turned, ran to the west window and leaned on the window sill as she looked toward Rocky Mount. Dense black smoke billowed high above the treetops. My God! Julia thought, the Yankees must be in both places! She knew her mother and father were aware of the presence of the Federals; they would keep her from further harm. Julia began to feel the weariness of the walk from Kingsboro and sighed as she returned to the west side window.

The brightness of the afternoon sun caused the translucent glass of the cupola windows to mingle a kaleidoscope of colors; purple, amber, cobalt and green reflected down the cupola staircase onto the second level floor. The brilliance of the colors increased and diminished as the breeze stirred the leaves of the oak trees, alternately allowing the rays of the sun to penetrate the colored glass window panes.

Julia found solace and peace in the sacred hues of the cupola. Time and space merged as Julia sat on the sill of the west window, one foot on the cupola floor and one knee drawn to her breast. Her head lowered onto her knee, Julia was lost in thought. The familiar sounds of home lulled her into security and contentment. No harm could approach her now; she was home.

Julia was startled from her thoughts by a thunderous roar echoing from Tarborough. Frank bolted from the porch and looked up to the cupola. "Julia! Can you see what's going on over at Tarborough?" Julia's father with his face lifted upward continued, "Can you tell what's happening?" Julia jumped from the window sill, ran to the east window, scanned the treetops, darted back to the west window and leaned out. "The only thing I can see is a lot of black smoke over Tarborough!"

Leaning farther over the window sill, Julia looked toward the west. The towering smoke had begun to disperse as the prevailing southern winds carried the gray smoke toward the north. Julia continued to keep her eyes on the road to Rocky Mount. A cloud of dust began to increase and the clattering sounds of hoof beats became more distinct as the cavalry column came into view. Oh, Lord! Julia thought, the Yankees are coming! Julia leaned out the cupola window and shouted, "Daddy! there's Yankees coming down the road!"

Julia dashed down the spiral stairs, rounded the grand staircase to the first level and bounded out the back door, shouting, "Daddy! Mama! the Yankees are on the road coming this way!" Julia, still barefooted, jumped to the ground and continued shouting, "They're coming this way! By my God! they're coming this way!"

Frank ran to the west side of the house, stopped and called, "Ada! Ada! Stay in the house!" Frank grabbed Julia by the shoulder, turned her around and pointed to the house. "You get in the house, too! I don't want you to get hurt!" Frank shoved Julia toward the house and yelled, "Get in the house, girl! Now!"

Nero and Esther ran to the main house from the barns, stopped and looked at Mr. Dupree. Nero called out, "You need us, Mr. Frank?" Frank waved his arm above his head and shouted, "Nero! You and Esther go back to the barns!" Dolly ran from the kitchen, stopped and called out, "Lord! What's all this 'motion 'bout!" Frank shouted, "Dolly! Get Nate and get to the back of the house!" Frank Dupree knew he was the only one who could handle the situation. He was the owner here; he was the one responsible for Coolmore.

Frank ran to the front of the house. He watched as the column of horses galloped nearer, turned into the path and moved in single file to the front of Coolmore. The cavalrymen reined their horses into the shade of the trees and waited for the artillerymen to move from the road. The oak trees sheltered the raiding party from the heat of the afternoon sun. One by one the men dismounted, secured their horses and sought the coolness of the oak grove.

Major Jacobs grasped the saddle pommel, swung his leg over the back of his horse and with one foot in the stirrup lowered himself to the ground. The major, his horse's reins in hand, led his horse to the front of the house. Major Jacobs glared at Frank Dupree and declared, "I am Major Ferris Jacobs of the Third New York Cavalry," and continued as he remained focused on Dupree, "and I assume you are the owner here! Is that correct?"

Dupree looked at the major and angrily demanded, "What is your business here? Yes, I am the owner! And I demand you leave! And leave now!" Dupree continued, "This is private property! You have no business on this land!"

Major Ferris turned to Captain Chamberlain, motioned and called out, "Captain! Join me with this man." The major looked at Dupree and demanded, "Your name, sir?" Frank stared at the major and shouted, "My name is Frank Dupree! Now get the devil off this land!"

Jacobs watched Chamberlain as he approached, turned to the captain and ordered, "Captain! Take a company and go to the rear of this house and see if there is any corn," and then Jacobs added, "and if there is, take it all! Our horses need feed and water." The major continued to direct the captain, "See that water is drawn and the trough filled." Chamberlain walked to the west side of the house, stopped and called out, "Company C! Check the rear of the house for water and corn!" The troopers quickly moved to the rear of the home, spread into the rear yard and began to search the buildings.

Julia and her mother watched from the partially closed front door. Julia saw Captain Chamberlain and immediately recognized him as the officer she had encountered on the train. Her anger began to rise, she turned to her mother and whispered bitterly, "That's the devilish man that put me off the train this morning! I won't ever forget what he looks like! I won't ever forget what he did to me this morning! No! Never!"

Sergeant Wentz ran from the rear of the house, stopped at the front west corner and shouted, "Captain!" Chamberlain answered, "Yes, Sergeant." The sergeant quickly added, "There's a half-full corncrib in the back!" Chamberlain held the reins of Blue Boy and walked closer to the sergeant. "Tear it down, Sergeant!" and without any hesitation yelled, "and be sure all the corn is out of the crib! See to it that our horses get the corn! Take what you want!"

Sergeant Wentz turned and started toward the rear of the house, stopped and called back to Captain Chamberlain, "Captain! there's some Negroes out back! What about them?" The captain quickly walked closer to the sergeant and responded, "Let's leave that decision to the major."

Julia ran to the back door, stopped at the side of the door, held onto the door facing and leaned her head to the side of the door. She saw the sergeant as he directed the troops as they ripped the boards from the sides of the corn crib. She watched the corn as it poured onto the ground. Julia felt the rage as it began to make her tremble. She bolted back to the front door, pushed her mother to one side, flung open the door and darted onto the porch. Julia stopped abruptly at the top of the porch steps, placed her hands on her hips and yelled angrily, "You thieving rogues! You plundering devils! You ain't satisfied 'til all we've got is gone!" She motioned to the back of the house and angrily continued, "Those thieving devils are chasing the chickens and letting the hogs out of the pen!"

Captain Chamberlain heard the shouting, pulled on Blue Boy's reins and quickly walked back to join Major Jacobs. The captain observed Julia on the porch as she shouted at the Major and immediately recognized the raging girl. My God, the captain thought, it's the same girl that hit me with the brass spittoon on the train. Not again, he thought! Chamberlain hesitated before he approached the major, observed the raging Julia and was smitten by her fiery beauty. Her chestnut-colored hair reflected the sunlight. He was struck by her features that were so animated in her rage. Her shrill voice seemed to pale as he continued to look at Julia as she moved from the top step to the ground. The captain forgot his mission for a moment and stared at Julia.

Julia stepped barefooted onto the ground, turned quickly and watched as Captain Chamberlain approached. "And you! You heathen of hell!" Julia continued and pointed at the captain, "You are a despicable Balaam's ass!" Julia continued to rant and shake her finger at the captain, "I remember you from this morning! And your soul be damned to hell!"

Frank trembling with anger, grabbed Julia by her shoulders, gave her a sudden shake and pushed her back toward the porch steps. Dupree shouted, "Let me take care of this situation! Get back inside with your mother, now!" Julia lifted her skirt, exposed her bare feet and started up the steps onto the porch. She reached the porch, turned and looked at the captain and shouted, "Yes! you're Balaam's ass!"

Seth stared at Julia as she stood on the porch raging. He shouted, "You Carolina Jezebel! You're lucky I don't burn this house down around your pretty little neck! That might shut your mouth!"

"Get in the house, Julia!" demanded her father, and added angrily, "You and your mother get to the back of the house and stay there, inside!"

Frank Dupree looked at Major Jacobs, his eyes glaring with

rage and demanded, "Now! Will you leave us alone! Haven't you caused us enough trouble for one day?" Major Jacobs stared steadily into Dupree's eyes and declared, "I can burn your house to the ground, and there won't be one thing you can do about it! I have the authority to destroy everything in my path!" the major continued, "And by God! I ought to do it!" Major Jacobs turned to Captain Chamberlain and ordered, "See that everything in the yard is burned! Leave no outbuildings standing! Burn everything!"

The captain pulled Blue Boy by the reins and started walking to the rear of the house. "Yes, sir!" Chamberlain responded as he rounded the corner of the house. Julia heard the captain yell, "Burn all the buildings!" The rage continued to build as Julia dashed to the first floor bedroom, bolted into the room, pulled open a closet door, reached and grabbed Frank's musket. She ran to the front door, burst onto the porch and tossed the musket to her father. Frank instinctively reached to catch the weapon. He knew the musket was not loaded. A shot rang out from the grove of trees. Frank dropped the musket, fell to the ground, grabbed his leg and screamed at Major Jacobs, "My God, man! Can't you control your men?" Frank drew his knee up, and saw blood as his pants began to absorb the flow from the wound above his knee. Dupree looked from side to side and yelled again, "Good God, man! Have you gone to shooting civilians, now?"

Julia and her mother burst from the front door, ran to Frank as he lay on his back at the bottom of the steps. Julia screamed at Major Jacobs, "Good Lord! You had no cause to do that!" Ada snatched off her apron, tore Frank's pant leg and pressed the apron on the bleeding bullet hole and shouted, "Dolly! Nathan! Get around here!" Ada, realizing her husband was helpless as he lay on the ground, screamed louder, "Nathan! Nero! I need you, now!" Julia ran to the rear of the house and yelled, "Nero! Nathan! For God's sake, help mama!"

Nathan ran from the barn, glanced at Miss Julia frantically crying and yelled as he ran toward the front, "I'm a-comin' Miss Julia!" Nathan continued to shout as he ran to the front of the house, "Nero! Nero! I needs some help!" Nero heard the frantic call, looked and saw Nathan as he ran to the front and yelled, "I'm with you, Nate! I'm comin'!"

Nathan and Nero rounded the corner, rushed to Mr. Dupree, knelt down, looked at Miss Ada and Nathan asked, "Does you want him in the house, Miss Ada?" Julia yelled at Nathan, "Of course, we want him in the house!" Nathan looked at Nero, placed his hands under Frank's arms and shouted, "Nero! Take Mr. Frank by the feet. We got to get him on the bed in the house!" Major Jacobs backed away from the two black men as they lifted Mr. Dupree and started up the front steps. The major looked to the troopers in the grove of oak trees, saw one of the troopers replacing his revolver into the holster and shouted, "That was stupid! You men stay put!" The major loudly added, "That was Stupid! Stupid! Stupid!"

Captain Chamberlain watched as Julia and Ada walked behind Nathan and Nero as they carried Mr. Dupree into the house. The numbness of the sudden wound began to wear off, Frank felt the pain as it radiated through his leg. Nero and Nathan placed Mr. Dupree on the bed and stood back as Ada and Julia cut the pants above Frank's knee, exposing the blood-soaked apron. Ada screamed at Nathan, "Get Dolly! Get her to boil some water!" Julia shouted at Nero, "Don't just stand there! Go get Esther! We need all the help we can get!" The two black men responded simultaneously, "Yes'um, we'll fetch 'em right now!"

Major Jacobs and Captain Chamberlain turned and walked ahead of their horses toward the middle of the oak grove. The troopers began to stir under the giant oaks. Noises of the troopers in the rear of the house intensified. Mixed sounds of chickens and pigs rose above the din. Major Jacobs mounted his horse, gently whipped the reins and galloped to the west side of the house and ordered loudly, "Sergeant Wentz! Sergeant Wentz! If you find any wagons and mules in the barns, seize them! We will need them on our way back!" The major continued to command, "Don't leave anything we can use!"

Captain Chamberlain remained restrained under the spreading branches of the giant oaks. He held Blue Boy's reins loosely in his hand. The captain's gaze was fixed on the architectural design of the house. He knew there was something familiar about this house; he looked upward to the cupola. Rays from the sun penetrated the colored glass of the arched windows. Dazzling dancing colors held him spellbound.

Captain Chamberlain observed the gables of the cupola. His eyes remained focused on the modillions under the eaves, the intricate details of the porch and the arched windows. The details looked amazingly familiar. He continued to stare at the architectural features of the house. The captain pulled on Blue Boy's reins, walked closer to the house and continued to gaze at the cupola. Great God! Seth suddenly remembered, this is the house I helped design. Yes! The summer I spent in Baltimore! How could I have forgotten the summer I was sent to Baltimore?

Captain Chamberlain quickly placed his boot into the stirrup, pulled himself into the saddle and snapped the reins on Blue Boy's neck. "Major Jacobs!" the captain shouted as he rounded the corner of the house, "We can't burn this house! I helped design this house myself! I knew it looked familiar! It just now came to my recollection!"

Major Jacobs stopped issuing orders, looked at the captain and retorted sarcastically, "So! That's supposed to mean something to me?"

Chamberlain tugged on the reins, steadied Blue Boy, dismounted and pleaded, "Major! This is one of the few things in the south that has my handiwork! God knows I'd hate to see it wiped out! It can't serve any military purpose! Can't we let it stand?" The captain again pleaded, "Who will know?"

The major looked at the captain and responded, "You and me!" Chamberlain interrupted, "But, Major, it's the work of my hands. Surely you can understand that! Nobody likes to see their creations destroyed. Years from now who will know the difference?"

"All right! All right!" responded the major, and ordered, "See to the rear of the house—see that everything else is destroyed."

The captain grasped the saddle pommel, pulled himself into the saddle and pressed Blue Boy to the back side of the house. He pulled his horse to a halt, watched the corn crib, barns and livestock enclosures being pulled down. He called to Sergeant Wentz, "Sergeant! Harness up two mules to the wagon under the shed. We will put it to good use on our return to New Berne!"

Captain Chamberlain urged Blue Boy back to the front of the house. He drew to the side of Major Jacobs and remarked, "What do you suggest we do about the two Negroes?"

The major shook his head and answered, "I don't know. Lincoln says they're free; I reckon our telling them will be sufficient. They can do what they see fit."

Chamberlain snapped the reins on Blue Boy's mane, galloped around the side of the house, pulled to a halt and called to the troopers, "To the front, men! We're finished here! To the front!"

He watched as the troopers mounted their horses and galloped to the front of Coolmore. He prodded his mount to the side of the porch and called out, "If the ball went through his leg, he'll be fit in no time!"

Captain Chamberlain nudged Blue Boy still closer to the porch and called as loudly as he could, "You darkies! Mr. Lincoln says you're free! You don't have to be a slave to nobody! You're free! Go where you want to go!" The captain hastily added, "With us back to New Berne, if you're a-mind to!"

Julia, hearing the captain, burst furiously through the door onto the back porch. She ran to the edge of the porch screaming, "Get away from here, you Yankee scoundrel!" She jumped to the ground, pointed at Seth and screamed again, "Rot in hell!"

Captain Chamberlain tugged at the lines of his horse, turned in the saddle and looked at the seething Julia. How could anybody so beautiful be so vengeful, so hostile? He stared at Julia as he rode past. She was boiling with rage, but still the captain marveled at her striking beauty.

Nero ran from the rear of the yard, peered from behind the kitchen and called to the captain, "What was dat you said, soljur?"

Captain Chamberlain turned to see where the voice came from and spotted Nero as he peered around the corner of the kitchen. "I said you're free! If you are a slave here, you are free! You don't have to stay here if you don't want to!"

"You sayin' I can leave anytime I wants?" asked Nero. "Me and my wife, too?"

The captain said a little louder, "Yeah! That's right! You and your wife, too." Nero drew back behind the kitchen and shouted, "Glory be! We's free! We's free!" Nero ran to the cabin, pulled the door open and yelled to Esther. "Let's go, woman! De Yankee says we's free! We can go wid him if we wants to! Let's go, woman!" Nero danced around in the cabin and shouted, "Woman, get your things and throw 'em in the old wagon bed!" He rushed Esther as she thrust her clothes into a burlap bag. "Hurry, woman! Dem Yankees won't wait all day!"

Esther grabbed Nero's hand as he extended it inside the cabin and pulled her out the door. Esther handed Nero the burlap bag, grasped his hand and both ran to the front of Coolmore. Nero rounded the corner of the house, paused, looked to see where the wagon was and jerked on Esther's hand. "There be's the wagon!" Nero called out and pulling harder on Esther's hand, excitedly added, "We's free! Let's go!" Nero ran to the wagon, grabbed the burlap bag, tossed it over the wagon rail and jumped onto the rear of the wagon bed. He reached for Esther and pulled her into the wagon.

The captain spurred Blue Boy to a gallop and pulled beside Major Jacobs in front of Coolmore. The major called out, "Column! Mount up! We're moving out to join General Potter!" Major Jacobs looked at Captain Chamberlain and smiled. "Captain, let's take the long way to the road! Let's go through the corn field. Maybe some of the men might pull a few ears for roasting tonight." Major Jacobs snapped the reins and pressed his horse into the corn field. The tall green stalks began to lean forward and fall as the major and captain made a path through the field. Jacobs' column of cavalrymen spread and widened the path. A wide swath was cut as the lumbering howitzer followed onto the road to Tarborough.

The late afternoon sun was at the back of the column as the troopers entered the Tarborough Road. Dust began to rise as the cavalrymen urged their horses faster. General Potter would be waiting on the road to Sparta.

Coolmore was quiet. The livestock was gone. The corncrib was torn down. The barns were in shambles and the corn was lying flat in the field from the house to the road. Nero and Esther were gone. It was only Julia, her mother and father, Dolly and Nathan.

"Julia, run to the kitchen and see if Dolly has the water hot on the stove, yet!" directed Ada, the tears running down her cheeks. Ada looked at Frank as he writhed in pain. The blood from the bullet wound continued to soak onto the white cotton sheets. Ada applied more pressure to the blood-soaked apron. Frank yelled in pain as Ada increased the pressure. She held the pressure on Frank's leg, turned toward the open door and shouted, "For God's sake! Hurry with the hot water!"

Julia appeared in the open doorway with ripped cotton sheets and reassured her mother, "Dolly is bringing a pot of hot water from the kitchen, now!"

Ada looked quickly at Dolly and directed, "Put that pot on the floor!" Ada glanced toward Julia and motioned, "Bring me some of those clean cloths," Ada continued to give instructions, "and dip them in the hot water and hand them to me!"

Frank stared into the eyes of his wife and sighed weakly, "Oh, Ada! This pain is unbearable!" Ada took a cloth from Julia, twisted the excess hot water from it, removed the bloodied apron and gently washed the blood from the wound. Frank stiffened his body and groaned, "Did the ball go through?"

Ada looked at the fresh wound and responded, "I can't tell for sure, Frank! I don't know." She removed the warm bloodied cloth and called, "Julia! Hand me another hot cloth!" Julia twisted the excess hot water from the cloth and handed it to her mother. Ada gently wiped Frank's wound again and called for a clean dry cloth. The bleeding had begun to slow; the wound appeared to be responding to heat and pressure. Ada removed the bloodied cloth, leaned over the bed, looked at the wound and called, "Julia! Get me some clean, dry cloths!" Her mother moved from the bed and continued, "We will try to stop the bleeding by keeping clean pieces of cloth pressed over the wound!"

Frank began to relax as the hot damp cloths soothed the bullet puncture. He sighed and asked, "Would somebody get me a dipper of fresh water? I'm burning all over!" Julia ran to the back porch, grabbed the dipper and plunged it into the bucket. She ran back to the bedroom and held the dipper over the bed. Ada lifted Frank's head as Julia placed the dipper to his lips. The water dripped from Frank's lips as he relaxed.

Ada lowered his head onto the bolster. "Thank you, Ada," Frank said weakly as his head rested on the bolster, "This has been a mighty miserable day."

Ada looked at Frank, saw his bloodied clothes and called, "Julia! Go and fetch Nathan and Nero! Your daddy needs to have his clothes off and his night clothes put on!"

Julia moved to the bed, looked at her mother and father and reluctantly told them, "I'm afraid Nero and Esther ain't here. I watched them leave with the Yankee soldiers. It's just Nate and Dolly, now."

"Oh, drat it!" snapped Ada, "Then, get Nathan in here to help me with Mr. Frank!"

Julia ran to the back porch, grasped a column, leaned from the porch and shouted, "Nate! Nate! Mama wants you in here to help her!" Nathan heard Julia screaming his name. He ran from the rear of the house and bolted onto the porch beside Julia. Julia pointed and said, "Daddy is still in the bedroom where you put him! Mama needs some help to get him undressed, and she wants you!"

Nathan pulled the back door open, ran into the hall, the door slammed behind him and he burst through the bedroom door. "Miss Ada! You need some help with Mr. Frank?"

Ada looked at Nathan, "I sure do, Nate! We need to get Mr. Dupree in some cool night clothes, and you'll have to help me lift him!"

Ada motioned, "Julia! Get your daddy's nightshirt from the bureau and bring it to Nate!"

Ada moved to the opposite side of the double bed. Julia stood back and watched as her mother and Nate removed her father's bloodied clothes. She dropped her head, began to cry and ran into the hall. She heard her father shriek in pain with every movement required to undress him and put his nightshirt on.

Julia ran from the hall onto the back porch and wept uncontrollably. Dolly heard her sobbing, ran from the kitchen and saw Julia leaning against a porch column. She walked to Julia, placed her arm on her shoulder and said quietly, "Yore daddy's gonna be alright. Me and Nate is gonna be with you and your mama!" Dolly reassured her, "We ain't goin' nowhere! this is home to us; we bees too old to take up and leave."

Julia, calmed by the presence of Dolly, rubbed her eyes with the back of her hands and darted back to the door of the bedroom. She looked at Nate and her mother as they pulled the sheet up to Frank's shoulders. Frank turned his head on the bolster, looked at Julia and assured her, "Julia, I'm going to be all right! Your mama and Nate has got this bullet hole under control." He settled his head onto the bolster and lamented, "Maybe I can stand the pain."

Ada looked at Nate, smiled and spoke humbly, "I'm much obliged to you, Nate. You and Dolly are a real help." Then she added sadly, "And now I reckon you'll be leaving, too."

Nate stepped back from the bed. He looked dolefully at the owner of Coolmore, glanced at Ada and asserted, "No, I reckon we ain't. This has been home in all my recollection. No need to move now."

Nate quietly left the room and walked to the back door. He opened the door, smiled at Miss Julia and went to join Dolly in the kitchen. Julia followed Nate into the kitchen. She looked at Nate and Dolly and asked meekly, "Nate, how does it feel to be free?" Dolly looked at Nate, waited for him to respond, then said, "The girl axs you a question, Nate."

Nate continued to hesitate, then slowly remarked, "I reckon it feels like the fly caught in the spider web; everybody says he's free, but the spider knows he ain't. It might looks like we bees free but hits a spider somewhere what knows we ain't."

A mantle of darkness slowly covered Coolmore. The moon began to rise above the surrounding tree tops. The pallid light dimly illuminated Coolmore. Coolmore's majestic oaks cast shadowy figures against the exterior of the house. Quietness cast a pall of forgetfulness over the harshness of the day. Ada quietly prepared for bed. Julia slowly made her way up the staircase to her room. The ever-present night creatures began their overture. The day was finally passing into yesterday; tomorrow would soon be today and there is always hope for tomorrow.

# CHAPTER FIFTEEN

General Potter pushed the reins through the pommel opening, looped the lines over the top of the leather hump and removed his slouch hat. He glanced at Cole and Clarkson. "Let's get back to New Berne and to a few comforts," he suggested. Major Cole set his boots tight in the stirrups, lifted himself above his saddle, turned and glanced at the column. General Potter inquired, "Major, does it look like the companies are forming behind us?"

Major Cole replied, "The column appears to be making up satisfactorily. Some of our men are without their horses, and they seem to be moving slowly."

Cole settled into his saddle, relaxed the lines, looked at Clarkson and asked, "What does it look like to you, Major?" Clarkson stood upright in his stirrups, turned and looked to the rear, "I can't tell how many of our men are having to walk. We lost a lot of our animals in that ambush. We should have known better than to follow after so few Rebs on that isolated road."

The general interrupted angrily, "How were we supposed to know we were being drawn into a trap by so many of them? Or that they could have arrived from Fort Branch so quickly?"

Major Cole saw the irritation in the general's demeanor, stared at Major Clarkson and moved his head to convey silence. Clarkson understood the meaning of Cole's facial expression and did not speak. Only the sounds of the animal harnesses broke the silence as the column advanced toward Sparta. The cavalrymen squinted and turned their heads as they pressed south in the glare of the afternoon sun.

General Potter put his slouch hat on, loosened the reins from the pommel and glared at the two officers. "Gentlemen, we will not return to New Berne by the same route we came.

I'm sure Whitford's Brigade has already blocked that road."

Major Cole turned, looked straight at the general and concurred, "I highly suspect you are correct, General. What did you have in mind?"

Potter pressed his heels to his horse and turned to Major Cole. "Major, at first light tomorrow morning we will strike our bivouac and proceed south of Greenville in the direction of Snow Hill and Hookerton." Potter glanced at Cole and Clarkson. "To be sure, no one will expect us to head in that direction. I doubt Whitford's brigade is in the area. We might be harassed, but that will be all I expect." The general asserted, "When we reach Swift Creek, we will be in our territory."

General Potter divulged, "I expect my request for pontoon bridges in the Street's Ferry vicinity to be honored and ready for my crossing." The general glanced at Major Cole and jestingly asked, "You want to put up with old Street again, Major?" Cole looked at Major Clarkson, smiled and quickly added, "No, sir! That we don't!"

Towering pine trees lining the rutted road began to cast refreshing shadows onto the column. General Potter pressed southward toward his final destination. He thought the site of the bivouac of the previous night would provide security for his troopers.

"Aren't we forgetting something? Where are Jacobs and Chamberlain?" inquired Potter. He turned to Major Clarkson and directed, "Major, dispatch Lieutenant Henderson to ride back toward Tarborough to see if Major Jacobs is in the rear."

"Yes, sir." Clarkson responded as he pulled his horse to the side of the road. "Jacobs and Chamberlain wouldn't appreciate being left here in this territory." Clarkson tugged his horse to a halt, held the lines tight as the column moved past. He waited beside the road as Henderson approached. "Lieutenant Henderson! Potter said to ride back toward Tarborough to see if there's any sign of Jacobs and Chamberlain." Henderson turned his mount out of the advancing column, pulled the reins and turned toward the rear of the column.

The lieutenant peered along the road and urged his mount past the advancing column. He kept his horse in the middle of the road to avoid the wagon ruts.

The shadows of the tall pine trees gave the road an appearance of alternating light and darkness as the lieutenant pressed his horse in a trot toward Tarborough. Henderson drew his horse to a halt and strained to listen for sounds of the detachment. He decided it might be better to press his ear to the ground than to wait for the noises of the animals.

Lieutenant Henderson dismounted, led his mount to the edge of the road and secured the reins to an extended tree limb. He knelt on both knees, leaned over and placed his hands on the ground before him. The officer removed his hat and placed it on a grassy area. He pressed one ear against the grassy ground and listened. Nothing. He pressed his ear to the ground again. Henderson expected a distant rumble to vibrate through the ground. A feeling of disappointment flooded him when he did not detect any vibrations. Suddenly, the faint hint of vibrations assured the major of some movement closing in on his position. He jumped to his feet, retrieved his hat and removed the reins from the limb. He grasped the pommel firmly, hurriedly placed his foot in the stirrup and pulled his frame onto the saddle.

Henderson goaded his mount into a trot toward Jacobs' approaching detachment. He rounded a sharp bend in the road, reined his horse to a slow gait and gazed along the straight section of the road. Henderson could see a rising column of dust. The lieutenant knew it was the detachment returning from Rocky Mount. The lieutenant snapped the lines hard on his horse's neck, leaned forward and broke into a gallop toward the advancing cavalrymen. He neared the column and saw Jacobs and Chamberlain riding in the lead. Henderson shouted as he approached, "Old Potter was worried about you two! Man! Am I glad to see you."

The junior officer urged his horse to the side of the road, and reined in beside Jacobs and Chamberlain. "Major, I am to report to General Potter if I locate you. I'm sure glad to see you've made it safely from your assignment." Henderson rode alongside the officers briefly. "Now, gentlemen, if you will excuse me I have to get back to the main column and inform the general of your presence." With his heels, the lieutenant pressed his horse into a gallop. He leaned over the horse's neck and yelled, "See you fellows at Sparta!"

Major Jacobs and Captain Chamberlain watched as Henderson disappeared into the narrow tree-lined road. Chamberlain turned to Jacobs, laughed and asked, "Do you think old Potter is really concerned whether we make it back or not?" Jacobs responded with a halfhearted laugh, "I doubt it." The major, without hesitation, added, "He probably doesn't think we can find our way to Sparta by nightfall."

The heat bore down on Henderson as he pulled his horse to a moderate gait. He felt it radiating from the sides of his horse and observed if the heat was affecting him, it was affecting the animal also. The lieutenant drew his horse to the side of the road.

Tall pine trees provided shade and relief from the July sun. Henderson reined his mount back onto the road and pressed south toward the main column. He rode steadily, rounded another bend in the road and sighted the lumbering cannon. Its brass barrel reflected the rays of the sun directly into the eyes of the lieutenant. A glare caused Henderson to slow his horse's gait. The lieutenant guided his mount behind the artillerymen and shouted, "Sergeant! Pass the word to the column ahead of you. Jacobs and Chamberlain are behind us!" He nudged closer to the cannon crew and shouted again, "Pass the word! Jacobs is behind us!"

Lieutenant Henderson listened as the word passed from the rear of the column toward the front. "Jacobs is behind us" echoed along the road, gradually becoming fainter as the message passed to the head of the column.

Henderson pulled his horse to the side of the road and waited. The lieutenant joined Jacobs and Chamberlain riding toward Sparta.

General Potter tightened the lines and turned toward Major Cole and spoke, "Now that we know Jacobs is on the road behind us, we can take our time to reach Sparta; we should be there by dark."

Cole looked at the general and with a weary sigh, groaned, "I could use some rest before we start back to New Berne tomorrow. This has been a long day."

Potter raised his short frame above the saddle, turned and looked toward the rear of the column. "Major, you're not by yourself. I think the men walking back there would share your sentiments." Then added solemnly, "Ughmm! I dread to report our losses. General Foster might not understand the full details of our engagement with the enemy."

Major Cole lightly goaded his horse and pulled ahead of the general. He turned in the saddle and informed General Potter, "Looks like our old camp from last night is just around the next bend in the road.

The general responded, "Excellent, Major. Make the turn into the area and secure the site for the night."

The major replied, "Yes, sir! I'll move on to the area."

Major Cole turned his horse and disappeared from the road into the wooded terrain. General Potter called to his aide, "Lieutenant Smithson! Secure the site we used last evening." Smithson spurred his mount, moved ahead of General Potter and turned into the wooded area behind Major Cole. Potter shouted as his aide moved ahead of him, "Smithson! See that my headquarters tent is set up."

In single file, the troopers moved into the bivouac site and dispersed into the pine trees. The artillerymen and the Mountain

Howitzer section followed and scattered into the wooded terrain.

Major Jacobs pressed his boots tight in the stirrups, raised his frame erect, turned and looked toward the rear of the detachment and called, "Captain! What do you think the general will have to say about those two Negroes we brought along?"

Chamberlain quickly turned toward Major Jacobs and replied, "Probably a lot. He did not make any plans for bringing back any freed slaves."

Major Jacobs glanced toward Chamberlain and Henderson, snapped the lines on his horse and called out, "Let's find out what we've got to face and get it over with, gentlemen." He stood erect in the stirrups and roared, "Close up! Close up the column!"

Jacobs pulled ahead of the captain and the lieutenant, turned in the saddle and added, "Move on, men! Move on. We've got to make Sparta by dusk."

Chamberlain and Henderson urged their horses behind the major, and galloped in the trailing dust of Major Jacobs. Captain Chamberlain watched as Major Jacobs reined his mount to a slow gait. The captain observed the major lift his arm above his shoulder and understood the halt sign.

Seth pulled Blue Boy to a stop, twisted in the saddle toward Henderson and observed, "Looks like we're about at our home for this night. Just for one night, I trust." The captain turned his horse behind the major, turned to Henderson and motioned, "Lead the column behind us, Lieutenant."

Henderson raised himself above the saddle and turned toward the column. He motioned toward the area of the night's encampment and announced loudly, "This is it, men! Turn in here." Henderson pulled on the reins and turned into the wooded area; the cavalrymen followed in single file.

The artillery unit followed the troopers and the wagon drawn by two mules with Nero and Esther entered last. The wooded terrain consumed the two columns as they merged in their bivouac for the night.

General Potter watched as the rear of the column entered the wooded bivouac area. He saw the mules drawing a wagon, noticed the two Negroes in the bed of the wagon and angrily shouted, "God Almighty! What are those two doing here?" The general yelled to his aide, "Smithson! Find Major Jacobs and tell him to get to my tent on the double!" Potter pondered, is this officer out of his mind? What are we going to do with these Negroes? Potter shouted again, "Smithson! Find Jacobs, immediately!"

Lieutenant Smithson disappeared in the woods calling frantically, "Major Jacobs! Major Jacobs!" The major hearing his name called, responded loudly, "Here we are, Lieutenant!" The general's aide hearing the major's response, ran in the direction of Jacob's voice. "The general wants to see you immediately, Major at his headquarters tent."

Jacobs acknowledged the order, "All right, Lieutenant! You can report back."

Major Jacobs fastened his horse's lines to a low-hanging limb and quickly walked to General Potter's headquarters site. "General Potter," the major reported, "You wanted me, Sir?"

Potter placed his hands behind his back, grasped his hands in a tight grip and asked abruptly, "Major! Just why in God's name did you bring them darkies with you?" The general ranted on, "Nobody said anything about bringing them back with us to New Berne. Free them, yes! But bring them with us, no."

General Potter continued to rebuke the major, "If they can't be left here, then by God, they will not be riding in that wagon tomorrow!" Potter walked from Major Jacobs, moved his hands from behind his back and turned toward the major. "My men who lost their mounts today will be riding tomorrow. Those two darkies will be walking if they have to return with us. I have to protect them—I don't have to transport them."

General Potter fixed his stare on Major Jacobs. "Major, I

have already informed Cole and Clarkson of our route of return to New Berne. We will not use the same route we used to get here. I'm reasonably sure that General Martin at Kinston knows where we are and has probably set some plan in motion to intercept us on our way back."

The general explained his directions, "At first light tomorrow I want this unit on the road south to Farmville, Snow Hill and Hookerton. We will keep away from Greenville and Whitford's Battalion. I suspect that Confederate colonel is already somewhere in the vicinity." Potter walked away from the major, then returned, "If we arrive at Swift Creek too late in the day we will bivouac there again." The general paused then added, "But if I learn that General Foster has honored my request, we will cross on a pontoon bridge near Street's Ferry." The irritated general rattled on, "I'm in no mood to confront old Street again!" General Potter calmed his rage and informed the major, "If we are not able to cross tomorrow, we will cross the following day, and I hope to God it's on a pontoon bridge!"

Nature's harbingers of night introduced their prelude to the dark—a sure sign of the coming of darkness. The orchestra of the forest inhabitants began in earnest their overture to the stars. Nature's sounds would rise and fall in relentless repetition until the rays of the morning sun dissipated the blackness of night into the brightness of a new day. Mother Earth would give solace and security to weary mortals as they laid their heads to her bosom and closed their eyes to the darkness and reality. The expected dawn of a new day would bring renewed hope and a day farther from the dangers of exposure in a hostile environment.

A day that began before the hint of light, merged again into lengthening afternoon shadows. The descending sun shed its light as the Federal column passed Fort Anderson and pressed on toward the vicinity of Street's Ferry and the return to New Berne.

General Potter urged his horse past the previous night's

bivouac area. His long column of cavalrymen and artillerymen followed. Coolmore's two mules balkingly pulled the creaking wagon over the rutted road. The unmounted cavalrymen sat in contorted positions in the bed of the wagon. Nero and Esther walked behind the wagon. The column pressed toward the Neuse River.

Major Cole noted the density of the trees and remarked, "General, it appears we may be approaching the river. The trees seem to be thinning out somewhat." General Potter remained straight in his saddle. He paused before answering, then responded, "Yes, Major, the river should not be very far now." The general shook his horse's reins and added, "Let's move on ahead. I want to make this crossing before dark."

The general looked at Clarkson riding beside him and directed, "Move ahead into the clearing and see if there are steamers and a pontoon bridge anywhere in sight. If there is a pontoon crossing, get back here fast and let me know!"

The major snapped the lines, prodded his horse sharply and trotted from the wooded terrain into the clearing. Clarkson looked to the south and spotted smoke rising from the stack of an anchored steamer. He observed the engineers as they secured the pontoons into position to both banks of the river. Clarkson jerked the lines, turned his horse and pressed his mount back onto the road toward the advancing column.

The major approached the column shouting, "General! General! It looks like we can cross before dark!" Clarkson urged his horse alongside the general as he advanced to the river. Clarkson commented, "By the time we reach the river, it appears everything should be completed for the crossing." General Potter acknowledged, "Bless God! General Foster did honor my request."

General Potter looked at Cole and then at Clarkson and ordered, "Have all the men dismount and lead their animals across the pontoons in single file." Then the general added,

"And direct two troopers out of the wagon to lead the two mules across the river behind the column."

Potter quickly spurred his horse, pulled away from the column and raced to the clearing at the river. Major Cole followed closely and tugged his mount to a halt beside the general and announced, "General, that pontoon bridge looks good to me!"

Potter's beard exposed a broad grin as he agreed, "Yes, Major, that's a fine piece of engineering. Thank God, it's here!" General Potter dismounted, led his horse to the edge of the river and called to the officers standing on the planking of the pontoons, "We're coming across!"

An engineer shouted to the general, "Lead the way, General, all is ready!" General Potter grasped the reins, stepped onto the undulating pontoon planking and led his horse across the bridge.

The general stepped from the planking onto the opposite river bank, led his mount farther from the river's edge and watched as the column followed across the bridge. He removed his slouch hat and shouted, "Hurry it up! I want this crossing completed before nightfall." The weary general raised his hat above his head, waved it side to side and shouted, "Thank you, engineers! Thank you."

General Potter mounted his horse and waited for Cole and Clarkson. The military objectives had been completed; New Berne loomed in the distance.

As the familiar structures came into view, Captain Chamberlain remarked, "I never thought New Berne would look so good." Major Jacobs looked straight at the captain and laughed, "Now, will you stop complaining about this duty and make the best of a bad situation?"

Seth loosened Blue Boy's reins, lowered his head, removed his hat and answered, "I'll try, I'll try."

# CHAPTER SIXTEEN

The predawn darkness began to lighten as the eastern horizon announced the arrival of another day. The open bedroom window on the west side of the house allowed the first hints of morning light to flood the room. Ada awoke, gently put her feet on the floor and quietly dressed for the new day. Awake, Frank tried to remain still to keep his leg from any sudden movements. The pain of the previous nights had been excruciating. Darkness seemed to intensify the pain.

Frank raised his head from the bolster and stared at the blood-soaked strips of sheeting and dropped his head back onto the bolster. "Ada," Frank called. He called again in a frantic voice, "Ada, I need some help!"

Ada ran from the kitchen, flung open the door to the hallway and dashed to the doorway of the bedroom. "Yes, Frank! I'm here! What can I do?" She looked at the blood-soaked sheet under his leg and exclaimed, "Good Lord, Frank! It looks like you're bleeding half to death." Ada darted to the bed, leaned over and stared into Frank's eyes. "Frank, something has got to be done. You just can't go on in this fix."

Frank looked at his wife and asked, "Just what in heaven's name do you think can be done? There ain't no regular doctor around any more; they're all in the army."

Ada sat gently on the edge of the bed. Looking sympathetically at her husband, she blurted, "It was Yankee soldiers that did this! I don't see why Doctor Jones at the Confederate army hospital in Tarborough can't do something for you."

Frank's pale complexion startled Ada as she listened to his weak voice. "Ada, I don't know about Jones. He's from somewhere else and he might not look kindly on us, seeing I ain't in the army." He remained quiet for a moment, raised his head to look around the room and wearily conceded, "I know, I know! I don't think I can go through another night like the last two." Frank raised his head again, looked at the bloody wrapping around his leg and sighed, "I reckon some clean wrapping needs to be put on my leg. The sheets are all bloodied, too." Ada placed her hand on Frank's forehead and reacted, "My Lord, Frank! you're burning up! Here in the middle of July, you're under the covers like you're cold and feeling to me like you're on fire."

Ada lifted herself from the bed and looked at her husband. She placed her hand on his forehead again. "I'll get Julia and Dolly in here to change the bedding. I'll take off the wrapping and put it all in the wash pot out back. We'll be boiling the wash this week." Ada walked from the bedroom, stopped on the back porch and called loudly, "Julia!" Pausing, she called again, "Julia!"

Julia ran from the back yard, jumped onto the porch and inquired, "Is daddy any worse off? You need some help, Mama?" Ada gazed into Julia's eyes and asked, "Will you help me get the wraps off your daddy's leg? It looks like all his blood has soaked right through the wrapping." Ada started for the door leading into the main house, stopped, turned to Julia and requested, "Julia, see if you can find some more old sheeting we can use to wrap your daddy's leg."

Julia followed her mother into the hallway and assured her, "I'll find something, somewhere, but I'll help you get daddy ready first."

Ada quickly moved to the doorway of the bedroom and walked to the side of the bed. "Frank, Julia and me will clean up your leg and the bed. You try to keep still so's you won't hurt any more than need be."

Julia followed her mother to the side of the bed, looked down at her father and screamed, "Oh, my Lord! My Lord! We've got to do something about your leg." Julia burst into tears and cried out, "Daddy! What in God's name are we going to do?"

Ada lifted Frank's leg slowly to remove the wrapping. Frank grabbed the top edges of the mattress with both hands and screamed in agony, "Good God, woman, it hurts! It really hurts!"

Ada gently began to unwind the wrapping from Frank's leg and looked at Julia. "Julia, we need to get hold of Doctor Jones at the Confederate hospital in Tarborough, and see if we can get him to come out here. I don't know of anything else we can do."

Frank continued to writhe in pain, raised his head from the bolster and relented, "Something's got to be done. I can't take much more of this pain."

Julia watched as her mother continued to remove the strips of sheeting from Frank's leg. Ada quickly turned toward Julia and motioned, "There is some hot water on the kitchen stove; get it in here, quick." Julia glanced at her father, dashed into the hallway, sprinted to the back door and ran from the main house to the kitchen. She looked at the kettle, saw the steam coming from the neck of the kettle, darted to the stove and picked up the kettle by the handle. The uncovered handle burned her hand. Julia reached for a cloth on the kitchen table, folded the cloth to double the thickness and removed the kettle from the stove. She moved carefully to the kitchen doorway, walked onto the porch and grabbed a basin from the table. At the back door she called, "Mama! Mama, open the door! I've got both hands full."

Ada rushed to the back door, pushed it open and Julia carefully moved into the hallway. Ada walked quickly ahead of Julia and moved to the side of the bed. "Frank, this ain't going to be easy, but it's got to be done," Ada cautioned. Julia placed the basin on a table by the bed, poured some hot water from the kettle into the basin and placed the kettle on the floor. She dipped the clean sheeting into the basin of hot water. Cautiously she lifted it from the basin with a hairbrush from the dresser.

She waited for the hot water to drip from the strips and twisted the excess water from the wrappings. Julia handed the wet cloths to her mother. Frank screamed as Ada placed the hot cloths to the open wound and wiped the blood from his leg.

Julia placed some fresh sheeting strips into the basin on the table, looked at her father, burst into tears and exclaimed, "I know we don't have no more wagons! I know our mules are gone! I know Esther and Nero's gone! But I know I'm going to get to Tarborough and get that Doctor Jones out here if I have to walk all the way there and back!"

Ada looked at Frank as he tried to lie still on the bed. "I don't know what else to do. If you're going, Julia, you best get started right away." Frank heard Ada and Julia discussing his pain and angrily interrupted, "No! No! To be sure somebody will be coming this way. There's no need for Julia to walk."

Julia wiped her tears with her hand, gazed at her father and asserted, "I'm going! I'm the only one that is able." Julia ran from the bedroom, called as she dashed up the rear stairway to her bedroom, "It won't take me long to get ready!"

Ada looked at her husband and reassured him, "Let the girl go! It's your only hope!" Frank relaxed his head on the bolster and relented, "Maybe you know best, Ada! Like I am, I'm not thinking right."

Julia was not concerned with quietness as she moved from one side of her room to the other. Moving quickly she thought getting to Tarborough was the important thing. She searched for her shoes and realized they had been pushed under her bed. She knelt on the floor, leaned and reached under the bed. Oh, Lord, she thought, where are my shoes? She strained her arm farther, felt her shoes and quickly pulled them from under the bed. With her shoes in her hand, she sat on the edge of the mattress. She lifted her foot and pulled on one of her shoes. With a short sigh she pulled on the other shoe and leaned to lace them. She stood with both shoes laced. Oh, my Lord, Julia thought, I forgot to put on my stockings. She quickly decided it did not matter; getting to Tarborough and getting the doctor to Coolmore was the most important thing. Julia grabbed her bonnet from the back of the door as she ran from the room and dashed down the stairs to the hallway.

Julia stopped in the doorway of Frank's bedroom and declared, "I'm going to get some help! I don't know who or where, but some help I'll find!" Julia looked at her father and reassured him, "I'll be back with some help this afternoon. Don't fret about me. I'll be safe enough."

Julia ran to her mother, embraced her tightly and broke into tears. "I'll be all right. We know everybody along the road to Tarborough. Somebody will help us. To be sure, somebody will help us." Julia ran from the room, dashed through the back door onto the porch. She jumped from the porch to the yard and ran along the pathway to the Tarborough road in front of the house.

The midmorning sunlight reflected from the dusty road. Julia placed her hand above her eyes and squinted as she looked toward Tarborough. She placed her bonnet on her head, pulled the strap under her chin, tied it in a neat bow and began walking east toward Tarborough. The heat of the July morning and the rays of the unrelenting sun reminded Julia of the walk she endured a few days earlier from the Kingsboro siding. The fresh memory of the events reminded Julia of the fact that it was the Yankee captain who caused all this hardship.

Julia glanced eastward toward Tarborough, noticed a cloud of dust in the distance and moved to the side of the road. She stopped, strained her eyes as she peered in the direction of the cloud of dust. Julia waited to see what was stirring the dust. Julia stood in the shade of the trees and observed the bend in the road ahead of her. Suddenly a horse-drawn buggy rounded the bend of the road.

The driver shouted, "Whoa!" Julia recognized Josh Mewborn as the buggy slowed. Josh pulled the horse to a stop, looked at Julia in amazement and asked, "Miss Julia, what in heaven's name are you doing out on this road by yourself? We heard what happened to you all and I was on my way out to see what was going on."

Julia looked up at Josh as he fumbled with the horse's lines and responded, "Daddy was shot in the leg. We need some help, bad!" She moved closer to the buggy and continued, "I'm going to town to see if I can get that Doctor Brown of the Confederate army to come and see to my daddy." She informed Josh, "All our stock is gone! They took our wagon and all I can do is walk to town."

Josh looked at Julia and with a tender voice offered, "Miss Julia, come around and get in the seat. I'll see that you get to the hospital where you might find that Doctor Brown." Julia moved quickly around the rear of the buggy, stopped at the side of the buggy seat, looked up at Josh and put forth her hand. Josh reached over the seat, grasped Julia by her hand as she stepped onto the buggy step, pulled her upward and into the seat.

Josh rattled the lines, urged the horse with an audible glick and guided the buggy to the side of the road. He pulled tight on the left line, tightened the bridle bit and turned the horse in the opposite direction. Julia leaned forward and with both hands drew her skirt securely under her.

Josh lightly tapped the reins on the back of the horse and adjusted the lines to hold the horse in the center of the road. The buggy rattled as it moved steadily along the ruts in the road. Josh turned to Julia, raised his voice above the clatter of the buggy and asked, "Is your daddy in any danger?"

Julia glared at Josh and responded, "Of course he is! I wouldn't be trying to get a doctor if he wasn't."

Josh apologized, "I'm sorry, Miss Julia, I didn't mean to make little of your trouble."

Julia smiled at Josh and responded, "I know you didn't, Josh. I'm a bit shaky right now."

Julia turned to Josh, "It's bound to be an act of the Almighty, you being on the road to our house at this time. Thank God, for your helping me in this terrible time! I could have been out here on the road for most of the afternoon." Josh nodded in agreement and thought, yeah, an act of God for both of us. He felt sympathy for Julia and her family, but it did provide him with the opportunity to be alone with her.

Young Mewborn continued to press the horse toward Tarborough. The buggy bounced in and out of the ruts. Julia was unable to maintain her balance as the buggy bounded out of a rut and she slumped onto Josh's shoulder. She immediately regained her balance and apologized, "I'm sorry. I'll hold tighter! Don't slow any." Josh thought as he lashed the horse onward, maybe I'll find me another rut if it will do that again. The softness of Julia's body against his was enough reason to look for more ruts in the road.

Josh snapped the lines on the horse's back, turned to Julia and smiled. "We're coming into Tarborough! I think Doctor Jones is using one of the homes in town for his Confederate hospital." He continued to reassure Julia, "I'm pretty sure I know where it is." Julia smiled and replied, "Josh, I'm counting on you! I don't have any notion where it might be." Josh tightened the lines, slowed the buggy and proceeded east on the main street through Tarborough. Julia sat quietly and watched as the buggy passed the elegant homes. Josh pulled on the left line, turned the horse from the main road into a connecting lane and guided the horse to the end of the lane. "Miss Julia, I believe this is where the hospital is. It ain't the biggest place, but it has been used somewhat in the past."

Julia focused her eyes on Josh. "Josh, can you wait here for me to find the doctor? I don't know what to expect at a place like this." Josh smiled, "I want to help you all I can. Sure! I will wait to see what you can do about your daddy." Julia lifted her skirt above her knee, placed her foot on the buggy step, grasped the metal bar around the seat and lowered herself to the ground.

She paused, brushed off her skirt and blouse and looked at Josh, "You are a real friend. I won't forget this—ever!"

Josh watched as Julia ran to the massive two-story white house and bounded up the steps onto the porch. She disappeared through the open double doors. He steadied the horse with the lines, held the lines in one hand and stepped from the seat to the ground. With the horse's reins in hand, Josh led the horse to the grove of trees beside the house. He observed uniformed men in various stages of convalescence and knew the home was being used as an army hospital.

Julia stopped in the wide hallway and scanned the lower floor. She cautiously walked farther into the hallway, stopped and looked through each doorway. The first floor was filled with men on cots, soldiers hobbling on crutches and men with bound limbs. "Yes, ma'am," a voice echoed in the hallway, "just who are you searching for?" Julia stared at the soldier. His wide galluses contrasted with his light colored underwear top. A full scraggy beard disguised a slight smile as the soldier asked again, "Ma'am, are you looking for somebody special?"

Julia suddenly realized she was gawking and quickly responded, "I'm looking for Doctor Brown." The confederate soldier looked to the top of the staircase and nodded. "The doctor is upstairs. He's been up there for quite a while, now. He ought to be back down here before too much longer." The wounded man cautioned, "He's in a contrary mood. Maybe you ought to wait here rather than go upstairs." Julia tried not to stare, turned toward the open front doors and answered, "Thank you, sir." She walked slowly toward the doors, turned quickly and fixed her eyes on the top of the stairway and moved aimlessly from side to side.

Julia waited for the doctor to appear at the top of the staircase. Minutes became agonizing as Julia continued to pace. Abruptly the stillness was shattered as a bearded man descended the steps and came to a stop at the bottom of the stairway. "Yes, young lady, and what do you want?" the gruff man blared. Julia gazed at his shirtless frame, noted the same light colored underwear, wide galluses and a bloodied apron around his neck. "Well, stop gawking and tell me what you want!" the doctor roared. Doctor Jones walked to the parlor entrance, glanced inside, returned to Julia and bellowed again, "What do you want? I don't have all day! There's some hurt boys here."

Julia's shock disappeared and she responded, "My daddy has been shot and he might be bleeding to death! We live on our farm between here and Rocky Mount. He was shot by Yankee soldiers two days ago and the bleeding won't stop." She excitedly stressed, "And he's as pale as a ghost."

Jones joined his hands behind his back, leaned toward Julia and asked sarcastically, "Does this look like a military hospital to you or do you think these boys are just here on furlough?" The officer stared at Julia and stormed, "Well! What does it look like to you?"

The frightened Julia fixed her eyes on the doctor and angrily informed the officer, "By God Almighty! It was soldiers that shot my daddy and not some discontented neighbor!" Julia regained her boldness and insisted, "It was soldiers, and it was what they came here to destroy that caused my daddy to be shot!" The furious Julia continued in a loud voice, "That makes it a part of what you can do to help."

Jones reached for the apron strap around his neck, removed it over his head, flung the bloodied apron to the floor and shouted, "I have no such responsibility—to you or anybody else! It's the army I'm in and not in private doctoring!"

The trembling girl gazed directly into the eyes of the doctor and blurted, "Do you mean to tell me that you will stand by and let my daddy die, that you will do nothing even though it was soldiers that shot him?"

Julia's wrath intensified as she raged, "What are we supposed to do when the Yankees hurt us when they are trying to hurt you? Are we just something that gets in the way? Don't you think you should have some concern for us, too?"

Doctor Jones frowned at the enraged Julia, pointed his finger and scolded, "Don't you come in here and tell me what I am supposed to do, young lady! Everybody has been suffering and I reckon you'll have your share of it, too. I can't be everywhere, and I can't do all I need to do. If I agree to go to your papa's place, I don't have the conveyance to get there and get back." Brown quickly concluded, "I can't leave the hospital now for any reason anyway."

Julia angrily accused the doctor, "You're only making excuses! I need somebody to help my daddy before he dies! We need some help, now!"

Doctor Brown recognized the uselessness of the argument, glared at Julia and demanded, "What is your name anyway? And who is your daddy?" Julia restrained her anger and answered, "Julia Dupree, and my daddy is Frank Dupree."

Colonel Brown lowered his voice and asked, "If I consent to sending Captain Baker, how do you propose to get him to your home," the doctor quickly added, "and back here before nightfall? I need my assistant surgeon. Captain Baker is the only assistant surgeon in my command."

Julia, elated at the offer, quickly assured the colonel, "I have a buggy outside and a driver; we can be out to my house and have him back way before dark."

Colonel Jones scratched his beard, hesitated, turned toward the open staircase and shouted, "Captain Baker! Captain Baker!"

Julia turned her head upward toward the top of the stairway, watched as a young captain bolted down the steps. "You called, sir?"

The colonel looked at the captain and instructed, "This girl's daddy was shot by the raiding party a day or so ago. From what she tells me the ball may still be lodged in his leg. God only knows what you'll find, but take a probe, some silk stitching and forceps. You've done this before; you will know what to do. God forbid, but be ready to remove his leg if you find it necessary." Colonel Jones reminded the captain, "She has promised to have you back here before nightfall, and I expect her to keep her part of the bargain."

Colonel Brown gestured with his hand toward the front door. "Miss Dupree, Captain Baker will do what he can, but he'd better be back here before night!" Brown quickly asked, "Do you understand that, Miss Dupree?"

Julia quickly acknowledged, "Yes, sir! I understand. The captain will be back before dark—I promise."

Captain Baker looked at the colonel. "Excuse me, sir, I'll get the instruments and be ready in a few minutes." Julia looked at the captain and smiled. "I'll be outside waiting with the buggy when you're ready, Captain."

"God bless you, Colonel! You were our only hope for daddy."

Julia turned and started toward the open front doors, stopped and again assured the colonel, "The captain will be back before dark, and we all are much obliged to you."

Julia briskly walked to the front doors, stepped onto the porch and looked to both sides of the house. She saw Josh and dashed down the steps onto the ground. "Josh! Josh!" she called loudly, "The doctor is sending his assistant with us!" Josh watched Julia as she approached, gazed at her every movement and thought if only she would show some token of interest.

Josh confessed as Julia stopped beside the buggy. "I am really surprised that Doctor Brown would give you any help, Miss Julia. I don't know of anybody the army has helped since they have been using this house."

Julia sighed, looked at Josh and said, "We were desperate

for some help, and I reckon he could tell that by my actions."

Josh, waiting by the buggy stretched his arm to help Julia onto the buggy seat. He felt the softness of her skin and gently squeezed her hand. Julia gripped his hand and steadied her body. She raised her foot to the step, grasped the seat and pulled herself into the buggy. Josh walked to the tree and loosed the lines. He held the lines in one hand, moved to the buggy and grasped the seat railing. He settled into the seat beside Julia. Josh tightened the lines, urged the horse backward and with a snap of the lines pulled the horse's head to the right. He guided the animal toward the front of the house. Josh turned to Julia, caressed her hand and reassured her, "I'll help you and your family in every way I can. I hope you know that!"

Julia, watching the open doorway answered, "Thank you, Josh, you may know that I am obliged to you, and my family is, too."

Captain Baker stopped in the door opening, tucked his shirt in his pants and pulled his galluses to his shoulders. He looked for Miss Dupree and the buggy, tightened his grip on his leather bag and moved quickly down the front steps to the buggy. "Miss Dupree, if you will move to the center of the seat I will sit on the outer side." The captain handed Julia his leather bag. He gripped the metal railing around the back of the buggy seat and pulled himself onto the seat beside Julia.

Julia looked at the captain, "Captain Baker, this is Josh Mewborn."

Josh reached in front of Julia, clasped the captain's hand and responded, "Good to meet you, Captain." Josh slipped to his seat and remarked, "We best be on our way."

Julia shifted closer to Josh as he lashed the lines and verbally urged the horse toward the road to Coolmore.

Josh tried to keep his eyes on the road, but the closeness of Julia made it impossible to concentrate on the center of the road. The buggy wheels slipping in and out of the ruts caused the buggy to tilt and jostled Julia closer to Josh. He could feel Julia's leg against his and that made an unpleasant ride exciting. Josh quickly looked at Julia, placed his hand on hers and gently squeezed it, "Don't worry! We'll be there in a little while." He gripped the reins with both hands, snapped the lines in rapid succession and shouted to the animal, "Yhoo! Yhoo!"

Coolmore came into view and Julia punched her elbow into Captain Baker's side. "There's home! There's home!" Josh tightened the harness lines, slowed the buggy and pulled the horse to the left into the path through the trees. The panting horse slowly pulled the buggy to the backyard.

Josh tugged the horse to a stop. "Miss Julia, take the captain in and I'll see to the horse." Captain Baker quickly leaped from the seat onto the ground. Julia handed him his leather bag, slid to the edge of the seat, grabbed the wheel and leaped to the ground. "Come on with me, Captain," Julia directed. She ran toward the back porch calling, "Mama! Mama! I got a doctor." The captain clutched his medical bag and followed Julia onto the porch.

Ada appeared in the doorway, opened the door and watched the captain as he approached. "Bless you! God bless you! My husband is in a bad fix. Come on with me to the bedroom."

Julia followed behind her mother and motioned to Captain Baker, "Come on! my daddy's here in his bedroom." The captain followed Julia into the room. He looked at Frank lying unconscious, placed his bag on the table beside the bed and began to remove the bloodied strips of sheeting from Frank's leg.

Frank roused from his stupor, gazed at the captain and reacted slowly, "Bless God! My Julia did find some help! Bless the Lord, oh my soul!" Ada and Julia stepped back as Captain Baker continued to remove the bloody wrapping.

"Get me some hot water, quick!" demanded the captain.

Julia responded, "I'll have it here shortly." Baker looked at Ada and directed, "Do you have any clean cloths?—this is a mess. Mr. Dupree's leg has got to be cleaned so I can see what the damage is." Baker removed the last of the stripping, tossed it to the floor and called out, "Where's the hot water?"

Julia, in the kitchen, heard the captain call. She grabbed a cloth from the kitchen table, gripped the handle of the hot kettle and responded loudly, "I'm coming with it!"

She cautiously ran from the kitchen, opened the hallway door and moved quickly to the bedroom. "Mama, will you put the basin on the table?" Her mother quickly reached to the floor, picked up the basin and placed it on the table.

Doctor Baker motioned to Julia and directed, "Pour some hot water in the basin and get those clean cloths good and hot!" Julia poured the hot water in the basin and Ada dipped the cloths. Ada twisted the cloths over the basin as Captain Baker adjusted Frank's exposed leg.

Captain Baker looked at Frank and glanced at Julia and her mother. "Mr. Dupree must have suffered through some long hours. This wound is in foul shape; I can already see that much." The young captain asked, "Is the water and cloths ready, yet?"

Julia answered, "Yes, sir! Are you ready for them?"

Captain Baker looked at Ada, leaned over Frank's leg and directed, "Hand me one of those hot cloths. This wound has got to be cleaned." The doctor touched the warm cloth to Frank's leg. Frank reacted with a shriek of agony, jerked his head from the bolster and cried out, "My God! My God! That pain is killing me!" Baker pushed Dupree's head back onto the bolster. "I know, Mr. Dupree, I know!" Baker continued to wipe the blood from Frank's leg.

Captain Baker stood erect, glanced at Ada and Julia and looked at Mr. Dupree. "Mr. Dupree, the ball is still in your leg." The captain hesitated and added, "I think the bone is shattered, too." The doctor reluctantly counseled, "This is in awful shape, Mr. Dupree. From the looks of things, your leg will have to be removed."

Frank reacted angrily, "Oh, no, you're not! No! No! No!" Dupree fell back onto the bolster. "I ain't going to spend the rest of my days without my two legs!" Frank attempted to raise his voice, "No! No! No!"

Captain Baker stared at Dupree intently. "Mr. Dupree, to keep your leg, you might not have the rest of your days. Do you want to take a chance of gangrene setting in on your leg?" Dupree glared at Baker and answered bitterly, "I don't care what sets in! My leg stays with me!"

Captain Baker looked at Ada and Julia. "He's your husband and your father. What do you want to do?"

Ada walked to Julia's side and placed her arm around her shoulders. "Julia, this has got to be left up to your daddy. We must do what he wants done. It's his limb."

Julia began to cry, looked at Captain Baker and agreed, "Doctor Baker, we'll do as daddy wants."

Frank glared steadfastly at the captain. "Doctor, take out the ball and leave the balance to God. He will provide."

Doctor Baker moved to the foot of the bed. "Mr. Dupree, I will do as you wish, but I must be honest with you. We do not have any laudanum for pain. The blockade has made it impossible for medical supplies to reach us." The captain continued to counsel, "And if gangrene sets in, it will be a godawful way to die."

Dupree raised from the bolster, fixed his stare on the doctor and rebutted, "Then, so be it, Captain!"

Captain Baker looked askance at Ada and Julia and motioned for his medical bag. "Get some more water heated! We'll do what we can."

"I'll get the kettle boiling," Julia offered as she left the room.

Ada walked to the side of the bed, leaned over her husband and caressed his forehead. "We will do exactly as you want, and we will do what we can to see you through."

Frank looked into Ada's eyes and smiled. "I know you will. I know you will do what you can. I love you, Ada." Frank settled back onto the bolster, looked at the doctor and in a reconciled voice, uttered, "Do the best you can, Captain, and God help us all!"

Captain Baker opened his medical bag and removed the probe and forceps. He fumbled in the bag, pulled out a small spool of silk thread and a curved needle. "Mrs. Dupree, this will not be a pretty sight, but I will need you and your daughter to help me."

The captain stared at Frank and nodded. "Are you sure about this, Mr. Dupree? Either way it's going to be a painful thing."

Frank responded, "I'm sure! Get on with it."

Julia doubled a kitchen cloth and removed the steaming kettle from the iron woodstove. She held her arm outward to balance herself and moved cautiously toward the porch. She slowly opened the kitchen door, walked onto the veranda and stepped carefully to the doorway to the house. She paused and held the kettle away from her side. She pulled the door open and stepped into the hallway. "Here's the hot water, Doctor Baker." The doctor responded, "Very good, fill the basin half way." Julia walked to the table, carefully lifted the kettle above the basin and slowly poured the steaming water into the basin.

Captain Baker picked up the instruments beside his medical bag and placed them into the basin of hot water. "Miss Dupree, spread out a bolster case on the bed. I will need a clean place to work from." Julia bolted to the chest of drawers, removed a bolster case, returned to the bed and spread it at the foot. "Thank you, young lady," acknowledged the captain. He walked to the table, reached into the cooled water and retrieved the instruments. Captain Baker placed the instruments on the bolster cover, looked at Dupree and asked, "Are you ready, Mr. Dupree? This won't be the easiest thing you've ever done."

Frank's body became tense as Captain Baker wiped the wound. Captain Baker picked up the probe. He held it as he would a pencil, inserted the pointed end into the pierced muscle and began to move the instrument to locate the ball. Dupree jerked his leg and shrieked in agony. The captain drew back, looked at Frank and firmly insisted, "Mr. Dupree, I can't get that ball out if you don't hold your leg in place!"

Baker quickly instructed, "One of you go get that Mewborn boy in here to hold this man's leg."

Julia reacted instantly, ran to the hallway, darted through the backdoor onto the porch and shouted, "Josh! Josh!" Mewborn ran from the rear of the house, rounded the corner of the kitchen and saw Julia standing on the porch.

He knew something was wrong. "Can I help with something, Miss Julia?"

The trembling girl quickly informed Josh, "Doctor Baker wants you to help hold down daddy's leg!"

Josh jumped onto the porch and followed Julia into Frank's bedroom. "Let me know what to do, Doctor!"

The doctor looked at Josh and ordered, "Get to the other side of the bed and hold down Mr. Dupree's leg just as firm as you can! Don't let his leg move an inch!"

Josh quickly moved to the opposite side of the bed, leaned over and firmly grasped Mr. Dupree's leg below the knee. "I've got his leg, Captain!"

The confederate surgeon began the probing again. Dupree stiffened, screamed and raised his shoulders from the bolster. He relaxed and dropped back onto the bolster. "Very good, Josh. You held his leg under control," the surgeon complimented.

Captain Baker drew back from Frank's trembling body. "It's not imbedded in the bone. I think I can get it out with the forceps." The captain reached to the bolster cover at the foot of the bed, picked up the forceps and leaned closer to Frank's leg. "Hold his leg down! I'll get the ball out this time." Baker inserted the forceps slowly into the open wound. Dupree's body stiffened; he screamed again from the piercing pain.

Captain Baker withdrew the forceps, held the bloody forceps in full view and declared, "There it is! It's out!" Frank relaxed onto the bolster, his face covered with perspiration. The captain noticed Dupree's pallid color and informed him, "That might have been the worst part, Mr. Dupree, provided you don't get gangrene." The Confederate surgeon apologized, "I'm sorry, Mr. Dupree, but we don't have any silver nitrate, either. I won't be able to cauterize that gash." Surgeon Baker quickly continued, "The bleeding may get worse."

Frank closed his eyes momentarily, sighed and remarked, "I'll just have to chance it. There ain't no other choice."

Doctor Baker moved to the bolster on the foot of the bed, picked up the curved needle and threaded the silk thread through the eye. "Mewborn!" the captain instructed, "hold his leg secure again. This hole will have to be stitched closed." Baker leaned over Dupree's leg, inserted the threaded needle through the outer skin, pulled the stitch closed and tied the silk thread. Josh gripped Mr. Dupree's leg. The surgeon pushed the needle through the skin again.

Frank jerked his head from the bolster, tightened his grip on the sides of the mattress and screamed, "My God! My God! Take it slow, Doctor!"

The surgeon looked at Julia and asked, "Do you have any scissors? These silk threads have got to be cut." Julia bolted from the bedroom, into the hallway and ran to the other downstairs bedroom. Julia pulled out the drawer of her mother's sewing table, grabbed the scissors and yelled out, "I got them! I'm coming!" She ran down the hallway, entered the bedroom and handed the scissors to the surgeon. The captain quickly snipped the two stitches and looked at Mr. Dupree. "One more left to close the wound." The doctor threaded the needle, snipped the thread to the length he wanted and leaned over Dupree's leg. "Josh, hold his leg tight one more time," the captain instructed as he pierced the outer skin with the curved needle.

Frank's body tightened as the captain pulled the stitch and tied the two ends. Frank moaned, loosened his grip on the mattress edges and asked, "Is that the last of this misery?"

Captain Baker placed his hands on the lower part of his back, stretched backward with a loud sign. "No, Mr. Dupree, that is not the last of it. Your leg bone has been smashed, and that means I've got to put a splint on that leg." Captain Baker nodded at Josh, "Mewborn, look out back for some boards; I need two about two or three inches wide and about two feet long." The surgeon advised Dupree, "This is only temporary until you can make better arrangements."

Josh looked at Julia and motioned, "Come on with me. You can find your daddy's saw while I look for some boards." Julia and Josh quickly left the bedroom, bolted onto the veranda, jumped to the ground and ran to the barn area. Julia shouted as she passed the back part of the house, "Dolly! Mama needs some help in the house!"

Josh saw the remnants of the corn crib, observed the boards and called to Julia, "Julia! These boards look just fine! Find your daddy's hand saw!" Josh looked toward Julia as she ran to the barn and quickly thought, my God, I called her Julia, not Miss Julia.

Julia knew where the saw was kept. She ran to the shelter attached to the barn, grabbed the hand saw from the peg and ran back to Josh. "This is the only one I know of." Josh took the saw by the handle, placed the board on his knee and cut a two-foot piece from the corncrib siding. "That looks about right!" Julia agreed and snapped, "Cut another one just like it." Josh placed another board on his knee and ripped the saw blade quickly through. He hurriedly grabbed the boards and darted back to the house. Julia ran ahead of Josh, jumped onto the veranda, flung open the door and held it open as Josh ran through. The two entered the bedroom as Julia instructed, "Josh, give the doctor the boards!"

The surgeon took the two boards, looked at them and lamented, "It'll have to do at least for the time being." Doctor Baker looked around the room and in exasperation asked, "Is there any quilting to wrap around these splints? They will be mighty hard next to his leg without it."

Julia quickly suggested, "I know where there is some old quilting! I'll be right back!" She ran from the room and dashed up the stairway. The sound of a closet door opening echoed down the staircase followed by the hurried steps of Julia as she shouted, "Here's some pieces! Here's some quilting!" Baker looked at Julia and instructed, "Rip it up and wrap it around these splints!"

Baker looked at Ada and asked, "Do you have any more clean sheeting? This wound is going to have to be covered before we can put the splints on his leg." Ada saw Dolly as she passed the doorway and called, "Dolly! Go to the other bedroom and rip up some old sheets." Dolly hurried to the bedroom, pulled some sheeting from a drawer, rushed back to Ada's side and suggested, "You'uns can rip it better than me." Ada snatched the sheeting from Dolly, grabbed the scissors from the bolster cover, snipped the sheeting and ripped it into strips.

The Confederate assistant surgeon reminded Ada and Frank of the medical supply shortage. "Mr. Dupree, I am sure you and your wife know we are short in all medical supplies. We are just about out of tincture of iodine. We have very little at the hospital and I don't have any with me at all. I don't know what to recommend to use on the wound. Our supplies are exhausted."

Dupree raised his head above the bolster and looked around the room. "We'll make out. God will provide. Go ahead and do the best you can." Dupree attempted to encourage the young captain with his reconciling counsel. "Captain, you've done all you can do—and we are obliged to you. Go ahead and put some covering over the hole and if you think it best, put the splints in place." Dupree continued to reassure the captain, "There ain't but so much you can do. We have to depend on the Lord for the healing."

Dolly heard the conversation as she remained outside the room in the hallway. "Mr. Frank," Dolly interrupted, "If'n you want, I have some poke salve what will draw out the poison from that ugly place. Me and Nate has used it many-a time and hit ain't done us no harm." Frank looked puzzled as he gazed at the surgeon. "What do you think, Captain? Do you know of any harm it might do?"

Captain Baker looked at Dolly and then at Mr. Dupree and replied, "I really don't know, Mr. Dupree. It may do well or it may do more harm than good. It's your leg, sir."

Frank looked at Dolly, then glanced at Ada and Julia. "Get your salve, Dolly, and put some on before it's wrapped." Dolly hurried from the room and ran to her quarters.

"While we wait for her to get back with the salve, we can go ahead and get ready to cover the wound and fix the splints," advised the surgeon. "I believe this lady promised Colonel Jones to have me back before nightfall," reflected the captain. Captain Baker backed away from the bedside and reminded the Duprees again, "Mr. Dupree, I have to tell you again—there is no laudanum to be had. I don't have any suggestions for you to take the edge off the pain. Our boys at the hospital are suffering, too." The Union commanders seem to think the more we hurt, the sooner we'll quit."

Dolly appeared in the doorway with a glass jar in her hand. "Mr. Frank, here it be. If'n the soljur will smear it on the hole it will surely draw the poison out." Mr. Dupree looked at Dolly and directed the captain, "Captain, put it on and cover it up." Captain Baker took the open jar from Dolly, dipped his finger into the contents and smeared it over the wound. "Mr. Dupree, I can only hope you don't get gangrene." Baker folded a strip of the cotton sheeting, placed it over the wound and began to wrap strips of sheeting around Dupree's leg.

"Get me those two strips of wood, Mewborn," directed the captain. Josh reached to the floor, picked up the boards and handed one to the doctor. The doctor further directed, "Young lady, hold your daddy's leg steady as I slide some strips under his leg to secure the two splints." Baker pushed three strips of sheeting under Dupree's leg, placed one of the quilt-wrapped boards alongside his leg and directed, "Mewborn, put the other board against his leg and hold both boards in place while I tighten the strips." Captain Baker drew the strips tight and tied the ends. "That ought to hold your leg in one place for a spell. You need to keep it still for at least a month."

Captain Baker picked up his instruments, placed them in his leather medical bag and looked at Josh and Julia. "You promised to have me back before dark. We best be on our way." Julia looked at Josh, smiled and asked, "Josh, can you take the doctor to the hospital on your way home? I think I best stay with mama now."

Josh nodded, "I'll help your folks anyway I can, Julia."

Ada walked toward Josh, reached out her arms and embraced the young boy. "We're much obliged to you, and the Lord bless you."

Julia reminded the captain, "I aim to keep my word. Are you ready, Captain Baker?" Josh followed the captain and Julia as they moved from the hallway to the veranda. Captain Baker looked at Josh and asked, "Where is the buggy?" Josh responded, "It's behind the kitchen," and quickly suggested, "would you wait for me there?"

Julia focused her deep brown eyes on Josh, smiled and moved closer. She lurched toward Josh and embraced him. "Josh, I love you for what you've done for me today."

Josh felt the softness of Julia's body pressed to his. He responded lovingly, "Julia—may I call you Julia? I hate all this has happened to you. I want you to know that you can call on me anytime." Julia released Josh, stepped back and smiled. Josh viewed her chestnut hair glistening in the late afternoon sun, stared into her deep brown eyes and felt all the emotions of a maturing young man. "Julia, if you only knew how I feel about you," Josh stammered as he reached and placed his cupped hands on her cheeks. He lifted her head to his face. Julia's inviting eyes spoke to Josh as he leaned his head and pressed his lips to hers. Time slipped into forgetfulness.

"Mewborn! Will you hurry?" reverberated from the rear of the kitchen. Josh looked longingly at Julia and asked, "May I call sometimes at your convenience?"

Julia reacted with receptiveness. "Yes, Josh. You are welcome here anytime."

Young Mewborn, elated with Julia's acceptance, turned and ran to the rear of the kitchen. "Sorry to keep you waiting, Captain!" Josh untied the reins from the post and leaped into his buggy. He pulled the lines to the left, turned the horse in the direction of the road to Tarborough and snapped the lines, "Gwick! Gwick!" The horse began to trot along the path beside the house. Josh waved to Julia as he urged the horse past the veranda. Josh full of excitement, tapped the lines rapidly, turned onto the road and urged the horse faster.

Julia watched the buggy disappear in a rising pillar of dust. She walked toward the doorway to the hall. She hesitated before entering the main house and reflected, my Lord, what a day this has been!

# CHAPTER SEVENTEEN

Ada walked around the foot of the bed, sat gently on the mattress at Frank's feet and stared through the open window. The sun was descending in the southwest and the tops of the trees obscured half the roundness of the blinding golden orb. Rays of departing daylight caused the room to dim in the corners as Ada thought of the coming darkness and the long night of pain in store for her husband. She stared at the sunset in a long period of silence. Frank raised his head, looked at Ada staring out the window and uttered weakly, "Oh, Lord, I do hate to see the night come on. I know the misery of this leg will make the night seem forever. There is nothing to ease the pain, and I don't want none of that whiskey, neither."

Ada turned from the window, looked at Frank sympathetically and responded gently, "I know, Frank. I know! I pray to God that you will be able to rest and not have to suffer through the night. Lord knows I dread this night for you."

Frank replied, "Ada, you and Julia have done all you could. There ain't nothing else that can be done. Maybe a breeze will begin to stir after the sun goes down and the night won't be so bad."

Julia stood quietly in the doorway as her father and mother shared their feelings. She walked to the bedside, leaned over her father and gently stroked his forehead and assured him, "Daddy, if there is anything that can be done to make the night more bearable for you, Mama and me will see that it's done."

Frank focused his eyes on Julia and in a hushed voice said, "I know you will, my little girl. I know you will." Frank's eyes closed momentarily, then opened gradually and a weak smile changed his countenance. He spoke slowly, "Julia, my dear little girl, you have suffered through a lot of things for the last few days. I don't think we could have done anything to stop it;

we would have stopped your hurt if we could. This war has made your life miserable. I wish your young life could be more pleasurable. It may be that our people, both north and south, will soon have enough of this suffering and we can go back to our way of life." He closed his eyes, remained silent for a moment, then with a weak smile rallied to continue, "I was lucky this time—I'm still here. There is coming a time when your mama and me will not be here, my dear Julia, and Coolmore will be yours and Willie's. I pray to the Lord Almighty that Willie will be spared in this war." Frank closed his eyes again and rested his head on the bolster. He slowly opened his eyes, looked at Julia as she stood over him and attempted a smile. "Julia, my Julia, there are times in life when things happen that we do not understand. Sometimes we make vain tries at trying to understand and we cannot satisfy ourselves with any answers. Now seems to be one of those times, and we must come to the place where we are made willing by God to admit what the Lord said."

Julia touched her father's hand, as tears swelled in her eyes and asked, "What did the Lord say, Daddy?"

Frank forced a smile and answered, "Even so Father, because it seemeth good in Thy sight."

Ada moved beside Julia, grasped her hand tightly and quietly watched as Frank closed his eyes and lapsed into sleep.

Ada constrained a smile as she looked at Julia and said softly, "I reckon your daddy is just plain tired, and sleep will give him a little relief."

Julia squeezed her mother's hand and moved from the bed. "I'll go out and check to see how Dolly is doing."

Julia walked softly to the hallway, turned toward the back door and quietly made her way to the porch. She carefully closed the door behind her and walked to the kitchen. Julia looked through the kitchen doorway and saw the empty kitchen. She stepped from the porch onto the steps and walked quickly to the rear of the kitchen. Julia stopped and watched Dolly as she lifted the clothes-laden paddle from the black iron wash pot. Steam floated upward as Dolly moved the paddle to an empty tin tub.

Dolly called out, "Nate! Draw me some fresh water from the well." Dolly let the steaming clothes drop from the paddle into the tine tub and shouted again, "Nate! I need some fresh water to rinch dis washin'."

Julia stood silently and watched Nate as he lowered the bucket into the well and hoisted a full bucket of water to the top. "Nate!" Julia called, "I'll get another bucket and tote the water to the tub for Dolly. You just keep drawing up the bucket." Julia observed a rusted bucket beside the well, joined Nate at the well and held the bucket for him to empty the water from the well bucket into hers. She felt the weight as Nate emptied the water into her bucket, and quickly moved to pour the fresh water into the rinsing tub.

Dolly reached to lift the last of the clothes from the wash pot, raised the paddle above the iron pot and carried the steaming clothes to the rinsing tub. Dolly began to stir the clothes in the rinse tub. She looked at Julia and spoke gently, "Miss Julia, I's been praying for yore daddy. I got a good feeling 'bout him. I b'leves he gonna be alright."

Julia watched as Dolly began moving the clothes around the rinsing tub with the paddle. Julia stood quietly as Dolly continued to stir the clothes.

Julia turned slowly, felt the abrasive soil in her shoes and realized the day had passed and she had worn no stockings. Gazing at the western horizon she reflected, where has this day gone? The day that was closing seemed to have had no beginning. The happenings from early morning until early evening were like a horrible dream; one from which she would awake and realize everything was all right.

Julia, lost in thought, was startled as Dolly shouted, "Nate!

Get over here and help me twist dese clothes! Dey got to be on the line 'fore dark."

Nate ran from the well, joined Dolly at the rinsing tub, looked at Dolly and sarcastically declared, "Well, git a handful and I'll hold one end whilst you twist."

Julia watched as Dolly began twisting the clothes. She moved closer to Nate and Dolly and meekly asked, "Dolly, can you fix some of that special tea that you boil sometimes for easing pain?"

Nathan, gripping one end of the twisted clothes, stared at Dolly and asked, "How'd she know 'bout that brew?"

Dolly glared toward Nathan and retorted, "She's been 'round long enough to watch how we take the edge off'n pain."

Dolly focused her eyes on Julia and in a tender voice asked, "You be thinkin' 'bout your daddy, don't you? You be wonderin' how he's gonna fare dis night, ain't you?"

Julia glanced at Nathan, looked directly at Dolly and admitted, "You're right, Dolly. I dread to see the night coming on 'cause I know what's likely to be. That bullet hole might fester and put Daddy in mighty tight straits."

Dolly untwisted the clothes and began separating the pieces. She glared at Nathan and directed, "Nate! On de other side of de tracks at de end of the path dere's a big willow tree. Fetch yourself a kitchen knife and strip me some bark from the bottom of the tree."

Dolly looked at Julia, stared at the lowering sun and instructed, "Nate! you best be 'bout it now; dark will be here 'fore long."

Nathan smiled at Julia and confidently added, "Don't fret none, Miss Julia, I know right where she's talkin' 'bout." Nathan smiled at Dolly, turned toward their quarters and ran down the path.

Dolly stopped separating the pieces of clothing, and looked

compassionately at Julia. "Miss Julia, I'll fix some willow bark tea when I fix supper tonight. It takes a spell to fix it right; hit'll be ready if'n yore daddy needs it tonight." Dolly began to separate the clothes, looked at Julia and shrugged her shoulders. "Dere ain't but so much de tea can do. Hit'll take the edge off de pain and dat's 'bout all."

Julia grabbed Dolly's wet hand, squeezed it with a pleasant smile and gratefully acknowledged, "Thank you, Dolly! Lord knows you're a Godsend."

Julia looked toward the western horizon as the sun was disappearing behind the treetops and watched Nathan as he made his way to gather the willow bark. She looked at Dolly and asked, "You want me to help you hang the washing?" Dolly shook her head and answered, "No, child, you go in and help yore mama. I 'spect she'll be needin' some help long 'bout now."

Julia looked again at the sun sinking behind the treetops and started walking toward the veranda. She detected the aroma of boiling cabbage as she neared the kitchen and thought how good that would be with some fried corn bread. The thought of cured ham crossed her mind, but she realized all the meat had been taken from the smokehouse by the Yankee soldiers. Julia wondered if her mother might be using pure lard as seasoning. Lard would be the only thing available now. As she neared the kitchen, the aroma became distinct as Julia realized she had not eaten since earlier in the day.

"Mama!" Julia called, as she stepped onto the veranda, "will we have enough for supper tonight?"

Ada replied, "I think so, but it sure takes a bit of doing to put something on the table when we've been stripped of everything. I expect all Frank will want is some cabbage soup."

Julia sat at the table, stared at her mother and asked, "Mama, is Daddy still resting?" Ada turned from the hot stove and wiped her face with her apron. "Julia, I expect he will be waking up pretty quick now and he might be hungry. Help me around here before you do anything else."

Julia got up from the table and offered, "What can I do, Mama?"

Ada directed, "Go to the garden patch and pull up some of those big onions and wash them off at the well. They will give these cabbages a little more flavor. Your daddy likes onions with cabbage and corn bread."

Twilight at Coolmore was Julia's favorite time. The blistering sun was obscured as it sank below the horizon. Only the brightness mingled with the dust hinted of the departing sun.

Summer breezes ceased as day dissolved into night. Without any wind moving the window curtains, darkness often meant a long sleepless night. Nature's creatures of the night steadily began their invitation to the darkness. The mighty oaks of Coolmore cast shadowy figures below their mantle of leaves as night swallowed the light. In the east a sallow light slowly lightened the treetops as a full moon emerged above the trees.

Grasping the oil lamp on the bureau, Ada removed the chimney from the lamp and set it beside the lamp. She looked at Julia standing in the bedroom doorway and asked, "Julia, will you get me some matches from the kitchen table. I forgot to bring some with me after we cleaned the table." Julia replied, "Yes ma'am, I'll be right back. There's enough light to see my way around in the kitchen."

Julia moved quickly to the kitchen and returned with the box of matches.

Ada glanced at Frank as he lay in the light flooding through the open window and assured him, "Frank, I'll have some light in here directly. I know you're tired of this dark room. I hope what you had for supper will hold you till day."

Julia appeared in the doorway, walked to her mother and

held out the box of matches. "You want me to strike the match while you hold the lamp?"

Ada picked up the oil lamp, turned the wick high in the mantle and held it out to Julia. "Julia, you put the flame to the wick."

Frank watched as his wife and daughter stood in front of the bureau. The mirror over the bureau reflected Julia placing the flaming match to the wick of the lamp held by Ada. He watched as the flame danced upward and the darkened room changed to a shade of dim yellow.

Ada placed the lamp on the bureau, carefully picked up the chimney and placed it into the clips of the mantle base. She turned down the wick and the flickering light became steady. The low dancing flame leaped to one side of the chimney and illuminated one wall, then danced to the other side of the chimney and lightened another wall. Light bounded from wall to wall in erratic order.

Julia laid the matchbox on the bureau and walked to the open window. "Daddy, I think I'll go up to the top and see what things look like at night."

Frank turned his head on the bolster and smiled, "You go right ahead. There's enough light you can find your way, alright."

Julia walked to the hallway, and made her way to the bottom of the stairway. She stopped, sat down on the bottom step and unlaced her shoes. With her shoes in her hand, her feet felt free as she darted up the steps to the second floor. The steep incline of the steps to the cupola slowed Julia as she made her way through the opening into the dome. Julia stepped carefully to the west windows of the cupola, leaned out and viewed the ashen colored landscape. The moonlight exposed the cotton field, trampled by the hogs that escaped the Yankee soldiers. She cautiously moved to the south window and viewed the destroyed barns and empty corncrib. A brighter light flooded the east window as Julia leaned out the window and observed the field of flattened corn. A feeling of bitterness overcame her as she thought, what in God's name are we going to do? Everything has been destroyed. Julia sat on the cupola flooring, pulled her knees under her chin and placing her arms around her knees began to cry. The moon moved from the eastern sky into the darkness of the southern sky. Time and space became a veil separating Julia from her thoughts and the reality of the night.

Julia's absorption was interrupted when Ada called quietly, "Juuulia! it's time for bed."

She got up from the floor, descended the steep stairs from the cupola and stepped quietly to the top of the steps. "Mama, I'm going on to bed, now. I don't need a lamp. It's bright enough by the moon."

Julia walked to her room, turned into the doorway and removed her skirt and blouse. The moon was behind the house. Julia's room was dark. She dropped her clothes onto the floor and fell on the feather mattress. Exhausted, Julia pulled the bolster under her head and sleep quickly engulfed her.

The quietness of the night was broken by a cry of pain. Julia awoke, lay still and listened to be certain what she heard was not a dream. "Ohhh! Ohhh!" Julia raised from the bed, put her feet on the floor and listened intently.

"Oh, my God!" Frank moaned. Julia ran to her bedroom door, stopped and listened again. "Oh, Lord! I'm cold!" Frank moaned again.

Julia dashed down the stairs and stopped in the doorway of the bedroom. She looked at her mother pulling the bedspread over Frank, "Mama, how can daddy be cold here in the middle of July?"

Ada turned toward the doorway and instructed, "Julia, light the lamp! Your daddy's got the agues! He's cold, but I can feel he's burning up!" Ada continued to wrap the spread around

Frank and directed, "Julia, run and get a quilt from the upstairs closet!"

Julia quickly turned and dashed up the stairs, flung open the closet at the top of the staircase and grabbed a quilt. With the quilt under her arm she bolted down the steps and into the bedroom. "Here's a quilt, Mama, what else can I do?"

Ada directed, "Light the lamp! We need some light in here."

Julia quickly moved to the bureau, removed the chimney from the lamp base and fumbled for the match box. She opened the match box, spilled the matches on the top of the bureau, retrieved a single match and struck it against the box. The light from the flickering flame reflected from the mirror as she placed it to the lamp wick.

Ada, spreading the quilt over Frank raised her voice, "Will you hurry, girl!" Julia blew the flame from the match, adjusted the lamp wick and placed the chimney on the lamp base. "It's done, mama! What else can I do?"

Frank attempted to turn on his side, rolled to his back and wailed, "I'm cold! I'm cold!—Good God, I'm cold!" He rolled to his side again, stopped and rolled onto his back again and cried out, "My leg is poundin' in pain! Ooh, my Lord, my leg is throbbin'!"

Ada glanced at Julia standing in the dim lamp light. "Girl! get a pan of fresh water from the porch!"

Julia bolted to the back porch, grabbed a basin and dipped the water from a bucket into the basin. She picked up the basin with one hand and walked cautiously to the door, opened the door with her other hand and stepped carefully back to the bedroom. "Put the basin on the table beside the bed, Julia," directed her mother.

Ada dipped a towel into the basin, lifted it above the basin and twisted the excess water from the towel and placed it on Frank's forehead. Ada stared at Julia and lamented, "I don't know anything else to do."

Julia dashed through the bedroom door, stopped and turned toward her mother. "Mama! I know something to do! Let me get my robe on and I'll be right back! Keep Daddy quiet if you can!"

Julia ran up the staircase, and in the dark darted into her bedroom. She hesitated as her eyes adjusted to the darkness, rushed to her closet and removed her robe. She searched her way from the bedroom and into the hallway. Julia hesitated at the top of the stairs, slipped one arm into the sleeve of the robe and twisted her body to slip her other arm into the sleeve.

With a quick tug on both arms she lifted the robe onto her shoulders. "Mama! I'll be right there," Julia shouted as she bolted down the steps.

Ada looked at Julia as she stood in the doorway. "Julia! What has got into you, girl?" The flame of the lamp danced atop the wick, casting a dim light from one side of the room to the other.

Frank raised his head from the bolster and groaned, "Oh, Lord! My leg is a-throbbin'!"

Julia glanced at her father, turned from the bedroom door and running to the back door, shouted, "Dolly's got something for misery. I'll be right back!"

Julia burst onto the back porch, grabbed the lantern from the doorfacing and ran back to the bedroom. She ran to the bureau, placed the lantern beside the lamp and pushed the lever to raise the chimney. Reaching for a match, she informed her mother, "Dolly was going to boil some willow bark tonight in case we needed some relief for daddy." Julia struck the match against the box and touched it to the lantern wick. The flame began to rise above the wick as Julia lowered the chimney into place. "I'll see if Dolly made it," Julia added as she adjusted the wick of the lantern.

Ada continued to secure the quilt onto Frank as he shouted, "Good God! I'm willing to try anything—anything!"

Julia held the lantern at her side, ran from the room and darted to the back door. She stopped on the veranda, peered into the darkness and jumped from the porch onto the ground. Steadying herself with the lantern in her hand she began running toward Nathan and Dolly's quarters. The sky was clear and the moon cast a pallid light over the back of the house.

Nearing the quarters, Julia began to shout, "Dolly! Dolly! Get up, I need you! Nate! I need you!"

Dolly jabbed Nate, "Get up and see what that young'un wants." Nate pulled on his pants, slipped his galluses over his arms and walked to the door. He opened the door and viewed Miss Julia holding the lantern above her head. "Good Lord, child, what ails you?"

Julia lowered the lantern to her side and in a quivering voice cried out, "Tell Dolly we need some of her tea! Tell her to come up to the house and fix it in the kitchen." Raising the lantern she quickly added, "Daddy's in a bad fix—a real bad fix!"

Dolly called out from inside the cabin, "Miss Julia! Start a little fire in the kitchen stove. I have to heat the tea! I'll be dere as fast as I can."

Julia moved from the cabin door, turned toward the main house and ran to the veranda. She stopped at the edge of the porch, gripped the lantern tight, raised her foot onto the porch and lurched onto the veranda. Steadying the lantern, she dashed into the kitchen and set the lantern on the kitchen table.

Remembering Dolly's directions, Julia placed some kindling and stove wood into the firebox and began to look for the matches. Oh, heavens, she thought, they're in the bedroom.

Julia ran from the kitchen, burst through the doorway into the hall and ran to the bedroom door. "Mama! Dolly is coming to the kitchen to heat some willow tea!" Julia went on frantically, "She told me to start a fire in the kitchen stove to heat the tea." Reaching for the match box Julia added, "I've got to get the fire started."

Ada rushed to Julia, grabbed her by her shoulders and demanded, "You be careful with a fire in the kitchen. Let Dolly see to it and you get back in here!"

Ada heard Julia as she flung open the door and acknowledged Dolly as both entered the kitchen.

Frank raised his head from the bolster, looked at Ada and asked, "What in the world is going on?"

Ada walked to the side of the bed, leaned over and tucked the quilt under Frank's shoulders. "Julia is helping Dolly fix some Willow Bark Tea for your pain. I just heard her and Dolly go in the kitchen. Maybe you will have some relief shortly."

Frank jerked in pain and cried out, "Oh, Lord! Anything to help—anything!"

Ada removed the damp cloth from Frank's forehead. She dipped it into the basin, twisted the excess water from the cloth, folded it and placed it back onto Frank's forehead. Frank yelled again, "This blasted contraption holding my leg stiff is a pure misery! If I live to see the light of day, it's a-comin' off."

Coal oil fumes from the lamp permeated the room. The air was still and the flickering flame of the lamp continued to cast its waves of dim yellow light onto the walls. Frank remained twisting in agony with every beat of his heart. Ada maintained her ritual changing of the damp cloth as time stretched the agonizing darkness.

Ada heard hurried footsteps in the hallway, looked and saw Julia and Dolly as they passed through the doorway.

Frank raised his head from the bolster and watched as Julia and Dolly approached the bed. Julia looked down at her father. "Daddy, me and Dolly fixed you some Willow Bark Tea. Dolly tells me it will take the edge off the pain. It might not get it all, but she says it'll make the suffering bearable."

Frank stared at Julia and in a barely audible voice, "Anything, Julia—anything."

Ada took the cup from Julia's hand and moved to the opposite side of the bed. She leaned and placed her hands under Frank's shoulders and gently raised him forward.

Frank shrieked in pain, "Good God, woman! Don't move me so quick!"

Ada looked hurt as she lowered his shoulders back onto the bolster. "Frank," insisted Ada, "I'll try to be a little easier this time, I reckon this tea is the only hope you got to ease off any. There is nothing else we know to do."

Ada placed her arm under Frank's head, slowly raised his head as Julia put the cup of tea to his lips.

Frank sipped the warm tea, lifted his hand and pushed the cup away from his mouth. "God! That's the worst tasting stuff!"

Dolly looked at Mr. Dupree and smiled. "I know Misster Frank, I know, but hit will take the edge off'n de pain." Ada continued to hold Frank as Julia pressed the cup to his lips again. Frank sipped and then swallowed as Julia kept the cup to his lips.

Dolly took the cup from Julia, saw it was empty and smiled broadly, "He took right smart. Hit ought to be working in 'bout a hour or so."

Ada gently lowered Frank's head to the bolster as he sighed, "Thank you! Thank you all, so much."

Julia stood erect, and looked at her mother and Dolly. "If that gives him any relief, we got Dolly to thank for that. She's the one that knew about it and fixed it."

Frank forced a smile, jerked in pain and slackened onto the bolster.

Dolly tugged on Miss Julia's arm and motioned with her

eyes. "Help me in the kitchen, Miss Julia."

Julia looked at her mother as she stood between the bed and the open window. "I'll be right back. I'll be with Dolly in the kitchen."

Julia walked down the hallway, through the door onto the veranda. She opened the back door and waited for Dolly.

Dolly passed through the door and went to the kitchen. Julia closed the door and followed Dolly into the kitchen. Dolly looked at Julia and instructed, "Miss Julia, leave de coals in de stove wid de pot on de top to keep de tea warm. In 'bout a hour give Mr. Frank another cup of de tea. I don't know if'n hit'll help, but dere ain't much else to do."

Julia, with tears in her eyes, embraced Dolly tightly. "Dolly, you are a blessing from the Almighty."

Julia leaned over the kitchen table and turned down the lamp wick. "Dolly, I won't bother you no more tonight. I'll leave the lamp on low for the rest of the night. Mama or me will have to be back in here, I'm sure."

Dolly smiled at Julia as she walked from the kitchen. "I best get back to Nate, Miss Julia."

The pale light from the moon cast enough light for Julia to make her way back to the bedside of her father. She entered the room, noticed the light from the lamp as it skipped from one wall to the other as the flame danced on the wick.

Ada, sitting in a chair beside the bed, looked at Julia as she came into the room. "Julia, you can go back to bed. I think I will sit up with your daddy for the rest of the night."

Julia stopped beside her mother and looked at her restless father. "No ma'am, I'll stay up with you. You might need some help when he wakes up." Ada reached for Julia's hand, pulled her close and quietly agreed, "I would feel better with you here, Julia; you use that rocker and maybe you can nap a bit."

Julia sat in the rocker, leaned forward and removed her

shoes. She gathered her robe around her waist and settled as the rocker leaned back.

Stillness and calm enveloped Coolmore. Julia was hypnotized as she watched the flame dart from side to side on the lamp wick. Her head dropped as a moment of unconsciousness overwhelmed her weary frame.

Frank's body suddenly convulsed, the quietness was broken by a loud cry, "Ada! Ada! I'm dying!" Ada leaped from her chair, looked at Frank and saw beads of perspiration on his forehead. "Julia, get some fresh water in the basin. Your daddy's mighty hot."

Julia picked up the basin, ran into the hallway and onto the porch. She stopped and placed the basin on the table beside the water bucket and ran into the kitchen. Opening the firebox, Julia thought, maybe I'd better stir the ashes to warm the tea. She reached for the stove poker in the woodbin and stirred the smoldering ashes. She closed the firebox door of the stove and ran back onto the porch. The frantic Julia dipped water into the basin, let the dipper fall onto the table and with the basin in one hand moved quickly through the doorway and down the hall to the bedroom.

Ada looked at Julia as she entered the bedroom. "Julia, put the basin on the table. I'll put some fresh cool water on your daddy's forehead."

Julia carefully placed the basin on the table, turned to her mother and asked, "Do you want me to warm up some of the tea that Dolly made?"

Ada, twisting the excess water from the cloth, responded, "I reckon so, that's all we can do."

Julia dashed from the bedroom, into the hallway and onto the veranda. She saw the dim light from the lamp on the kitchen table, hurried into the kitchen and clutched a large cup from the cupboard. She moved to the stove, removed the pot lid and dipped the cup into the warm tea. The tea dripped from the cup as Julia moved cautiously to the door.

Julia pushed the kitchen door open, cautiously walked onto the porch and carefully stepped to the door of the hallway. She paused, opened the door with one hand and balanced the cup of tea with her other hand. "Mama! I got the tea!" Julia called as she moved through the hallway to the bedroom.

Ada watched as Julia approached the bed with the dripping cup of tea. "Julia, you stand on this side of the bed and I'll go to the other side and raise his head so's you can put the cup to his mouth."

Ada quickly made her way around the foot of the bed and stopped at the head of the bed. "Julia, I'll lift his head and you see that he gets the tea."

Ada gently slipped her arm under Frank's shoulder and slowly lifted his head. Frank, racked with pain cried out, "Oh, my Lord! Death will be a relief."

Julia placed her hand behind her father's head and with the tea cup in her other hand raised it to his mouth. She tilted the cup as Frank sipped the tea. Julia looked at her mother as she supported Frank's shoulders. "Mama, this is a bigger cup; it might do better than the other."

Frank continued to sip as Julia encouraged him to consume the tea. He blinked his eyes and mumbled, "Enough." Ada relaxed her arm and gently lowered Frank to the bolster. Julia removed her hand from her father's head and with the empty cup said, "Mama, he sipped it all. That's good, maybe he can get some relief."

Ada gently tucked the quilt close to Frank and reached for a fresh wet cloth from the basin. She twisted the cloth, folded it and placed it gently over his forehead.

Julia returned to the rocker, settled again as the rocker leaned back and drew her knees up close to her body.

Ada walked to the open window and  stared at the ruined

cotton field. She moved from the window to the chair beside the bed.

The light of the lamp continued to dance from wall to wall in irregular sequences. The quietness again covered Coolmore as the vigil continued.

Ada's head drooped as sleep touched her weary body. Julia twisted in a contorted position as the rocker leaned. Frank was restless as the willow bark remedy caused him to lapse into a stupor.

The dimly lit room began to lighten as the morning light flooded through the open window. Frank suddenly raised his head from the bolster and shrieked, "Ada! Ada!"

Julia jumped from the chair and watched as her mother lunged from her chair to the bed.

Frank flipped the quilt from the top of his body and moved the sheet from his neck. "Ada! My gracious, I'm hot—get this cover off!"

Ada pulled the quilt from the bed, turned back the sheet and placed her hand on Frank's forehead. "Frank! you're not hot like you were a few hours ago. It looks like the agues is gone. Bless God!"

Julia joined her mother at the bed, looked at her father and sighed happily, "I do think Dolly's cure worked!"

Julia glanced at her mother, focused her gaze on her father, smiled broadly and walked into the hallway. She stopped and looked at her mother at Frank's bedside. "Mama, I'm going on the back porch to see what the clouds look like in the east. Maybe it will be a little cloudy and today won't be as hot. "Thank the Lord for bringing us through the night. Today has got to be a better day!"

# CHAPTER EIGHTEEN

Seth awoke to the sound of rain falling steadily onto the veranda roof below the bedroom window. A breeze gently stirred the frayed lace curtains hanging from the worn rod across the top of the window facing. The usual sounds from the river were absent. The gray overcast sky veiled the morning sun. Seth remained immobile and listened as the constant drops fell from the top of the Alcock house to the roof of the veranda. He closed his eyes, and reflected on the events of the past days. A sudden gust of wind from the river made him feel clammy and he arose from the bed and walked to the open window. The quay was quiet and still. The leaves of the trees listed in the wind to provide a glimpse of the rippling river surface. Seth lingered as he remembered the encounter with the girl on the train. He had graphic mental pictures of the young woman raving on the back veranda of the Coolmore farm. Why couldn't he get the mental picture of her on the train and on the rail tracks out of his mind? Seth moved from the window, feeling a tinge of guilt as he realized it was Melissa he should be thinking of. Remembering Melissa, he wondered if the mail packet had arrived while his unit was away. Seth heard the officers stirring, pulled his uniform from the bedside chair and began to dress. He paused, looked at the stirring curtains and reminded himself of the bath he would indulge in tonight. The thoughts of a bath and shave heartened Seth as he continued to dress for the day.

Floyd Clarkson stood at the bottom of the stairs, looked to the top and shouted, "Seth! Don't forget we've got to report to General Potter this morning and give our reports." Seth heard Clarkson and answered, "Alright, Clarkson! I'll be right down."

Seth walked onto the front porch, turned and looked at Clarkson. "Well, Floyd, do you want to see what is available at the mess tent? It will at least be something for breakfast."

Clarkson smiled and nodded, "Yeah, it will be better than what we had to make out with while we were away."

Seth walked to the edge of the porch, stopped and turned to Clarkson. "The street to the mess area looks to be pretty much of a mess itself—a muddy mess, that is. By the time we get to Potter's headquarters our boots will look like we've been walking in the mud all day."

Clarkson grasped a porch column with one hand, leaned from the porch and stretched his hand outward. "Oh, it's not raining much, Seth. We've seen worse weather; at least it's not as hot as it has been!"

Seth nodded in agreement, "Let's get the day started." He stepped from the porch, placed his hat on his head and carefully avoided the pools of water as he made his way to the mess area. Clarkson stepped from the porch, felt the water dripping from the roofline, quickly put on his hat and picked up his pace to join Seth.

"I can't tell what is being cooked this morning, but it smells pretty bland—whatever it is," Clarkson noted as he sniffed the air. He lowered his head, pulled the brim of his hat over his face and quickened his pace. "Seth," asked Clarkson, "do you suppose Old Potter will keep us all day?"

Seth maintaining his fast pace, responded, "Probably so, he'll probably be praising himself all day."

The two officers entered the canvas-covered area and removed their hats. They simultaneously struck their hats on the side of their legs to remove the accumulation of water from the brims. George Cole rose from a bench beside one of long tables and exclaimed sarcastically, "Breakfast this morning is from Chamberlain's raid on somebody's pantry!" Cole laughed and continued his mockery, "And all he could find was cornmeal and a couple of darkies to show him how to prepare this Carolina mush!"

Seth stared at Cole and rebutted, "Major, I'm glad to know you recognize fine food. Maybe it makes you feel at home."

Cole, sensing the agitation in Chamberlain's voice, returned to his seat at the table and countered, "It is better than rations in the field!"

Clarkson walked ahead of Chamberlain, picked up a tin plate from the table and moved to the steward by the steaming pot. "Private, whatever it is, let's have some on the plate."

The mess steward responded, "Yes, sir!" as he dipped the ladle into the steaming yellow mush, "and do you want a full plate?"

Clarkson looked at the private, smiled and joked, "I never eat much of anything I haven't tried before—no, I don't want much!"

Seth looked at the mess steward, smiled and added wittily, "Since I'm the one that provided this, give me a heaping portion." The steward lifted the ladle from the pot and emptied it into Chamberlain's plate, "Captain, you deserve all you want of this."

Seth looked at his plate, smiled and motioned to Clarkson, "Let's join these appreciative fellows for a hot breakfast." Seth placed the steaming plate on the table, looked to both sides of the table and remarked, "You fellows don't seem carried away with the generosity of our Carolina friends."

Major Cole watched as Chamberlain quietly spooned the cornmeal mush into his mouth. "Old Potter is probably feasting on cured ham while we get the meal mush."

Seth looked at Cole and asked, "Do you suppose he'll share with us when we report this morning?"

Cole pushed his plate away and laughed, "I think we all know what he'll share with us—anything he doesn't want himself!"

"This slow rain makes things miserable for us," noted

Chamberlain, "but it fills the cisterns in this part of the state for drinking water, so it is not all bad." Seth walked toward the outside, turned and looked at the seated officers. "Well, fellows, let's get this ordeal behind us!"

Major Cole rose from the bench, reached for his hat on the center tent pole and concurred, "Yeah, let's get this over with."

Seth waited for Major Cole and smiled as he approached, "After you, Major, I believe you outrank me." The staff officers walked from the shelter, put on their hats and quickened their pace to General Potter's headquarters.

Seth stared at the front of the house used by General Potter. The similarities of the design of the house used by Potter and the house near Tarborough were surprising. As he gazed at the house, he could visualize the raging girl on the porch. For some mysterious reason he could not block her features from his mind. Everywhere there was something to remind him of his encounters with her.

Major Cole stepped onto the porch and looked at his boots. He knew the mud could not be tracked into the presence of General Potter. The major extended his foot and scraped the mud from the bottom of his boots on the edge of the porch. The officers observed Cole as he scraped his boots, moved to the outer edges of the porch to scrape the mud from their boots. "When you fellows are finished scraping, come on in!" Potter shouted.

Major Clarkson looked at Lieutenant Henderson and grinned. "You've been mighty quiet this morning, you want to go first?"

Henderson shook his head, "No thank you, Major, you can have the honor." He moved ahead of the officers and opened the door. The lieutenant gestured with his hand as he held the door open, "After you, gentlemen."

General Potter looked at the officers, placed his hands behind his back and moved away from his desk. "Well! Are you boys satisfied with what you did in Rocky Mount and Tarborough?" The general glanced at the officers and turned his back toward them and shouted, "Well, By Jove, I am!" He abruptly turned and faced the officers and added, "You gentlemen did a fine job—a fine job!" General Potter removed his hands from behind him, placed them on the desk and leaned toward the officers. "I will make my report to General Foster after I have received your reports. It looks like six were killed and thirty one wounded or captured. I don't know what General Foster will think about the seventeen horses killed. I expect that to be confirmed by your reports." The general continued to gaze at the staff officers. "I want your reports at your earliest opportunity." General Potter moved back from the desk and a broad smile surfaced through his beard. "Very good, gentlemen, you are dismissed."

Seth felt a sense of relief as he moved quickly for the door. "Hold up, gentlemen!" General Potter roared as the staff headed for the door. The general turned to his aide, "Smithson, get me my dispatches." Lieutenant Smithson walked to his desk, reached for the dispatches and handed them to the general. Potter pulled an envelope from the dispatches and announced, "A letter was placed with my messages by mistake. It looks like the packet *Muskegon* came while we were away. There's a letter here that looks like it might be from a delicate lady of refinement. The handwriting is a sure sign of gentility." The general deliberately moved the letter close to his nose and joked, "It ain't from somebody's mother, either." Seth looked at the general as a feeling of resentment began to surge through his body. The general looked at Seth, grinned and asked, "Mr. Chamberlain, you been expecting a letter from some pretty little thing back home?" Seth felt his face flush as anger began to build. General Potter looked at Seth again and grinned, "Well, Captain, have you been looking for a letter?"

Seth angrily blurted, "Everybody knows I've been expecting a letter!" Seth restrained himself quickly and added, "Sir!"

Potter gazed at the officers at the doorway and asked, "Do you think he needs this letter, gentlemen? It might make him even more unhappy. We don't want the captain unhappy, do we, gentlemen?"

Seth's irritation began to surface as he eyed General Potter and cattily retorted, "You, Sir, I believe know what is best."

Potter grinned through his scraggy beard, laughed and remarked sarcastically, "Oh, alright, Captain! Take your letter! I was just joshing with you, anyway!" The general looked at the stilled officers and instructed, "Gentlemen, have your reports ready as soon as possible. Thank you."

General Potter handed the letter to Lieutenant Smithson. "Give this envelope to the Captain." Smithson grasped the envelope and walked toward Captain Chamberlain. "Sorry, Captain, I don't know how it got in with the general's papers."

Seth snatched the envelope, turned toward the door and quickly moved to the porch. He turned, gave General Potter a backward glance and bolted from the porch into the muddy street. Seth pushed the letter into his shirt pocket, placed his hat on his head and pulled the front of the brim to secure it to his forehead. The rain slowly beat against Seth's face as he hurried to his quarters.

The Alcock house looked bleak as Seth approached. The sunless sky and the haze over the river gave a dismal appearance to the beginning of a wearisome day. Seth thought as he stepped onto the porch, but I have this letter from Melissa—what can possibly upset my day now.

Seth scraped the mud from his boots, removed his hat and walked into the house. He stopped at the bottom of the stairway, felt to be certain he had Melissa's letter in his pocket and took the stairs two at a time. He removed his hat, tossed it onto the bed, nervously pulled the letter from his shirt pocket and laid it on the table. The once irritated captain was now calm. Slowly and deliberately he adjusted himself in the chair and nudged nearer to the table. He plunged his hand into his pocket and pulled out his cavalry knife. He looked at the address on the letter and recognized Melissa's handwriting. His heart pounded as he opened the knife and placed the blade in the top of the envelope.

Cautiously he pulled the blade from one side of the envelope to the other, exposing the folded pages inside. With tenderness he grasped the pages and pulled them from the envelope. At last, he thought—at long last he could feel the presence of his dear Melissa. Seth sighed in relief as he spread open the folded sheets, placed his arms on the table and leaned forward.

Dear Seth,

I am in receipt of your last letter and am relieved to know that you are well. I know you must be very homesick being so far from New York.

The news is good regarding the war. There was a time when all the news was bad, but now there is some good news.

Seth, I must tell you something that I regret to divulge while you are so far away. I would tell you personally, but I do not feel it would be honest of me to wait until the war is over and you return home.

Please believe me when I say I was sincere when I accepted your request for marriage. It pains me greatly to retract my consent to your proposal. I do so desire to be honest with you and it would be dishonest should I continue to lead you to believe I would honor your request.

I would also be dishonest if I led you to think there was no one else. I must be perfectly honest with you and say, there is someone else. You do not know him, but I have come to realize that it is he that I am in love with.

There is no easy or kind manner in which to inform you and still be honest in the matter.

I cannot ask or expect you to understand. I can only hope that you will find someone who will appreciate and love you. You are truly a good man.

Please find it in your heart to forgive me for not finding an easier way to let you know of my decision.

May God bless you to return home safely.

Affectionately,

Melissa

Seth folded his arms and dropped his head onto the table. He suppressed the urge to scream aloud an oath of contempt. Seth slowly allowed the tightness in his throat to relax and his eyes overflowed with tears. Captain Chamberlain raised his head, gazed through the open window and thought, how could she do this? The breeze gently stirred the leaves, exposing the mist hanging low over the river. The gray hazy morning weighed heavily on Seth as he picked up Melissa's letter. In a burst of rage, Seth shouted, "No! No! By God, no, I won't read it again!" He snatched the pages, ripped them into shreds, walked to the window and flung the pieces from the window. Seth screamed again, "No! By God, no! It will never be read again— by nobody!" Seth dropped into the chair, folded his arms in front of him and lowered his head on his arms. The tears rolled down his cheeks as he suppressed his outbursts.

Major Clarkson heard the commotion, ran to the stairway and shouted. "Seth! What's wrong up there?" He dashed half way up the stairway and called again, "Seth! Are you alright?"

Seth heard Clarkson, raised his head and yelled, "Yeah! I'm alright! Just leave me alone! I'm alright!"

Clarkson turned and slowly stepped down the stairway. "Alright, Seth. If that's what you want."

Seth heard Clarkson as he made his way down the stairway. He thought, no one will know about this letter. Captain Chamberlain did not like the thought of being ridiculed by his fellow officers. He rose from the chair, walked to the window and stared toward the river. Briskly he turned from the window, walked to the doorway and bounded down the stairway. The captain stopped at the bottom of the steps and shouted, "Well, gentlemen! Are you ready to get the day started? It may be wet, but this army can't stop because it's wet!"

Major Clarkson looked at Major Cole and glanced at Lieutenant Henderson. "The captain's letter must have revived his spirits! I do believe he feels better already, yes I do!"

Seth looked at the officers, forced a smile and exclaimed, "Yes, gentlemen, I'm just great. Let's see that our reports find their way to old Potter's desk."

The heavy murky morning clouds opened and allowed the rays of the midmorning sun to shed its beams on the port city of New Berne. Sunlight reflected from the wind-blown ripples on the river as the quay began to come alive.

Summer evolved into autumn, the brilliant colors of the gum trees mixed with the ever present maples. The Carolina autumn merged into bitter windy days of winter. Army life remained dull as the days changed to weeks and the weeks to months. News from the Army of the Potomac in Virginia was changing for the better. Another spring season arrived as the Union Army continued to fortify New Berne. The Army of Northern Virginia was withdrawing from the Petersburg fortifications and moving west toward Lynchburg. Daily the telegraph brought news of Confederate losses and withdrawals. Spirits were uplifted and hopes were high. Soon this carnage would be over and home was the subject of every conversation.

April was a lovely month in North Carolina. The gray days of winter had yielded to the warm southern sun. Nature's floor began to send forth the yellow ushers of another Carolina spring. Daffodils were waking from their long night of sleep and bursting from their earthly beds onto winter's barren floor. Scents of new life overcame the receding musty reminders of the wintry blasts. A new spring with its new expectations infused the dreary soldiers.

The clatter of the telegraph in General Foster's headquarters continued constantly with information concerning the movements of the armies in Virginia. Each day brought news of Grant's successes. General Johnston and his Army of the Tennessee was moving west from Smithfield to Durham. The new nation born of economic necessity was convulsing in its last gasps due to economic deprivation. Scott's Anaconda had squeezed the life from the dying nation.

"General Foster! General Foster!" the telegrapher shouted, "Lee has surrendered to Grant! The war's over!" Lee had surrendered at Appomattox Court House; it was April 9, 1865.

Nature neither acknowledges nor approves man's insanity. She silently absorbs the blood of the victor and the vanquished and moves forward. The inevitable progression of the seasons continues despite mankind's folly. This fateful year would be no different.

Captain Chamberlain had contained his personal disappointment. There had been no inquiring into the details of his letter and he had offered no explanation. The captain resolved in his own manner that he would not return to Albany. He did not know what he would do, but he would not return to Albany.

Days merged into weeks as the population of New Berne shrank. The presence of the Union Army diminished with the departure of each ship from the Neuse and Trent Rivers into the Pamlico Sound. The blossoms of spring were emerging into the blooms of early summer.

Major Ferris Jacobs approached the Alcock house, spotted Captain Chamberlain sitting on the floor of the porch leaning against a column and called, "Seth! I'm finishing up all my details and getting ready to go home." The major walked up the steps onto the porch and sat beside Seth. "I have not heard you say what you intend to do. You have been very reserved for the last months and I did not want to invade your private thoughts." Jacobs reluctantly asked, "But don't you think it is about time you let somebody know what your plans are? After all, we've been together since we enlisted in Albany." The major adjusted himself on the porch floor allowing his legs to hang to the ground and added, "Seth, something has been eating at you for well over a year, now. Do you want to talk about it? We've been through a host of tough times together and I think I have a right to know."

Seth pulled up one leg, drew his knee close to his face and propped against the porch column. His other foot dangled as he situated his frame in the warm April sun. He waited as he observed Jacobs twisting from the glare of the sun. "Ferris, I have not spoken of this since the summer we made that raid to Rocky Mount and Tarborough—I know I have got to let my intentions be known sometime and I suppose now is as good a time as any." Seth nudged closer to the column and lowered his head. "Do you remember that angry girl at the plantation we almost burned down? The house that I pleaded with you not to burn because I had helped design it?"

Jacobs looked at Seth and acknowledged, "I remember the incident well, and I remember the girl and her father; I believe their name was Dupree."

Seth raised his head and glanced at Jacobs, asking, "Do you remember the girl's name?"

The major placed his finger under his chin, thought for a moment and answered, "If memory serves me correctly, her name was Julia. I could be wrong, but yes, I think it was Julia."

Seth folded his arms, adjusted himself again to the porch column and focused on the major. "Ferris, I have not been able to get her off my mind since the day we returned from that expedition." Seth, sensing a friendly listener, displayed a willingness to talk and continued, "That's right, everything I have seen reminds me of her. I can't get her out of my thoughts.

I don't know why, but I feel a special attraction to her. Call me mad if you will, but I can't shake it off."

Seth turned from the direct sunlight, pushed closer to the porch column and looked at Jacobs again. "Do you recall the day that Potter made a big joke about the letter he had gotten by mistake and the show he put on about that?"

Jacobs lowered his head and answered, "Yes, Seth, I remember that, and I know it was embarrassing for you and I felt badly about the display of poor taste."

Chamberlain, feeling unrestrained, confessed, "That was a letter from Melissa."

Jacobs looked startled and asked, "A letter from Melissa, in Albany?"

"Yes," answered Seth. "A letter telling me she was withdrawing from our engagement. I have not spoken of it since that day. I hesitate to speak of it even now, but now that the war is over, I am going to have to make some decisions about returning home to Albany."

Major Jacobs looked sympathetically at the captain. "Seth, why have you harbored this all these months? You should have known I would have understood."

Seth continued to gaze at Jacobs. "Yes, Ferris, I should have, but I won't be played the fool again—like I was in Potter's headquarters."

"Seth," the major continued, "we have been together for a long time, and I am interested in your ambitions. I'm sure Colonal Jourdan will disband the unit when we get back to Albany. What do you intend to do when you get home?"

"Ferris," Seth declared, "I plan to resign my commission."

"You plan what?" exclaimed Jacobs.

"Yes, Ferris," Seth resumed, "I will submit my resignation to the Secretary of War from Foster's headquarters here in New

Berne. I do not plan to return to Albany. There is nothing for me there anymore. There is no reason for me to return to New York."

Major Jacobs looked stunned and quickly asked, "Well what, pray tell, do you plan to do? There is certainly no future here in the south. I would think you would have to go somewhere."

Seth pulled his dangling leg onto the porch, twisted his frame and raised himself to his feet. He leaned against the column and turned toward the sun. "Ferris, I have some money saved from my army pay. I believe there will be some opportunities here in the south as they rebuild—and they will rebuild! It may be I can accumulate something here quicker than going back home and starting all over."

Jacobs moved closer to Chamberlain, folded his arms against his chest and asked. "Well, just what do you have in mind? The whole wretched place is in shambles."

Seth focused his gaze on the major. "This was an agricultural region before the war and it will be an agricultural area after the war. The land will come back—it always has!" Seth, maintaining his focus, added, "And somebody has to provide the means."

Jacobs laughed and belittled the captain, "And how do you think they will find the means? With their goodwill for former soldiers! Especially for soldiers who ripped their property apart?" Jacobs continued to make light of Seth. "No, Seth, you have to have more security than that. Security does not come in the form of goodwill."

Seth lowered his head in embarrassment and countered, "Land, Ferris, land! That is the security. If I can supply the means to rebuild the land and have the land as security, therein lies the opportunity!"

Jacobs walked to the edge of the porch, paused and returned to Seth's side. "Seth! Are you sure it's opportunity knocking at your door or that Dupree girl knocking at your heart?" The major then quickly turned and apologized, "I'm sorry, I should not have said that."

Seth laughed and admitted, "I'm not sure I know the difference."

Seth moved farther from the edge of the porch and out of the direct sunlight. "Ferris, I have given some thought to asking you to be my contact for the tools that will be needed. They will all have to come from up north."

Jacobs moved from the edge of the porch and looked at Seth. "Are you asking me to be a partner in your venture?"

Seth smiled and responded, "Yes, I'm asking you if you want to take a chance in this."

The major walked to the edge of the porch, paused and slowly walked back to answer the captain, "Seth, if I did not know you so well, I would swear you were mad. You may be right—there has got to be opportunities here. Where else can the place go but up?" Jacobs looked squarely at Seth and asked, "Just where do you propose to mark out your territory? No, don't tell me, I think I can guess—that little town on the Tar River where that pretty little girl would just love to hang you from one of those big oak trees on the place."

Ferris laughed again and apologized, "Seth, please forgive me, but the thought of her hurling insults at you when we were by her home crossed my mind and I can just see her welcoming you to the section." Jacobs looked seriously at Seth and in a calm voice counseled, "I have always heard that land is wealth, and in any country, wealth is power." Ferris walked closer to Chamberlain and added, "And power is the tool to exercise influence. Now I see where you're going. Yes, indeed, provide the people with the means to rebuild the land with their land as security and if they fail, you acquire the land and the power. If they succeed, you still have wealth and the power. A scheme well-calculated, I must admit. Yes, I would like to be a part of that."

Seth walked to the edge of the porch and turned his face into the sunshine. "Ferris, we can use the river to bring in the tools. It's not that far from Baltimore to Washington on the Pamlico and up river to Tarborough. But it will require me to be here in North Carolina and you to be New York. You have reason to go back and I don't. It ought to work to our advantage."

The April sun was refreshing as Seth and Ferris strolled in front of the Alcock house. Seth raised his face to embrace the warm rays of the sun and inquired, "Ferris, have you noticed that gig under the shed in the backyard of the Morris house?"

Jacobs thought a moment and responded, "Yes, I think I have seen it a time or two. Why? Have you been admiring it from a distance?"

Seth looked in the direction of the Morris house and answered, "I think I will ask if it is for sale. I intend to ask Colonel Jourdan if he will authorize my request to purchase my horse, Blue Boy. That gig and Blue Boy would fit well together."

Jacobs fixed his eyes on Chamberlain and remarked, "You have been thinking about this for a long time, haven't you? You already have it planned, don't you?"

Seth turned and started toward the rear of the house. "Yes, it's been on my mind for quite some time."

Jacobs joined Seth as he walked around the Alcock house to the veranda in the rear. "Alright, Seth. Before I leave I will give you a bank draft to help get started. I'll consider it an investment in our future."

Seth smiled and assured Jacobs, "You can rest assured that I will be in contact with you when I am organized and ready to begin shipments of what will be needed."

# CHAPTER NINETEEN

Seth felt the exhilaration of a free spirit. His resignation had been accepted by the Secretary of War and now Blue Boy was his. He folded the quartermaster's authorization papers that Colonel Jourdan had secured from General Foster and tucked them in his shirt pocket. He quickened his gait on the brick streets of New Berne in the direction of the military stables.

Seth was elated that he now owned Blue Boy. Blue Boy had been with him on many expeditions in North Carolina and now the two were about to begin a new adventure. He pondered as he moved along the narrow street why the army had chosen a stable site near the old Tryon Palace. The merchants of prewar New Berne were beginning to ply their occupations in the old Colonial town. Union soldiers still patrolled the streets and waterfront. The signs of an army occupation remained.

The Heber Morris house came into view as Seth neared the stables. He remembered having seen a gig under a shelter in the rear yard of the house. Seth bounded from the street onto the front steps which swept from the edge of the street up to the small covered porch. Seth concluded Mr. Morris must have built his house first and then the bricks were laid to make the street more passable. The bricks were laid in Flemish style to give the house a European touch. Seth rapped the brass door knocker and waited for a response. He turned and looked down the street. Today was different. Everything looked different.

A rattle from inside the door alerted Seth and he turned toward the door. Slowly the door opened and Seth heard an irritated voice. "Yeah! Yeah! What do you want?" The door opened wider and Mr. Morris asked again, "What's your business here?" Seth looked at the hunched man in the doorway. "I see you have a gig under your shelter in the back.

Would you consider selling it?" The elderly man, with the collar of his white shirt buttoned at the top and wide galluses, stepped onto the porch. "It might be, seeing as how I can't use it anymore. As you see, I'm taken with the rheumatism."

Seth looked sympathetically at the gentleman and expressed his regrets. "I'm sorry, Mr. Morris. I'll be glad to give you a good price for the gig."

Morris looked at Seth, "And what is your idea of a good price?" Seth hesitated and proudly answered, "Twenty-five dollars—United States dollars!"

Morris reflected and answered, "That don't include the harness and collar."

Seth smiled at the bent man and offered, "Five dollars for the harness and collar."

Mr. Morris dawdled then responded, "Alright, but I make no promises as to the shape it's in."

Seth restrained a smile. "I understand that, Mr. Morris, then it's a deal?"

The old man replied, "I suppose so."

Seth reached into his shirt pocket and drew out some folded bills and held out a twenty-dollar bill and a ten-dollar bill. Mr. Morris stretched his bent arm through the doorway and Seth placed the bills in his hand. "Mr. Morris, I'm on my way to the stables to get my horse. Will it be alright for me to hitch my animal to the carriage on my way back past your house?"

The crippled gentleman grunted as he lifted his head. "I suppose so. The harness and collar are hanging in the shelter."

Seth glanced at the elder Morris, "Thank you, Mr. Morris! I'll be back in a short while and move the gig." He turned toward the street and bounded down the steps.

Seth stepped up his pace as the stable area came into view. He had requisitioned Blue Boy often, but today would be the last time. Blue Boy was his now. He slowed his steps as he neared the corral adjoining the large barn-like structure. Stopping at the corral, he looked into the enclosure and shouted, "Blue Boy! Blue Boy! Over here, boy!" Blue Boy reacted to Seth's voice, turned with a neigh and trotted to him. Blue Boy extended his neck over the top corral timber to greet Captain Chamberlain and snorted. Seth clutched the horse's bottom lip, held it securely and stroked the forehead of the animal. "You belong to me now, old friend," Seth declared.

The stablemaster walked from the barn toward Captain Chamberlain. "Going somewhere today, Captain? I haven't been notified of any need for animals today." Seth smiled at the sergeant and stroked Blue Boy's head again.

"Sergeant, when Blue Boy and I leave here today, we won't be coming back." The sergeant looked puzzled and asked, "Just what do you mean by that?"

Seth reached into his shirt pocket, removed the quartermaster bill of sale and handed it to the sergeant. "This animal belongs to me now, Sergeant."

Looking at the paper and recognizing the signature of General Foster, the sergeant acknowledged, "Yeah, I reckon he does."

Seth extended his hand, "I'll be needing that paper back. I might need to prove I didn't steal this animal."

The stablemaster glared at Seth and looked at Blue Boy. "Well, Captain, do you want me to bring him from the stable or do you want to go in and get him?"

Seth braced himself against the corral timbers. "Bring him out; just a bridle and halter will be enough. I'll walk him back to my quarters." The sergeant disappeared into the stables. Seth watched the horses stirring in the corral, propped his foot on the bottom rail and thought how good it would be to have Blue Boy hitched to the gig.

Seth anxiously watched as the sergeant led Blue Boy from the barn in his direction. "Sergeant! If this horse is as glad to get out of the army as I am, we'll both be happy together." Seth reached for the reins and drew Blue Boy closer. "Thank you, sergeant. I wish you luck, now that the war is over."

The stableman responded, "Good luck to you, Captain."

"Let's go, old boy," Seth said as he tugged on the reins. The sergeant watched as the two moved toward New Berne's merchants' district. Chamberlain walked ahead of Blue Boy holding the bridle lines taut. "I hope you don't mind being hitched to a carriage. I know you're not used to that. We both are going to have to get used to things we haven't done before." Seth mused, good Lord, what am I doing talking to a horse? The sounds of Blue Boy's hoofs changed abruptly as they moved from the dirt pathway onto the bricks of the residential street. At the Heber Morris house he pulled on the reins and led the animal to the rear yard. Seth looped the bridle lines around the shelter post and walked under the shelter. He stood between the two shafts of the gig, turned and faced away from the gig. Looking at Blue Boy he muttered, "I'll pull it out from the shelter and then it's yours." Seth stooped between the two shafts, picked them up with both hands and leaning forward, pulled the gig from the shelter.

Seth looked at Blue Boy as he would a friend. "I don't know how you're going to take to a collar and harness." Back in the shelter, he reached for the collar, removed it and returned to Blue Boy. Approaching his horse slowly, Seth stretched the hinged collar open and placed it over Blue Boy's neck. The horse remained still as Seth stooped to secure the buckle strap under the collar. "Good, good boy," muttered Seth. He stood up, spotted the hames in the shelter, removed them and returned to his horse. "This is something that will make it easy for you, old boy," Seth whispered as he placed the hames on the collar and secured the buckle attachment. He gathered the harness parts, pulled them to the side of Blue Boy and began to assemble the harness on the animal. Seth released the reins from the shelter pole, and carefully stroked his horse between his eyes and gently pushed on his head, "Back, boy, back." Blue Boy slowly reacted and moved backward between the two shafts of the gig. Seth stroked his horse, moved to the animal's side, stooped and picked up the shaft. He steadied Blue Boy and pulled the leather strap over the shaft. He moved around the front of the horse and secured the other gig shaft. Seth moved his hand along Blue Boy's back as he walked toward the front of the rig.

"Good boy, good boy," Seth said aloud as he visually checked the harness. Grasping the reins, Seth remarked as he began to lead Blue Boy toward the street, "We're on our way, old boy! We're on our way!"

Seth walked ahead of Blue Boy, turned onto the brick street and started toward the Alcock house. The sounds of Blue Boy's hoofs and the creaks of the gig's wheels sounded strange to Seth as he proceeded toward his quarters.

Nearing the Alcock house, Seth saw Major Jacobs on the front porch. Jacobs watched as Seth led Blue Boy and the gig around the side of the house. "I see you got what you were after, Seth," shouted the major.

"Sure did," yelled Seth, "come on to the back and take a look at it."

Major Jacobs followed Seth into the rear yard, examined the gig and remarked, "With a little tightening here and there, this rig ought to serve you well."

Seth looked at Major Jacobs, "Major, you've been a good friend for a long time. But this is not the end; we've still got a lot of things to accomplish. I'll be leaving first thing tomorrow morning. I'll be busy for the rest of the day and we might not have the chance to talk again." Seth stretched his hand toward Jacobs. "You will be hearing from me." The major extended his hand and the two cavalry officers exchanged firm hand shakes. The two in agreement said, "Good luck!"

Chamberlain inspected the gig, noticed the loose bolts and unharnessed Blue Boy. He began to tighten the bolts. He was glad he had taken the time earlier to get himself outfitted at the sutler's tent. He did not want to be on the lonely road in a Union uniform. There were many details to take care of before sunrise tomorrow.

Seth's tapestry bag was bulging and heavy. The revolver was hidden under the clothing. He placed the bag at the foot of the bed and went down the stairs to the veranda and into the rear yard. Seth dipped some water into a bucket and carried it to Blue Boy. "Well, old boy, tomorrow it's going to be just you and me."

The sounds of New Berne were always the same. Every night nature was on schedule. The river creatures united in a collective endeavor to lift their monotonous strains in competition with all other night creatures. Seth settled onto the worn mattress, gazed through the open window and welcomed the image of the Dupree girl to his mind.

The early hints of light penetrated the window of Seth's room. The dull colored walls of the bedroom absorbed the light as Seth aroused to greet the day. He got out of bed and walked to the window to see if Blue Boy was still guarding the gig. He hurriedly dressed in his new civilian clothes, clutched his bag, placed his blanket under his arm and dashed down the stairway. Seth stopped on the veranda, looked into the kitchen and saw the officers drinking coffee. Seth placed his bag and blanket on the floor of the porch, stepped to the kitchen door and asked, "Can you share a bit of coffee, gentlemen?"

Clarkson turned and looked at Seth, "Sure, come on in, this one last time." Seth walked to the stove, lifted the pot and poured a cup of coffee, moved to the table and asked, "Clarkson, while the stove is hot, I think I would like to heat some water and shave off this beard. I see your razor on the table. Mind if I use it?"

Clarkson nodded, "Go right ahead, Chamberlain. This might be the last favor I can do for you."

The June sun was beginning to dissipate the lingering fog as Seth placed his bag and blanket in the foot of the gig. He moved alongside Blue Boy to lift the shafts into the leather straps. He stroked Blue Boy as he secured the snaps and rings to the harness. "Today's the day, old friend, today's the beginning of all our tomorrows." He examined the harness over Blue Boy's back and pulled himself into the seat of the gig. He snapped the lines, looked toward the Alcock house and raised his hand. "So long, boys! Good luck!"

Seth turned Blue Boy onto the dirt street and guided the gig toward the west. He passed through New Berne, glanced at Potter's headquarters and pressed on to the road to Street's Ferry. He turned and looked to the rear and watched as the familiar buildings disappeared in the dust.

Seth was alone with his thoughts as he urged Blue Boy toward the ferry crossing. He no longer thought of Melissa, but the image of the Julia Dupree filled his mind.

The landscape had changed little since he had traveled this road two years before. He was able to recognize some scenery as he approached Street's Ferry. Not too much farther, he thought as he rounded a bend in the road. Seth tightened the lines to restrain Blue Boy as the ferry landing came into view.

Seth walked from the gig to Blue Boy's head, and looked at the empty ferry. "Anybody here?" he shouted.

He heard a rustling sound coming from the wooded area and a voice called out, "Yeah! Somebody's here! Just be patient." Seth looked toward the wooded terrain and saw Street as he emerged from the shaded thicket. "What's my chances of getting to the other side of the river, Mr. Street?"

Street walked closer to Seth and grinned. "About a twenty-five per cent chance—you got the quarter?"

Seth pulled Blue Boy's halter line taut to steady the horse, reached into his trouser's pocket and pulled out the quarter. He handed it to Street while holding the lines of his horse. "Yes sir, here's the quarter."

Street looked at Chamberlain and nodded. "Well, take your rig on the ferry." Seth gripped Blue Boy's halter and led the animal onto the ferry. Street loosened the mooring line, warned Seth to hold steady and shouted toward the opposite river bank, "Pull 'er across!" The rope attached to the ferry snapped taut and the ferry began to move toward the opposite bank. Seth remembered the crossing with his column two years before and steadied Blue Boy. He felt a bump and realized the crossing was complete. He waited for the helper to remove the wooden slat from the front of the ferry and pulled on the bridle lines and led Blue Boy and the gig from the ferry to the top of the riverbank. He turned and waved to Street on the opposite bank. With the reins in one hand, he gripped the seat and pulled himself up and guided the gig from the riverbank onto the Vanceboro road.

Minutes merged into hours as Seth proceeded on his journey. He remembered some scenery but there were some vistas he failed to recognize. He became thirsty and thought surely there would be a branch to cross on the road ahead. The last water he had seen was at the ferry. He twisted on the seat, relaxed the lines and allowed Blue Boy to follow the road. Spring had come to eastern North Carolina. The fading blooms of the white dogwoods stubbornly remained as the emerging young green leaves forced their appearance from the unyielding remnants of early spring.

Unclothed maples from winter's harshness were imperceptibly donning their new raiment in a renewal of life. The air was fresh and free of stifling campfire smoke.

A sudden jolt aroused Seth from his reverie. He leaned over the edge of the gig to see if any damage had been done. He noticed that Blue Boy had strayed to the side of the road, reached for the reins and pulled him into the center of the road.

Seth looked into the wooded terrain, saw a shallow branch and tugged on the lines. Holding the lines in one hand Seth leaped to the ground, gripped Blue Boy's halter and led him into the thicket. The water in the branch flowed slowly. Leaves from the previous winter covered the surface of the water. Seth removed his felt hat, stooped and swept the leaves from the water with his hand. He dipped his hat into the water, allowed it to fill and raised up with the water-filled hat in both hands. He placed the water under Blue Boy's head. Seth's faithful companion slurped the water from the hat as Seth held it to his head.

The tall pine trees offered the travelers a canopy of shade as Seth placed his wet hat back on his head and stooped beside the branch. He cupped his hands and dipped them into the water and drew them to his mouth. The water was refreshing and again he cupped his hands and dipped them into the clear water. Seth stood beside the branch, looked at the sun shimmering through the trees. It was time to get back on the road. The pause had refreshed him. Seth led his horse from the branch back onto the road. He settled in the seat, tapped the lines and continued north.

Seth directed Blue Boy to the side of the road as an approaching wagon neared. The driver of the wagon responded by guiding his mule to the opposite side of the road. The two men came abreast and Seth raised his hand. The drivers stopped and Seth looked at the man in the wagon and asked, "Do you know of any inns or lodges near Greenville?"

The disheveled man looked suspiciously at Seth and curtly answered, "No, no I don't." He snapped the lines on the back of his mule and moved away from Seth. Chamberlain gently whipped his lines and speculated to himself, I hope there are more civil persons here than that one. He considered the possibility of having to bed down in the forest if no lodging could be found.

Greenville did not appear hospitable and he passed through. The road to Sparta and Tarborough appeared familiar as he pressed on. The sun began to disappear as the shadows of twilight changed the scenery. Seth recognized the crossroads, remembered the encampment of two years earlier and said to himself, why not?

The early morning sunrise brought renewed vigor to Seth as he placed the harness on Blue Boy. His gig was a rough riding carriage, but today would be the end of the constant bouncing. The pretty little town of Tarborough waited as Seth led Blue Boy onto the road. He pulled himself into the seat, lightly snapped the lines and announced, "My friend, let's have our next meal in Tarborough."

Seth tried to recall the houses of Tarborough and the scenery as he peered ahead toward the town. Nothing looked familiar and a feeling of disappointment stirred his emotions. He strained to see farther along the road and suddenly remembered, he had not entered Tarborough two years earlier from this direction. His column had used this road to leave Tarborough. He felt encouraged as he rattled the reins and noticed the small neat houses lining the dirt street leading to the center of the little town. The oak trees gave the appearance of being planted mainly for lining of the street. Seth urged Blue Boy on to the railroad tracks, crossed the tracks and immediately observed the storefronts lining the main road through the town. He issued an audible sigh of relief as he thought, finally a place that looked a little familiar—and by God, I hope a little friendlier.

Seth turned onto the road, glimpsed what appeared to be an inn or lodge and guided Blue Boy to the front of the house. He urged his horse to a position beside other carriages in the yard. He noticed an aged horse harnessed to a worn shay. He admired the two-story boarded house with a veranda along the sides and across the front. The plain railing balusters surrounded the veranda. Seth continued to admire the simple but efficient design of the house as he climbed down from the gig. He gripped the horse's halter and led the animal to the front of the house and secured the lines to a vertical wooden post. Chamberlain glanced upward and noticed the open windows and thought how good it would be to rest in a clean room and a decent bed. Two days of accumulated dust needed washing off.

The weary Chamberlain walked slowly up the steps onto the veranda and rapped on the doorfacing. A neat, well-dressed lady appeared in the doorway and warily looked at Seth. "Yes?" the lady acknowledged.

Seth smiled and backed from the doorway. "I thought this might be a lodging house from the looks of the carriages in the yard. I surely hope it is."

The lady in the doorway responded, "It is, but with the war just over, there's not much to offer. The dreadful Yankees took just about everything we had."

Seth recoiled from the accusation, gained his composure and responded, "Yes, ma'am. I know how things have been with you and I sympathize with you. But I need somewhere to spend a few days and most anything will do."

"Very well, I'm Mrs. Andrews; my husband is William Andrews," she acknowledged.

Seth smiled and held his hat behind his back. "I'm Seth Chamberlain from New Berne." He looked to both sides of the porch and stepped closer to the doorway. "Would you be kind enough to direct me to the local hostler?"

Mrs. Andrews nodded and directed, "Go back up the street and turn left at the mercantile store; you will see the courthouse. The stables are a little down the road from the courthouse." Seth stepped from the doorway and placed his hat on his head. "Thank you, ma'am, I'll see to my animal and carriage and I'll walk back."

Mrs. Andrews nodded in agreement saying, "You can leave your bag and blanket here on the veranda until you return. It will be safe. All the Yankee thieves are gone now!"

Seth walked to his carriage, loosened the reins, stroked Blue Boy and pulled his hand along the animal's back as he walked to the carriage seat. Seth muttered, "Well, old boy, it looks like we both have a place to rest for the night." He raised his leg into the gig, pulled his frame onto the seat and pulled Blue Boy's reins. Blue Boy pranced back momentarily, turned and with a snap of the lines trotted into the street. Seth looked for the mercantile building, pulled on the left line and turned toward the courthouse. He saw the brick courthouse, turned east and spotted the hostler stables.

Seth directed Blue Boy to the front of the stables and guided his horse to the entrance. "Anybody here?" Seth shouted.

A gruff voice sounded from the entrance door, "Yeah, yeah, somebody's here!" Seth looked toward the entrance and watched as a shabbily dressed man appeared. "You need a place for your animal and rig for the night?"

Seth still holding the reins answered, "More than one night, maybe a week."

The bearded man looked at Seth warily. "I get payment in advance from folks I don't know, and I don't think I know you." Stepping from the gig, Seth handed the man Blue Boy's reins and reached into his shirt pocket. "How much did you say?"

The stable hand answered, "A week will be three dollars."

Seth counted out the bills and placed them in the man's hand. "If my animal requires more, I'll take care of that, too." Seth stroked Blue Boy's mane, looked at the stablehand and turned toward the courthouse. The afternoon sun glared in his eyes as he passed in front of the courthouse. Seth looked at the brick building and thought, I'll have to be here in a few days to find a lawyer. He continued walking toward Mrs. Andrews' house. The thoughts of a clean bed encouraged him and he quickened his pace.

Seth arrived at the Andrews' house, looked for his bag on the veranda and did not see it. Good Lord, he thought, she said it would be safe. He hurried to the house, bounced up the steps and met Mrs. Andrews at the front door. "My bag, Mrs. Andrews—where is it?"

Mrs. Andrews smiled at Seth, "Mr. Chamberlain, I carried your bag to the room you will be using for the night."

Seth felt relieved and nodded, "Thank you, Mrs. Andrews, and I wonder would it be possible to find a bite to eat for supper tonight?"

Mrs. Andrews smiled, "I'll be fixing a little something for Mr. Andrews for supper. It's not much, but it's the best we can do in these hard times. You're welcome to join us."

Seth followed her into the hallway, saw the stairway to the second floor and asked, "Is it alright if I go on up and rest a spell?"

Mrs. Andrews pointed to the top of the stairs. "You will see your bag on the bed at the top of the stairs. I'll call you when supper is ready."

# CHAPTER TWENTY

S eth was startled from a deep sleep by Mrs. Andrews' loud voice from the bottom of the stairs. "Mr. Chamberlain! You want to wash up? We've got a little something to eat." He rose from the bolster, turned and put his feet on the floor. He leaned and pulled his shoes closer to the bed then looked through the open window and observed the dusty street. He remembered the street from earlier in the day and thought it would not be difficult to return to the stable for Blue Boy.

"Thank you, I'll be right down," he called. He placed his hand on the banister and slid his hand along the rail as he descended the steps.

Mrs. Andrews motioned with her hand, "You can wash up on the backporch. Mr. Andrews and I use the kitchen, since it's just him and me most of the time."

Seth followed Mrs. Andrews through the hall and saw the porch at the end of the hallway. "Thank you, I'll wash up and be right with you. It is very kind of you to invite me to your table."

Seth observed a worn table at the edge of the porch, noted the bucket with the dipper protruding and a tin basin hanging on a nail in a porch column. He reached, gripped the dented basin and placed it on the table. Grasping the dipper, he filled the basin with fresh water from the bucket and began to rinse his hands. Leaning over the basin he splashed water on his face and straightened to reach for the towel that hung on the post column. Seth was drying his hands and face when he heard a voice behind him.

"Mr. Chamberlain, my wife tells me your name is Chamberlain."

Seth turned, looked at the small-framed man, noticed his

tidiness and offered his hand, "Yes, that's right, I'm Seth Chamberlain."

Mr. Andrews grasped Seth's hand tightly and smiled, "I'm William Andrews, but most folks call me Billy and I'm glad to meet you. Charity, that's my wife's name, tells me you'll be using one of our rooms for a few days."

Seth nodded, "Yes, sir, I hope I can make more permanent arrangements in a few days."

Andrews started toward the kitchen door. "Come with me, Mr. Chamberlain, Charity ought to be about ready. It won't be much; this war's drained everything from us."

Seth reflected on the events of two years earlier and hesitated, "Yes, sir, I know it has been difficult for everyone."

Mr. Andrews opened the door. "Come on in and take a seat at the table." Seth saw Mrs. Andrews placing a single bowl in the middle of the table.

"Where do you want me to sit, Mrs. Andrews?" She pointed to the end of the table.

"Use that end, Mr. Chamberlain. Mr. Andrews will sit at this end."

Andrews leaned toward the center of the table, drew a deep breath and settled back. "Stewed chicken and pastry. That ought to be good. Mr. Chamberlain, serve yourself from the bowl and help yourself to a piece of the cornbread." Seth lifted his plate, held it close to the bowl and dipped the pastry and chicken pieces into his plate. He set the plate down, picked up the fork and began to lift the dripping pastry to his mouth. "My gracious, Mrs. Andrews, this is delicious. I have never eaten anything like this before. May I have some corn bread?"

Mrs. Andrews picked up the plate of corn bread and passed it to Seth. "Mr. Chamberlain, you must not be from around here, or you would know what chicken pastry is. We haven't had a lot of anything else owning to the war and all."

Mr. Andrews moved his plate close to the bowl, dipped the spoon deep into the pastry and lifted it from the bowl into his plate. "Mr. Chamberlain, did I understand you are from New Berne?"

Chamberlain lowered his head and responded, "Yes, sir, New Berne."

Andrews continued, "Were you in the army in New Berne?"

Seth stopped eating, placed his fork on the side of his plate and replied, "It's been a very trying time and right now I really do not wish to talk about the army. That's something I want to forget and put behind me."

Andrews glanced at his wife, "We can understand that, Mr. Chamberlain. Please forgive my intrusion."

Seth picked up his fork and fumbled with a strip of pastry in his plate. "I'm sorry, but there are some things we all best forget."

Billy Andrews reached for the corn bread, twisted his fork into the pastry strip and leaned to keep it from slipping from his fork. "Yes, sir, there are some things I'd like to forget, too. About two years ago a Yankee raiding party came through and destroyed the depot, some rail cars and the bridge. I was there that day and I barely got away from that Yankee riff-raff."

Seth nodded, "Yes, I'm sure you have something you would like to forget, too." He considered it would be unwise to reveal his true identity. He pushed from the table and looked at Charity Andrews and smiled. "That was a truly delightful meal. I thank you for your hospitality, and now could I trouble you for a kettle of hot water? Tomorrow is Sunday and I would like to clean up a little. I would like to see the balance of this pretty town."

"Yes, Mr, Chamberlain, if you will have a seat in a chair on the porch, I will call you when the water is hot. Mr. Andrews will join you on the porch." Andrews pushed away from the table, reached into his shirt pocket and removed a cigar.

Seth followed Andrews onto the shaded porch. The sun was sinking below the tree tops in the west and the east side of the house was shaded. Seth pulled a rocker from the wall, turned and lowered himself into the chair. "Mr. Andrews, I trust I will be able to secure some business space in the mercantile district. It is my intention to start bringing in guano and farming tools."

Andrews moved from the edge of the rail-lined porch to the wall, pulled a chair next to Chamberlain and sat down. "Mr. Chamberlain, I hate to discourage you, but the farmers in this part of the country don't have anything left to purchase those things with."

Seth rocked forward in the chair and stopped abruptly. "Mr. Andrews, I intend to give the farmers until the next harvest to settle up for the supplies and equipment."

Andrews struck a match on the arm of the chair and raised the flaming match to his cigar. He puffed on the cigar as the smoke billowed above his head. "Mr. Chamberlain, that's all well and good, but I doubt very much that anyone will take you up on your offer. Most of the folks around here are a mighty independent breed."

Seth allowed the rocker to lean back. "It would seem they would have to secure those things from somewhere." Andrews gazed at Seth. "Most of them would rather do without and make-do with what they have."

Chamberlain leaned forward and placed his hands on his knees. "I'm going to try, Mr. Andrews. I am sure going to try."

"Mr. Chamberlain," Mrs. Andrews called, "the kettle of hot water you wanted is ready. You can come to the kitchen and get it when you're ready."

Seth turned in the chair and smiled. "Thank you. I'll be right in." He turned to Mr. Andrews. "Will you excuse me, I think I will get cleaned up a little. There's a lot of road dirt on me right now."

Billy Andrews leaned back in the rocker and puffed his cigar. "Go right ahead, I hope you have a good rest tonight."

Seth walked to the kitchen, picked up the kettle of water and walked to the bottom of the stairs. He cautiously made his way up the stairs to the bedroom. He moved carefully to the bureau, and poured the hot water into the bowl, gripped the pitcher and dashed down the stairs to the back porch. Seth placed the kettle on the table and dipped water from the bucket into the pitcher. "Thank you, Mrs. Andrews," he called out as he hastily made his way up the stairs. He poured the cool water into the bowl until the mixture was warm to the touch. Chamberlain sat on the edge of the bed, removed his shoes and stood upright. He pulled his suspenders over his shoulders and let them drop by his side. As he began his bath he thought, my God! I'd better keep who I am to myself.

Seth pulled back the spread and sheet, fluffed the bolster and sat on the edge of the mattress. He turned and allowed himself to drop onto the mattress. The bolster held his head above the mattress and he joined his hands behind his head. Twilight was giving way to darkness. Tarborough was quiet. A gentle breeze rustled the young leaves of the oak trees in the front yard. Another spring had been born. Seth felt free and excited.

The early morning air was fresh as Seth flipped the sheet and placed his feet on the floor. He sat by the open window and contemplated spending the day looking around the town. He looked along the quiet street and visualized what it would be like to have his own establishment somewhere in the area of the courthouse. Everyone had to come to the courthouse.

Seth walked to the closet, removed his bag and placed it on the foot of the bed. As he opened it, he was reminded it was Sunday morning. He removed a white shirt from the bag and laid it on the bed. He neatly laid his gray corded trousers beside the shirt and visualized himself fully dressed with his new suspenders and Trilby hat.

Seth pulled the sheet and spread to the bolster and tucked the ends under the bolster. It was not that well made, but it was the best he could do. He walked to the bureau, saw the water in the bowl from the night before and picked up the bowl. He stepped cautiously down the stairs, pushed the door with his foot and walked onto the porch. At the edge of the porch he tossed the water into the yard.

Charity Andrews appeared at the back door and instructed, "Mr. Chamberlain, just leave the bowl on the porch table; I'll take care of it later. You're welcome to have some breakfast with us, if you will. It's not much."

Seth placed the bowl on the table and smiled. "Thank you, I would like a cup of coffee, please."

Mrs. Andrews gazed steadily at Seth and apologized, "I'm sorry, Mr. Chamberlain, but there is no coffee to be had. We have learned to make out with molasses stirred into hot water. It's tasty once you get used to it."

Seth forced a smile. "Thank you, I will try it. If it is sufficient for you, then it's all right for me." He walked into the kitchen, sat at the table and watched Mrs. Andrews pour hot water into a cup in front of Mr. Andrews. "Mr. Andrews, how much molasses do you use in your cup of hot water?"

He looked at Seth as he reached for the jar of molasses. "A good teaspoonful usually does it for me. It has to be stirred real good to get mixed in well with the hot water."

Seth watched Mr. Andrews dip the spoon into the molasses jar and mix it in his cup. "I think I'll try it just like you did. It does look good." Seth dipped his spoon into the molasses, moved the jar over his cup and placed the spoon into the cup of hot water. He began to stir the mixture and watched it turn from dark brown to a lighter brown as the molasses mixed with the water. Seth lifted the cup to his mouth and sipped the hot liquid.

He looked at Mr. Andrews and remarked, "Excellent! Very good. It looks like you have found something to take the place of what you're not able to get."

Andrews reached for the plate of baked corn bread and suggested, "You might try dipping some bread into the cup. Cornbread and molasses is pretty good, too."

Mr. Andrews finished drinking the cup of hot molasses and water. "Well, Mr. Chamberlain, our town ought to be real quiet today. You should be able to walk at your leisure. I don't know what Charity will have for dinner, but you're welcome if you're a mind to join us."

Seth stood up and straightened his braces."Thank you, sir, I don't know if I will be back or not. If you and Mrs. Andrews will excuse me, I would like to see what your town looks like."

There was a freshness in the air as Seth stepped from the porch onto the steps. He stopped and gazed past the oak trees. He observed the hard dirt road that divided the town. The store fronts on both sides of the road gave the appearance of two mercantile districts. Seth walked past the trees in the yard of the Andrews' house and entered the road that ran east and west through the town. He walked along the south side of the road, paused and observed each business establishment as he leisurely moved toward the east. The warm rays of the sun felt good as Seth turned toward the south and continued walking toward the railroad.

Seth's reverie was interrupted as he neared the rail tracks. He heard the low tones of singing in the distance, focused his eyes on a simple wooden building beyond the tracks and stopped. He peered into the yard of the building and observed horses, mules and buggies tethered under the trees. Seth quickened his steps and walked closer to the modest building. The musical tones became louder as Seth neared the white building. He was certain the melodies were hymns, but he had never heard such strange words. The sounds were harmonious but the words were not understandable.

Walking past the front of the building, he realized it was a church. Seth looked at the two front doors and wondered why there were two. He stopped and was struck by the strange words coming from the building. He noticed a cemetery beside the church. A canopy of trees shaded the graves as he walked to the side of the church and stood in the shade. The church windows were open and the familiar melodies and strange words were clear. Seth stood motionless and listened at the open window. He recognized the tune, but not the words. He moved closer and listened intently.

Sol, la, do, mi, do, la, sol, do, re, mi, re, do, ti do. He recognized the tune as "Rock of Ages," but he did not recognize the words. Suddenly the words changed and he heard the hymn in syllables he was familiar with. Seth remained mesmerized with the haunting melody and remained still as the hymn was completed. He heard a voice from the building call a number and a loud response echoing the number. Seth listened intently as a voice sounded, fa, so, la, do! The voice paused and the strange words began in harmony. Me, re, do, do, la, la, sol, do, mi, re, re. The first stanza was sung in the odd-sounding words. He recognized the melody as "Nearer My God to Thee." Seth continued to listen as the hymn was begun over again using words he could understand. Incredible, he thought, it is "Nearer My God to Thee."

Seth, fascinated by the strange method of singing hymns, walked to the front of the building and stepped inside the door nearest the cemetery. He looked toward the apse of the modest building, saw that everyone was seated and sat on a back pew. Seth listened as hymn numbers were announced. He observed an old man on a front pew make the strange sounds to begin the hymns. Seth could feel the floor vibrate from tapping feet at the beginning of each stanza. He was startled by the tapping sounds coming from the balcony. Seth turned slowly and looked up. My Lord, he thought as he gazed at the blacks in the balcony, they didn't all leave; that must be the reason for two doors. As the familiar words began to resound through the building, the tapping stopped but the melody continued. Seth reflected, how different this is, yet how beautiful. He looked toward the raised platform, noted the plain wooden pulpit and scanned the congregation. Everyone remained seated and the singing continued.

How very odd! Seth pondered, as he observed the pews beside the pulpit. They were shorter and arranged along the wall facing the pulpit on both sides of the rostrum. He noted three on one side occupied by women and three on the opposite side by men. Seth continued to stare toward the podium. His gaze was broken as a man rose from one of the side pews and walked toward him. He watched askance as the man limped past him. Seth nodded in response to the man's smile as he passed in the aisle. Chamberlain reflected, where have I seen that face before? I know I have seen him, but where? Seth studied the man's features as he limped toward the front pews. Seth felt his face flush and his heart began to race as he remembered a day two years before. Now Seth knew where he had seen that face. It was Frank Dupree, the owner of Coolmore. Seth winced, oh, no! I didn't expect to see him here! If he was here, then his daughter must be here. Seth felt his face flush as he stared at the backs of the ladies' heads.

Seth fumbled with his hat and tried not to gape at the men and women occupying the pews in the center of the church. He cautiously raised his head and slowly scanned the rows. He looked at their backs and tried to picture Julia's face in his mind. His eyes moved from one end of a pew to the other. Abruptly his eyes centered on the woman wearing the pork pie hat. Below the flat top and wide brim a bun of chestnut colored strands caught his attention. He stared at the back of her head and visualized her face as he sat mesmerized. Seth looked to the front, observed Frank Dupree and looked again at the woman with the wide brim hat. He watched as she turned to whisper to the man beside her. It is her! He recognized her face. His heart raced and he felt flushed as he continued to stare at the back of her head, but a feeling of disappointment flooded him as he concentrated on the young man sitting next to her.

The singing stopped and a man dressed in a black suit stepped onto the podium. Seth was aware of words being said and a hymn being sung. He fumbled with his hat and tried not to gawk. His thoughts crowded out words and time passed. Suddenly the movement of the congregation's standing broke Seth's mesmerized thoughts. He glanced at Julia Dupree, noticed the young man beside her and picked up his hat. He started toward the door and felt a tap on his shoulder. He turned, and saw the man that had spoken from the pulpit earlier. "It's good to have you with us this morning. I am Robert Hart, pastor of the church."

Seth stretched his hand toward the minister. "Thank you, sir, I am Seth Chamberlain. I have just arrived and I haven't met many of the people yet."

Hart responded, "We hope you will find our town acceptable. After what we have been through, with the war and all, things are not as they used to be."

Seth nodded, "I know, I know." He walked to the door, put on his hat and stepped into the street. He stopped and looked toward the doors of the church and saw Julia and her father. He watched Julia holding to her father as he limped toward him. Seth's heart pounded as they neared. Dupree extended his hand, "Good morning, sir."

Seth gripped his hand, "Good morning to you, too, sir." Seth tried not to stare at Julia as Dupree added, "This is my daughter, Julia. My wife Ada is still in the church house. It's good to have you with us this morning."

Seth looked at Julia and tipped his hat. "It's nice to make your acquaintance, ma'am." Julia nodded, gazed at Seth and responded, "It's good to meet you, sir."

Seth attempting to steady his hands, secured his hat. "If you will excuse me, I have to get back to take care of my horse." Seth smiled at Julia, felt his face flush and turned to leave.

Seth felt relieved as he walked from the church. He had not been recognized! Suddenly he heard a loud voice, "That man! That man! I remember that man!" He turned and saw Julia pointing at him and screaming, "I know that man! He may have shaved his beard, but I know it's the Yankee that burned our farm!" Seth remembered the seething Julia of two years before and the vivid mental image returned. He turned to walk away when he felt a tug on his shoulder. The man who was sitting beside Julia pulled at his shoulder again.

Seth turned and warned, "I wouldn't push my luck, boy!" He heard the man shout, "You Yankee buzzard!" as he drew his arm back. Seth recoiled from the strike. Chamberlain instinctively stretched his arm and deflected another blow.

Elder Hart, hearing the confusion, rushed toward Josh Mewborn, grabbed him by the arm and pulled him away. "My God, Mewborn! This ain't no way to act on the church ground!"

Mewborn backed from Chamberlain and shouted, "The buzzards have come back to pick the bones!"

Elder Hart drew Seth from the irate Mewborn and apologized. "I'm sorry about this. I hope you can understand the feelings of the folks around here. It has not been easy. Feelings still run deep." Hart motioned to the mumbling bystanders, "Go on home! That's enough for today."

Frank Dupree gripped Julia's arm and pulled her toward the church. "Go get your mama and let's get on home."

Julia turned toward Seth and railed, "You're not wanted around here! Haven't you hurt us enough?" Frank raised his voice at Julia. "I said, 'Go get your mother!' Meet me at the wagon."

Seth watched Julia as she moved toward the church

building. He stared at the gathered crowd and shouted angrily, "Are you all like that?" He turned and walked toward the mercantile district. Seth seriously wondered if he should have gone back to Albany.

Frank limped to the wagon, untied the lines and looked at Ada and Julia. "Go on, get in the seat. We best get on home before Julia starts something else." Julia climbed into the seat and mumbled, "He ought not to come back here! I won't forget him." Julia extended her hand to her mother, "Catch on, Mama, and get up here!" Frank snapped the lines and the mule pulled the wagon onto the road. Frank looked at Ada and remarked, "I wonder why that Yankee came back here! I wonder what he wants."

Julia turned and waved to Josh as the wagon moved from the church toward the main road through Tarborough. Frank turned the wagon west and snapped the lines. "Let's get on back home." Julia watched as they passed the Andrews house and saw Seth walking up the steps to the porch. "My Lord, the man must be staying at the Andrews house. To be sure, he's not planning to stay here!"

Frank looked toward the Andrews home, looked at Ada and added, "The war has brung some strange things our way."

# CHAPTER TWENTY-ONE

Billy Andrews heard the sound of running feet up the front steps. "Charity, it sounds like somebody is on the front porch." He wiped his mouth with the cloth napkin and pushed back from the table. "I'll see who it is; go ahead with your supper." Loud rapid knocking could be heard. "I'm coming! I'm coming! Be patient!" he shouted. Looking through the open doorway, he saw Josh Mewborn pacing nervously on the porch. "Yes, what do you want? We're having dinner, won't you come in?"

Josh motioned to Mr. Andrews, "Can you step out here on the porch?"

Andrews stepped onto the porch, "What can I do for you, Josh?"

Josh moved closer and in a hushed voice asked, "Did you know that Chamberlain man was a Yankee soldier? He was one of the soldiers that came through here two years ago and tore up the place." Josh studied Andrews' face to ascertain his reaction.

"No! I didn't know that! Are you sure about that, Josh?"

Josh spoke excitedly, "Yes, sir! I'm sure! I just had a run-in with the man, and Elder Hart broke it up! He came in the church while services were going on!"

Mr. Andrews' face began to redden and he stared at Josh. "Thank you, son. I'll take care of the situation." Josh bolted down the steps, leaped into his buggy, snapped the reins and turned toward the river bridge.

Andrews returned to his seat at the table and glared at Chamberlain, "Mr. Chamberlain, I reckon you knew we were bound to find out about you, sooner or later." Mr. Andrews turned toward his wife and elaborated, "We have been used by this man, Charity. He was a Union soldier during the war. He was one of them that came through here and burned everything."

Mrs. Andrews' penetrating stare frightened Seth. "I should have known he won't from New Berne; he had no idea what chicken pastry was."

A scowl changed Andrews' thin face. "Chamberlain, get your things and leave. You and your kind are not wanted here. I don't want any trouble."

Seth's countenance changed and he said defensively, "My money is as good as anybody's and better than that Confederate scrip that's not worth a thing now!" Seth stood and glared down at Andrews. "I will leave, but you people have got to accept the fact that you lost the war!" He started for the stairs, stopped and continued, "Whether you like it or not, you are going to have to deal with us. You can do it now, or you can do it later. Suit yourself." Seth gripped the stair rail and stepped to the top of the stairs. He snatched his bag from the closet, stuffed his clothes in the grip and fell onto the bed. He pondered as he lay still, where will I go for tonight?

Charity Andrews' eyes reflected the intensity of her thoughts. "Mr. Andrews, you know very well your pay from the railroad is never on time and sometimes does not come at all. Don't you think we could use some money to get by on? At least for a little while? I know folks are going to talk, but we've got to eat."

Billy focused his eyes on Charity and asked, "Do you realize what you're saying? That would be almost disloyal!"

She stared into her husband's eyes and declared, "The war is over and done! We've got to go on living and do the best we can." Billy's scowl changed to a quizzical expression, "Are you willing to tolerate the whispers of the town if we keep him here?" Charity glared intently at Billy and queried, "Do you have another way of making it with what we have?" Billy paused, reflected and answered, "Oh, alright, I'll take a chance for a day or so and see how things work out. When he comes down, I'll tell him he can stay on a while."

Seth got up from the bed, gripped his closed bag and started down the steps. He stopped midway on the stairs, saw Mr. Andrews waiting and announced, "I'm leaving! Tell me how much I owe you for the night, and I'll be out of your way."

Andrews looked at Seth and drawled, "Not too hasty now, Mr. Chamberlain. Charity and I have talked it over and we decided we may have acted too quick." Seth remained still on the steps, held to the rail and questioned Andrews, "Are you saying you are willing to risk me staying here for a spell?"

Billy Andrews lowered his eyes and responded, "Yes, we want to do the right thing, not only for you, but for ourselves also. Charity is agreeable."

Seth had reached the bottom of the stairs and apprised Mr. and Mrs. Andrews, "I will try to find a more permanent place just as quick as I can. I regret not being totally honest with you about my past, but I really do want to get it behind me and start a new life." Andrews turned toward the kitchen and called out, "Charity! Mr. Chamberlain will be staying."

Seth retraced his steps to the bedroom after informing Mr. and Mrs. Andrews of his plans, "Thank you, I will unpack my bag and rest a while. I expect to start early tomorrow and get down to the courthouse first thing."

Mr. Andrews nodded. "Rest upstairs or on the porch—suit yourself."

Seth placed his bag in the closet and stretched out on the bed. He closed his eyes and the image of Julia came to his mind. Restless, he got to his feet, put on his shoes and went to the front porch. Billy and Charity Andrews were sitting in rockers. "May I join you? The rockers in the shade look comfortable." Andrews turned and looked at Seth. "Yes, please do. This time of the afternoon is always cool on this side of the house."

Seth pulled a rocker beside Mrs. Andrews and sat down. "I will try to be situated somewhere else just as fast as possible. I think I can understand your situation." Seth continued,

"Perhaps you can explain something to me. I heard something this morning at that little church I have never heard before."

Andrews looked puzzled. "And what was that?"

Seth began to rock slowly. "I always thought organs were used in churches. Those people did not have one."

Andrews puffed on his cigar and answered, "You were at the Primitive Baptist church. Some folks call them 'old schoolers.' I'm not much of a church goer myself. They are pretty popular in this part of the state."

Seth reflected, "I was impressed with the singing. It was inspiring." Then hesitated and added, "What took place later wasn't all that inspiring."

Mrs. Andrews' dark penetrating eyes focused on Seth. "If you plan to be around here for long, you'll have to get used to that way. Most of the folks around here are of that persuasion. Oh, it's getting late; I'd better get a little something on the table for supper," Mrs. Andrews remarked as she rose from her chair and walked to the door. "I'll call when it's ready."

Seth smiled at Mr. Andrews. "Go right ahead and enjoy your cigar. I can enjoy viewing the beauty of your little town." An early evening breeze swept over the porch and time faded."

"Supper's on the table," resounded from the hallway.

Sitting down at the table, Andrews remarked, "Sunday night is pretty light at supper."

Seth volunteered, "I have done with less." Mrs. Andrews joined them at the table, "Just some warmed over gravy to put on the cornbread and white potatoes."

Twilight yielded to darkness and the day would soon become yesterday. The porch was dark as Seth rose from his rocker. "I think I will get to bed. It has been a trying day and tomorrow may be even more so. I have many things to take care of in the morning."

The ashes on Andrews' cigar reddened as he puffed steadily. "Goodnight. I hope you will rest well." Mrs. Andrews added, "Goodnight, Mr. Chamberlain."

Seth ascended the stairs, sat on the edge of the bed and removed his shoes. He undressed, placed his clothing over a chair and pulled back the spread and sheet. Sighing, he quietly lay down and stretched the full length of the bed. His thoughts leaped into tomorrow and embraced the plans that he anticipated.

The brightness of the morning sunlight surprised Seth. He was not accustomed to sleeping past the early signs of daybreak. Sounds from the kitchen resounded up the stairs. Seth stretched his arms, walked to the window. Today was the day he had been waiting for. Today he would start putting all the plans together. He dressed hurriedly and gingerly dashed down the steps. "Good morning!" Andrews, drinking his hot water and molasses mixture looked at Seth. "Good morning! Looks like you're ready to get a big day started." Seth walked to the table, sat down and asked, "May I have a cup of that molasses and water, too?" Mrs. Andrews poured his cup full of hot water. "The molasses is on the table, help yourself. The biscuits will be ready in a bit."

Andrews smiled as he added, "Hot biscuits and molasses makes a mighty good breakfast." Seth hurriedly emptied his cup and rose from the table. "That was delightful, thank you so much. I must be on my way."

Billy Andrews looked astonished. "Why so early? The town isn't up good, yet."

Seth turned from the table and headed for the front door. "I want to take a look around the courthouse." The door slammed behind Seth as he bounded down the steps into the yard. He stopped, glanced at his shoes and adjusted his suspenders. With a brisk swagger Seth started toward the courthouse.

Chamberlain scrutinized the stores and offices in the courthouse area. He was looking for a lawyer and the area of the courthouse was where to find one. He stopped in front of the courthouse, looked to both sides of the building and then turned around. Ah, yes, he thought, there is a lawyer's office. Exactly where it should be—across from the courthouse. He walked to the front of the office, looked at the sign and knocked on the door. "Come on in, the door's unlocked," sounded from the inside the building.

Chamberlain pushed the door open and walked into the room. He looked at the nattily dressed man behind the desk. "I'm looking a lawyer."

With a grunt the man at the desk rose to his feet and extended his hand. "Then you've found one—I'm Tom Burgess."

Seth gripped his hand across the desk, "I'm Seth Chamberlain. It's good to meet you, sir."

Burgess nodded at Chamberlain and smiled. "Pull up a chair and we'll see if I'm what you're looking for."

Burgess pushed away from the desk, leaned forward in his chair and asked, "Well, what do you have in mind this Monday morning?"

Seth tilted his chair toward the lawyer and began, "I want some papers drawn up for debt security. I will be wanting land to secure loans and to cover credit for plows and farming tools."

Burgess looked at Chamberlain and laughed. "Are you crazy? Ain't nobody around here got enough of anything to secure a debt. And besides, they know there ain't nobody around here crazy enough to loan them any money."

Seth tipped his chair back and peered at Burgess. "I'm crazy enough! And if I can find a building to work from, I'll prove it!" Burgess pulled his chair closer to the desk and folded his arms on the top. "You do know you'll need a surveyor?"

"I know that. Is there one in this town?"

The lawyer unfolded his arms and swiveled in his chair. "Yes, I think there is."

Seth stared at Burgess and ordered, "You just fix the papers and leave the rest to me, and besides isn't all the land plots on record at the courthouse?"

The lawyer looked stunned. "Alright, Mr. Chamberlain, come back tomorrow and I'll have them ready. How many do you want?" Seth rose from the chair and instructed, "Let's start with four, and if I need more, I'll let you know."

The lawyer grinned. "They'll be two dollars each, Yankee dollars!"

Seth leaned over the desk and glared at Mr. Burgess. "Spell my name right—that's Chamberlain, C-H-A-M-B-E-R-L-A-I-N, Seth Chamberlain."

Seth walked toward the door, stopped and turned back toward Mr. Burgess, "By the way, where is the bank?"

Burgess motioned with his hand, "Go around the corner to the next street and you'll see it."

Chamberlain nodded and smiled, "Thank you, I'll be back in a day or so."

Burgess signaled agreement and inquired, "Oh, by the way, Chamberlain, won't you be needing some space to start your enterprise?"

A quizzical expression crossed Seth's face and he replied, "Yes, I will. Why do you ask?"

Burgess responded, "I own this building and there's some space next door. You might like to look at it."

Seth stepped back to the desk "Can I see it now?"

Burgess moved toward the door. "Yes, just come on with me and we'll go right now. If you think it will suit your needs, you can have it at four dollars a month."

Seth followed Burgess through the door and into the street. Burgess pulled his key from his pocket and unlocked the door. Seth watched and quizzed Burgess, "Ever given any thought to putting a porch across the front to keep it dry at the doors?"

The lawyer opened the door and motioned to Seth, "No, not really. Come on inside and see if it will do."

Seth scanned the front room, noticed the dusty desk and walked to the door between the rooms. He pushed the door with his foot and walked through. "Is there a flue connection in this room for a stove?"

Burgess answered instantly, "Yes, it connects to the same chimney my stove uses."

Seth walked back into the front room, and affirmed, "Looks like it'll do just fine. I'll clean it later to suit my needs."

Burgess pulled the key from the lock and handed it to Seth. "It's yours! But the four dollars will be in advance."

Seth reached into his shirt pocket, pulled out some folded bills and counted out four dollars. "Here's four American dollars!"

Burgess took the bills and started toward his law office. "Thank you, sir, I'll be expecting you in a day or two."

Seth walked past the law office, and toward the main street of Tarborough.

Seth stopped at the mercantile building on the corner, looked east toward the river bridge and noticed a freshly painted sign protruding from one of the building fronts. The sign glistened in the sunlight as if to announce it was the Guaranty Bank. He walked briskly to the front of the bank and entered the opened door. Seth approached the counter in the center of the room. "Yes, sir! Can I help you?" echoed from the back of the counter.

Seth replied to the voice, "Yes, I need to talk with someone about depositing some money in this bank."

A loud voice from the back room called out, "Send the gentleman on back here!" The man behind the counter opened the railing door and directed, "Right through that door, sir."

Seth walked to the door and pushed it open, "May I come in?"

A well-dressed gray-haired man rose from the desk and answered, "Come on in, sir." He extended his hand across the desk and added, "I'm Claude Dickens, please pull up a chair."

Chamberlain gripped his hand and responded, "Chamberlain, Seth Chamberlain, sir."

Seth sat facing Mr. Dickens. "I need to deposit some cash and a draft."

Dickens smiled and nodded, "Very good, Mr. Chamberlain. I think we can handle that for you. Do you wish to draw upon it?"

Seth looked seriously at the banker and snapped, "Of course I do. How else can I do business?"

Dickens' face flushed, "I apologize, sir, I wasn't aware of your business."

Seth countered, "Pardon my rude behavior; it's hard to realize nobody knows me, but I have been in town such a short time."

Mr. Dickens smiled and acknowledged Seth's request. "And where, may I ask, are you from?"

Seth breathed deeply, hesitated and answered, "Albany, New York."

The silence seemed to stretch as Seth gazed at the banker. "New York! Good heavens, man, what are you doing here? Don't you know there's bitterness around here for people from up north?"

Chamberlain admitted, "I'm beginning to realize just how bitter, the longer I'm around." Seth proceeded, "My plans have already been put into operation and it's too late to back out now."

Dickens shook his head in doubt. "Well, then, just what are your plans, if I may ask?"

Seth spoke deliberately, "I aim to buy land that may go up for sale. I intend to bring in guano and farming tools and I plan to sell them to the farmers. If they can't pay cash for it, I propose to extend them credit until the harvest."

A scowl covered Dickens' face as he reacted, "And what do you suggest they use as security for all your goodwill? Their goodwill?"

Seth answered, "Their land as recorded at the courthouse."

Dickens leaned closer and advised, "I hope you've got the money to back your dream, 'cause that's all you've got is a dream!" Seth stood upright, reached in his front trouser pocket and pulled out a folded envelope. He opened the envelope, removed the bills and began to place them one at a time on the desk in front of the banker. "Do you want to count the one-hundred dollar bills along with me, Mr. Dickens?" Seth counted out the bills, folded the envelope and returned it to his pocket. "Will this do, along with this draft on a New York bank?"

A flabbergasted Mr. Dickens replied, "Yes, sir! That will be just fine. We will handle it for you."

Seth nodded at the banker and added, "I'll need a receipt for that. I've got to start my own bookkeeping. I will need some drafts, also."

Dickens got up, walked toward the door and turned to Chamberlain. "Come on with me and I'll see that you get all you need."

Mr. Dickens walked with Seth to the front door and extended his hand. "Thank you, sir! A belated welcome to Tarborough to you! We'll be looking forward to seeing you again."

Seth gripped the banker's hand and replied, "I hope so, sir! I hope so." Seth walked into the street, glanced at the sign and proceeded toward the Andrews' house.

Seth walked directly into the glare of the late afternoon sun. He pulled his hat down to shade his eyes and walked to the shade of the trees in the Andrews' yard. Seth moved slower than usual up the front steps, removed his hat, hung it on the back of the rocker and slumped in the chair. A long, tiring day, he reflected, as he leaned in the rocker.

"Mr. Chamberlain, you can wash up for supper," sounded from inside the house.

Seth had dozed and not heard Mr. Andrews come in the rear door. "Yes, ma'am," he answered, "I'll be right there." On the back porch, he dipped some water into a basin and washed his face and hands. Reaching for the towel he called, "Is Mr. Andrews already at the table?"

Mrs. Andrews answered, "Yes, come on and sit down." Seth walked into the kitchen, glanced at Mr. Andrews and noted, "I didn't hear you come in. I think I dozed off on the porch. It's been a long day, but I got a lot of things done. Perhaps I won't be a burden on you much longer."

The porch on the east side of the Andrews' house was shaded as the sun receded in the west. Twilight ushered in a refreshing breeze as Seth quietly kept his rocker moving. "Mr. Andrews, I started early with Mr. Burgess, the lawyer. He is doing some work for me and I will be renting a part of his building for my use."

Mr. Andrews stopped his rocking motion. "Tom Burgess? Yep, old Tom has been around here quite a spell. He's alright, but he's still a lawyer."

Seth continued, "I got acquainted with Claude Dickens, too."

Andrews listened and answered, "You did make some acquaintances today, I must say."

"Mr. Andrews, what kind of shape are the telegraph lines in at the railroad station?"

Andrews sighed and answered, "Not very good; I can only get to Rocky Mount. I don't think they can get much farther than Weldon. The lines to Richmond have been down for almost a year now." Seth remarked, "I need to contact a friend of mine in Albany, New York, and I don't know the best way to do it. Do you have any suggestions?"

Andrews puffed on his cigar and replied, "I suppose the best way is to give a letter to one of the river captains to take to Washington and try to get it to Baltimore and then to Albany. It's a risk at best. Our mail has been stopped for a long time—but you ought to know that!"

Seth noticed the quickness in Andrews' voice and cautiously remarked, "I need to get word to my contacts about shipping me some new plows and replacement plowshares, moldboards and plowtails. If I can get them here, I can be my own plow-wright."

"I would suggest you give a river captain your letter and wait and see what happens. Nothing is working like it ought to since the war started," remarked Andrews and added, "I can keep you informed about the telegraph, but I wouldn't expect too much."

Seth began a slow rocking motion. "Well, in any event, I've got a lot of work to do in the place I rented from Mr. Burgess to get it ready, not only for an office, but a place I can live in the back room." Seth looked at the cigar smoke spiraling above Mr. Andrews' head. "Tomorrow I want to check on my horse and rig. I will also want to see if there is any information on land for sale at the courthouse."

Darkness covered the porch as Seth got up from the rocker and walked to the door. "Goodnight, I think I'll go upstairs and write that letter you suggested and get it to the riverfront as soon as the next steamer leaves for Washington. That seems about the only thing I can do." Seth walked back to Mr. Andrews and asked, "May I have a match to light the lamp?" Mr. Andrews answered, "Sure, and stop at the hallway table and get a pencil and some paper. Maybe Mr. Burgess will give you an envelope. We don't have any."

Seth stopped at the table, picked up a tablet and pencil and carefully ascended the dim stairsteps. He entered the bedroom, placed the paper and pencil on the bedside table and sat on the bed. Reaching in his shirt pocket he pulled out the match and stood to light the lamp. The flame danced upward as he adjusted the wick and settled in the chair. Somehow this seemed futile, but what else could he do?

Seth finished the letter to Major Jacobs, and placed it in his shirt pocket. He removed his shoes, slipped his suspenders over his shoulders and removed his trousers. Placing them over the back of the chair, he reflected, what have I gotten myself into? He removed his shirt, and blew out the light. The lingering oil odor filled the night air as he pulled back the sheets and dropped onto the bed. Four days in Tarborough and his only sight of Julia had been marred by an ugly incident he preferred to forget.

The warm spring days unfolded into uncomfortable mid-summer. Seth's time was consumed in the preparation of his rented space and an occasional trip into the country. Seth was grateful to the Andrews for allowing him to remain a guest until he could complete his space for his living arrangements. He restrained his emotional urge to call at Coolmore. He knew the only way to reconcile the Duprees was to face them directly. But still he hesitated, and in his mind he used every excuse not to call at Coolmore.

# CHAPTER TWENTY-TWO

Frank Dupree pulled the soiled cloth from his hip pocket, wiped the perspiration from his face and looked overhead at the blistering sun. "Dinnertime! Nate! It's dinnertime."

Nate stepped across the row of tobacco plants, raised his arm and dropped the green leaves he held against his body onto the burlap sheeting. "I's be glad to git to de house for a mouthful of sump'n t'eat. My Lawd, it bees hot!"

Frank wiped his face again and stepped from the rows of plants. He looked at the pile of green tobacco leaves on the guano bags sewn together and glanced at the field. "We better get the leaves before they dry on the stalk. I do pray that it will rain soon." Nate started toward his and Dolly's quarters. "Yassur, I ain't seen it dis dry in a spell now."

Dupree put the sticky rag back into his hip pocket. "This is gummy tobacco this year! Seems like more so than usual. Let's go get a bite to eat and get out of this heat for a while."

Nate followed Dupree toward the house. "You bees right, Mr. Frank. Hit's gummy dis year. I hope hit'll cure decent."

Dupree added, "Yeah, me too. This is all we got. Looks like the corn and cotton have already dried up."

Frank stepped onto the porch and walked to the table. "Julia! Julia! Get out here on the porch!"

Julia ran from the kitchen, noticed her father's dirt-smeared face and asked, "You going to wash up for dinner?"

Frank glared at Julia and walked to the edge of the porch. "Bring the bucket and the dipper over here." Frank gripped a porch column and leaned over the edge of the porch. "Julia, dip the water on the back of my head until I say quit!" Julia quickly filled the dipper and poured it on the back of her father's head.

"More!" shouted her father, "More!" Julia filled the dipper again and poured it over his head. He shook his head, wiped his face with his wet hands and pulled himself back from the edge of the porch. "Bring me that drying cloth!" Julia placed the bucket on the porch, grasped the drying cloth and handed it to her father. He snatched the cloth and with both hands began to dry his face and head. "My, my, my! It's hot out there today!"

Julia took the drying cloth, returned it to the nail and moved to the kitchen. Frank followed Julia into the kitchen and sat at the table. "Ada, the sun is drying everything in the fields. I don't know when I've seen it so hot and dry."

Ada placed a bowl of peas and potatoes on the table. "Julia, you and your daddy, go ahead and eat."

Julia reached for the bowl and looked at Frank. "I heard that Chamberlain man is still staying at the Andrews and is fixing up that place beside lawyer Burgess." Julia handed the bowl to her father and added, "I even heard he's planning to stock some farming tools."

Ada sat down and asked for the bowl and frowned at Julia. "Every time Julia goes anywhere she always hears something. Usually something not worth repeating."

Frank, silent, began to eat and listened as Julia continued, "Well, I did! I heard he even has a horse and a nice gig at the stables in town."

Frank abruptly stopped eating, glared at Julia and shouted, "Good heavens, girl! Everything you seem to hear is about that Yankee soldier! Can't you talk about something else?" Frank looked at Ada and rolled his eyes. "You'd think she'd find something else to talk about! That's all I've heard for the last month!" Frank returned to his dinner. "Our corn is drying up! Our cotton is withering! The well is drying up, and all she can talk about is that dratted Yankee!"

Julia, shocked by her father's irritation, pushed from the table and began crying, "I'm sorry, I didn't mean no harm."

Frank rushed through his dinner, walked onto the porch and placed a chair close to the back wall of the house. Propping his feet on the rungs of the chair, he tipped it back and yelled, "Don't fret none, girl! No harm done!" The shade of the veranda relaxed Frank as he sat silently.

Julia began removing the dishes as Ada filled the dishpan with water. "Let your daddy rest a spell," Ada reminded Julia.

Julia wiped the tears from her eyes and remarked, "The worse things get in the fields, the worse daddy's temperament gets!"

Ada, washing the dishes, responded, "Well, trying to make-do with what we got ain't exactly the easiest thing I ever tried to do. We had to look to the neighbors last year for corn. The only meat we've had is a squirrel or rabbit now and then. The lard's gone and there weren't no hogs last winter. Your daddy ain't got nothing to be happy about."

Julia slinked to the door and observed her father resting. "Yes, ma'am, I reckon he's got enough to keep him worried."

Ada added, "And your constant chatter about that Yankee in town don't help none."

Julia closed the door quietly behind her and walked to the edge of the porch. She observed a dust cloud rising from the Tarborough road. Julia did not relish the thought of disturbing her father, but the cloud of dust appeared to be nearing Coolmore. She peered along the path from the road as a horse-drawn rig turned from the road. The well-groomed horse slowed as the two-wheeled rig approached the house. Julia uttered in a low voice, "Good Lord, it's that Chamberlain man!"

Julia ran from the side of the porch, the vibration roused Frank and he snapped, "What is it now, girl?"

Julia, frightened and excited, sputtered, "It's that Chamberlain man!"

Frank jumped to his feet, raced to the side of the veranda

and observed Seth directing his rig to the rear of the house. With a frown on his face he yelled, "Julia! Did you know about this?"

Julia, trembling, replied immediately, "No, Daddy! I don't know what he's doing here!" Julia and Frank stared as Seth stepped from his gig, secured his horse to a tree, and slowly approached the veranda.

"What the devil are you doing here? What do you want this time?" shouted Frank.

Julia leaned over the edge of the porch and yelled, "You're not welcome here! Leave! Get off this place now!"

Seth moved deliberately toward Frank and extended his hand. Frank backed from the edge of the porch and yelled, "I ain't shaking hands with you!"

Julia ran to the kitchen door and called, "Mama! Daddy needs you out here on the porch!"

Ada rushed to the porch, glared at Frank and Seth and muttered, "Oh my heavens! What a mess this is going to be!"

Julia gripped her mother by her arm and pulled her toward Frank. "Mama, what's daddy going to do?" Ada shook Julia's hand loose and replied, "I don't know, Julia!"

Frank, quivering with anger, demanded, "I'll ask you again, what do you want?"

Seth remained at the edge of the porch and answered slowly and deliberately, "Mr. Dupree, I simply want to talk with you. I mean no harm. I just want to talk business with you."

Dupree's eyes blazed as he reacted, "Business? What business can I possible have with you? Your business was completed here two years ago!" Dupree motioned, "Just look at this place! Thanks to you, we've come close to perishing to death! And you want me to talk with you?"

Seth backed from the porch and focused on Dupree, "Yes,

sir, I want you to talk with me."

Frank gripped a porch column and steadied himself. "Our Willie didn't come home—he's dead and buried and only God knows where! Our fields are drying up, our livestock was run off by you and those with you and our mules and wagon stolen! Just what in God's name have we got to talk about?"

Seth stepped toward the porch, glanced at Julia and Ada and spoke directly to Frank. "About getting your place back into the shape it was in."

Julia gazed at Seth; bitter, vivid memories surfaced. Suddenly it was as if she were seeing him for the very first time. Her anger diminished. What was happening to her? Julia realized she was gawking and was embarrassed. Turning to her mother, she suggested that they leave Frank and Seth to discuss the farming arrangements. Ada and Julia returned to the kitchen, but Julia found a spot where she could watch. She could not take her eyes off of Seth. She was fascinated by this Yankee soldier-turned-farm-supply-merchant. Being in his presence no longer disturbed her. Her bitterness and resentment drained from her.

Seth forced a smile and pleaded, "Can we talk, Mr. Dupree?"

Dupree glared at Seth and relinquished, "Talk? Alright! Then you can leave," Dupree added quickly, "but you stay where you are and talk from there." Dupree leaning on the porch column ordered, "Well! Talk and be done with it!"

Seth moved closer to Frank and looked up to him as he stood on the porch. "Mr. Dupree, I am expecting some shipments of guano in the fall. I have rented some space to store it for the spring season. I hope to have some plows and replacement parts, too." He continued cautiously, "I know things have not been easy, and I'm willing to let you have what you need and wait for the harvest to settle."

Seth glanced at the kitchen door, saw Julia watching as he talked to her father and tried not to stare. He wanted to see Julia, he wanted to talk to her, but now was not the time. He felt a flood of disappointment at the lost opportunity. He sensed her eyes focused on him and felt the intensity of her stare. He glanced at her and smiled; he thought he saw her smile in return, but the distance made him unsure.

Dupree folded his arms and re-braced himself on the column. "Oh, you are—how gracious of you!" Dupree continued sarcastically, "And what do you want in return for your generosity?"

Seth felt his face redden and responded, "Just sign a note of debt."

Dupree forced a laugh and asked, "And what do you expect to back that up when the crops don't make?"

Seth answered, "Just a little land." He quickly added, "I bought a piece of land over near Prospect Hill meeting house; the owner wanted to sell."

Dupree lunged from the column and shouted, "I thought there'd be a trick! It's land you want! Old Williams over near Prospect Hill might want to sell, but we don't! Now that you've talked, you can leave!"

Seth glanced quickly at the kitchen door, saw Julia still gazing at him and felt his face flush. He smiled at Julia and waited for her to reciprocate. She remained motionless and continued to stare. Seth felt the sting of embarrassment and turned his eyes away.

Seth stepped back from the veranda and apologized, "I'm sorry, Mr. Dupree, I thought we might could get together." Seth turned and walked toward his gig, "We're going to have to learn to get along. I'm here to stay, too!"

Julia watched from the kitchen door as Seth untied the reins, stepped into his gig and snapped the reins. She watched the carriage move from the house onto the road to Tarborough and followed with her eyes until it dropped out of sight.

Julia felt a tinge of disappointment. She did not dare reveal her feelings, but for some strange reason she had for a moment wanted her father to have a friendly conversation with Seth. Julia felt guilty for not wanting Seth to leave. After all, he was responsible for the sad condition of their farm, but there was something about that man!

Frank walked from the edge of the veranda, drew the dipper from the bucket and gulped the water. He moved close to the side of the veranda and scattered the water from the dipper. "Can you imagine that? He had the nerve to expect me to go for an offer like that!" Frank shook his head and wiped his face with the gummy rag. "I best be getting back to the field. Me and Nate got a lot of leaves to pull." He looked at Julia and instructed, "You best get Dolly and get on down to the barn. The leaves have got to be tied on the sticks and put in the barn."

Frank walked into the yard, started toward the tobacco field behind the house and shouted, "Nate! Time to go!" He watched for Nate to meet him in the path to the field.

"Daddy! Daddy!" Frank heard Julia shouting.

He turned quickly and raced to the house. Panting, he inquired, "What's wrong, girl? You look like you seen a ghost!"

Pointing toward the main road, she screamed, "He's coming back! I saw his carriage coming back!"

Frank leaped onto the veranda, ran to the opposite side and jumped onto the ground. "At least you're right about one thing. Somebody's coming up the path. I can't tell yet who it is for sure." Frank peered toward the road. "By God! It is him—what does he want this time?" He quickly moved to the center of the path and held up his hand. "Hold it right there!"

Seth drew the lines tight, stopped Blue Boy and remarked, "If we can't get together on business, can I at least find out about your church meeting times?"

Frank, surprised by the question, hesitated as Seth settled his horse. "Why are you asking such a question? What else do you want?"

Seth watched Dupree as he walked to the side of his gig. "I have never heard singing like that before. I was impressed."

Frank placed his hand on the side of the gig and doubtfully asked, "Impressed with what—the difference or the sound?" He moved from the gig as he heard, "The sound—the sound! It was quite moving!"

Frank felt his resentment subside as he thought, why would he be interested? He regained his poise and purposely asked, "Are you being deceitful or do you really want to know?"

Seth countered, "I suppose only time will make that clear."

Frank stepped away from the gig, glanced at Julia and answered, "Tarborough on the first Sunday and Old Sparta on the fourth Sunday. They're the ones closest by." Julia standing on the veranda, added, "Don't forget Prospect Hill and Town Creek!" Frank glared at Julia and frowned. "Yeah! Them, too. We'll see how your interest runs."

"Thank you, sir! I'll be on my way now." Seth glimpsed Julia staring at him as he pulled Blue Boy's reins and turned the gig in the direction of the road to Tarborough. Completing the turn, he glanced at Julia and remarked, "We'll see, we'll see!" Seth snapped the lines and guided his horse from the house.

Frank watched as Chamberlain turned onto the main road and walked toward the veranda. "The war brung some strange things, but the end of it has brung even stranger things."

Julia leaped to the ground and ran to meet her father. "What do you think he has in mind, asking all those questions?"

Frank placed his gummy arm across Julia's shoulders. "The Lord moves in mysterious ways—who knows?"

Julia broke from her father's embrace and ran toward the veranda. "I'll go get Dolly and meet you at the curing barn."

Ada walked from the kitchen to the edge of the veranda. "I

heard those questions," she remarked, "and I don't know what to make of it."

Frank started toward the curing barn, passed Ada on the veranda and added, "Me neither, me neither."

Julia, in her bare feet, leaned and picked four green tobacco leaves from the burlap sheeting. She placed the stems together and handed the leaves to Dolly. Dolly, standing beside a rack supporting a four-foot long stick, gripped the leaves and twisted the string around the bundle and looped them onto the stick. Julia leaned again and picked four leaves and placed the stems together and handed them to Dolly. "You won't believe what happened today."

Dolly looked puzzled, "I 'spose I wouldn't." She looked at Julia and waited for another bundle of leaves. "You goin' to tell or you goin' to keep quiet?"

Julia looked to see if she and Dolly were alone. "Do you recall when them Yankees came here two years ago?"

"Yes'um, I remembers dat."

"Well, one of those soldiers has come back and started some kind of business in town. He came to the house about dinnertime and talked to daddy about guano and plows." Julia leaned for more leaves, handed them to Dolly and continued, "Daddy turned him away, but he came back again and asked about our church meeting times." She continued handing the leaves to Dolly, "Daddy didn't put a sting on him the second time and we wonder what he wants."

Dolly paused and frowned at Julia, "I don't know, girl! I don't know!"

Nate, a sheetful of tobacco on his shoulder, walked to the shed at the barn and dropped the tobacco ladened burlap sheet onto the ground. "Deres more where dis come from." Nate reached and grabbed the bottom of Dolly's apron and wiped his sweaty face. "I best be gittin' back to the field."

Ada finished covering the table with a large linen cloth. The bowls on the table gave the table cover an uneven appearance. The vinegar cruet protruded high, giving the appearance of a mountain peak. Summer months abounded with insects hovering over the leftover food. A table cloth helped, but still the insects persisted. She walked from the kitchen to the shed where Julia and Dolly were getting the tobacco ready to hang in the curing barn. Approaching the shed, Ada judged it would soon be time to start the curing process. She dreaded that part of the preparation time because it kept Frank at the barn for most of the night. The fire in the stone kiln had to be stoked with wood to maintain the heat in the flues.

"I'm finished in the kitchen; I can hand some tobacco," volunteered Ada.

"I'm tired of bending," Julia remarked as she moved from the pile of tobacco.

Dolly scowled at Julia, "You ought to be 'shamed, Miss Julia. Yore mama ain't as able as you are. You git back here and hand me de 'bacca."

Julia glanced at her mother and answered, "Oh, alright! I'll do it." She lifted the leaves, matched the stems together and handed the bundle to Dolly. "I've been telling Dolly about that Chamberlain man," she volunteered.

Her mother stooped and picked up some leaves. "I suspect you've been telling Dolly a lot of things. I saw how you eyed that man when he came to the house." Ada handed the matched leaves to Dolly and added, "You've got something going on in your mind. I haven't raised you all these years not to know a little something about your actions."

Dolly gripped the bundle of leaves from Ada's hand and shook her head. "My Lawd, Miss Ada! Has dat young-un got another man on her mind?"

Ada returned to lifting the leaves and bunching them together. "My heavens, I hope not. Every time we go to church that Mewborn boy's right in the way."

Julia frowned at her mother and countered, "Mama, you know that's not so. He says he's just trying to help."

Ada added sarcastically, "Yes, young lady, I know what sort of help he's trying to give."

Dolly grinned at Julia and nodded, "Yes'um, if'n it won't for de war killin' off the boys, dey'd be here like ants to de sugar bowl—onliest thing, we ain't got no sugar."

Ada laughed as Julia ran from the shed. "Let her go pout a little bit. She'll get over it."

Frank approached the shed, looked at the pile of green leaves and advised, "After that pile is tied, that ought to be a plenty for today. Nate and me are getting tired and it'll soon be suppertime." Frank looked around and asked, "Where's Julia? She ought to be helping here."

Ada answered, "She just ran back to the house. Me and Dolly teased her a little and she's pouting."

Frank pulled his gummy rag from his pocket, wiped his face and informed Ada, "We'll stop at the end of the row we're working; that ought to give you time to fix supper."

Frank turned to Dolly and advised, "Nate will be ready to leave when I do; he's worn out, too."

Ada glared at Frank, shuddered at the gum and dirt and suggested, "You best take a wash rag to your whole frame before supper."

The late afternoon sun glared on the veranda as Frank walked from the kitchen. "That was a good supper! I think I'll move a chair from the veranda and sit in the shade in the yard."

Ada called out, "Julia and I will be right there when we finish the dishes." She glanced at Julia and added, "You are going to stay here and help me finish up in the kitchen!" Julia's face showed a scowl as she replied, "Alright! Alright!"

Frank tipped his chair against a tree, placed his bare feet on the rungs and dropped his hands onto his legs. He removed his gummy shirt and sat with his underwear exposed. He watched as Julia and Ada carried a wooden bench from the veranda. Frank motioned to Ada, "Bring it over here; the shade is real good under this tree."

Julia sat on the bench and motioned to her mother, "There's room for both of us."

Ada broke the silence. "Where do we expect to go to church this coming Sunday? There's a meeting at Old Sparta."

Frank reacted slowly, "The nearest place suits me. I have to be back to feed the stock 'fore dark. I don't want to get too far from home."

The quiet of the evening was abruptly shattered as Julia yelled, "There comes a buggy down the road! To be sure that man's not coming back again!"

Frank tipped his chair from the tree and peered toward the road. "It isn't that fellow again! That's Josh coming out here. He's taken a liking to Julia."

Julia blushed and countered, "No he's not! He's coming to see us all!" Frank watched the buggy as it neared and added, "Yeah, yeah, I know all about that."

Josh pulled his horse to a stop, jumped from the buggy and led his horse to a tree. He secured the lines and walked toward the Duprees. "Evening all!" Josh greeted. "What kind of a day have ya'll had?"

Frank responded, "Evening, Josh! Its been a mighty hot and tiring day."

Josh looked at Julia, smiled and walked closer to her. "You been busy today, Julia?"

She got up and walked to her father's side. "It's been a mighty busy day—and hot, too!"

Josh looked at Mr. Dupree and glanced at Julia, "I hear you had a visitor today."

Frank jerked his head and snapped, "That bad news sprouted legs!" He glared at Josh and asked, "I reckon it's all over the county by now."

Josh looked at Julia and smiled sheepishly, "Yes, sir, I reckon it is."

Frank tipped his chair and announced, "Well, all he wanted was business. He's in some kind of business in town."

Josh focused his eyes on Julia and admitted, "Yes, sir, that's what I heard." Josh continued to gaze at Julia. "Just business? That's neighborly, yes, just business." Julia lowered her eyes and looked toward her mother. "Yes, Josh—only business. Farming business!"

Josh, recognizing the embarrassment, changed the subject. "Julia, I will be going to Old Sparta Sunday. Can I come by and we can go together?" Julia reflecting on the question asked by Seth earlier in the day, hesitated before answering. "I believe I will go with Mama and Daddy. Maybe I'll see you at the meeting. I believe they will have dinner spread at the church Sunday."

Josh looked disappointed. "Are you sure? It won't be any trouble coming by here to pick you up."

Julia looked toward her mother and answered, "Yes, I'm sure. I'll go with them Sunday."

Josh felt his face blush as he looked at Julia. "Alright, I hope to see you there." A feeling of disappointment filled Josh as he walked to his buggy. He jerked the lines from the tree, leaped into the buggy, angrily snapped the lines and guided the buggy toward the road.

Frank stood up, watched the buggy disappear at the end of the path and turned to Julia. "You know what you just did, Julia?"

Julia lowered her eyes and asked, "What did I do, Daddy? I just told him I wanted to go with you and Mama."

Frank glanced at Ada and asked, "Do you expect your mama and me to believe that?" He glared at his daughter and inquired, "What have you really got on your mind?"

She bashfully answered, "Nothing! There's nothing on my mind."

"Well, young lady, since you will be going with us tomorrow, I reckon you know we'll have to be up and about before light."

Julia deliberately looked away from her father. "Yes, sir, I know that. I'll go ahead and clean up for tomorrow." She walked to the porch, picked up the bucket of water and carried it to the kitchen. Julia stirred the hot ashes in the stove and put on a kettle of water. Saturday night was a refreshing time; a time for a complete bath. Walking to the kitchen door she mentioned to Frank and Ada, "I'll be done here in the kitchen before you are ready to come inside."

Julia began to undress as she reflected on the questions Seth had posed earlier. That might, he just might, be at the meeting tomorrow crowded out any thoughts of her rejection of Josh's request. Julia heard Frank and Ada stepping onto the porch and called out, "I'm all finished." With both hands she gripped the basin of bath water and walked to the veranda. She stepped to the edge and tossed the water into the yard. Julia glanced at Ada and Frank and declared, "I'll go on upstairs and get ready for bed. I really do want to go with you tomorrow."

Julia bolted up the spiral staircase and darted to her room. She selected a hairbrush from the dry sink drawer and began to brush her hair. Looking into the mirror over the dry sink, she imagined what she might look like tomorrow if the Chamberlain man was there at the meeting house. A fleeting thought disturbed her as she reflected, what will everybody think if she is too friendly? No, no, that just would not do.

Finishing her hair, Julia pulled the locks over the front of her shoulder, twisted her body and watched the mirror reflect her movements. She removed her dress, chose a cotton nightgown from the bureau drawer and pulled it over her head.

No need to light the lamp, she thought, as she walked to the window. The sun was disappearing in the west. The east side of Coolmore was evolving into darkness. The metamorphosis process of the July insects resounded from the majestic oaks. Nature's cacophony of change filled the night. Julia flipped the sheet to the foot of her bed and fell onto the mattress. She pulled the bolster under her head and thought of tomorrow.

# CHAPTER TWENTY-THREE

S eth awoke, turned on his side and peered through the open window. The eastern horizon was beginning to lighten. His attempts to sleep had been interrupted by fleeting thoughts of his conversation with Frank Dupree. The vivid image of Julia standing in the kitchen doorway invaded his senses with every restless movement. He judged the time by the clarity of the trees in the yard. A feeling of confidence permeated Seth as he reflected on yesterday's occurrences. He had done what he feared, yet had been anticipating. He felt secure as he recalled arranging with the hostler to have Blue Boy ready early Sunday morning. He was restless as the emerging light slowly illuminated the room. The Andrews house was still. Seth rose carefully, moved to the bureau, poured water into the bowl and splashed it on his face. He gripped the linen towel lying beside the basin and walked to the window. His heart quickened as he dried his face and anticipated the day. He was deliberately quiet as he began to dress. Considering the early hour, He moved softly to avoid disturbing the Andrews' Sunday morning.

Seth tucked his shirt, adjusted his suspenders and leaned to inspect his shoes. He walked to the bureau, buttoned his shirt collar and picked up the black ribbon-like tie. Seeing himself in the mirror, he raised the narrow collar, put the black strip around his neck and turned his collar down. He tied the narrow black strip into a small bow and adjusted it. Backing from the mirror, he dipped his hands in the bowl of water and smoothed his brown hair. Leaning toward the mirror he reflected, maybe he should not have shaved his beard, but a clean shave was more comfortable. He listened as sounds began to come from the kitchen and walked to the top of the stairs. Bounding down the steps he greeted Mrs. Andrews. "Good morning! And where is Mr. Andrews?"

Continuing to organize her activities, she answered, "He'll be here shortly. It is Sunday morning, you know."

Seth recognized her irritation and countered, "Oh, I'm sorry. I'll wait on the porch. I was up early this morning and I tried to be quiet."

She continued to put her utensils in order. "I'll let you know when to come in."

Mr. Andrews walked onto the porch, looked at Seth standing next to the railing and observed, "You're looking rather dapper, going some place special today?"

Seth leaned against the low railing and admitted, "Yes, sir, I think I will head out for Old Sparta today. I hear they have a big meeting today, maybe even dinner on the ground. I don't know what that means, but it sounds like some big picnic."

Andrews sat in a rocker, struck a match and lit his cigar. "You might get invited to eat, but you sure as the devil won't be invited to socialize." He continued to advise, "You'll probably get treated like an angry sore spot—nobody can stand to touch it."

Seth felt his enthusiasm drain and he countered, "Well, I'm going to try it anyway."

Rising from the rocker, Andrews came back, "I'm sure you will! I'm sure you will!" Walking to the door, he motioned, "Come on, Charity ought to be about ready with breakfast."

Seth barely touched anything at breakfast. He stirred the molasses in the hot water, gulped the sweet mixture and thanked Mrs. Andrews. He walked to the front door and called toward the kitchen, "Have a nice day! I'll see you all later." Seth leaped down the steps and walked sprightly toward the hostler's stable. He neared the stable, peered toward the front entrance and saw Blue Boy secured at the front. His gig was attached and everything looked in order. Fantastic! He had asked the groom to have Blue Boy ready, but he didn't expect it to be this soon. He reasoned that the groom must have wanted to go back to bed. My good luck, he concluded.

He loosened the lines, patted his horse on the forehead and tugged on Blue Boy's halter. Leading his horse into the street, he declared, "We're going to have a great day, old boy!"

Seth gripped the lines, bolted into the gig and enthusiastically snapped the lines. The road toward Sparta looked familiar. The scenery had changed little since the day he led the column returning from Rocky Mount. Approaching Old Sparta, Seth mused, it was almost like meeting an old friend, this coming back to Sparta. He gently rapped the lines, guided his horse out of the ruts and pressed on.

The midmorning sun began to intensify and the dust settled slowly behind his gig as Seth approached the crossroads. He tugged his horse to a stop and scanned the roads. Seth watched as a buggy approached and waited as it turned in front of him. He observed the man and woman and decided they must be on their way to the meeting house. He snapped the lines and guided his gig behind the buggy. Seth restrained Blue Boy to keep his gig away from the dust of the buggy. He followed the buggy, watched the driver turn the horse into the yard of the meeting house and turned behind the rig. Seth noticed the wagons and buggies encircling the building and guided Blue Boy to a spot which looked unoccupied. He carefully jumped from the gig, secured his horse to a small tree and gazed at the freshly painted meeting house. The tall windows of the building reflected the sunlight and the glare from the white sides interrupted Seth's focus as he moved toward the building.

A crudely dressed man stepped from the gathered men in front of the building and walked toward Seth. "Good morning, sir." Extending his hand, he continued, "I don't think I know you."

Seth gripped his hand and agreed, "No, I don't think we have met before." Seth studied the man's face and waited for his response.

"From the sound of your talk, you ain't from 'round here."

Seth, struck by how unrefined the man was, answered, "No, sir, I'm not a native of this section."

The man visually examined Seth. "My name is Thomas O'Berry. I'm not ordained, but I speak here at times. Folks 'round here call me Tom-O."

Seth strained a smile. "Well, it's a pleasure to meet you, sir."

Tom-O returned to the gathered men as Seth walked to the steps. He observed only one entrance and wondered, why the building at Tarborough had two doors and this building only one?

Seth stepped inside, removed his hat and sat on a rear bench. He noticed the stark white plastered walls and the same short pews beside the pulpit platform as the Tarborough building had. He pondered the contrast as the building began to fill. This house felt cold and foreboding. No one stopped to greet him as the pews filled. A roar echoed through the building as voices intensified in unintelligible sounds. Seth observed the gathering congregation and glanced over his shoulder toward the door. His face flushed and his heart beat faster when he glimpsed the Duprees as they entered. He tried not to gawk, but turned his eyes to determine if Julia was with them. Frank and Ada walked down the aisle and glanced at Seth, but said nothing. Seth felt discouraged as the Duprees passed. He glanced again and his spirits were lifted as he saw Julia come in. She walked toward the front, glanced at him, passed and made no acknowledgment. He noted her full green skirt and white, high-necked blouse, topped with lace. The follow-me-lads streamers trailed from her straw pork-pie hat as she passed. Her chestnut-colored hair in a neat bun glistened under the brim of her hat. Seth gazed at Julia as she edged into the pew with her mother and father. The roar increased as the building continued to fill.

Seth's attention was drawn to the front of the meeting house as the O'Berry man called out a number. The roaring stopped, the standing congregation quickly sat and Tom-O repeated the number. Tom-O walked to a side pew and sat with the men. Seth listened as the vibrations of a tuning fork resonated through the building. He gazed intently toward the front as an old man commenced to hum. His humming became louder as the pitch blended with the resounding vibrations. The old man raised the black book close to his eyes and started to sing. Quickly the congregation's voices blended with the old man's words. Seth picked up the black book on the bench, thumbed through it and saw it was a book of poems. He turned to the number that Tom-O had announced and saw it was the familiar hymn "Amazing Grace." Was this the same kind of singing that was so inspirational before? This singing is as mournful as a death march. This is depressing!

The light from the open door behind Seth suddenly dimmed and he turned to determine the cause. His face flushed again as he observed the Mewborn boy enter. He quickly looked toward the front as Josh passed in the aisle. Josh glanced at Seth, stopped, glared at him and walked to the front. Josh motioned to Julia, edged in beside her and sat down. Julia leaned toward Josh and whispered. Josh turned, gazed at Seth and whispered to Julia. Seth's earlier exhilaration was dampened. The mournful singing and now the young boy and Julia together added to his disappointment.

Thomas O'Berry walked from the side pew, stood beside the table below the pulpit and began to speak. Seth recalled Elder Hart and attempted to compare Hart with O'Berry. What a difference! Seth lowered his head, thumbed through the little black book and glanced at Julia. His spirits drooped and the dragged. Finally, it was over, Seth concluded, as he heard Tom-O announce, "Dinner has been brought. Ya'll are welcome to stay."

Seth walked to the door, listened to the final verse of the mournful hymn and stepped outside. He walked to his gig, adjusted Blue Boy's lines and watched the women remove their baskets from the buggies and wagons. Suspended between two trees Seth observed rough-sawn boards. The boards were quickly covered with white tablecloths and dishes filled the length of the boards. Tom-O muttered some words and the scattered crowd converged at the makeshift table.

The shade of the oak trees obstructed the direct rays of the sun as men and women began to mingle. A muffled roar resounded from the crowd as Seth observed a man walking toward him.

"Come on and have some dinner," he motioned to Seth.

"It does look very good, and there appears to be enough to feed an army," Seth remarked.

"There's a-plenty! Come and help yourself."

Walking to the table, Seth added, "Thank you, I believe I will." He glanced toward Julia, observed the young boy watching him and picked up a plate. He followed behind an older man, and selected from the food spread on the cloths. He balanced the plate, placed his fork on the plate and moved away from the table. Standing alone, he began to eat as he glanced around the milling crowd.

Seth observed Josh furtively, saw him move from Julia and approach Tom-O. He maintained his oblique gaze and saw Josh speaking to O'Berry. Tom-O stopped eating, looked toward Seth and nodded his head. Josh moved from Tom-O to another man, drew close and spoke into his ear. Seth observed the man and Josh looking toward him. Seth felt the severity of their stares and walked to the table to return his plate. He continued to keep Josh in his sight as he walked to his gig, thinking, Mr. Andrews was right!

He surveyed the gathering and noticed Josh walking toward him. Seth loosened the lines and stood beside his gig. No need to look frightened now. He kept his gaze on Josh as he neared. Josh stopped directly in front of Seth and looked straight into his eyes. "I know who you are! I think I know what you want! And right now, I'm telling you to stay away from Julia

Dupree!" Then he added angrily, "And better still, stay away from Tarborough! Your kind ain't wanted, and you might not live to see another day! Carpetbaggers ain't wanted around here!"

Seth's face began to redden. He restrained the urge to physically strike back as he angrily countered, "I don't know your name, but I do know your kind! I don't plan to go anywhere! If you make any advance toward me, I'll make you regret the thought!"

Josh's face flushed as he stepped back from Seth and added, "You just keep yourself away from Julia!"

Seth gripped the lines and examined the silent assembly. "You and your Christian friends need to realize you lost the war!"

Seth glanced toward the crowd and saw Julia emerge and run toward his gig. He watched Julia as she gripped Josh's arm and pulled him toward her, "I don't want no embarrassment here, Josh Mewborn! Come on, let's get home." She tugged his arm again and added, "You can take me back home!"

Seth glared at Josh and concurred, "Yes, Josh, if that's your name, you'd be wise to take her advice."

Josh lunged toward Seth, Julia restrained him and angrily screamed, "Stop this! Take me home, now!"

Josh calmed his rage, stared at Seth and yelled, "You stay away from Julia and you stay away from me!"

Julia motioned to her father, "Somebody come here and help me!" Tom-O and Frank darted from the crowd, seized Josh and pulled him back to the table. Frank shouted at Josh, "That's enough, boy!" The gathering resumed their conversations and the muffled din dimmed the confrontation. Seth gripped Blue Boy's halter and led him to the road. He looked back at the people, gripped the side board and pulled himself in the seat. He snapped the lines rapidly and guided his horse into the center of the road.

Passing the crossroads of Sparta he reasoned that he should have listened to Mr. Andrews. He knows these people better than I. Pressing Blue Boy toward Tarborough, he mused that at least Julia did intervene and that was a good sign.

Seth's despondency was buoyed by the recollection of Julia walking in the aisle. The brightness of the interior of the building had etched the sight of Julia indelibly in his mind. He smiled as he remembered her pulling at the Mewborn boy. Snapping the lines he reasoned, if the Mewborn boy thought he was interested in Julia and Mr. Dupree held the same notion, then why should he continue to guard his secret yearning?

He pressed Blue Boy steadily toward Tarborough. The afternoon sun still had a long time to shed its light before descending in the west. This day was not completed. Seth judged there was much he could do before the twilight announced the close of the day. He urged Blue Boy to the stable, guided the gig to the front entrance and leaped to the ground. "Anybody home?"

A voice sounded from the interior of the stable, "The door's open! You know where to put your horse. Close the door behind you!" Seth gripped Blue Boy's halter, led him inside the barn and unharnessed the rig. He pulled Blue Boy to a stall, removed his halter and stroked his forehead. "Rest well, old boy." He walked from the stable, closed the door and moved toward his space beside Lawyer Burgess' office.

Seth pulled the key from his pocket and unlocked the door. He stepped inside the room and braced the door open with a chair. A musty odor lingered in the room. He sat at the worn desk, pulled a drawer and removed a sheet of paper and pencil. The late afternoon sunlight reflected from the dusty street through the two windows and door. He untied his bow tie and unbuttoned his collar. Adjusting the paper and positioning the pencil, he began to write.

July, 1865
Tarborough, N.C.
Ferris Jacobs, Jr.

I have not been in recp't of any correspondence from you. A letter was dispatched by way of a river boat captain in the expectation you would receive it.

One cannot imagine the privations the people here are experiencing. It is even more difficult to imagine the indignities the southern people are suffering at the hands of our own people.

It is disheartening to witness the subjugation the central government is fostering on these people. I think you should well be glad you are not part of the occupying force.

I have secured a parcel of land in the northwest part of the county in your name. When the legal papers are complete and I am in touch with you, I will apprise you of the details.

There is much resentment toward us here. Sometimes it is very discouraging, but I have done what I have done.

I do not know if you will receive any of my correspondence, but I must try. In my last letter I asked you to send a number of implements. I hope you received the request. I can only wait.

All telegraph lines are down and there is no way to communicate. Times are very difficult. The people are a determined lot. I would think Albany is cooler than it is here.

Your obedient servant,
Seth C.

Seth tipped his chair back and stared out the open door. The shadows were beginning to lengthen. Tarborough was quiet as a peaceful Sunday drew to a close. Seth straightened in his chair when he heard the rumble of a wagon on the main street. He listened as the rumble became louder. Looking through the doorway, he glimpsed a buggy as it rounded the corner. Seth, startled by the sudden appearance of the buggy, jumped from his chair and darted away from the doorway. A loud crashing sound broke the silence as a rock crashed through the front window. Seth dashed to the door, leaped into the street and watched as the buggy disappeared in a cloud of dust. He peered down the street as the buggy turned out of sight. Blast it all! It looked like that Mewborn boy, but who will believe me? He looked at the smashed window and walked into the room. Mr. Burgess will just love to see this tomorrow! Seth closed and locked the door. Discouraged, he walked to the Andrews house. A Sunday which had begun so encouragingly was waning in gloom.

Billy Andrews watched from the porch chair as Seth slowly ascended the steps. "You look like it might have been better if you'd stayed in bed today."

He lingered on the steps and responded, "You were right! I got a little something to eat and that was all. They looked at me like I was a snake in their hen house. It was a good thing they didn't have a hoe in their hands." Seth stepped onto the porch and sat in a rocker. "A little while ago, somebody rode by in a buggy and hurled a big rock through my window. I know Burgess won't like that." Seth tipped the rocker and continued, "I think it was that Mewborn boy, but nobody will believe me. He threatened me at the Meeting House today."

Andrews frowned and responded, "Threatened you? How did he do that?"

Seth leaned forward in his rocker, "He threatened me harm if I did not stay away from Miss Dupree."

Billy puffed on his cigar, "Frank Dupree's girl?"

Seth's rocker tilted back as he answered, "Yes, Mr. Dupree's daughter."

Mrs. Andrews appeared in the doorway and announced, "Supper's ready."

Seth leaned forward in the rocker and averred, "I'm not hungry; I think I'll stay on the porch awhile. You go ahead. Thank you anyway."

A shadow began to extend from the east side of the house onto the front yard. Seth reclined in the rocker, mulled over the events of the day and concluded, I'm here and I intend to stay here! The Duprees were probably back at Coolmore by now. He determined he would inform Julia of the rock tossing incident since she had heard the threats at the meeting house.

Frank pulled the line in his left hand. "Haw! Haw! The mule reacted and turned into the path from the Tarborough road. He lightly snapped the ropes and urged the animal to the rear of Coolmore. "Ada, you and Julia get off and I'll put up the mule and feed up."

Julia lifted her skirt and leaped to the ground. Ada cautiously slipped to the edge of the seat, gripped the side and called, "Julia! Help me down from the wagon. That ride made my bones stiff." Ada gripped Julia's hand and lowered herself to the ground. Julia ran to the veranda and darted up the steps. She flung open the hallway door and dashed to the spiral staircase. Julia looked up, saw the rays of light filtering through the colored glass and raced up the steps. Stopping on the second floor, she glanced at the colors dancing in the dome and sprinted to her room. Panting, Julia unbuttoned her skirt, let it fall, unbuttoned her blouse and flung it on the bed. She unlaced her shoes, tossed them in the corner, removed her stockings and pitched them on top of her shoes. Clothed in her undervest and pantalettes, she raced to the staircase and double stepped the narrowing spiral steps to the cupola.

Julia dropped to her knees, twisted and sat on the cupola floor. She placed her arm on the window sill and rested her chin on her arm. Relaxing in the draft rising from the bottom of the staircase, she reflected, Josh sure made a show of himself today. She wondered if anyone would have tried to stop Josh if she had not intervened. Julia wondered whether Seth had noticed her in any way other than restraining Josh.

The colored glass transformed the cupola into changing multi-colored patterns as clouds passed between the sun and the cupola. Julia scanned the parched fields, noted the twisted stalks of corn and the thirsty cotton plants. She judged the cotton ought to be twice as tall. A warm breeze caressed her as she stared through the open window. She reasoned, if this heat and dry spell keeps up, then daddy will sure enough need some help come fall. Julia continued to study the distress of Coolmore for the spring planting season. She was aware of her father's independent disposition and reasoned it would be useless to mention looking for assistance until the next harvest. Julia surveyed the fields and surmised that if this year's harvest fails, we fail. Time faded into space as Julia's thoughts digressed to the day's happenings. Why had she intervened in the encounter between Josh and Seth? What galvanized her into that action?

The treetops to the west of Coolmore were beginning to obscure the sinking sun. The cupola colors dimmed. Looking down the spiral staircase, Julia noted the proportion of darkness at each floor. She cautiously stepped from the cupola onto the winding stairs and quickened her steps as the staircase widened with each turn. Stopping on the second floor, she heard her mother call, "Julia! Get ready for supper." Julia entered her room, removed an old gingham dress from the bureau drawer, put it on and buttoned the front. She looked at her dress and shoes on the floor. I'll put them up later she decided. In her bare feet, she dashed down the stairway to the main floor and onto the veranda. Frank, washing his hands and face, looked at Julia and remarked, "I'm glad this day is over. I don't know what the people thought when you pulled Mewborn from that Chamberlain fellow. I hope they don't get the notion that we're getting too friendly with him."

Julia walked to the table, picked up the basin and tossed the water into the yard. She dipped fresh water from the bucket and began to wash her face. "I really don't care what they think. No matter what we think of him, he may have what we are going to need to get by on." She dried her face and continued, "It looks like we're going to lose everything in the fields from the dry spell."

Frank frowned at Julia, "Good Lord, girl, your twenty-two years don't entitle you to know what's best for this place!"

Julia hung the drying cloth on the nail. "I can see what's happening around here, Daddy. It don't take no Solomon to see we might not have enough to make-do with." She opened the kitchen door and remarked as Frank entered, "You and Nate can't do all the work around here." He sat at the table and motioned to Ada, "Come on and sit down, Julia here has got our problems figured out."

Ada pulled her chair to the table and asked, "Oh, she has, has she? What does she want you to do?" Julia interrupted, "I don't want him to do anything! I just made mention we might not have the crops to harvest to carry us through the winter."

Frank pushed his chair closer to the table. "Go ahead and eat and let me worry about that."

The earlier breeze through the oak trees ceased; the leaves became still and a veil of darkness covered Coolmore. The ever- present creatures of the night launched into their nocturnal repetitive clatter.

The veranda was quiet as the conversation diminished. Julia walked to the doorway and announced, "I'm tired, I'm going to bed."

Frank responded, "So are we. It's going to be a hard week upcoming."

Ada nodded and asserted, "All the weeks are going to be hard, and all the months and years are going to be hard! We don't have much to look forward to. The best way for us to handle the hardships is to live one day at a time and not borrow trouble from tomorrow."

# CHAPTER TWENTY-FOUR

The heat of summer stubbornly relinquished its grip as autumn announced its arrival. Seth, standing on the courthouse steps admired the brilliant colors of the leaves. He had seen the seasonal changes in New Berne, but autumn here presented a variety equal to that of New York. He lingered at the top of the wide steps and gazed at the morning sun through the stirring leaves. The stimulating hint of cooler weather invigorated him as he heard his name called, "Mr. Chamberlain! Mr. Chamberlain!" He looked toward the river and spotted a young boy running toward the courthouse shouting, "Mr. Chamberlain!"

Seth quickly stepped to the bottom of the steps and stopped the boy. "Yes, young man! I'm Chamberlain! What are you so excited about?"

Huffing, the lad blurted, "The boat captain wants you at the dock!"

Seth gripped the lad by his shoulders and inquired, "Are you sure, boy?"

The dusty-faced lad answered, "He's calling for a Mr. Chamberlain!"

Seth reached into his pocket, pulled out a coin and placed it in lad's hand. "Thank you, son! I'll see to it right now!"

He watched the boy as he skipped off, "Thank you, sir! Thank you!"

Seth walked to his office, closed the door and headed toward the dock. He wondered as he walked faster if this could be the shipment from Jacobs. Could it be after all these months that his letters had reached the major? Approaching the dock, Seth saw a man pacing and he called out, "Captain! Captain!"

The bearded man removed his cap as Seth approached and asked, "Are you Mr. Seth Chamberlain?"

Chamberlain responded, "Yes, sir!"

Putting on his cap, the captain explained, "I've got some boxed cargo for you," then added hastily, "but the shipping charges are for you to pay, and you will have to remove it from the dock." Seth, elated, responded, "Get it on the dock! I'll be right back with a wagon and a bank draft." Seth asked excitedly, "Where's it from?"

Walking toward the steamer, the captain answered, "Up north, somewhere, that's all I know."

Chamberlain, alternately walking and running went toward the stables. He entered the opened door and shouted, "I need a mule and a wagon, quick!"

The stable hand looked at Seth and asked, "How quick?"

Seth glanced toward the stalls and responded, "Just as quick as I can get back from across the street!" He dashed through the opened doors and ran to his office. Opening the unlocked door, he ran to his desk and opened a drawer. He groped for his bank drafts, sighted one and removed it from the drawer. He shoved the drawer closed, bolted through the doorway and left the door ajar. Panting as he entered the stable, he shouted, "Is that wagon ready to go?" Seth paced impatiently, looked to the rear of the stables and shouted louder, "Is that wagon ready?"

The stablehand drawled, "Don't be in such a rush, Mister! It's still early in the day."

Seth grabbed the lines from the hostler, tugged on the halter and led the mule into the street. He gripped the lines and leaped onto the wagon seat. Snapping the lines, he clucked, "Gwick! Gwick!" Chamberlain felt the wheels revolving, impatiently whipped the lines and shouted, "Move out! Move out!"

Tom Burgess watching from his law office, observed the stubborn mule and walked outside. "Hey, Chamberlain! Don't you know how to talk to a mule?" He laughed and advised, "Just guide him, he ain't going but so fast."

Seth bounced the lines, glared at Burgess and called, "Send me some help down to the dock! I think my things have come in."

Burgess gestured with his hand, "Alright! I'll find somebody."

Seth accepted the nature of the animal and directed the mule toward the dock. Approaching the bank of the river, he stood in the wagon and tugged the mule to a stop. "Gee! Gee! He shouted as the pulled on the right line. The mule turned and stopped. Frustrated, Seth leaped from the wagon, grabbed the halter and pulled the mule away from the river bank. He extended the lines to a tree and secured the mule. Seth walked down the steep bank to the dock. He watched as the river men moved the boxes onto the dock. "Captain!" Seth called loudly. "Yes, sir," sounded from the steamer as the captain emerged from the hatch. He looked at Seth and asked, "You find anybody to load these boxes for you?"

Chamberlain looked at the crates and replied, "Somebody will be here shortly to load them on the wagon." He pointed to the wagon at the top of the bank. "We can get them up there to the wagon." Seth reached into his shirt pocket, pulled out the bank draft and asked, "Where is the bill of lading?"

The boat captain motioned, "Come on aboard and I'll go below and get it."

Seth stepped onto the rocking boat, observed the giant, round paddle-wheel at the stern and noted what a difference there was between this boat and Street's Ferry on the Neuse River. He walked cautiously beside the cabin to the bow of the steamer and looked down to the waterline. The dark green planking of the side of the steamer was peeling. Brown water lapped at the hull as the boat rocked against the dock. He watched the mooring lines fall to the water and tighten as the boat rocked with the river waves. Seth wondered why the wheelhouse was near the bow of the boat. He smiled as he mused, that it looked like a bulldog. Seth judged it must be because the river pilot had to view the shallow river to avoid debris. He carefully stepped alongside the wheelhouse to the center of the steamer and noted the metal stack emerging from the deck behind the wheelhouse. A gray wisp of smoke wafted upward in the still autumn air. Seth recalled the steamers tied to the quay at New Berne and was reminded of the usual two stacks of the larger steam ships. The white paint of the wheelhouse was dull and peeling. Seth wondered if the guano he ordered would arrive on a river boat like this one.

The faint odor of burned wood attracted Seth's attention as the wheelhouse door opened. "Here it is, Mr. Chamberlain," the grimy captain called as he emerged from below and presented Chamberlain with the bill of lading. Seth looked at it and saw the shipper was F. Jacobs, Albany, N.Y. "Very good, captain! Here's my draft for the cost." He placed the draft on the steamer cabin roof and completed the draft. "You just get the boxes on the dock; I'll take it from there." Seth leaped from the steamer onto the dock. "Thank you, captain! I hope to see you again!"

Seth looked toward the top of the river bank, observed two black boys scampering down and called out, "Did Lawyer Burgess send you boys here?"

Reaching the dock, the two announced, "We's here, sir. What you want done? Mr. Burgess 'rected us here."

Seth gestured to the mule and wagon above the dock. "I want all these boxes put on that wagon. I'll be up there to show you where to put them."

Seth watched the two boys as they leaned to grasp the boxes. "Umph! What might dis be? Hit's heavier than a dead hog on de gallowses."

Seth laughed and affirmed, "It's something to work with. Just get them up the hill."

He observed the boys as they moved the crates to the

wagon. "Dis is de last one," noted one of the boys as they slid the box onto the wagon.

Seth reached in his pocket and pulled out two coins and handed them to the boys. "Thank you, lads!" Walking to the tree to loose the lines, Seth looked at the animal and muttered, "Reckon you can pull this?" He secured his foot on a wheel spoke and pulled himself onto the seat. Snapping the lines, he pulled the right line and shouted, "Gee!" The wagon wheels sank in the sand, stopped and suddenly lurched with the pull of the animal. Seth directed the mule to the center of the road and urged the beast toward his office.

Chamberlain pulled the lines tight, stopped the mule and leaped from the wagon. He gripped the lines and walked to the front of the mule. Gripping the mule's bridle, he pulled the animal nearer the front of the two offices. Burgess stepped from his office and laughed as Seth pulled on the mule. "That's about as close as you're gonna get that beast." Burgess gazed at the boxes in the wagon and inquired, "Where do you aim to store them crates?"

Irritated, Seth retorted, "In that blasted space I rented from you, I suppose!"

Burgess pointed to the boarded-up space beside Seth's room. "You can use that for the time being." Seth walked to the front of the boarded window and looked at Burgess. "I suppose it would be best to leave it boarded up. Somebody might hurl another rock at me!"

The lawyer walked to the side of the wagon and looked at the crates. "Looks like your friend in New York got your letter. He's got more faith in you than the folks around here do."

Seth walked to the side of the wagon, folded his arms on the side boards and stared across the crates. "Burgess, don't confuse faith with survival. Faith is talking. Survival is working." Seth maintained his gaze at the lawyer. "I have what the farmers need to survive! They'll come around soon enough." Burgess laughed and conceded, "Oh, alright, I'll get some hands and you can get this wagon unloaded."

A crisp breeze rustled the drying leaves of the trees as Seth tugged on the mule's halter and guided the animal to the stable. "Here's your mule back!" yelled Seth.

He waited as the complaining stablehand approached. "Maybe you ought to have kept the beast all night! I'm ready to get on home!"

Seth handed him the lines and responded, "Sometimes we all have to do what we don't like. Goodnight, sir!"

Seth, fatigued, trudged to the Andrews' house. Stopping at the steps he looked, saw the porch vacant and stepped to the front door. He walked to the back porch, filled a basin and washed his face and hands. Drying his face, Seth called, "Is anybody here?"

He detected the aroma from the kitchen, turned and heard Mr. Andrews, "Yes, we're here in the kitchen. Come on in and sit down."

Seth sat at the table and announced, "Those implements I ordered arrived today by a steamer. I didn't know whether to look for them or not."

Andrews reminded him, "I told you a riverboat captain would get your letter off. These days with everything down, it certainly is not convenient."

Seth nodded in agreement, "Yes, sir, you're right and tomorrow I'll have to start getting things in order; and I'll have to do it myself."

_____

Seth was excited as he viewed the tops of the crates. He forced the hammer claw under a board and heartily pried the board loose. Looking at the raised nail head he tapped the board down and wedged the nail head between the hammer claws. He put pressure on the handle and pulled the nail from the board. He dropped the hammer, gripped the loose board and jerked it free. He gazed at the plowshares and visualized the assembled plow.

Chamberlain removed his military frock coat, tossed it over a crate and proceeded to open the boxed implements. A wagon rolled past the front of the building and Seth flinched. Recalling the rock incident, he watched the wagon continue toward the river. Seth knew Saturday mornings were social occasions. The streets were filled with mules and wagons secured in front of the shops along the main thoroughfare. He reasoned, why not ramble the streets like the local people? Yes, why not! They made no effort to dress in any special fashion and he would not either.

Seth walked to the doorway, stepped into the street and felt the warmth of the sun. He decided to leave his frock coat in the building, reached into his pocket and pulled out the key. Locking the door, he concluded, why not enjoy the warmth of the day? He brushed off his trousers, adjusted his suspenders and briskly walked to the main thoroughfare. The sun felt good as he strolled  and observed the chatting groups. Seth detected the fading conversations as he neared the groups and sensed their silent gaze as he passed. He tipped his hat and moved along the street.

Seth crossed the street and turned to walk toward his business. The glare from the midmorning sun blurred his vision as he peered along the store fronts. Passing into the shade of store front, he spotted Julia Dupree. His heart began to pound as he neared her. He stopped, took off his hat and waited as Julia approached. Seth, captivated by Julia's comeliness, maintained his gaze as she stoically passed. He quickly put on his hat and called, "Miss Dupree! Miss Dupree!"

Julia stopped, turned toward Seth and responded, "Yes?" Seth's attention was drawn to her chestnut-colored hair glistening in the sunlight. Her hair, the last time Seth had seen her, was twisted tight to the back of her head. She glared at Seth, her poke bonnet shading her deep brown eyes and repeated, "Yes, Mr. Chamberlain?"

Seth continued to admire her tresses flowing from the back of her bonnet onto her shawl. "Miss Dupree, may I have a word with you, please?"

She stared at Seth and replied, "I don't think we have anything to talk about."

Seth stepped closer, detected a hit of magnolia essence and gazed into Julia's eyes. "Miss Dupree, I am aware of the differences we have had and I certainly understand your feelings."

Julia frowned and responded, "Do you, now? Do you really think you understand how we feel?" She motioned and continued, "Just look around at our misery and tell me you understand how I feel!"

Seth fumbled with his hat and replied, "Well, not really, but I do know about disappointments. Deep disappointments."

Julia walked from Seth, turned and snapped, "I will not be rude. You asked for a word with me—what is it you want? I don't want to be seen talking with a carpetbagger."

Seth searched Julia eyes for any sense of acceptance. "Miss Dupree, I know things have been difficult for you and your family, with the war and all. I know I was a part of your hurt." Seth felt sheepish as he continued, "That was then and this is now. I have gotten some farming tools that will make your daddy's farming a lot easier. Especially now that there are no field hands to do most of the work."

Julia's face formed a scowl as she replied, "And what do you think we will pay you with?"

He stumbled for words and replied, "I'll be willing to wait for the next harvest."

She countered, "What do you demand for security?"

Seth quickly remembered his words to Major Jacobs about using the land for security. "I have heard that folks around here do business with a handshake. Mr. Dupree's word is good enough for me."

Julia made a movement to walk away, halted and concentrated her stare on Seth. "I suppose you have a place of business in town?"

He quickly answered, "Yes, it's across from the courthouse. I've got a lot of work to do to get it in shape for next spring."

Turning to walk away from Seth, she remarked, "Daddy knows what's best." Seth, sensing the rejection, watched Julia as she moved farther along the street, and he returned to his rented space.

Seth opened the door, glanced at the opened crates and searched the floor for the borrowed pliers. He pushed a crate with his foot, exposed the pliers and leaned to pick them up. The early afternoon sun warmed the interior of the building. Seth's military frock coat that felt warm earlier in the day was becoming uncomfortable as he stooped to assemble the plows. He stood upright, removed the coat and draped it over the desk chair. Returning to his knees he continued to tighten the nuts on the bolts with his fingers. Securing them finger tight, he picked up the pliers and twisted the nuts tighter. The plow was beginning to take shape. The shape of the plowshare caught Seth's attention as he stood and imagined the finished implement. A very big improvement on the earlier shapes, he concluded.

Returning to his knees, Seth resumed assembling the plow. The sunlight entering the doorway dimmed and attracted Seth's attention. He looked up and saw Julia standing in the doorway. He rose slowly, gripped a plow handle and stared at her. The image of Julia, framed in the open doorway by the reflected sunlight, stunned Seth. He noticed her bonnet was dangling by its straps down her back. The shawl which earlier covered her shoulders was missing. Her glistening hair flowed over her shoulders and disappeared under the bonnet. Julia's laceless collar exposed her satiny skin. Seth glanced at the sleeve cuffs and viewed her silky hands. Her print calico dress emphasized the porcelain texture of her skin and the color of her eyes.

Seth was jolted into reality as Julia stepped into room and remarked, "I heard your window was smashed by a stone thrower."

Seth brushed off the front of his shirt and responded, "Yes, that was last Sunday evening. I think I know who it was, but I'm sure nobody around here will believe me." Then he added, "It really is not doing me any harm, it really does harm to Lawyer Burgess. It's his building, you know."

Julia spitefully reminded Seth, "Didn't I tell you that you and your kind weren't wanted? I told you that you had done us enough harm already." Julia's face flushed with anger. "Don't you know when you're not wanted? Can't you see our people will never accept you!" She glanced through the open doorway and added hatefully, "Those people out there don't want anything you've got!"

Seth fastened his eyes on Julia and declared forcefully, "Miss Dupree, I do not intend to leave! I do not intend to be intimidated or frightened into leaving, and the sooner you and your friends accept that, the better off we all will be." His eyes blazed as he advised Julia, "I have some implements now! I will soon have the guano that your daddy and everyone else is going to need next spring. Yes! You will come to me for that, and you'd better get used to it!"

Julia fired back, "Oh no, we won't! We got along before you came, and we'll get along after you're gone!

Seth proudly pointed to the unfinished plow, "There is nothing like that in this part of the state. It can break more new ground than anything around here! Change the share and it will bust middles all day long." He spitefully added, "And I've got extra shares for the ones that get broken, and that, Miss Dupree, will bring your stubborn people here!"

Julia rushed to the doorway, turned and shouted, "I'll dig

the rows with a hoe before we'll need anything here!"

Julia stepped into the street, observed the staring crowd and stomped from the doorway. She watched as the crowd dispersed and Josh ran toward her. "Julia! You know I don't want to see you with that man! It looks like every chance you get, you always show up where he is!" Josh pointed toward the building and admonished, "I've told you not to go near that fellow, and I ain't going to tell you again!"

Julia's cheeks flushed as she glared at Josh and exclaimed, "What do you mean, you've told me? You don't tell me anything! You might not like what I do, but you sure as the devil are not going to tell me what to do!" Julia glanced toward Seth's office, glimpsed him in the doorway and continued in a loud voice, "You, or nobody else, is going to tell me where I can and cannot go!"

Josh backed from Julia and apologized, "I didn't mean to boss you! I thought we had an understanding!"

Julia glared at him and added, "Yeah! We've got an understanding, and you best understand I don't need a master."

Josh reached to touch Julia's hand, "I said I'm sorry! Ain't that enough?"

Julia jerked away and snapped, "Just so you know you don't tell me what I can or can't do!" Julia quickly mingled with the Saturday afternoon crowd.

Seth, observing from the open doorway, watched Josh as he made his way toward him. He stood in the open doorway and gestured with his hand, "Stop right there! I don't want any trouble." Josh remained motionless as Seth advised, "I'll tell you the same thing! I go where I want to, when I want to!" Then he warned angrily, "Any more stone throwing just might get you hurt!"

Josh turned and blurted, "How do you know it was me?" Seth countered, "I didn't! You just told me! If I were you, I'd get back to milling what little corn is left around here." Seth watched as Josh rounded the corner to join the Saturday afternoon throng. Seth smiled to himself, well, at least he knows where he stands, too. The shadows extended farther along the street as Seth stepped from the doorway, pulled the key from his pocket and locked the door. He felt the coolness of the late afternoon, unlocked the door and secured his frock coat. Stepping back into the street he locked the door and began walking to the Andrews' house. Flinging his coat over his shoulder, he questioned, are all my days destined for this?

# CHAPTER TWENTY-FIVE

Autumn's magnificent parade of colors had vanished. Layers of wet leaves covered the ground beneath the sweet gum and maple trees in the pine thickets that lined the road to Coolmore. Green towering pine trees stood as living sentinels of a sleeping nature. The naked tree limbs bared their branches against a gray February sky. Winter's icy hand gripped the landscape with its colorless fingers. The bitter winds swept the dry broom sage in the barren fields. Chimneys spewed black billowing smoke high into the air and a pall of gray smoke hovered over the houses dotting the barren landscape. Obscured by heavy clouds, the sun struggled to lighten the shortened hours of daylight. Seth reasoned as he snapped the lines on Blue Boy's back, he must talk to Mr. Dupree and return to his room before darkness veiled the road to Tarborough. His gig lumbered in and out of the spongy ruts. Winter rains turned the rutted roads into hidden mire. Chamberlain cautiously pressed west from Tarborough toward Coolmore.

Seth's trilby hat, knee length great coat and knit wool gloves thwarted the wintry blast as he moved from the tree-lined protection beside the road into the open spaces. His blue wool army blanket protected him from his waist to his feet, but cavalry boots gave his numb feet little comfort. Seth squinted as his eyes became wet from the icy wind. He rapped the lines on Blue Boy's back and urged him on toward Coolmore.

The form of the Coolmore house emerged from the wintry murk as he neared the entrance. Seth's spirits rose as he viewed the gray smoke ascending from the brick chimney towering above the house. He imagined the roaring fire in a massive fireplace and Julia with her mother and father sitting close to the flames. Seth pulled on the left line and muttered, "Haw!" He steadied Blue Boy as the horse trotted along the path to the house. Nearing the veranda, Seth pulled the horse to a stop and flipped the blanket from his legs. He jumped from the gig, gripped the horse's halter and led Blue Boy behind the house. Detecting the protection from the wind, he tied his horse to the woodshed behind the kitchen and walked to the veranda. On the veranda Seth scraped the mud from his boots and walked to the rear door. A bitter blast of wind from the west blew across the veranda as he rapped on the door. He heard motions from inside and felt the vibrations of steps become stronger under his feet; he moved away from the door and listened as the knob turned and the door opened.

Frank Dupree peered from behind the slightly ajar door. "Good heavens, man! This ain't no time to be out in the cold. Are you in some kind of bad fix?"

Chamberlain, his eyes wet from the icy wind, responded, "I came out here to see you, Mr. Dupree. I admit my choice of times isn't the best, but I didn't expect it to be this cold." Seth shivered and waited for a response.

"Well, I ain't so cruel as to make you stand out in the cold; you can come on in." Dupree opened the door wider, stood back as Seth entered the hallway. "Yes, sir, this is wicked weather. I should have stayed put in Tarborough."

A puzzled expression crossed Frank's face as he invited Seth, "Come on with me to where we're sitting around the fire." He followed Dupree in the hallway to a closed door. He heard Julia and her mother talking. Frank opened the door, walked in the room and motioned, "Come on in by the fire. You can thaw yourself before you have to go back to town."

Seth removed his hat, looked at Julia sitting in a rocker and greeted her, "Good afternoon, Miss Dupree." He looked at Ada and nodded, "Good afternoon to you, Mrs. Dupree."

Ada rose from her chair and remarked, "I'll fetch another chair."

Julia interrupted, "I'll get it, Mama. You keep your chair."

Seth moved to the open fireplace and commented, "That's quite alright, I'll stand here in front of the fire. I don't think I will be here very long."

Julia sat in her chair and looked at her father. "I suppose he's here to see you. Mama and me will go to the kitchen if you want to talk privately."

Frank responded, "No, you and your mama stay here. He won't be here that long." Frank moved beside Seth in front of the fireplace. Frank, standing on one side of the fireplace looked at Seth at the opposite side and asked, "Well, Mr. Chamberlain! What business do you have here?" Julia and Ada sat away from the fire and observed the two men as they faced each other.

"Mr. Dupree," Seth began, "I will come directly to the point and tell you why I came out to see you. I have received a good shipment of farming tools from New York, and I'm offering to supply you what you will need to start your crop in the spring. I have some very good plows and parts for them." Seth glanced at Julia, observed the shawl around her shoulders and her rapid rocking motions, he sensed her hostility. He looked at Ada and continued, "I expect a shipment of guano any time. I don't know a lot about farming, but I believe you do need all those things."

Julia stopped rocking and interrupted, "There's a whole lot you don't know anything about!"

Frank frowned at Julia and admonished, "That's enough, Julia!" Dupree looked at Chamberlain and agreed, "That's right, I will need all those things." He leaned forward and placed his hand above his knee and continued, "But Mr. Chamberlain, I'm carrying around with me every day a very good reason why I should not patronize you in any manner. Two years ain't long enough to forget."

Seth's head dropped and he confessed, "Yes, sir, I recall that day, and I wish I could call it back and change it. That man was punished and that's all I can say; I know it doesn't help you very much."

Frank rubbed his leg and grimaced. "This cold weather don't help it none neither."

Seth unbuttoned his great coat and moved away from the open fire. "I have already bought some land and sold some plows. Some of your neighbors have signed notes of indebtedness for the tools." He glanced at Julia and directed his remarks to Dupree, "However, I am prepared to let you have what I can spare with only your word. Like all the rest, I do expect a payment when the harvest is in next fall."

Julia jumped from her chair and interrupted, "And what if we can't pay next fall?"

Frank angrily motioned to Julia, "I said 'be quiet!'" Frank looked at Seth as Julia returned to her chair. "She does have a good point. What about that question?"

Seth acknowledged, "I have been getting some farmland as security, but I'm willing to have a surveyor mark off a fair amount of land to cover what we both agree is a fair security and not secure the whole farm."

Julia leaped from her chair and blurted sarcastically, "Well, bless his heart! He's going to do us a favor."

Frank motioned with his hand, "Will you hush for a spell, Julia!"

Julia was morose and mumbled, "Yeah, he's here for our benefit."

Ada stopped rocking, glared at Seth and asked, "Did our neighbors also agree to get enough guano to start the spring planting with?"

Seth stepped farther from the heat and responded, "Yes, ma'am, most of them agreed my terms were more liberal than Dickens at the bank. I'm not asking you to make up your minds right now, I'm just trying to see if we can do business. That's all I'm asking."

Seth paused, listened as the mantel clock prepared to strike, looked at the ornate scrollwork around the clock housing and remarked, "Sounds like it's getting ready to tell us the time of day." In rapid succession the clock struck three times and the ticking continued. "No doubt about the time; it told us real quick it's three o'clock." He leaned toward the fireplace, rubbed his hands near the fire and buttoned his coat. "I best be on my way back to town. I don't want to chance that road after dark."

Frank glanced at Ada and Julia and turned his back toward the fireplace. "Chamberlain, I never did give you an answer. Do you want to leave without me letting you know what I will do?"

Seth looked at Frank and shook his head, "No, I would rather know what you feel you are able to do."

Frank pointed to the window. "Those fields out there will soon have to be broken up, and Nate and me are the only ones to do it. Two old mules and two old men to tend all this land; that ain't much to look forward to." Frank glanced at Ada and turned toward Seth. "I won't say for sure right now, but looking at things like they are, we might be able to get together." Holding the palm of his hand toward Julia, he anticipated her reaction. "Just hold your tongue, girl!"

Frank gripped the metal poker beside the open hearth, stirred the embers, returned the poker and looked at Seth. "Looking at the circumstances, this is what I'm seeing. My old plows are worn out, we ain't got no money for guano, and if we break a plowshare we ain't got an extra one in the barn. We might can find some seeds, but then we might not. We can't pay for the seeds now anyway and the land has got to be worked, regardless of what we harbor in our minds. It looks like that don't leave us much of a choice, does it?"

"Times are hard for everybody," Seth interjected and quickly added, "you aren't the only ones caught in this plight; we all are affected in some fashion. You are bound to tend the land, and I've made the choice of staying." He looked at Julia and emphasized, "Yes, in spite of what your daughter thinks, I'm bound to stay." Julia scowled, rocked rapidly and remained silent.

"Shed your coat," Frank invited, "there's something I've been wanting to ask you about."

Frank waited as Seth removed his coat and pointed to an empty chair. "Just lay your coat over that chair." Frank moved close to the roaring fire and motioned to Seth. "Get a little closer to the fire, you'll need to be good and warm when you step outside to go back to town."

Dupree feigned a smile and stated, "I've lived long enough to learn that weeds of bitterness will soon choke out everything else trying to sprout in a man's heart. And too many weeds will kill off a good crop of anything. I've noticed you have not been to any of our meetings since you were at Old Sparta last summer. Did the quarrels you met with discourage you?"

Seth reacted quickly and replied, "Well, wasn't that enough to discourage anybody?"

Frank agreed, "Yes, I suppose it was. But you know we humans don't get over things as fast as we ought to. We lost a lot of family members and as you can tell, we're still under the heel of northern oppression. You can see that for yourself, and for some reason you stayed while others left. I don't like having to do business with you, but I have got to accept it. Sometimes accepting something ain't all that easy, but you do what you have to do to survive."

"You're right, sir, I haven't been to a meeting since that day at Old Sparta. I don't know if I want to put myself through that again," Seth commented. He looked at Julia and continued, "The singing at the Tarborough Meeting House was moving, but the other didn't move me in any direction, but out."

Frank restrained his amusement and explained, "The singing

is different at each meeting house. Some use one hymn book and some use another. Some have a lot of talent and some don't. Some feel good about their faith and some don't. Some always manage to see something good in life and some don't. I suppose everybody is about that way."

Seth pretended a smile and answered, "Yes, sir, I suppose you're right. Folks are about the same wherever you go."

Frank nodded at Seth, "You might want to try another time and another place."

Ada stopped rocking, pulled her shawl tighter around her shoulders and looked at Seth. "We've heard that the Falls of Tar River Church over at Rocky Mount will be having a general fellowship meeting in May. If it's anything like it was before the war, then a lot of ministers will be there from all over."

Frank interrupted, "That is, if the railroad has been fixed all the way. It used to be that we would have visitors coming by boat from Baltimore and taking the train from Norfolk. But the war stopped all that." Frank felt his resentment beginning to surface and he suppressed the feeling. "But that was in the past!" Waxing philosophical, he added, "We can visit the past, but we cannot live there." Frank's eyes welled with tears, "We miss our dear Willie, but we can't dwell on him, we have got to go on and do what we can with what we got." He pulled a soiled kerchief from his hip pocket, wiped his eyes and turned to Seth. "Now let's see what we've got and move on."

Julia jumped to her feet, glared at Seth and exclaimed, "Are we giving in to this scalawag? He's coming out here offering his charity—and for what?" She looked at her father and pointed to his leg, "How easy do you think it will be for you following a mule all day with that gimp leg? Thanks to him!" She moved from the chair and stood in front of Seth and her father. "I still remember being thrown off the train! I still remember my daddy being shot! I still remember the barns being burned!" She stepped to the window beside the fireplace and pointed out, "I remember them deliberately stomping down the corn! Yes! by God, I remember Esther and Nero following along behind them soldiers like biddies following a hen." Julia slumped into the rocker, "I remember it all!"

"That's enough, Julia! I'm your daddy and I know what's best here and you best keep quiet!" Julia gripped the arms of the rocker and, began rocking rapidly and stared out the window. Seth intentionally remained silent and gazed at Julia. She quickly turned from staring out the window and fixed her eyes on Seth. He felt the intensity of her stare, but could not resist maintaining his eye contact with her. She quickly turned her head and gazed through the window in silence.

Seth moved to the center of the hearth and nodded to Ada, "I know your husband has probably been through a real ordeal with his leg. We all carry with us some scars from the past." He looked at Julia, "I think we can all remember a lick I took across my head, yes ma'am, a brass cuspidor, I believe it was— a lick that left its mark on the back of my head." Julia stopped rocking, subdued a grin then resumed rocking. Seth watched as Julia slowly turned her eyes toward him. He consciously maintained his gaze into Julia's eyes and faked the hint of a smile. "We all have a little something to take with us through life as a reminder of the past."

The springs of the mantel clock began to prepare for the hourly strike. In rapid succession the clock struck five times. Seth walked to the chair for his coat. "It's beginning to get dark outside, I'd better be on my way back to town. You know where to find me if you have a mind to take me up on my offer." Seth looked at Julia as he pulled his coat over his shoulder and adjusted his arms in both sleeves. "I hope we can forget the hatreds of the past and get on with making a life for ourselves." He reached for his hat, pulled the gloves from his coat pocket and moved to the door. "I have a real desire to see this beautiful house one day. I vaguely remember the plans with its grand circular staircase leading to the cupola." Seth deliberately reminded, "I'm glad I had a chance to save it from destruction two years ago."

Seth stretched his hand to Ada, "Good evening, Mrs. Dupree."

Ada stood, gripped his hand and responded, "Thank you, sir, I hope you get back to town before it gets too dark."

Seth turned to Julia, extended his hand and looked into Julia's eyes, "Good evening, Miss Dupree. It has been a delight seeing you again." Julia hesitated, stood and extended her hand. Seth gently gripped her hand, felt the smoothness of her skin and placed his other hand on top of hers and with obvious sincerity declared, "I do wish that you will have a most pleasant evening."

Julia realized he was gripping her hand beyond the customary greeting and pulled away, "Thank you, I assure you I will."

Seth walked back to the fireplace and held his gloves close to the flames. "I'll warm them before I have to make the cold trip back to town." As he turned to leave he remarked to Frank, "I really hope you can see fit to consider what we have discussed."

Frank walked to the door and entered the hallway. "We'll see how things turn out."

Seth followed Frank into the hallway and caught a glimpse of the spiral staircase. He walked to the door, turned to Frank and put on his gloves. "I'll get my horse and rig from behind the kitchen and be on my way." Walking across the veranda he turned and nodded, "Thank you, Mr. Dupree." Seth stepped from the porch, hurriedly moved to the rear of the kitchen, loosed the lines and gripped Blue Boy's halter. He tugged at the halter and directed the horse into the path beside the veranda. Seth looked at Dupree on the porch, pulled himself into the seat and flipped the blanket across his legs. He motioned with his hand toward Dupree and snapped the lines on Blue Boy's back.

Moving past the house, Seth shuddered as a wintry gust vibrated the gig. He guided Blue Boy onto the Tarborough road, pulled the collar of his great coat to the back of his neck and pressed into the fading murkiness of twilight.

Frank walked to the side of the veranda and watched as the rig turned from the path onto the road to town. He shivered as he walked back to the warmth of the fireplace. Standing with his back to the flames, Frank looked at Ada and glanced at Julia. "Well, what do you think? Both of you heard everything that was said. As much as I hate to say so, he's right. We ain't got much of a choice if we expect to tend the land this spring."

Ada rose from her chair, walked to the fireplace, turned her back to the flames and pulled the hem of her dress from the hearth.

"In the book of Esther the question was asked, who knows whether or not Esther was sent for such a time as the Lord's people were in? Who knows whether this man was sent for such a time as this? The Lord moves in mysterious ways." She walked to her chair, pulled her warm skirt close and sat down. "Frank, you're the one that knows what's best for the fields."

Frank moved away from the fireplace, stared through the two windows on both sides, and scanned the gray eastern horizon. Then he asked, "What will our neighbors have to say? To be sure, there will be talk a-plenty if we seem to be taking to that Yankee."

Julia rose from the chair, walked to the fireplace and stood next to her father. "It will soon be time to start breaking the land, Daddy. What folks say doesn't really make much difference. I don't like this either, but what else can you do? Old Dickens has had his eye on this land a long time. At least this man seems willing to settle for some of the land and not all of it."

"I suppose it will be just me and Nate to break up the fields. We've got one mule left and I reckon I could make arrangements to get another one. Me and Nate will just have to break the land from light till dark."

Frank moved from the front of the fireplace and gazed through the window. "It won't be long before the winds of March will be drying out the land. It's for certain, if we are aiming to tend the land, then we're going to have to make some preparations. I may go into town next week and see what Chamberlain has to offer." He walked back to the front of the hearth. "He did make me a mighty tempting offer. He seems to trust me more than I trust him."

Julia rose from her chair, walked to the window and stared toward Tarborough. "I reckon all the farmers around here are in the same fix. But it does seem like he's mighty generous with us. I can't help but wonder what it is he's after."

Frank suppressed a faint smile and looked at Ada. "The last time he was at the meeting house, he couldn't keep his eyes off Julia."

Ada stopped rocking and looked at Julia. "That Mewborn boy didn't like that one bit, either."

"Oh, good Lord! Don't put the blame on me!" Julia blurted. "First thing you know everybody will be talking and looking down on me." She walked to the window, and changed the conversation. "Looks like it's about time for supper. Mama, do you want me to start the fire in the kitchen stove?"

Ada answered, "I suppose so, and your daddy can bring in a turn of stovewood from outside."

Frank walked into the hall, removed his coat from the hall rack and returned to the fireplace. He held the inside of his coat toward the dancing flames and commented, "That wind is howling a gale out there, I don't want to forget my hat when I go for the wood." Donning his canvas coat, and buttoning the front, he declared, "I'll catch the first decent day and go to town and talk to Chamberlain. I may as well go on and get it done with."

# CHAPTER TWENTY-SIX

April's warm winds swept away the memory of winter's unrelenting grasp. The icy grip of long nights and short days loosened, yielding to the annual surge of nature. A sense of renewal filled the air as the scent of newly turned earth drifted across the countryside. The colorless terrain was responding with a renewal of emerging colors. Nature's feathered harbingers of warmth darted through the budding branches of the waking trees. The lethargy of yesterday was transformed into revitalization as the hint of a new burst of life rolled across the land.

Tom Burgess stepped from his office into the street, deliberately breathed deeply and called out, "Hey, Chamberlain! Open the door and let some of this Carolina air lift your spirits." Seth looked up from his desk, peered through the window and saw Burgess walking toward the door. He pushed his chair from the desk, walked to the door and opened it fully. "You want to come in, or do you think I ought to come out?"

The lawyer gestured with a heavy breath, "Take in a little of this invigorating air. Come on out in the sun. It's been a long cold spell!"

Seth stepped from his office, imitated Burgess with a deep breath and looked upward. "You're right, Counselor! This looks like a day to enjoy a new birth of freedom—freedom from having to stay inside near the fire."

Burgess, with fervor, remarked, "Old boy, I see where you've had a steady flow of folks looking at your equipment. I wouldn't have thought so, but they're showing interest. Maybe there's hope for you yet."

"It's going to take more than hope to move all that guano I got stored in that building you told me about. If we don't see some wagons carrying it off, then we're both in trouble." Seth smiled at Burgess and asked, "Did you hear what I said? I said, We're both in trouble if that guano stays where it is?"

Burgess grinned and replied, "Yeah, I heard you, but from the terms I hear you're offering, I think you'll get shed of it quick enough. It looks like you're the one who has the most to lose."

Seth shook his head in doubt. "You're right, I'm the one sitting on a dead limb." He quickly assured Burgess, "But! Like this burst of springtime, if that limb shows some life, then I'm the one that's going to feel alive."

Burgess stepped closer to Seth and placed his hand on his shoulder. "Chamberlain, if you persuaded Frank Dupree to go away with two of your plows, I don't think you have to worry about your guano." He removed his hand from Seth's shoulder, looked him squarely in his eyes and grinned. "Folks are saying you got an eye for old Dupree's daughter." The lawyer, still grinning, added, "Your judgment of looks sure is better than your judgment of books. You can close the lids of your ledgers, but you might can't close the lids on her."

Seth grinned sheepishly and replied, "From my meetings with her, I wouldn't know which side of the ledger to put her on, the assets or the liabilities."

"Well, at least most of my plows are gone and I've got some spare shares in two sizes. That won't feed me till the crop comes in, so I'll have to stretch it a bit." Seth laughed and added, "You might have to do a little stretching, too!"

Seth called to Burgess as the lawyer walked to his office. "Do you think I ought to be checking my securities?" Burgess stopped and turned toward Seth.

"Yeah! Won't nobody be in town today! It might be Saturday, but in planting time everybody's working in the fields."

Walking to his office Seth shouted to Burgess, "I'll see to

my investments!" Seth stepped into his office, placed his ledgers in the desk drawer and closed the door behind him. He hesitated at the front of the building and called to Burgess, "I left the door unlocked if anybody wants to get in." Seth walked to the hostler's stables, stopped in the open doorway and shouted, "I'm getting my horse and rig! Any objection?"

The stablehand peered over the back of a horse he was grooming. "No! Go ahead and get your animal. You know where everything is. The more you do for yourself, the less I have to do for you."

Seth walked to the stall, opened the gate and stroked Blue Boy's neck, "Want to take a stroll in the countryside today?" He removed the bridle from the post, placed it over Blue Boy's ears and secured the bit in the horse's mouth. Tugging on the bridle he muttered, "Come on fellow, this will be an easy trip." He guided the horse to the gig and harnessed Blue Boy to the carriage. Seth flipped the lines onto the seat and led his horse and gig from the barn. Placing his foot on the wheel spoke he pulled himself into the seat, gripped the lines and shouted, "See you later this afternoon." Snapping the lines, Seth guided Blue Boy in front of the courthouse and turned toward the main road through Tarborough. Seth stopped his gig, looked toward the east and pulled on the right line, "Glick! Glick! Let's go, fellow!" He directed his gig into the center of the road, rapped the lines gently and moved along the road toward the Dupree place.

The midmorning sun warmed the side of Seth's face. He removed his hat, placed it on the seat and absorbed the soothing warmth of the sun. Seth tightened the lines, restrained Blue Boy and scanned the terrain as the gig lumbered over the dried ruts. He reflected that what was mire last February was now ribbons of dry ridges. The air was filled with the scent of freshly tilled soil. Nature's melodies echoed from the changing forest announcing its continuing renewal. Seth relaxed the lines, scanned the road ahead and visualized Julia greeting him from the veranda.

The question raced through Seth's mind as he pulled Blue Boy into the path leading to the main house—what reason would he use to justify this visit? He tightened the lines and maintained Blue Boy at a slow pace as he neared the veranda. "Whoa! Whoa!" Seth called loudly, expecting his voice to be heard. He put on his hat, jumped to the ground and walked to the front of Blue Boy and waited. He glanced at the kitchen door, stroked the side of his horse's neck and called, "Anybody home?" Seth watched askance as the kitchen door opened. He turned his head toward the fields and attempted to survey the newly plowed ground. "Yes, sir, what brings you out here on Saturday morning?" asked Julia as she walked to the side of the veranda.

Seth fidgeted with the lines and stared at Julia. "Do you think my horse will stay put if I don't tie the line someplace?" Julia recognized the circumstance and said impulsively, "Tie your horse at the back." He gripped the halter, led the animal to the rear of the kitchen and secured the lines. Walking to the veranda Seth asked, "Where's your daddy? I'd like to know if the plows are working to his satisfaction."

Julia, knowing her mother was in the kitchen answered loudly, "He's in the east field with Nate. They're both breaking land."

Ada opened the door, looked at Seth and walked to the side of Julia. "You can walk to the field if you're a-mind to. I don't expect Frank here till dinnertime."

Fumbling with his Albert chain attached to a buttonhole of his shirt, he pulled his watch from the watch pocket of his trousers. "That looks to be about an hour off. The fields look good! Do you mind if I walk to the edge of the field?"

Ada glanced at Julia and looked at Seth, "No, not at all. Frank's right proud with how things are coming along."

Walking toward the rear of the kitchen, he suddenly stopped

and looked at Julia. "I've never seen the finished work of this house. Would it be asking too much to see what it looks like? I've seen it on paper and that's all." He walked toward the veranda and continued, "This is a fine example of skilled architectural work. There's not many homes this finely detailed."

A quizzical expression crossed Ada's face. Julia looked at her mother in surprise and asked, "Mama, you want me to show him the house?" Ada stepped from the edge of the porch, paused and looked at Julia, "Yes, I suppose so. It's not the cleanest right now, cause we've been tracking in mud. But if he wants to see it like it is, then go ahead."

Julia looked at Seth at the bottom of the steps and motioned, "Alright, come on in."

Seth stepped on the bottom step, turned and scraped his shoes and remarked, "I don't want to track any more mud in your house."

Julia walked to the doorway, turned and motioned, "Mind going in the back door?"

Seth responded, "No, not at all."

Julia opened the door and stood back as Seth entered the hallway. She closed the door and stood beside him. "I suppose you know where the rooms are, since you said you helped plan it. You wouldn't have planned it so big if you knew you'd have to clean it."

Seth laughed, removed his hat and hung it on the rack beside the door. "I guess you're right about that, Miss Dupree."

Julia walked to the middle of the house, stopped at the bottom of the grand circular staircase and pointed upward. "Most folks think this is the oddest stairway they've ever seen."

Seth gripped the bannister, twisted his head and looked toward the top of the spiral steps. "I did not remember these steps going the full way to the cupola. These spiral steps get smaller as they wind their way to the top." He stepped from the staircase and looked at Julia. "It may be odd, but it sure is beautiful to me. I can readily see the work that went into finishing it."

Julia pointed toward the front of the house, "Come on and I'll show you the rest of the house." Seth followed Julia as she moved from room to room, watched her every movement and seized every opportunity to comment on the house.

Julia walked to the bottom of the staircase, pointed upward and remarked, "In the summer, with the windows in the dome open, it draws a draft through the house like a chimney."

Seth looked at Julia and smiled, "That must be refreshing to sleep with."

Julia lifted the front of her dress and stepped on the bottom step. "I reckon you want to see the rest of the house."

Seth responded, "Yes ma'am, that would be very kind of you." Julia delicately stepped one step at a time, lifting her dress with each motion upward. She stopped, gripped the railing and looked down on Seth. "And, don't call me ma'am. My name is Julia."

Seth struck by the curtness of her the comment, responded, "Yes, ma'am." He caught his response and quickly corrected, "I'm sorry!" and added, "Julia!" Realizing the opportunity, Seth countered, "and my name is Seth!"

Seth gripped the banister and carefully placed his foot on each step as he followed Julia to the next floor. He stared at Julia's every movement as she ascended each step. His heart pounded as he realized he was on these truly magnificent steps with Julia. She reached the second floor, moved from the staircase and stated, "All the bedrooms are on this floor. There's windows all around to bring in the air." Julia walked to the front of the hallway and motioned to the front yard. "We can see the whole front yard from here."

Seth looked through the window and remarked, "A fantastic

view of the oak trees."

Julia turned and walked to the rear of the hallway and looked out the window. "We can see right across the top of the kitchen and all the way down to the railroad tracks."

Seth remarked, "I'm sure with just you and your mother, this is a big house to take care of."

Seth sensed Julia's penetrating stare as she commented, "Nathan and Dolly stayed here when Nero and Esther followed off with you and your crowd."

Seth quickly changed the subject, "Then I suppose you depend on this Dolly to help?"

Julia started toward the staircase and muttered, "That's right, we count on her and Nate."

Julia stopped at the winding stairway and glared at Seth. "You want to see the whole place from the top of the house?"

Looking up the winding steps he answered, "I don't think I could leave here today without seeing the entire place. It's absolutely beautiful."

With both hands Julia lifted her dress above her shoes and carefully ascended the narrowing spiral staircase. Nearing the entrance into the cupola, she gripped the railing, looked down toward Seth and cautioned, "These turns get a little narrow the closer we get to the top."

Seth gripped the railing and responded, "I've never seen anything quite like this before." He continued to gaze at Julia as she reached the top of the steps.

The colored glass of the cupola windows filtered the sunlight as Julia moved from the steps into the cupola. Seth's eyes were riveted on Julia's features as he viewed her standing at the cupola entrance. The dancing colors reflected from her hair. Her face radiated with each movement in the changing light. Awed by Julia's breathtaking loveliness, Seth stopped near the top of the steps and stared into the dome of dazzling colors. Julia extended her hand and remarked, "You'll have to come on in to see everything from here." Seth gripped her hand and quickly stepped into the cupola. Julia warned, "Watch how you walk around the sides up here, there isn't much space between the steps and the walls of this place."

Seth leaned on the window sill and peered to the east. "This is the most magnificent view I have ever seen."

Julia stood beside Seth and pointed, "There's Daddy and Nate plowing out there. They've been at it since sunup." Julia gazed through the window and remarked, "Sometimes I come up here for hours at a time. I can watch everything going on and I can be alone with my thoughts."

Seth detected a hint of Julia's essence as the spring wind floated through the cupola. He turned to Julia and gazed into her eyes. The filtered colors reflected from her chestnut tresses and gripped Seth with an overwhelming sense of passion. His inhibitions evaporated as he reached and drew her unresisting body to his. Her lips rose to meet his as he wrapped his arm around her waist and with his other arm pulled her tight against his body. Seth felt the pulsations of her heartbeats against his chest and the softness of her body. The sensation of her tightened arms around him stirred Seth's human passion. Time was lost in the moment. Bitterness and resentment melted into oblivion. Julia's resistance relaxed in a flash of human ecstasy.

Julia pushed away from Seth, looked through the cupola window and saw Frank and Nate coming from the field. "I've got to get back to the kitchen and help Mama with dinner."

Seth looked startled and asked, "Is that all you can say?"

Julia began to descend the spiral steps. "I don't want to talk about it! I don't want to talk about it!" She gripped the railing with one hand and raised the bottom of her dress with the other and quickly stepped down the spiral staircase. Panting, she stepped onto the last step, turned and watched as Seth descended the widening spiral stairs. "Daddy's in the backyard if you want to talk to him. I've got to go help Mama." Seth stood at the base of the grand staircase and watched Julia as she ran from the hallway onto the veranda. He walked to the hallway door, reached to the hall rack for his hat and walked onto the veranda. He watched as Julia disappeared into the kitchen.

Frank Dupree, washing his hands and face, looked up from the basin and inquired, "Did Julia give you the grand tour of the house? If you helped plan it, then I know you wanted to see it finished." Frank dried his hands and face, looked at Seth and joked, "I reckon we could put another cup of water in the cabbage likker, if you're a-mind to stay." Seth shyly looked at Frank and answered, "No thank you, Mr. Dupree, I just came out to see if your plows were working to suit you. I didn't expect the pleasant surprise of getting to see this magnificent house."

"I would say the plows are doing real good. The points seem to hold a good edge and go deep when we need them to. Old Nate thinks it's about the finest thing he's ever had holt of."

Seth stretched his hand toward Frank. "I hope you continue to be satisfied with them. Your fields are beginning to take fine shape." Seth walked to the side of the porch, jumped to the ground and walked to the rear of the kitchen. He looked through the open window, saw Julia and her mother and called out, "Thank you, Mrs. Dupree. Julia gave me a delightful tour of your home." He loosed Blue Boy's lines, gripped the halter and guided the horse to the side of the kitchen. Tossing the lines onto the seat, he placed his foot on a wheel spoke and pulled himself into the seat. Snapping the lines he urged Blue Boy into the path leading to the Tarborough Road. Passing the veranda he called, "If you have any trouble, let me know! Good day!"

Frank finished eating, placed his spoon in the empty bowl and looked at Julia. "You've been mighty quiet at the table. Has anything happened to upset you? Did you have another mix-up with that Chamberlain fellow?"

Julia lowered her eyes, hesitated and answered, "No, everything is alright. I showed him the house like Mama told me to. He said he remembered the plans but he wanted to see the finished house."

Frank pushed from the table and commented, "I suppose that'll hold me till dark. The rows seem to get longer and longer." He walked onto the porch, sat on the floor, pulled one leg to his chest and leaned against the wall of the house. The shade lulled Frank's senses as he nodded in the stillness.

Ada quietly opened the kitchen door, looked at Julia, motioned with her hand and whispered, "Don't wake your daddy, come on out in the yard with me." Julia followed her mother as they carefully stepped from the porch to the yard. "Give him a few more minutes to rest.

Moving from the shade of the porch into the sun, Ada remarked, "This sunshine feels mighty good to these bones." Julia agreed, "The sun makes me feel better than the cold dreary days."

Julia peered along the path to the road and noticed a black man and woman walking toward the house. "Mama, there's somebody coming this way. I can't tell who it is. It looks like a black man and woman."

Ada stared at the couple as they moved slowly toward the back yard. "Good Lord, that's Nero and Esther."

Julia reacted excitedly, "Nero and Esther?"

Ada examined the couple closely. "Yes! It is for sure, Nero and Esther!" Julia dashed toward the couple and grabbed Esther around the neck. "Good Lord, Esther, I didn't think I'd ever see you again." She glanced at Nero and added, "and you neither!" Julia gripped Esther by the arm and pulled her toward the back yard. "Come on, Mama spotted you coming! She knew it was you!"

Frank, roused by the voices, slowly rose from the porch floor and walked into the yard. "Well, I wish you'd look who's back. What's the matter, Nero? Ain't the Yankees doing you any favors?" Nero glanced at Esther, looked down and answered, "Bein' free is just fine, but some folks don't see it dat way. Me and Esther, here, has walked all de way from New Berne and rite now, I don't see no 'vantages in bein' free when we's hongry."

Esther sensed Ada's sympathetic gaze. "Yes'sum, and we ain't got no place to live." Ada looked at Julia and nodded, "Go get Nate and Dolly and tell them who's here." Julia responded, "Yes, ma'am!" She ran toward the barns, shouting, "Nate! Dolly! Esther and Nero's back!"

Nate heard the shouts, ran from his quarters and stopped Julia. "Did I hear you shoutin' sump'n 'bout Nero?"

Julia excitedly blurted, "Really! Nero and Esther are back! Come on to the house!"

Nate ran back to his quarters and called, "Dolly, come on up to de house! Esther and Nero's back!"

Julia dashed to the house and motioned to Nate and Dolly. "Hurry! Come on over here to see Esther and Nero."

Nathan looked at Nero and grinned, "Hit won't what you thought it was, was hit?"

Nero's head drooped, "Naw! hit shore won't." Dolly reached and embraced Esther. "I reckon dis place looks rite good to you, now." Dolly looked at Ada and glanced at Frank. "Dere old place is still empty, if'n you will let dem use it."

Frank hesitated and glared at Nero. "Are you looking to hire yourself out? You're free now, you know. You belong to yourself; you can do what you want to do."

Nero meekly answered, "I knows I can do what I wants to do, but dere ain't nothin' away from here I can do."

Julia interrupted excitedly, "Can Nero and Esther stay where they used to stay?" Frank looked sternly at Nero and Esther. "I ain't able to pay wages till next fall when the harvest is in. It may be that a few things can be provided in the meanwhile. But I can't make no promises."

Nero nodded and responded, "Dat's alright. We just needs a place to live rite now, and a little sump'n t'eat. Esther and me earns our keep."

Frank paused and reflected. Ada and Julia remained silent. Dolly and Nathan whispered with Nero and Esther. Frank broke the hushed discussions. He focused on Nero and then glared at Nathan. "You know your names will have to be changed?"

Nate looked puzzled and asked, "What you mean bys dat, Mr. Frank?"

Frank nodded toward Nero and Esther. "Nero, your name is on the church rolls as 'Dupree's Nero'. Esther, your name is on the rolls as 'Dupree's Esther'." He nodded at Nathan and Dolly, "Yours is on the church rolls as 'Dupree's Nathan and Dupree's Dolly'." Frank gazed at the Negroes. "You can take any last name you want to take. You don't belong to no man any more." He counseled, "I would keep your first names, but you can use any last names you're a-mind to." He continued, "Any children you might birth will have the last names that you choose to use."

Nathan looked at Dolly and waited for her response. Dolly stared at Nathan and hesitated. Nathan fixed his eyes on Frank Dupree and announced, "I think I'd be pleased wid Nathan Dupree." Dolly smiled at Julia and followed, "I 'bleve I'd like Dolly Dupree."

Julia darted to Dolly, wrapped her arms around her neck and shouted, "Oh! Lord that's good to hear!"

Frank turned to Nero and asked, "Do you aim to stay?"

Nero glanced at Esther and replied, "Yassur, we aims to stay."

Dupree hesitated and asked, "Well, what do you want your name to be?" Esther looked at Nero and answered, "Esther

Dupree is a fine soundin' one to me." Nero smiled at Esther and added, "I reckon I be's a Dupree, too."

"I'll see that your names are put on the church records the way you want them to be. Now, remember, all your young-uns will bear your same last names, just like everybody else. You ain't no different."

Frank smiled at Ada and Julia. "We best be about our chores and let them get their living places set up." He looked at Nate and said, "You and me better get back to the fields, they can get things here." Frank headed for the barn, stopped and called to Dolly and Esther, "I'll show you a place to start you a garden. We have to grow our rations, now. There ain't much money to buy anything with."

Julia, smiling at her mother, started walking toward the kitchen and asked, "Do you suppose Seth will let Daddy have another plow for Nero? With all three in the fields we could have things like they used to be."

"Oh! It's 'Seth' now, is it? It hasn't been too long ago, he was 'Mr. Chamberlain' or 'that man'! What happened to change your tune, young lady?"

"Stop it, Mama! You know what I mean. I'm thinking of how much ground could be turned by three men."

Ada frowned at Julia and advised her, "You best keep your conniving thoughts to yourself."

# CHAPTER TWENTY-SEVEN

Seth heard the rumble of a wagon, listened intently as the turning wheels slowed and became more distinct. "Whoa!" sounded from the street in front of Seth's business. He looked up from the ledger on his desk, saw Frank Dupree slowly moving from the wagon seat and closed the ledger. Seth pushed back the chair, rose and walked to the open door. "Good morning, Mr. Dupree." He signaled to Frank, "Tie your animal to the porch post and come on in. Burgess finally built a porch to cover the store fronts." Frank gripped the mule's halter, pulled the animal close to the post and tied the lines around the post.

"This is a pleasant surprise," Seth noted, "I didn't think I'd see you again so soon." He continued, "How's your wife and Julia?"

Frank walked closer and responded, "They're both doing fine. Julia got off at the mercantile place, but she'll be here before we get through talking."

Seth gestured, "Come on in, Mr. Dupree. I don't have a fancy place, but it works fine for the time being."

Frank slowly stepped inside the building, looked around and noted, "I see you still have some plows lined up against the back wall."

Seth smiled and pointed to the wall, "Yes, and I've just unpacked some plow points. I suspect a hidden root might break a few of those this spring."

Seth pointed, "Take a chair and tell me about how things are going."

Frank pulled a chair close to the desk, turned it toward Seth and sat down. Frank leaned forward, placed his hands on his knees and gazed at Seth. "I don't know what's going on, but the darndest thing happened the other day when you were out at the place. It was right after you left."

"And what was that?" asked Seth as he settled in his chair and tipped back. He joined his hands behind his head and inquired, "What is it that's got you puzzled?"

"I'd like to forget this, but when your crowd came through about three years ago, some of my hands went back with you. I had not seen nor heard about them until the day you were out at the house." Frank feigned a smile and straightened in the chair. "Not long after you left, two of my former slaves came to the house. They had walked all the way from New Berne." Frank tipped his chair back and continued, "It was Nero and Esther; they're man and wife. They were looking to hire out, seeing as how they couldn't seem to make it." Frank leaned toward Seth and placed his hands on his knees. "I explained the situation to them and told them I couldn't give no wages till fall, but they could stay at their old cabins if they wanted and we'd do the best we could."

Seth moved his hands from behind his head, placed his arms on the desk and leaned toward Dupree. "That means you've got two hired hands and their wives." He folded his arms and tipped his chair back and remarked, "Well, Mr. Dupree it sounds like you're about back to the way it was."

Frank forced a smile and answered, "Well, no, not quite. I don't have the worry about seeing to their rations. That's their worry now. We'll all do the best we can, but there's not but so much anybody can do."

"Well, I won't take a lot of your time," noted Frank, "but things like this always happen after you've been around. When you were here the first time, they left. Now that you are here again, they came back. I don't claim to know why, but that's the way it is." Frank glanced around the building and focused his gaze on Seth. "Now I've got all this land that's got to be tended or it'll grow up in weeds. Now, here's another family wanting to work. That leaves me needing another mule and plow." Frank tipped his chair back and folded his arms. "Julia has been slyly hinting at seeing if you had another plow you might would add to my debt." Frank straightened his chair and added, "All I can hear from her is tend the whole place and not let it grow over, but things are not what they used to be"

Seth smiled and nodded, "She may have a point. The land will certainly not do you any good sitting idle. I suppose you could say, the more you cultivate the more you will harvest." Seth added, "I hear there will be big demand for cotton this year since little has been produced lately for the foreign market."

"Well, you see the situation," Dupree remarked, and continued, "no need for me to take any more of your time."

"Hold on now, I've got plenty of time, and I am interested in helping you solve this. After all, I've got something to lose, too." Seth pointed to the plows and plowshares. "They won't do either one of us any good in here." He opened his ledger and pointed at the book, "I'll take a chance on it on the page and not on the wall."

Frank rose from his chair and extended his hand. "I'll shake and sign for another plow."

Seth gripped Frank's hand and nodded in agreement. "That's the last one I've got. Maybe a good year will replenish your needs and mine, too."

Frank walked to the door, stopped and turned toward Seth. "Oh, can you put me down for some guano. I've got my mule and wagon out here. If I'm going to owe my soul to you, I may as well owe it all. If I am in debt to you, you might as well go with me and help load the wagon."

"Sure, I'll ride with you to the storage building near the river docks," Seth suggested. He looked at Frank and inquired, "But what about Julia? Will she know where you are?"

Untying the lines, Frank glanced toward the corner and

nodded, "There's Julia, now. I thought it was about time for her to show up."

Seth quickly turned and gazed toward the corner building and saw Julia walking toward them. "It's good to see Julia again, too. She's looking well. I want to thank her again for that grand tour of your home."

"I don't know what your seeing our house had to do with anything, but Julia ain't been the same since," Frank commented. He looked at Seth and suggested, "Maybe she's glad to see somebody who helped plan it."

Seth smiled and tipped his hat. "Good morning, Julia. I'm delighted to see you again."

"Good morning, Seth," Julia responded and added, "I didn't think we'd be in town this quick, but Daddy decided he needed to talk with you." She looked at Seth and smiled. "Daddy knows more about what's best to do when it comes to the land."

Seth nodded and smiled, "I'm sure he does, I'm sure he does."

"Mr. Chamberlain is riding with us to his storage building to load some bags of guano," Frank informed Julia and directed, "You best ride in the middle and hold the mule while we load the guano."

Seth gripped the sideboard of the wagon bed and extended his hand. "After you!" Julia gripped his hand, stepped onto a wheel spoke, lifted the bottom of her skirt and pulled herself onto the seat. Seth placed his foot on a spoke and pulled himself onto the seat. Frank gripped the lines and walked around the front of the mule. He handed the lines to Julia, stepped on a spoke and pulled himself into the seat. "I'll take the lines now."

Julia jostled between Seth and Frank. Seth detected her closeness, looked at her and smiled. "Mr. Dupree it's the last building on the left before you get to the river docks."

Frank rapidly snapped the lines and looked at Julia. "We

won't take long; we'll be home 'fore dinnertime."

Seth touched his shoulder against Julia, looked into her eyes and smiled. "I want to thank you again for such a grand tour of your house." He smiled and nodded, "I assure you I shall never forget it." Julia blushed and responded, "You're welcome. I'm glad you liked our house."

Frank turned the wagon in the direction they had arrived, handed Julia the lines and directed, "Hold the animal steady while Chamberlain and me load the guano." She watched her father and Seth remove the bags from the warehouse floor and place them onto the wagon bed.

Seth pulled himself onto the seat, smiled and gazed into Julia's eyes. "Now we'll stop at my business. Your daddy and I will load the plow on top of the bags."

Julia asked in a puzzled fashion, "Did Daddy get a plow?"

Frank glared at Julia and faked a laugh. "Like you didn't know I was going to get a plow!"

Frank pulled the mule to a halt, leaped from the seat and tossed the lines to Julia. "Chamberlain and me will load the plow and then we'll head for home." Seth gripped Julia's hand and gazed into her eyes. "I hope to see you again, soon." He leaped from the seat and walked to the building. Entering the door, he turned and called to Frank, "Come on, Mr. Dupree, we'll get this loaded and you can be on your way."

Julia watched her father and Seth remove the plow from the building and secure it on top of the bags of guano. "Daddy," Julia whispered, "don't forget to tell Seth about the meeting in May at Rocky Mount."

Frank stood beside the front wagon wheel, gripped the seat and looked at Seth. "I thank you for this trust. Maybe we both can make a go of it." He looked up at Julia and directed, "Now you tell him about what you wanted to."

Julia fumbled with the lines and looked at Seth. "The last

Sunday in May there will be a big meeting at the Rocky Mount church. I hear some preachers from up north plan to be there. You might see some from New York." She added, "We will go on Saturday and spend the night with some kinfolks and be there both days."

Frank gripped the sideboard, steadied his foot on a spoke and looked at Seth. "If you have a mind to go, you can make the ride to Rocky Mount early Sunday morning and be back 'fore dark. Your horse and rig ought to be up to the trip. It might interest you to meet some folks from New York and New Jersey." Julia interrupted, "Yes, sir, preachers from Delaware and Maryland, too."

Seth extended his hand, gripped Frank's hand and responded, "Maybe I will, maybe I will. It sounds interesting."

Frank pulled himself into the seat, took the lines from Julia and looked at Seth. "The church is located on the Hilliardston Road. Only a little ways beyond the river bridge."

Seth felt his face flush as Frank mentioned the directions. He moved from the wagon and called out, "Give Mrs. Dupree my regards!"

Seth watched as the wagon disappeared. Astonished, he remained in front of the building and reflected, the Hilliardston Road! The river bridge! If Frank Dupree thinks strange things are happening to him, what would he think of this?

Tom Burgess walked from his law office and called out, "Chamberlain! It looks like you're scattering your guano all over the county." Seth walked toward the lawyer and extended his hand toward Burgess. "That leaves me with one plow and a few bags of the guano." Burgess gripped Seth's hand and responded, "Well done! Now you wait and hope for a good harvest."

# CHAPTER TWENTY-EIGHT

Seth snapped the lines on Blue Boy's back, turned around in the gig seat and peered toward Tarborough. The eastern horizon was beginning to lighten the treetops. He looked westward onto the Rocky Mount road and strained to view the outline of the wheel paths. Seth cautiously paced his horse slowly into the darkness. The wheels rumbled in and out of the unseen ruts and jostled Seth as he stiffened his legs to maintain his position. The quietness of the countryside lulled Seth into pondering what events might confront him at this Sunday meeting. He reflected on Julia's emphasis of the visitors from New York and New Jersey.

The emerging light caused the blackness to dissipate. Seth could detect the form of the tree limbs over the road. He distinguished the sides of the road and guided his horse to the center. His gig bounced as the wheels rolled in and out of the ruts. Seth rattled the lines and returned to his thoughts. Seth looked into the developing light as he passed Coolmore and reflected, they're not home this morning. Julia said they were spending the night in Rocky Mount.

The green fields came into focus as Seth pressed along the road. Three years earlier, these fields had been filled with ripening corn and the road filled with the dust of the cavalry column. Seth observed the early morning activity as he passed the farm houses beside the road. He reminded himself, he could not have known he would pass this way again.

The brightness of the sun dispelled all hints of night as minutes merged into hours. Seth reached into his watch pocket, pulled out his timepiece and observed the hour. He returned his watch and looked at the sun and judged, it looks to be about half past eight. He reached into his coat pocket and pulled out the handkerchief-wrapped biscuit and uttered, "Thank goodness."

He recalled Mrs. Andrews' reminding him the night before to bring it along.

Seth passed the homes, observed the wisps of smoke from the kitchen chimneys and pressed toward Rocky Mount. The houses began to be closer together as he neared the town. He rattled the lines and urged Blue Boy toward the railroad. The scenery was beginning to look familiar. Three years had not erased the memory of deeds he committed while he was in the army.

He pulled his horse to a halt at the tracks, looked to the south and reflected, I wonder what it looks like now. He looked to the north and speculated, I suppose the railroad bridge has been rebuilt. He snapped the lines, moved across the tracks and turned onto the Hilliardston Road. Trees now obstructed the view toward the old flouring mill. He rattled the lines and pressed north along the road.

Rounding a bend in the road, Seth saw the stone hull that remained of the mill. He pulled Blue Boy to a stop, stared at the mill site and noticed the interior was being rebuilt. He shook the lines and moved past the mill to the river bridge. Seth tugged his horse to a halt, noted the planking had been replaced and urged his horse across. The clatter of the horse's hoofs and wheels of the gig crossing the gapped planking gave Seth an uneasy feeling.

Seth whipped the lines and urged his horse along the road. He recalled Dupree saying the church was just beyond the river bridge. Seth peered ahead and looked for a clearing in the terrain. He restrained Blue Boy, glanced to both sides of the road and glimpsed a large white building. He noticed a worn path leading to the building, pulled on the left line and guided the horse toward the building. Seth observed the front of the meeting house did not face the Hilliardston Road. He noted the wagons and buggies tied behind the building and pulled his horse to the right and steered Blue Boy to the rear of the meeting house.

Seth gripped the lines, held to the seat and jumped to the ground. Grasping the halter, he led his horse to the edge of the wooded thicket and secured the lines to a tree. Walking toward the building, Seth paused, readjusted his shirt and brushed off his trousers with his hands. He scrutinized the milling crowd and walked to the front of the building. Nearing the entrance he heard the odd sounding singing and stopped. He glimpsed someone approaching and turned as the man extended his hand. "Good morning, sir! Don't that singing sound good from out here?" the man asked.

Seth looked at the man and responded, "Indeed it does. Indeed it does." He walked to the entrance, looked up and reasoned, this meeting house is tall enough for a balcony also. He stepped inside, noticed the steps leading to the balcony and listened for the rhythmic foot taps. Seth removed his hat and sat on a back pew. He noticed the similarities of the Primitive meeting houses.

Seth scanned the congregation, searching for the Duprees. His eyes stopped as he spied Julia's straw pork-pie hat with the follow-me-lads streamers. He fixed his stare on her chestnut chignon and imagined her sparkling brown eyes. He watched as Elder Hart moved to the front of the building and called out a number. Seth maintained his focus on Julia as the strains of familiar hymns echoed through the open windows.

Elder Hart stepped into the apse, moved to the high pulpit and announced, "We have been blessed to have with us for three days, Elder Gilbert Beebe of New York, Elder Silas Durand of Pennsylvania, Elder Philander Hartwell of New Jersey and Elder R. C. Leachman of Virginia." He gestured to the Elders on the side pews. "Would you come to the stand, please?"

Seth watched as the men rose from their seats, walked to the apse and stepped onto the high platform. He observed the chairs lining the wall of the apse and noted each man as he selected a chair. Seth scrutinized the attentiveness of the congregation as the men settled into their chairs. Seth's attention was concentrated on Julia as Elder Hart began to speak. He watched Julia stand to sing a hymn. He glanced at the standing congregation and steadied his eyes on Julia. He sat down as the congregation finished the hymn. Focusing on Julia, he reflected on the day in the cupola and her change of heart.

The stirring of the congregation startled Seth. His mind was absorbed with other things and other places. He listened as Elder Hart announced, "Dinner has been prepared and everybody is invited to have dinner with us. The good sisters have gone to a good deal of trouble, and they don't want you to leave hungry."

Seth walked to the door, put on his hat and stepped outside. He heard the last hymn as he stood at the front door and recalled, now this is singing as it should be. Walking to the rear of the building his attention was drawn to sawhorses supporting wide boards and covered with white tablecloths. He noticed the women were busy arranging the bowls on the make-shift table and that the men were talking to the visiting ministers and leaving the women to prepare the table. He looked for Julia and caught a glimpse of her and her mother approaching the table.

Frank Dupree walked from the crowd of men and extended his hand to Seth. "I'm glad you made it today. I don't reckon you had any trouble finding the meeting house."

Seth gripped Frank's hand and responded, "No, none at all. It was a little farther than I thought."

Frank gestured, "Come on with me, I want you to meet somebody you might find interesting." Seth followed Frank to the assembled men and waited as Frank merged with the talking men. "Mr. Chamberlain," Seth heard, "I want you to meet Elder Beebe from New York."

He watched as Frank ushered the elderly man toward him and extended his hand. "It's good to meet you, Mr. Beebe."

The elder looked at Seth and remarked, "I hear you're from New York."

Chamberlain nodded, "Yes, sir. I'm originally from Albany."

Beebe responded, "I'm from Watertown, and I would say we're both a long way from home." The old man inquired, "Are you visiting down here?"

Seth hesitated and answered, "No, sir, I'm making my home down here now."

Beebe looked puzzled and asked, "May I ask why you moved down south? I have a son that moved some years ago to Georgia."

Seth responded, "Well, I really didn't have any reason to go back north—I thought I would try a new life in the south." The elder detected his intrusive question. "I'm sorry, that's none of my concern. My son had his reasons and you have yours."

Seth looked at Elder Beebe and remarked, "I hope your son did not have the trouble being accepted that I am having." The elder fixed his penetrating eyes on Seth and asked, "Were you in the army before you decided to live here?"

Seth looked amazed and responded, "Yes I was. How did you know?"

Beebe smiled and replied, "That's about the only thing that would bring a young man here amidst all the trouble."

Elder Hart shouted, the roar of the crowd stopped, and he called for Elder Durand to return thanks.

Beebe looked at Seth and smiled. "Let's get a little something to eat. These good sisters have done the best they could, and we don't want to disappoint them, do we?" Seth followed the elder to the table. He reached for a plate, located Julia and smiled at her, moved along the table, filled his plate and stepped away from the table.

Seth glimpsed Frank approaching with a younger man. "Mr. Chamberlain, I want you to meet Elder Silas Durand from Pennsylvania."

Seth stooped, placed his plate on the ground and rising extended his hand. "Very good to meet you, Mr. Durand."

The young minister advised, "Go ahead and eat, Mr. Chamberlain. We can talk while you eat. I understand you're from New York and you're living near here, now."

Seth tried to balance his plate and answered, "Yes, that's right, but I must admit it's a difficult thing to be accepted. I can't help but notice how Mr. Beebe and Mr. Hartwell as well as yourself are accepted by everyone here." Seth continued to elaborate, "We're all from the northern states, but with you it doesn't seem to make any difference."

Durand looked over his wire-rimmed glasses and his mutton-chop beard amplified a smile. "My friend, it's you that wants to be accepted by them. It's not them wanting to be accepted by you." The young minister added, "We are accepted by these people because we're like they are. We believe like they do and we behave like they do. The rich man does not accept the poor man; he tolerates him but never truly accepts him. The refined man never accepts the crude man; he tolerates him." Durand continued, "If we want to be accepted by another, then we must become more like he is and stop trying to make him accept us as we are. After all, it's you that wants to be accepted, not them."

The elder adjusted his glasses and smiled at Seth. "Why don't you try believing like they do and see what happens?"

"Thank you, Mr. Durand! That sounds like good sense to me." Seth smiled at Elder Durand and chuckled. "I hope your talking to me does not hurt your reputation." The minister shook his head and assured Seth, "Don't fret about me; just remember what I said."

Seth continuing to balance his plate, saw Elder Hartwell was not engaged and walked to the elder from New Jersey. "Mr. Hartwell, I heard you are from New Jersey. I am Seth Chamberlain from Albany, New York. It sure is good to see someone from some of the northern states."

Hartwell looked at Seth and asked, "Did you make the trip from Albany by train?"

Chamberlain explained, "Oh no, sir, I live just a few miles from here. I was invited to the meeting today."

The elder asked, "What brought you here from New York?"

Seth glanced around and responded, "I stayed after the war."

Hartwell stopped eating, glared at Seth and inquired, "Don't you find that a little unsettling."

Seth responded, "I see that you and the other ministers from the northern states are accepted—why should it be unsettling?"

Elder Hartwell stared intently at Chamberlain and answered, "Son, we believe like they do. North, south, east or west—the same faith makes us all one body, and consequently accepting one another is not a problem." Hartwell continued, "This is the first general meeting since the end of hostilities. Do you see any animosity toward us?"

Seth placed his fork on the empty plate, held the plate in one hand and extended his other hand. "Thank you, Mr. Hartwell, you and Mr. Durand have been a big help. He told me about the same thing."

The elder gripped his hand and advised, "If you're going to live with these people, then you best try to change yourself instead of trying to force them to accept you." Seth moved to the table, scraped his plate into a wooden tub and placed the plate and fork on the table.

The crowd began to disperse into the shade and into the meeting house. Seth glimpsed Julia as she approached. "That was a nice dinner, Julia. I'm glad you and your daddy asked me to come today. I met the ministers from the other states and they were very cordial."

Julia looked at Seth and smiled, "Everybody noticed how well the elders took to you and how much you all talked."

Seth responded, "They gave me some pretty good advice and I was glad to listen."

Seth smiled at Julia and pulled his watch from his pocket. "I don't think I'm going to stay for the afternoon service. I think I will walk down to the river. When I rode in this morning I was attracted by the water falls on the river. I want to see them before I leave, but I want to be back to town before nightfall."

Julia straightened her hat and adjusted her reticule. "I've been there many times. It's a most peaceful place."

Seth smiled at Julia and asked, "Would you mind showing me the way?"

Julia glanced around and hesitated, "Oh, alright, just come on with me."

Julia gripped Seth's arm and directed, "Let's walk down to the road and cross at the end of the path. We'll have to go a short ways through the thicket, but there's a good path down to the river."

The brightness of the midday sun penetrated the new growth emerging from the tree branches, causing intermittent light and shade as Julia and Seth moved through the wooded thicket to the river. She gripped Seth's arm with one hand and lifted her skirt  from the ground with her other hand. Julia pushed a limb from her face, stopped and looked at Seth. "This place at the river is used for baptizing. That's why the path is so worn."

Seth stopped and listened intently. "Isn't that water I hear?" Julia gripped his arm and responded, "Yes, we're just about there. You can hear the water from here." The shade disappeared, the brightness of the sun glistened on the water cascading over the boulders. Only the sounds of nature penetrated the peaceful surroundings.

Julia released Seth's arm and stepped onto a boulder next to the high river bank. "Sometimes I step from boulder to boulder. You want to come?"

Seth jumped onto a boulder and joined Julia. "You're right, this is beautiful!"

Julia pointed to a large smooth boulder near the top of the river bank. "I can climb to that place, can you?" Julia carefully stepped from rock to rock and stood on the boulder. Seth followed her to the boulder and wrapped his arm around her waist. "It's even more beautiful from here."

Julia pressed her dress to the back of her legs, sat on the boulder and pulled her knees to her chin. "I've sat here many times and daydreamed. It's so peaceful here."

Seth sat beside Julia, pulled one knee under his chin and looked at Julia. "There is something I want you to know, Julia."

She looked at Seth and asked, "What is that?"

Seth looked at Julia's face, shaded by the straw pork-pie hat and admitted, "I did not come back to this county just to do business."

Julia looked puzzled and inquired, "Then what did you come here for?"

Seth looked toward the falling water, paused and stared at Julia. "I came back because I'm in love with you."

Julia pretended shock and responded, "You what!"

He grasped Julia by her hand, looked into her eyes and repeated, "Yes, Julia, since the day I passed by your home for the first time, I have not been able to get you off my mind." Seth paused and nodded, "I made the choice to come here because I don't think I can be happy without you."

Julia removed her hat, placed it on the boulder and turned to Seth. "I must admit to you, Seth, since that first meeting on the train, it's been difficult putting you out of my mind." She turned her head upward into the sun, her chestnut hair glistened as she responded, "I must admit I love you, too." Seth placed his hand behind her head, gently lowered her onto the sun-drenched boulder and with his other hand around her waist pressed his lips to hers. He felt her arms as she squeezed him tight to her bosom. The sounds of water rushing over the rocks faded as the moment dissolved in timeless ecstasy.

The sounds of laughing boys roused Julia and Seth. Seth quickly jumped to his feet, extended his hand and pulled Julia to her feet. She reached and picked up her hat and suggested, "We'd better get back before somebody comes looking for us." Seth gripped her by the hand and led her over the boulders to the river bank. He leaped to the top, extended his hand and pulled her to the top of the bank. Julia gripped Seth's hand and gestured, "Let's go back to the meeting house."

Seth pushed the limbs from their front as they moved along the path, turned to Julia and suggested, "May I take you home from here? I'm going that way anyway. Your mama and daddy can bring your grip." Julia, gripping his hand, replied, Yes, I'll ask them to bring my valise with them."

Crossing the Hilliardston Road, Seth turned to Julia and asked, "If you'll tell your folks, I'll get my gig and we'll start for Tarborough."

Julia moved quickly toward the front of the meeting house, spied her father and mother and joined them at the door. "Seth's taking me home. My valise is in the buggy. I'll be home when you get there."

A frown covered Frank's face as he scolded, "Oh, good Lord, if you weren't a grown girl I'd wear you out. Go on! We'll be home 'fore dark."

Ada looked at Frank and shrugged her shoulders. "We might as well agree, she's going to do it anyway."

Julia watched for Seth, saw him leading his horse by the halter and ran to the gig. "They said it would be alright."

Seth grasped the lines, moved to the side of the gig and extended his hand. Julia gripped his hand, placed her foot on the gig step and pulled herself into the seat. Seth moved around the front of the horse and pulled himself into the seat beside Julia. he snapped the lines and guided Blue Boy into the path toward the Hilliardston Road. Seth pulled on the right line and directed his horse toward the river bridge. He felt Julia as she nudged nearer and turned to her and smiled. "I love you so much, Julia." Julia slid her hand onto his and responded, "I love you, too, Seth."

Seth and Julia approached the river bridge. He pulled Blue Boy to a stop and looked at Julia. "One day I'll tell you about this bridge, and why we should never burn bridges in our lives. Only God knows when we might have to use them again for our happiness." He snapped the lines and rumbled across the gapped planking.

Julia nuzzled nearer Seth, placed her arm next to him and gripped his arm with both hands. Seth pressed his horse along the Hilliardston Road toward the rail tracks and the road to Tarborough.

The hours passed as the gig bounced in and out of the wagon ruts. The miles and the hours of the earlier trek passed as only minutes. Time again became inconsequential.

Seth turned and looked at the ebbing light. "Coolmore should not be too far, now. I know you'll be glad to get back home." Julia looked at Seth and beamed. "It's been a good day! I hate for it to end."

Seth gripped Julia's hand and reacted, "A better day for me."

Julia peered into the distance and declared, "There's home! There's home! I can see the oak trees!"

Seth snapped the lines and urged Blue Boy into a trot. "We'll be there in a few minutes."

Pulling on the lines, Seth restrained his horse and asked, "Do you want to go to the front or the rear of the house?"

Julia glanced at the house and answered, "Tie your horse in the front and I'll go through the back and open the front door."

Seth tightened the lines, pulled the horse to a halt, leaped from the gig and secured the lines to a tree. He moved around the back of the gig and extended his hand to Julia. She gripped his hand, lifted her skirt and stepped to the ground. Looking at Seth she said, "I'll go through the back and unlock the front door."

Seth watched Julia as she raced to the rear of the house. He thought, what a glorious day this has been!

He watched as the front door of Coolmore opened and Julia appeared on the porch. His memory was jolted to the first time he viewed her. It was here, exactly here on this porch. Seth walked to the porch, stepped up, wrapped his arms around Julia's waist and walked through the door.

Seth's attention was drawn to the grand spiral staircase ascending to the cupola. The light of the afternoon sun filtered through the colored glass and cascaded down the staircase. He walked to the steps and looked to the cupola, "What a beautiful sight!"

Julia stepped onto the first step, pulled her dress close to her legs, turned and sat on a step. She pulled her knees under her chin and stared at Seth. He stepped back, fixed his gaze on her and proclaimed, "My Lord, you're beautiful! The colors from the dome transform you into an angel."

Seth walked to the staircase, sat beside Julia and wrapped his arms around her shoulders. "Julia, I know my presence here has placed you in a difficult position." He maintained his gaze into Julia's eyes, "But I must ask you now or the opportunity may not come again."

Julia stared into Seth's eyes and questioned, "Ask me what?"

A smile beamed from Seth's face. "Julia, will you marry me?"

Julia smiling, continued to gaze at Seth, "The answer to that question is in the cupola!"

She jumped to her feet, dashed up the staircase, paused on the second floor and watched Seth as he gripped the railing and followed. Julia lifted her dress above her shoes and rushed up the spiral steps to the cupola. She knelt on the cupola floor beside the top of the steps and watched as Seth ascended. The colored glass of the cupola windows filtered the sunlight into a multitude of mingled colors.

Julia watched as Seth stepped closer to the top, waited for his face to be level with hers, and touched his shoulder. He paused, looked at her and asked, "Well?"

With her hands on her knees, Julia leaned toward Seth and with a scampish smile, responded, "I seem to recollect being called a Carolina wench who could not do anything but scream. Now, that Carolina wench could say, No!"

Seth remembered the incident on the train and with a dejected look remarked, "Yes, she could."

Julia looked deep into Seth's eyes, beamed and answered, "But she won't!"

Julia leaped to her feet and stepped from the cupola entrance. "No, she will not say, No! She thinks 'Mrs. Seth Chamberlain' rings with style."

Seth rushed up the last steps, wrapped his arms around Julia and drew her close. He smiled, tilted his head as she raised her face to meet his lips.

The scent of spring at Coolmore merged with the dancing colors in the cupola, Julia's peaceful sanctuary.